The lagoon be... ...ic of the waterfall filling her with pleasure. On impulse, she threw off her garments and plunged into the water for one last swim.

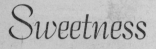

Sweetness

At last she swam back, climbed out, and reached for her discarded clothes. She looked up in fear. Domino stood just at the entrance to the lagoon, eyes intent upon her.

Surrender

For a moment their eyes locked. How long had he been there? She returned to the lagoon, and fled to the opposite shore. But there too, he was waiting. And even as she looked, he came in after her. . . .

MARY KAY SIMMONS

With Rapture Bound

A KANGAROO BOOK
PUBLISHED BY POCKET BOOKS NEW YORK

Another *Original* publication of POCKET BOOKS

POCKET BOOKS, a Simon & Schuster division of
GULF & WESTERN CORPORATION
1230 Avenue of the Americas, New York, N.Y. 10020

ISBN: 0-671-81018-9

First Pocket Books printing July, 1978

Trademarks registered in the United States and other countries.

Interior design by Sofia Grunfeld

Printed in the U.S.A.

Part
One

Chapter One

London in June of 1761 was a capital city gay with the growing affluence England's far-flung colonies provided and secure in the knowledge that British right and British might would conquer. The long French war was rumored to be nearing its end. British naval power had outshone the French and, save for the Indies, the battles for which were still to be waged, nearly all of the American colonies were now in English hands. On the other side of the world, the great subcontinent of India was slowly but surely being brought under subjugation, thanks as much to the adroit manipulation of the enmity between Hindu and Moslem as to the fierce fighting of Britain's disciplined troops. Perched on the edge of Europe, binding the nations of Cornwall, Scotland, Wales, and Ireland to her, England was rising to the peak of her power. Such affluence and such triumphant victories lent an air of universal well-being to the country as a whole; and London, heartbeat of the growing empire, was filled with both the old aristocracy and the growing and wealthy merchant class.

George III had been on the throne for nearly a year. He had just celebrated his twenty-fourth birthday and his betrothal to Princess Charlotte of Mecklenberg. Though George might be young, and the product of his foolish father, the late Frederick, Prince of Wales, and his unreasonably doting mother, Princess Augusta, he had already seized some control of his government, and under the prodding of his mother and the clever tutelage of his old mentor, John Stuart, Lord Bute, he gave every promise of remaining a strong influence in that government.

Those merchants and nobles and politicians who had

lacked the foresight to curry favor with Bute found themselves caught unaware by the upheaval of Whig power and the growing importance of the old Tories.

Sir Bertram Rowland, of Rowland's Imports, was not one of the unfortunates. He had managed to stay on the right side all during the reign of George II, without overlooking the very realistic fact that the hostility between George II and his son Frederick would surely result in governmental changes once the old king died. So adroit was Sir Bertram at maintaining favor that his position was held as well under George III.

Thus, on the sixth of June, 1761, his own wealth growing as steadily as the national treasury and fresh honors awaiting him through his old friend Bute, Sir Bertram left his offices near the Thames embankment between the Tower and London Bridge and stepped into his sedan chair for the short journey to Lloyd's Coffee House, on Lombard Street.

His two bearers, Joseph and Patrick Murphy, lifted the chair smoothly, and, with Sir Bertram standing, his head and shoulders above the open sedan top, they trotted off with their burden.

Everything pleased Sir Bertram this morning. The air was soft and warm, the sky cloudless, and his bearers were of the best. The fashion among the gentry of hiring only Irishmen as chair runners was rooted in the fact that they were the strongest and most trustworthy of this particular kind of manual laborers culled from the provinces.

As they turned up past the monument to the Great Fire, the Murphys slowed down to avoid collision with a draycart pulled by a plodding, weary old nag, its head bowed resignedly under the whip of the driver.

Sir Bertram turned away indifferently as the dray inched past him. His eyes fell on the monument's inscription: " . . . perpetual remembrance of that most dreadful burning of this Protestant City, begun and carried on by ye Popish faction."

Both monument and inscription had been familiar to him from early childhood. He had first seen them when he was a lad of six and his grandfather brought him to view the monument to illustrate his story of the Great Fire.

"Twenty I was then," his grandfather had said, "and living in Pudding Lane, and 'twas there it all began—

John Farynor's house. King's baker, he was, and no papist nor yet a Frenchman. But 'twouldn't do to mention that, Bertram. For when those of us living nearby told the truth, we was stoned for French papists ourselves. Aye, what people will believe, they will believe. But 'twas no popish plot. 'Twas Farynor's carelessness with his damnable ovens, and twasn't the first fire in that house. 'Twouldn't have been the last, either, had old John been up and about and putting the fire out."

Sir Bertram smiled with a sense of his superior knowledge. He had accepted his grandfather's story then and did now. It was not the words "Popish faction" that pleased him, but the words "this Protestant City." He was not a religious man, particularly, and he held little interest in sermons and the like. But facts were facts; there was no doubt that this Protestant city in this Protestant nation was faring far better than her counterpart among those countries still giving allegiance to Rome.

"Damn me," he muttered aloud, "but I mind I am counting my blessings this day." He beamed unconsciously as the sedan chair moved smoothly over the cobblestone streets, not seeing the ruder dwellings or the crowds of poor that clung close to the sides of the buildings in order to avoid being run down by dray or phaeton, as well as being soaked by pails of human waste tossed from upper windows.

As they neared Lombard Street, Joseph, who was in the lead, swerved suddenly. The sedan chair wobbled and nearly capsized as Patrick, behind, stumbled under this unexpected maneuver. Sir Bertram banged his arm against the opening and swore at Joseph. A second later, a large shower of matter from a chamber pot splashed in the street beside them and Sir Bertram realized that he had narrowly missed receiving the foul stuff over his head.

Good man, Joseph, he thought, and Patrick, too. Come year's end, he would see to a ten-shilling increase in their yearly wages. Well, five each. No reason to spoil them.

Lloyd's was noisy and crowded, the tables filled, and the overflow of brokers and clients and ships' captains pressed together, impeding the flow of traffic in and out of doors.

Sir Bertram raised himself on the balls of his feet and surveyed the room for the men he was to meet. He saw the insurance broker, Forbes, first. He was at the far corner, his bony frame wedged into a chair. Seated beside him, his weatherbeaten face relaxed and calm in the middle of the flurry, was the *Princess Charlotte*'s captain, William Ramsey.

Setting his shoulders, swinging his cane with seeming negligence so that he tapped the legs of those who prevented his passage, Sir Bertram made his way through the crowds.

"Strike me blue," he said as he came to the table. "I notice you have outgrown Lloyd's, Mr. Forbes." He seized the man's extended hand in a firm grasp and nodded at Ramsey as he lowered himself into the seat reserved for him.

"Well, Captain Ramsey, and how is my ship?"

"Spick and span, Sir Bertram," Ramsey replied with a gleam of amusement in his eyes. In the years he had sailed for Rowland, Ramsey could recall no single instance in which Sir Bertram had not greeted him with the same remark—"my ship," in prideful ownership, as if he, Ramsey, were merely a caretaker. It had long since ceased to rankle him.

"My apologies for my tardiness, gentlemen. I was detained on a combination of business and pleasure." Sir Bertram paused and smiled. "My daughter Caroline is to be wed this week, and she and her husband will sail for Virginia Colony on the *Charlotte*."

His smile broadened at the murmured congratulations.

"Which brings me to business," he said. "This voyage is the last the *Charlotte* will make on the Plymouth-to-Nassau-to-Barbados run. When she stops at Virginia Colony this voyage, it will be to load tobacco and cotton. From then on, she will sail exclusively between England and Virginia. Safe enough from the hazards of war, eh Forbes?"

Mr. Forbes, a thin, saturnine man with a nervous habit of drumming his forefinger on the table, tapped twice as fast and replied in a melancholy voice, "Safe enough. Aye, I venture it will be, but only if the *Charlotte* stays on the Plymouth-Norfolk route. Barbados, Nassau . . ."

"Come, come, Forbes. England controls all the northern colonies, as well as Nassau and Barbados and . . . "

"Controls, controls," Forbes murmured. " 'Tis true enough we have little to fear from the Frenchies above

Martinique, but we have always to fear the pirates and privateers and the tropical storms, as Captain Ramsey will tell you."

"Aye." Ramsey nodded in agreement. "But when have I lost ship or cargo to either, Mr. Forbes?"

"Never," Forbes admitted.

"What is more," Sir Bertram went on, "I am prepared to prepay for each two voyages, and Mr. Welles will additionally secure his cargo on the return voyage."

"Mr. Welles?" Forbes inquired.

"My daughter's betrothed, Joshua Welles, of whom you have surely heard."

"Joshua Welles!" Ramsey interjected. "Aye. He is known to me by reputation." Welles, he was thinking privately, what a husband for the eldest of Rowland's three daughters. Welles, forty if he was a day, and a Colonial in the bargain. Business and pleasure, Sir Bertram had said: business in the tobacco, but little pleasure for the bride. He had never seen Caroline Rowland, but he had heard of her. She was spoken of as too intelligent for a woman, as beautiful, as spirited, as mischievous and as hot-blooded; equally, she had been described as cruel and heartless and cold. He had heard it rumored that her family was making every effort to marry her off to one young blood or another and always without success, for the girl herself was headstrong. There had been stories of importunate suitors lost in the maze at Abbey Hall, whence Caroline led them and then fled, as well as of the unluckier men pushed (she always swore they fell by accident) into the fishpond or sent sprawling along a ballroom floor, unaccountably tripped while dancing. And this was the girl who had agreed to marry Joshua Welles.

" . . . say you, Ramsey?" Sir Bertram was speaking.

"Er, I beg your pardon, Sir Bertram, I confess to daydreaming."

"Do you estimate the sailing day yet?" Sir Bertram asked.

"First good tide and fair wind in a fortnight's time. Loading will be completed then, the ship in readiness."

"There would be some drop in rate for prepayment of future voyages and for additional cargo insurance, which, of course, cannot be determined in advance," Forbes said.

"It can. Mr. Welles assures me the tobacco yield is

steady, and he himself brokers the cotton of small farmers. Now, to the price, Forbes." Sir Bertram said.

"Well then, sir, taking all into account and Captain Ramsey . . ." Forbes paused and nodded at the captain, pursing his mouth and stretching it thin while he calculated.

The final figure was agreeably lower than Sir Bertram expected. Ramsey saw him stifle his grin of pleasure.

And not by prepayment, he thought, but on my reputation. It was time to brace Sir Bertram for an increase in his own share. For whatever was hatched between Rowland and Joshua Welles was bound to be profitable to both. He himself would never engage in partnership with Welles, but then business was never his interest. The sea, the ship, and his own captaincy were his business and his real interests. With his children grown, his wife preferred to remain ashore most of the time and occupy herself with grandmotherly interests, as once she had occupied herself with her own children. A good woman, his wife. Good company and affectionate during their brief times together. He had not tired of her. Still, as the end of each sojourn ashore neared and his ship was ready to sail, he was glad enough to leave the pleasant influences of his home and not particularly sorry to kiss his wife good-bye.

Sometimes, he would wonder how life would be when he was too old to be insured by Lloyd's, but at forty-two that time seemed remote. He came from a long-lived stock—his own father was still alive and only recently retired from the sea—and he had no reason to suppose he did not have twenty years and more before the mast.

He caught mention of his own name and brought his attention back to the business at hand.

"One run," Sir Bertram was saying, "to Nassau, Barbados, Virginia, and then straight back to England."

"One run and mayhap the last. There is fighting in the Indies," Forbes said.

"Nonsense," Ramsey broke in. "There has been no recent naval engagement anywhere near Nassau or Barbados, nor will there be. There is little left to fight over in the Indies, anyway. The Virgins are as neutral as Guadeloupe. Martinique will fall like ripe fruit, and when it does, Dominica, Lucien, Grenada, and St. Vincent will topple after it."

"Indeed, yes," Forbes agreed dryly, "but not without a fight. And that is why the rates for this run are higher than those to come. I repeat, quite apart from naval engagements, there are the pirates. Who, indeed, has not heard tales of them, seen ships return all cargo, and sometimes half the crew and passengers gone God knows where? Do not tell me, Captain Ramsey, that you have not heard of the infamous Captain Domino, as he calls himself?"

"I have heard of him," Ramsey said shortly. "But the *Charlotte* has thirty guns, Mr. Forbes, and a good crew, and my gunnery officer, young Mr. Hardin, is a sound man."

Mr. Forbes remained half-convinced and in the end conceded only a little. Still, it was something to be thankful for.

A few moments later, the business concluded, the three at the table rose and said their farewells.

"You will see that my daughter's voyage is a good one, Captain," Sir Bertram said, as if ordering a glass of ale.

"I will," Ramsey replied.

"Safe voyage, then," Sir Bertram said. "We shall meet on your return." He was gone, pushing his way back through the coffee shop as he had entered it.

He was smiling as he reached the street. It had been amusing to outwit Ramsey. The good captain had been ready to speak of more money. Sir Bertram had observed him during Forbes' negotiations, negotiations that had made it clear the lower rate was owing to Ramsey's reputation. Three times had he engaged pirates, and three times come through unscathed and cargo intact.

Standing once more in his sedan chair, Sir Bertram's gaze settled over the crowded streets with benign affection.

It is done, he thought, the Welles agreement and Caroline's betrothal, and neither was brought about easily. He reflected that the business had been less taxing than Caroline. She had been difficult to bring to heel, not that he had ever tried to break her spirit.

He owned to himself that she was above all his children, the most like himself, especially in her stubborn determination to get her own way and in her adroitness in managing to do so. She was his favorite. Her sisters, Jane and Anne, were small and wren-like, very much like their mother. Caroline was tall and arresting. Where her younger sisters were timorous, Caroline was bold. He had spoiled her outrageously, taking secret pride in her beauty and quick wit.

He had grumbled and said no when first she had sought to join her brother in his tutorings, yet he had eventually given in. She had proved a quick student and soon outstripped George William, five years her junior. By the time George William was ready for Eton College, Caroline had absorbed all she could from the tutors and had begun to beg for further studies.

Anne and Jane had been content to learn reading and simple figures and a smattering of French, not so with Caroline. She had to have history and geography and advanced courses in mathematics, as well as Latin. She had become completely proficient in French.

And she had become completely enamored of the French tutor, he remembered wryly. It was one of many of Caroline's infatuations he had dealt with, one of the two elopements he had foiled.

The last one had been a near thing—young Geoffrey Lyons, the old colonel's son. Fortunately, he had been apprised in time by one of Caroline's dismissed suitors, young Lord Redleigh. Sir Bertram despised Redleigh—improvident, foppish, and sinking so low as to bring gossip like a garlic eater in search of reward. But he listened and took action.

How angry Caroline had been. She would have married Geoffrey in spite of her father's threats to disinherit her. But, of course, Lyons was easy to bribe. Poor, in spite of his family connection with the Carterets, he had been eager to forfeit a dowerless Caroline for an army commission and a yearly stipend.

The chair slowed as they neared the junction at Threadneedle Street. Sir Bertram stirred, remembering his own childhood, as he always did in this part of the city. How he had hated that house with his father's shop and offices below. Crowded between the homes of other rich merchants, it was a constant reminder of his ambition to move up and out and beyond where all of fashionable London had moved by that time. Then, the West End had beckoned as the Elysian fields. Now it was his own home.

Well, he had climbed a high mountain since those

days. The boys at school who had scorned him, as men now sought him out. At twenty-three, on his father's death, all of Rowland's had passed to him.

It had always been a lucrative trade, but during the past thirty years he had made it a foremost shipping and import house. His father had left two small second-rate ships. He had multiplied that fleet to twenty large first-rate and merchant frigates. His father had mostly imported and exported goods for his shops. Sir Bertram dealt in everything from cinnamon to slaves.

The old house in the city had long since been leased to others. His new imposing town house, purchased from the late Lord Redleigh during one of his financial panics, sat in the middle of the elegant lawns and gardens of Gray's Inn Fields.

And even Redleigh Castle in Surrey was not as grand as his own estate in Kent. There was an estate that befitted his ambitions. The old king's conferring a baronetcy on him when he bought the lands had been only a step in the fulfillment of his dreams. George III, young, malleable if one knew how to get around him—and, thank God, neither Pitt nor Newcastle knew how to get around him—would be conferring a greater honor before long.

First, however, more money was necessary. And more money was to be had now, thanks to Welles and thanks to his own final triumph over Caroline. Welles had made her hand a condition of their agreement—eager to bind the business with family connection, as, indeed, Sir Bertram himself had been. If Caroline ever learned that . . .

He acknowledged that in this manipulation of his daughter he owed much to Elizabeth James, who knew Caroline's nature better than anyone. Elizabeth had been his mistress since the time George William was born, nearly fourteen years now. That was the year Agatha had retired from her marital duties under the guise of poor health, occasioned by a difficult birth.

Elizabeth, newly widowed when she met Sir Bertram, had never attempted to retire. She had borne him a son less than a year after George William arrived, a boy whose father was supposed to be the late Francis James. Christopher was very much Sir Bertram's son, although thankfully he had inherited his mother's looks, if not her tiny frame. Younger, sturdier, and more clever than his legitimate heir, he was a boy after Sir Bertram's own heart.

Elizabeth had had no other pregnancies, claiming she owed this to a mixture of herbs and fungus, which she obtained from what she laughingly called a "Scottish gypsy." "After all, Bertram, 'twould be unseemly to claim endless posthumous births." And there the matter rested.

They were crossing Cheapside into Newgate. On his left St. Paul's rose, its elegant spires soaring up against the sky. Quite soon now they would pass the Holburn Viaduct and be on the road to Gray's Inn Fields. South and west lay Elizabeth's residence in Lincoln's Inn Fields.

Elizabeth . . . how pleased she would be at his news. On impulse, he ordered his bearers to turn left and go down to Ludgate Circus.

"To Fleet Street," he ordered, "and across the bridge as far as Kingsway."

When they reached the road that curved up on the far side of Lincoln's Inn, he ordered the chair stopped.

"I will walk a bit," he said, climbing out. It was a small concession to convention and to his wife's feelings. Agatha knew of Elizabeth but pretended not to know. She was thankful enough to be spared her marital duties. From the beginning, she had found no joy in their physical union. He had always known that, but, bent on rearing a family and most especially of siring a son, he had ignored her inclinations.

As long as he remained discreet, he could enjoy his mistress, as well as his reputation for being a devoted family man.

In many ways Elizabeth would have been a far more suitable wife for him. Daughter of a Scottish doctor and cousin to the Cameron chief, she was lively, witty, and intelligent. It was she who had introduced him to Bute, she who had advised him of Bute's friendship with the Prince of Wales and his tutelage of Frederick's son George, then heir presumptive.

Sir Bertram could talk to Elizabeth. She admired him, flattered him, advised him, listened to his troubles, and —more important—she had never turned him away from her bed.

He was a simple man himself. The strain of mistresses

who were greedy and demanding had proved too much before he met Elizabeth. He was not prone to womanizing, and if Agatha had been more compliant, he would scarcely have considered straying. Elizabeth provided him with the missing ingredients of his marriage, and he was as faithful to her as he had intended to be to Agatha in the beginning of their marriage.

When he impulsively ordered the stop at Kingsway, he had meant only to spend half an hour in quiet talk, reviewing his day, but as he lifted the small brass knocker, his thoughts veered to Elizabeth herself, and he pulled out his watch. Nearing half past five. He had time.

She opened the door herself, saying, "I saw you from my window, Bertram. What brings you here this evening?"

Her bright brown eyes held an anxious look and she reached out a hand to him to draw him indoors.

"You brought me, m'dear," he replied with heavy gallantry. "It has been a most successful day, most successful."

She smiled at him, lifting her face for his kiss. Then, taking his hat and cane, she laid them on a chair and led him up the stairs.

He followed, watching her hoops swaying, anticipating the moment when she would begin to undress. He liked to lie in the bed and watch her. Sometimes she would tear off the clothes with impatience, sometimes come to him to loosen her laces. Sometimes she would stand behind the Oriental screen he had presented to her and he would see the clothes, piece by piece, come to rest across the top; other times she might stand with her eyes on him, removing each garment with tantalizing slowness, so that when she finally came to him he would seize her eagerly.

This evening she sensed his impatience, and without any appearance of haste she was soon beside him. The physical attraction between them had mellowed but not waned. When his family was down at Abbey Hall and there were no duties calling him home, they would be leisurely, but on a night such as this they abandoned such playfulness. He knew very well how to arouse her quickly, knew that she loved the sensuality of long preliminary caresses and of variety. Equally, he knew that she liked the swiftness of harsh entry from time to time.

He pressed her to him and then pushed her on her back and attempted to mount her. They wrestled silently for a few minutes, she making every effort to avoid being taken until he had mastered her with superior strength. As he forced her, she cried out sharply and then gave in with wild abandon, twisting and turning with the rhythms of his body until the final spasm of pleasure.

They lay panting afterward, still clasped in an embrace. At length he rolled away and she said, "I never cease to wonder at you, Bertram."

He felt a glow of expansive pride, thinking privately that for a man on the very near side of sixty, he was as good as many a young dandy around, and better than most.

It was what she had intended, and it both amused and pleased her that he never guessed she flattered deliberately. She did so not out of a sense of obligation, but out of genuine feeling.

In the early days of their affair, she used to dream of one day taking her place as his wife. As the years progressed, she had come to see that such thoughts were idle fancies. Agatha, with her everlasting care of herself, would live to be one hundred. And now that Elizabeth was over forty, she had come to enjoy her life as it was. She often thought that perhaps, after all, she was meant to be a mistress. She had not needed money, and because of that she felt free to love as she chose. She had loved her husband, if not at the peak of excitement, as least with quiet affection, but she had been restless under the bonds of duty. It was vastly different with Bertram. They had no claims on each other beyond their mutual fondness and physical attraction. It worked very well.

Beside her, Bertram stirred and said, "I want to tell you how clever you are, m'dear. I followed your advice and let Caroline have her way. I pretended to despise Welles for being a Colonial, and by the time young Lyons had been bribed away, she took Welles out of defiance." He gave a reminiscent chuckle. "She still believes I am disappointed. May she not learn otherwise, at least until after the nuptials."

"I am happy for you, Bertram," Elizabeth replied, stifling a twinge of guilt. Poor Caroline—she must give her some very special gift. She liked the girl and ordinarily would have abetted her. But Bertram's wishes came first now, as they always had.

She placed herself against him and murmured, "Tell me about your day, Bertram. Tell me about everything." As he talked she stroked him affectionately and then voluptuously, and at last the talk dwindled and they loved once again before he left.

Chapter Two

On the following afternoon, Caroline Rowland was seated in the large reception gallery of her father's home, somewhat apart from the gathering of friends who had come to entertain her while Sir Joshua Reynolds put the finishing touches on her portrait.

Dressed in a sky-blue gown that spread over pannier hoops to reveal snowy underskirts and wearing a wide-brimmed shepherdess hat on her thick wheat-gold hair, she was to the casual observer a model of gentle innocence.

On closer inspection, however, the gentleness faded a little and revealed an impish sparkle in her clear blue eyes that matched the spirited set of her head. There was a willfulness about her full lips and firmly molded chin that was in direct contrast to her placid pose.

The master's eyes had not missed the contrast. Indeed, the simple costume and the shy demeanor had been his own idea; they were a perfect foil for the vital electric quality in Caroline's personality.

" . . . and will you love the colonies as much as the Colonial himself?" young Edward Redleigh, Earl of Redleigh, said with a laugh that barely concealed his malice.

"I shall love my husband's home," Caroline answered demurely, "although I shall miss the maze at Abbey Hall."

An amused titter followed the remark and Redleigh's face flushed, although he laughed with the rest and said casually, "As, indeed, will all those of us who have adventured with you there."

15

There was a murmur of approval from the others for this adroit turning of Caroline's words back upon her. Redleigh acknowledged it with a mocking bow. Privately he seethed, recalling the afternoon he had followed her so willingly only to have her desert him, leaving him to blunder deeper into the maze. It had been two hours and more before a gardener's boy heard his cries and came to lead him out. Caroline had made a fool of him, and, worse, she laughed about it later.

Caroline slanted her eyes at him and saw that despite his quick rejoinder, he still smarted. She tossed her head with a light laugh.

"Do not move again, Miss, or I shall ask the ladies and gentlemen to leave," Reynolds barked. Caroline at once returned to her pose. One did not contradict Sir Joshua. It had been a singular honor that he had agreed to paint her for he accepted few commissions these days. Caroline cared less for the honor than for the fact that ever since his illness in Austria last year, Reynolds had been nearly stone deaf.

This misfortune to the artist was not without its blessings on those whom he consented to paint. Now it was possible to relieve the tedium of sitting without distracting the master.

Idly, she wondered if he barked at royalty when it moved, as he did at her. He had painted the Hanovers. Did he bark at King George? Surely not. She could imagine him doing so and George summoning the palace guards to have him ejected. The thought deepened the mischief in her eyes and Reynolds murmured, "Yes, that is what I wanted," in a pleased way. He became absorbed once more in his canvas and did not appear to notice the general stirring and the greetings as Joshua Welles entered the gallery.

Caroline, fearful of moving again, saw him from the corner of her eye, and beneath her stiff bodice she felt her heart quicken. As always, this response bewildered her, reminding her as it did of the days when she had, by every artifice at her command, attempted to dissuade Joshua's suit. For if Joshua was tall and well formed, he had grown thick around the middle. There were lines radiating from his shrewd gray eyes, and his powdered wig, worn full, bespoke an effort to hide a balding pate. How she had made a complete turn-around, she did not know. When she had first met Joshua, there had been Geoffrey, but then he somehow had become less interesting. There had been several heated arguments with her father when she spurned Geoffrey, and it was all so bewildering. She had not imagined that her father would favor Geoffrey, poor as he was, when he had been ill disposed toward others better endowed.

When had it happened that Joshua became more exciting than anyone else? She was never quite sure. Partly, she conceded, it had happened because her ill humor, her impudent remarks, and her pose as a mannish woman interested only in books and knowledge had amused Joshua rather than annoyed him. And he had promised a life in which she would be free to learn anything she cared to learn and a library that he assured her was the equal, if not superior, to that which her father possessed. And all of it would be open to her, as her father's had not been. Never again would she hear, "It is not seemly for a young woman to read such as Fielding's *Tom Jones*."

And, she thought now, never again would she be forced to sit for an evening while her father read aloud from Richardson's piously dull *Clarissa Harlowe*. Nor would she feel alien to all the family as her father's voice thickened over the lugubrious sorrows and her mother and sisters retired to their individual chambers to weep over the idiotic Clarissa's misfortunes.

Still, it had not only been books and promises of a freer life that had resulted in her capitulation. It had indeed also been that last effort to put Joshua off. She had seized the opportunity for an evening stroll through the gardens of Abbey Hall to lead Joshua, much as she had Redleigh into the maze. There, however, Joshua had outwitted her and there he had first touched her. She could not recall the incident without a racing excitement. He had known so surely how to stir her passions. One moment he had been the Colonial she was eager to be rid of; the next moment he was an ardent lover who evoked an exhilarating response.

Where former suitors had been fumbling and gentle, he had been expert and bold. She would have succumbed completely, so great was her newly awakened desire, had he willed it. Vividly, she saw her stomacher lying beside her, her bodice undone; again she felt his hands upon her breasts, his mouth covering hers, and at that moment when she would gladly have abandoned gown and petticoats and knickers, along with the stomacher, he had ended it all. Nor had he, since their betrothal, followed up that night with anything more than a kiss.

"I'll have no man count the days from my wedding to the birth of my son and find it wanting by so much as an hour," he had said to her startled protest, and although he had laughed, she never doubted he was serious.

A week less a day, she remembered, unaware that her thoughts had set her breast to heaving and brought the color high in her cheeks.

"And it is finished," Sir Joshua barked suddenly, bringing her out of her reverie. "My art is not equal to your present beauty, Miss," he added dryly.

"You flatter me, sir," Caroline said, rising and sweeping a curtsy.

She saw Joshua approaching, and, anxious to regain control before she faced him, she hurried forward to Reynolds, as if to see him to the door.

"It is not necessary, Miss. I may be deaf, but I am not yet lame," Reynolds said with a return of his brusque manner. "You may look at your portrait now." And before she could answer, he ordered sharply, "Touch nothing. It will be many months before it will be dry enough to touch."

Welles moved towards Caroline and they stood side by side at the portrait. With her back to the rest of the assembly, Caroline turned to smile at her betrothed.

"The portrait is perfect," Welles said in an undertone. "He has captured you truly. But I prefer the living flesh." He touched her arm and she quivered slightly, at which he smiled and whispered, "Soon."

She turned away, flustered, to face the rest. She saw them as if in a tableau: her sisters looking at her half-amused, half-envious, as alike as if they were twins; Redleigh, his sulky face sulkier, his dark eyes cold above the flush; Viscount Fortescue, Redleigh's odious boon companion, smirking knowledgeably; Lady Sarah Lennox, slightly withdrawn from the rest, her face sad, as befitted her present state as the beloved, but, for reasons of state rejected, of the king.

The tableau held a moment and then broke as Reynolds departed and they hurried forward to exclaim over the painting.

Admist this confusion Sir Bertram made his appearance. Caroline, with a murmured excuse about changing her costume, escaped to her own chamber, where Dobbs, her maid of four years, waited.

Caroline felt feverish and cross and jerked impatiently over Dobbs' ministrations. Then, seeing the girl's look of distress, she said in quick repentance, "Oh, Dobbs, I am sorry. I don't know what has come over me lately. I realize I am not myself at all these days."

" 'Tis the marriage, Miss," Dobbs said wisely. "You'm be a bride so on. It be so for all girls, so says my mother, her be knowing such things better'n you or me."

Caroline laughed, her humor restored. "And soon I'll be knowing better, too, is that it?"

"Yes, Miss," Dobbs said, a shadow crossing her face.

"What is it?" Caroline asked.

"It be nothing, Miss. I be thinking only how 'twill seem in Virginia, and if I will I see home again."

"Oh, of course you will. Papa says I am to bring home the first baby, at least. I am to come to England every few years. So you shall come, too, on Captain Ramsey's ship. And that is another thing. Thrice each two years it will call at Virginia. Joshua says that 'twill come straight up the James River mouth and to his own dock. Fancy that? 'Twill bring packages and letters from home, and if we are of a mind, we can step aboard and sail away."

As she spoke, Dobbs' face cleared and she smiled a little. "You be good, Miss," she said. " 'Tis why I must go with you."

"Must? But I thought you *wanted* to come with me."

"Aye, Miss, that I do," Dobbs said hurriedly. "Be you ready for the powdering now? 'Twill soon be time for the reception. And . . . ."

"And tomorrow we leave for Abbey Hall," Caroline said excitedly. "And on Saturday I will be wed, and the following week I shall be in Plymouth. . . ."

"Aye, and if you don't soon come to the powdering room, none will happen," Dobbs warned.

Sighing, Caroline wrapped herself into her negligee and took the cone from Dobbs.

"If only I were you, Dobbs. How lucky you are not to powder your hair and have to awaken with the gritty stuff on your pillow and then brush and brush to get rid of it and then powder all over again the next evening."

"Yes, Miss," Dobbs said quietly, following Caroline into the powdering room.

"When I am married," Caroline said, "I shall never wear powder." She buried her face well into the cone and submitted to Dobbs' ministrations.

Clouds of the fine starch rose in the air, settling on maid and mistress alike, leaving the one muttering into the protective paper and the other coughing as a fine film settled over her dark brown curls and the rough dark linen of her gown.

"There," Caroline said when it was over. "That leaves me only four more days of powdering."

In her room again, she slipped out of the negligee and stood before the long mirror, watching critically as Dobbs knelt and placed gold silk shoes with bright red heels upon Caroline's feet. She buckled the straps deftly and rose.

"They be beautiful shoes, Miss," she said as she reached for the pannier hoops. She tied them and then secured a pale green faille stomacher over the reed-stiffened bodice in such a way as to leave the soft mound of Caroline's pushed-up breasts outlined above it.

Upon the stomacher tiny golden embroidered birds pecked their way across Caroline's bosom. The golden gown that matched the shoes was draped very carefully, parting to reveal the elegant frothed underskirt and show to best advantage the multi-jeweled tails of embroidered peacocks.

Surveying herself fully clothed, Caroline had to admit that the long powdered ringlets of her coiffure were effective, curling whitely against her creamy shoulders and enhancing the gold and jeweled effect of her costume.

"I will wear no ornaments tonight," she said to Dobbs. "The gown glitters quite enough as it is."

"Yes, Miss."

"And, Dobbs . . . "

"Yes, Miss?"

"I will wear the blue cloth indienne tomorrow, the one of French design. It has a small tear above the hem that needs mending."

"Yes, Miss."

"Oh, dear," Caroline sighed as she passed from the room, "I am famished, and it is still hours until supper."

Seated next to Joshua that night at supper, Caroline observed the glittering array of guests with a curious sense of detachment. Her mother, at the far end of the long dining table, was more animated than usual, making every effort to entertain Lord Bute, the guest of honor. On the other side of the minister, Elizabeth James had turned her attention to Robert Clive, the former governor of India. Her sisters sat, their faces animated, beside the two young men who had already spoken for them, Jane smiling up at Guy Olden, Anne demurely flirting with Lord Bute's nephew.

She had heard enough gossip to wonder if it were true that Mrs. James, for whom she had a deep affection, was her father's mistress, but seeing how closely placed Mrs. James was to her mother, she decided it was gossip and nothing more. Her mother was far too puritanical to countenance such a social arrangement in her own home.

Across from her and slightly to the left, Redleigh and Fortescue made merry conversation with Lady Sarah, who sat between them.

" . . . and of course it was the usual musicale," Fortescue way saying.

"Which means?" Lady Sarah prompted, laughing.

"Pure Hanoverian," Redleigh said with audacity, "Haydn and Bach and the rest of the Teutonic group. Something new by Handel—a piece he calls the *Fifth Clavier Suite,* though why I make no pretense at knowing. The man is bent on supplying us with endless music, and I, at least, have been oversupplied, I fear, without having made a single demand."

"You overlook the large Colonial who was present," Fortescue said in a loud enough voice to claim Joshua's attention. "Powdered wig, damn me. Lace cuffs to his boot tops and jeweled buttons. Fancied himself a proper dandy."

"And his lady fair covered in jewels . . . a goodly number of jewels it took to cover her, too," Redleigh added. "And 'twas only a few short years ago that she was the loveliest of her London crowd."

Caroline, knowing that she and Joshua were meant to overhear the remarks, turned to Joshua with a brilliant smile.

"I shall be happy to leave the close confines of London

society," she said in a clear, carrying voice, "if only to remove myself from the useless fops who so befoul the air."

"We have our useless fops in Virginia Colony, as well," Joshua answered blandly. "Still, they are paid as little attention there as they are here." Their eyes met and Joshua added, in an undertone, "We have made at least one mortal enemy. Redleigh has turned an unbecoming shade of puce."

"I despise him," Caroline answered through barely moving lips.

"You have made that plain," Joshua replied. "Ah, I believe I see the first of the meal," he added as the footmen marched in, bearing the first-course trays.

Caroline ate steadily throughout the meal, taking more than one offering from each course. Delicately flavored oysters were followed by haddock baked in a rich sauce. Boiled beef, roasted pork, vegetable marrow and beans, and new Irish potatoes all disappeared from her plate.

The only things she refused were the baked woodcocks. She could never bear to pop them into her mouth, crunching bones and all, always unable to forget the small game birds she saw flying high over the Abbey woods. It made her ill to see them lying in rows upon the serving platter, their claws turned up in pitiful supplication, the odor of burned feathers still upon them.

However, she dined well and fully on everything else. By the time the gooseberry fool arrived, her stomacher felt tight, yet she finished it and partook of strawberry tartlet and the small spice cakes, as well.

Joshua, she noticed, had a better appetite. The bits she left on her plate to be scraped into the slop bowl for eventual distribution to the beggers at the gate were of a size consistent with politeness. Joshua seemed unaware of this practice and polished each course off with gustatory appreciation.

"You cannot be in love, after all," her sister Anne teased as they followed the other ladies into the parlor.

"And pray, why not?" Caroline asked.

"Your appetite—I hear that maids in love cannot eat."

"Love has always increased my appetite," Caroline answered with a laugh.

"Then you've loved always."

"And you never," Caroline said, "for you pick like a sparrow."

"Oh, Caroline," Anne said, "you are ever the one who can turn the word to her own advantage. Whatever shall we do when you are away? No one to tease. No one to argue with Papa. No one to make Mama change her mind. We will miss you sorely. Will you miss us, too?"

"Of course." Caroline smiled at Anne's serious face. She had answered automatically, answered as it was expected she would and realized all at once that she had not spoken the truth entirely.

I am different from them, she thought with a strange sadness, even from Papa. I cannot wait to begin my life, to be free. I long to visit far-off places. Mama? Why, I suppose I love Mama, but . . . but I don't really like her —not as much as I do Mrs. James, for example. And I would prefer the company of many others to my own sisters.

What was it, this difference? If she thought about it, all her nineteen years had been spent anticipating something she could scarcely name, something that was more than adventure, more than freedom. She had never been content to learn the housewifely arts, although she had mastered them. She had wanted learning. She still wanted it. That was something that held no interest for her mother or her sisters, and, she rather suspected, not for her brother, either, who would have been far more content without books. Even Papa. There it was again—"even Papa." If she had been his pet, he had been her favorite. Yet the prospect of leaving him and his protection struck no real sorrow in her.

Ahead, the future beckoned with half-realized dreams. When she left her father's house, she would leave all the chafing bonds of restriction behind her. I do not feel sad, she thought, because I am going where I want to go to live a life I long to live. Surely there was nothing strange in that. Still, Anne would not understand such feelings. She was full of sentimentality. Poor, dear Anne.

Aloud, Caroline said, "But of course I will miss all of you. How can you think otherwise?" And she patted her sister's arm as they joined the other ladies.

The light chat of the ladies, the foolish gossip, and the endless concern over food and fashion and entertainment, broken only by the maternal reports of the more besotted parents, washed over Caroline without effect during the hour the gentlemen lingered over their Spanish port and snuff.

Her spirits lifted as she heard them coming along the wide passageway to the parlor, and when Joshua's head and shoulders loomed above the others, her heart gave its customary start.

She rose from her place beside her mother and began to thread her way through the guests toward Joshua. Snatches of conversation came to her as she passed. " . . . better to be on the right side, and he has always been clever enough for that." Fortescue. " . . . which will give us Lord Stour in the Lords, by the new honors list, I'll be bound." Redleigh.

These sneering allusions to her father made her smile.

"Caroline," Elizabeth James said quietly from behind her, and Caroline turned.

"I have a small gift for you, my dear," Elizabeth said, "not your official gift, something extra, something I urge you to keep to yourself." She pressed a small silk pouch of considerable weight into Caroline's hands.

"Why, Mrs. James, what can it be?" Caroline murmured.

"A purse, my dear, in the shape of a pirate's chest. I have put coins into it. I remember my own wedding and those early days of my marriage. I grew weary explaining each purchase to Francis, and I used to dream of pocket money of my own that was out of his safekeeping."

"Papa has taken all the money gifts to add to my dower," Caroline said.

"We will have this gift be our own secret, then," Elizabeth smiled. "Promise me that?"

"Of course I promise," Caroline said warmly. "You are too generous to me. You have always been so."

"Not as generous as you believe," Elizabeth said enigmatically. "Slip the pouch loop over your wrist. There, I do believe that may start a new fashion," she added with a laugh as the cloth-of-gold pouch was in place.

"It is truly heavy," Caroline remarked.

"Use it wisely." Elizabeth patted her free arm and slipped away.

"And what is this?" Joshua asked as Caroline came up to him a moment later.

"Oh, 'tis a small gift from Mrs. James. She fancies it will begin a new fashion. But I find it awkward."

"Then why wear it?"

"She has only just given it to me."

"Put it away, then. I thought we might take a walk in the garden." His pale eyes were half-veiled, the tone of his voice intimate.

"I know I should enjoy that," she answered lightly.

"I will wait for you in the Chinese room," he said.

Joining him a few moments later in the dimly lit room, she found him examining an intricately carved and inlaid table that had been executed personally by Mr. Thomas Chippendale.

"Mama's favorite piece," Caroline remarked, coming up behind him.

"Is it? It is quite beautiful, but I prefer that screen"—he nodded at the tall Coromandel—"and the divan."

He slipped an arm around her as he spoke and led her across the room. "We will sit here," he said. "The garden can be chilly these spring evenings."

He moved a little apart from her once they were seated and said, "We have not been alone much these past weeks."

"No," she said, her pulse racing.

" 'Tis good, or I might have married a woman, not a maid."

"And now?" she asked, intending to be provocative.

"And now?" he repeated as he drew her across his lap. "Now, what?" His mouth came down softly on hers and he kissed her voluptuously. "These wicked robes," he murmured against her lips as his hand met the resistance of her bodice.

"You are adept at the unlacing," she said unevenly as his mouth wandered down her throat to fall on the newly exposed flesh. And then she said no more, unable to speak, thrilling to the remembered sensations that were somehow new.

Suddenly it was as it had been in the maze. Her heart pounded, a dull roaring filled her ears, and her body strained closer to him. She felt his hands slip between her knees and press them apart, to travel slowly upward and press between her thighs. She uttered incoherent sounds, oblivious to the time or place, the half-formed thought that anyone might enter dying before it was born.

She was reclining against him, her head thrown back, her body stretched full length, her fingers kneading at his arm as sensation followed sensation. And then when her body felt that it must explode, he stopped. Before she had a moment to understand what was happening, he had smoothed her skirts and laced her bodice, saying, "You are so ripe for love, my dear, and I will taste the sweetness soon."

Once more sitting erect, Caroline felt dizzy and slightly ill, as if she had gorged on sweetmeats with her appetite unappeased.

"I feel . . ." she began.

"I know," he replied. "But 'twill be the last time. I shall not see you until our wedding day. And that night . . . " —he drew a light finger along the line of her bodice— " . . . that night we have all to ourselves."

He rose and smiled down at her, extending a hand. "Come," he said, "we would not be the cause of sportive jests at our expense." He drew her to her feet, steadying her, and they strolled back to the others, separating as they reached the door.

Long after the guests had departed, long after she had sent Dobbs away, Caroline paced the floor of her chamber, unable to sleep. Through the open windows the sharpened night wind blew in, stirring the curtains, laying cool fingers along her flushed cheeks. In the distance, an animal awoke to cry out its complaint to the full moon.

At last she lit a candle and, taking the pouch Elizabeth James had given her, she withdrew the small chest. It was cunningly designed, a skull and crossbones worked in mother-of-pearl across its ebony top.

Opening it for the first time, she found it contained sixty gold sovereigns, as well as some florins and pieces of eight—a veritable treasure. The sight brought a gasp of astonishment to her lips. All for herself alone. How much Mrs. James must think of her to give such a gift! Keep it secret. But how?

After some thought she decided to sew the money into one of the new bodices. There was a white one, embroidered with round gold medallions. It would suit perfectly. And if all the coins didn't fit, she could sew the balance on either side of her pannier hoops.

It was nearly dawn before she finished and laid aside her work, ready to sleep at last.

Chapter Three

The road from London to Abbey Hall wound past the parklands of great houses and through Kentish village high streets where small dwellings and shops and inns clustered close together. On the morning of Caroline Rowland's wedding, the roads were filled with coaches and phaetons and chariots, with the sedan chairs of close neighbors and the blooded stallions of young gentlemen. Scarcely a well-known figure or name in English society went unrepresented. Sir Bertram had spared no expense in the preparations for the wedding of his eldest daughter.

"One would think," Redleigh said to Fortescue as they paused at Ashford to rest their horses, "that the fair Caroline was uniting with the king himself."

Fortescue yawned. "These early morning rides fatigue one so."

"I wager, Fortescue, that within the year Caroline will find herself longing for her old home." Redleigh went on as if his companion had not spoken: "Welles is not apt to indulge her as Sir Bertram has."

"Redleigh, you are overmuch preoccupied with the greengrocer's daughter. The members of this merchant class may wax rich, but we need not attach too much importance to them."

"An eye for an eye," Redleigh answered with a laugh. "One day I shall have mine—one day soon, I fancy."

"Do you still leave England this week?"

"Aye, one year away, looking over some land my aunt assures me will recoup the family fortunes. Will you not change your mind and come with me?"

"I, sir? Leave England for a deserted island and to live on coconuts? No, sir, not I."

"Then I shall buy a mulatto woman for you and bring her back as a gift."

"No, thank you. If you must bring back a gift, let it be the gold idol from some heathen temple. I assure you I shall fondle it more closely. Dear me, it is warm."

"We are two miles above the Abbey," Redleigh said. "I will race you for six sovereigns."

"Done," Fortescue agreed, his indolence vanishing. He spurred his mount as he spoke and the animal leaped ahead of Redleigh's, clouds of dust rising in its wake.

Caroline had awakened early that morning, before the rest of the household stirred. She lay for a time quietly, halfway between rising and falling back into slumber.

Her room was no longer familiar to her. The last of the cases and chests had been sent on to the *Princess Charlotte* two days before. Save for those things she would need until boarding the vessel herself, the room was empty of personal belongings.

Every conceivable article of clothing—from morning robe to ball gown, from French sack to negligee—had filled chest after chest. Her mother had ordered and purchased as if Caroline were never to see a hint of civilization again: pair after pair of brocaded shoes, clogs for rainy weather and—Caroline's greatest joy, won after a battle—long, soft leather riding boots made in gentleman's fashion.

China, silver, linens, yarns, and even bolts of cloth against the day she might fancy yet another gown filled other chests.

"You may be going into the wilderness of the colonies," her mother had said, "but you need not live as a savage."

Her mother's coaching and admonitions on running her own establishment had been endless. But of the realities of the union itself and all that it would mean, she had little to say beyond the oft-stated fact that a wife must allow her husband his marital rights, since her chief duty lay in providing heirs. Save for hinting that this was at best an uninspiring task and that the sooner the heirs reached a suitable number, the sooner it might be dispensed with, Lady Rowland would say nothing more.

Caroline, still struggling between ardent desire to be in

Joshua's arms without hindrance and the worry that somehow such desire was something to fear, had grown tense and nervous.

But when she mentioned this to her mother, Lady Rowland only said, rather sourly, "Well, it appears you will not be too displeased."

Now that the day was upon her, however, Caroline felt calm and contented. Gone was the feverishness, the tension, the worry, and the wondering.

She rose from her bed and went to lean against the frame of the opened windows and drink in the gentle beauty of the morning.

Summer had overtaken spring prematurely, and all of Kent, from Margate to Folkestone, sparkled in the sun. The parks and woods around the Hall were a fresh and dewy green. Soft breezes, sweeping in from the North Downs, rifled leaves and grasses. The sky was high and clear and intensely blue. Beneath it, field and combe burgeoned with new life. Wild roses rioted over fences and foxglove purpled beneath hedgerows. Nearby, Caroline heard the thrushes trilling, and above the distant woods a lark poured out its song.

A perfect day. The beginning of a new life. All she dreamed of awaited her. Caroline felt the stirrings of happy excitement beneath her dreamy calm.

Dobbs, coming in a few moments later with pails of water, said, "Happy the bride the sun smiles on, Miss." She poured the water into the round oaken tub and gave a little shiver. "'Tis very cold, Miss. It be summer in the sky, but the stream don't know it."

"I don't mind." Caroline smiled. " 'Tis only in winter when the rooms are drafty that I mind."

"It be'n't good, this washing all over," Dobbs said. "The fever can come then. Be there that woman in the woods what bathed in the stream and died, you remember that."

"Nonsense—stuff and nonsense. She was old. I am young. And I hear that Madame du Pompadour, King Louis' mistress, bathes each day in icy water."

"Her be a Frenchie," Dobbs sniffed.

"French or not, she has yet to die of the fever."

"Her will die one day," Dobbs prophesied darkly. "And you will, too . . . washing hair one day and body the next."

"Come, Dobbs, we will all die one day." Caroline laughed, removing her robe and stepping into the frigid water. She shivered and began scrubbing herself until her skin tingled with the warmth.

Someday, she thought, I will go to France, someday when the war is over. The silly war . . . bloody and expensive, the king had said. And he was right. She cared not at all who won. Let the French have Canada . . . a wild and woolly place from all she knew. England had all the rest—the best of the New World. Why, Joshua had said Williamsburg was as gay as London. And his lands were larger than her father's. And he had a hundred slaves and two houses, one in Williamsburg and one like Abbey Hall, called Wildwood. The very name delighted her.

"How shall I my true love know?" she sang. "By his silver cap and shoon."

Still humming, she stepped from the tub and into the wide linen cloth Dobbs held. "Dobbs, maybe you will find your true love in the Virginia Colony."

"Yes, Miss," Dobbs said without conviction. "Be you ready for dressing now?"

"Dressing, yes, powdering, no. Mama says I need not, and when today is over I need never do it again. I shall be like you, Dobbs—simple clothes and plain hair."

"Be you in simple clothes like me, Miss, there will be many fine gowns to waste in chests."

"No," Caroline said as Dobbs reached for the bodice into which she had sewn her coins, "not that one. The pink faille, please."

"This be heavy," Dobbs said.

"Too heavy," Caroline answered. And suddenly impatient, she added, "Oh, hurry, Dobbs. I must go to Mama when I have finished dressing.

The wedding ceremony and the feast that followed passed like a blur before Caroline's dazed eyes. Whenever she tried to recall it, only small incidents stood out: the rector of the tiny village church questioning; her own hand trembling on Joshua's rigidly held arm; the villagers, lining the roads to see the phaeton pass and return, cheering; the swirl of guests pressing forward and falling back with their felicitations.

All of it seemed like a dream, a happy and yet disturbing dream. Only when at last they retired to the

Dower House and Dobbs came to her did Caroline come to her senses with a small shock.

It was over. She was married. Her wedding gown was being carried away by Dobbs and she stood in the center of the large, strange bedchamber, her lacy white gown and robe covering her, her hair loosened and falling in waves around her.

Beyond the closed door was Joshua. Soon he would come to her and then . . . Her face and body were suffused with heat, and her hands and feet suddenly felt cold.

In one instant she poised to flee, and then the door opened and Joshua, himself dressed for bed, his wig gone and his thin, sandy hair combed back, came into the chamber.

Caroline stepped back as he approached, and, reading her anxiety, he laughed softly. As he gathered her to him, she stiffened for a moment and then, as his mouth covered hers, she grew limp.

There were no hoops, no bodice, no petticoats to obstruct his way with her tonight. The negligee was soon rustling to the carpet and the gown followed. Feeling his hands warm and firm upon her bared flesh, she uttered a little moan and began to tremble uncontrollably. Joshua lifted her up and carried her to the bed. He placed her upon the coverlet, where she lay, her eyes closed, body waiting. He straightened up and looked down at her for a long moment before bending to blow out the candle on the bedside table.

Darkness enveloped the room. She heard the whisper of his garments and then he was lying beside her, his flesh burning into hers. She moved against him, her desire rising. As she began to writhe beneath his caresses, he drew one of her hands to his member and she heard him groan with pleasure as her innocent fingers closed around it.

At first this act gave rise to startled reluctance, but as his hands kneaded between her thighs and his lips found her breasts, it faded, leaving in its place a sensual agitation she had not experienced before. All at once, he ceased his efforts to arouse her and flung himself upon her, spreading her legs wide and thrusting himself between them with ferocity, his breath hoarse and uneven.

The initial excitement of his entry was suddenly pierced and broken by pain that tore her apart. He was hurting her and she cried out, but her pleas only served to make him thrust more savagely. She screamed, but that only seemed to excite him more. "No, no!" she cried, twisting and turning frantically, but he held her helpless. Any idea of pleasure was forgotten for her. The more she struggled, the more powerful his thrusts became, and the intensity of the pain made her grow dim and faint. Yet the pain continued for a short time longer and then he groaned mightily and fell upon her. It was mercifully over.

His weight was suffocating. Beneath her, a wet stickiness spread and became part of the misery of the experience. At last he rolled away from her. Rising, he lighted the candle and held it up over her.

"A virgin, after all," he said with satisfaction. "It is pleasant to have proof." He blew out the candle and climbed back into bed.

"The greatest pleasure is in forcing a virgin," he said, as if in explanation. She only half-grasped his meaning and made no reply. Not long afterward he fell into a deep and sonorous slumber, leaving her to lie awake and wonder that the thrill of his caresses should result in so wretched an aftermath.

Twice more before they rose to face the morning, he awoke to repeat his performance. The searing agony of that first encounter was not repeated, but her flesh grew increasingly sore. Finally morning came and she fell into a troubled sleep.

Joshua had touched her desires, had shown her a different life, but in the same way he had left those desires raging unspent inside her, and so had he failed to inspire a deep and abiding affection.

From that day until their departure, the routine at night hardly varied and nothing occurred to assuage her physical or mental misery.

Her mother, seldom perceptive, was astute enough to observe Caroline's unhappiness, so that when Caroline sought her out before leaving, hinting that all was not well and that she wished it were possible to remain longer in England, Agatha said with poorly concealed satisfaction, "I warned you, Caroline. It is the way of life. We all suffer it. You will find once you are big with child you will have respite, and for a few weeks after the child is born, as well. When you have enough children, by that time you will find that he makes fewer demands, and, perhaps at last, none at all."

"Then I might as well be a broody hen or a cow in the field screaming under the weight of a bull."

Her mother stiffened. "Really, Caroline, such cant is unseemly. Ladies do not scream."

"Some women enjoy the flesh," Caroline retorted. "And what of the women who become mistresses?"

"They do it for the money and protection."

"But what of those who do not need the money? Gossip tells of many such."

"Not many—a few, perhaps. They have sex like animals, and, like animals, they seem to take some sport in it. But they are unnatural women. You must see that."

Then I am unnatural, Caroline thought bitterly. I do enjoy the flesh. And I want to enjoy all of it, as Joshua seems to. Aloud, she said, "I cannot bear to think of a life where I must suffer nightly for years. I *will not* suffer it."

At this Agatha grew alarmed. "You will not disgrace us. Your father has business with Joshua and your marriage seals it. . . . You—" She stopped at a startled ejaculation from Caroline when Sir Bertram walked into the room. And for the first and perhaps the last time in their life together as husband and wife they exchanged firm glances of their resolve to set their daughter in her place.

"Well," her mother went on more quietly, "it doesn't matter that you know now you are safely wed. This marriage was of your father's making. And mine. For once, Caroline, you did as we wished. Though I feel, had you known, you would have eloped with the fishmonger's boy first." She smiled thinly. "Never forget, however, you asked for the marriage."

It was true, and Caroline had to acknowledge that. She had imagined she had fought for the right to marry Joshua. She had been pleased at crying down her father's protestations that he was nothing but a humbug Colonial with pretensions. She had been flushed with triumph when, after many a tearful and stormy battle, her father had given his reluctant consent. And, as it turned out when she confronted him, he was full of good humor, affectionately paternal. She turned to her father with anger but before she could utter her protest at being tricked he stopped her.

"But Poppet, 'twas for your own good. I saw you were

smitten and knew were I to encourage it you would spoil your own happiness," her father said sweetly.

"Spoil my happiness," she said bitterly. "I *am* unhappy. Nothing is the way it seemed 'twould be."

"Come, come," her father said testily. "You are but a bride. Joshua may have been my choice for you, but never forget that he was your choice, as well, however it came about."

"If I do not like Virginia any better than I like marriage, I will soon be back on your doorstep," she lashed out.

At this, Sir Bertram's expansive good humor vanished. "You will find no welcome here, Poppet. You will not disgrace your family and expect to find succor among us. Your duty is with your husband, and it is he now who has charge and control of you. He is not, I fear, as indulgent as I. Make no mistake, daughter, were you to attempt to embarrass Welles by leaving, 'twould go hard for you, and I could not and would not lift a hand to spare you."

At the sight of her stricken face, he softened. "There, Caroline, once you are on your way to the Colonies, you will feel differently. How often have you begged me to travel abroad? There are many wonders ahead . . . wonders you only hoped to see. You are no longer a girl; you are a woman. The carefree days are over."

To this she had no answer. And as she journeyed down to Plymouth, she began to see more clearly the course open to her. If nothing else, she had the adventure she longed for ahead. Perhaps in the settling of the new life some of the misery would be abated. Perhaps in the very act of sailing across the Atlantic, of seeing the Indies, meeting new people, it would all once again seem worthwhile. And there would be children. Thinking of that and what it meant, she suddenly began to hope that she would soon be with child, then soon after with another. Children would ease the burden. And if Joshua were not all she hoped, at least he was offering her things she wanted. Cheered at this line of reasoning, she slipped her arm through her husband's.

Feeling the pressure of her hand, Joshua smiled to himself. He had done well, far better than he had dared believe. The proud and haughty Caroline Rowland, the minx who had used every artifice to discourage him, as she had so many before, was his at last.

Sir Bertram fancied it was his own cleverness, but he did not know his daughter as well as he, Joshua, did. Early, he had seen the slumbering sensuality beneath Caroline's cool and clever facade. It was the very look Reynolds had captured so adroitly—that half-realized passion, so ready to be fully roused. And Joshua had played to those very innermost desires to pique her interest. How it pleased him to make love to her and find her panting and eager in his arms. He frowned slightly. There had been no time like that first time, however. He could still remember the ardor she had shown and then the cries and writhings. By heaven, she could be a wanton when all was said and done. But since that first night, she had grown silent, and it taxed his ingenuity to make her resist, move, stiffen, and so increase the pleasure he took in the final consummation.

In ways she reminded him of Susan Ormonton . . . Susan Redleigh, then. That was twenty years ago now. Then he was a youth lately come into his inheritance from his uncle in Virginia and anxious to be away from the decaying splendor of his father's mansion and the poverty that was his as the youngest son.

Susan had been like Caroline then, easily aroused, only he had not bedded Susan, nor wedded her. The daughter of a lord, and a lord who was proud of his ancient title, was never to be the bride of an impoverished baronet's son . . . not even when the lands in Virginia became his.

Joshua recalled the last interview with the old lord as readily as if it had been yesterday. Redleigh was haughty and disdainful and, most of all, condescending. His son, the present earl's father, told the story of his rejection as if it were the greatest joke in London. And now the young Lord Edward Redleigh, a babe of three at the time, had been baiting him as recently as two weeks ago.

Well, time had been his champion. Both of the elder Redleighs were gone, dying young from the dissolution of wine and women and gambling excesses. And the present earl was almost certain to follow.

The Redleighs had deprived him once, but with his marriage to Caroline he had turned the tables neatly. It was Redleigh who needed a rich bride, and among the old nobility he could find no suitable one. He had turned to the newly rich merchant's daughter and had been despised by the very family he sneered at.

And Susan . . . poor Susan. Joshua remembered pleading with her to elope and come to Virginia, but she had no courage. Well, she had eventually settled in the Colonies, where she happily married Sir Alfred Ormonton, who leased the Nassau Colony from the Crown, hoping to make a fortune. Young Redleigh, even now, if rumor were to be credited, considered himself fortunate to win the hand of the dowdiest girl of London society, whose father's wealth was half that of the Rowlands'.

And he, Joshua, had both the loveliest of the London beauties and the richest, and a partnership with the most powerful merchant in England. He was Rowland's son-in-law. He had been received by King George himself. One day, if all went well, he would be honored with wealth and title through this fortuitous marriage. Caroline's dower was handsome; the share to come to her on her father's death was even more handsome.

She was young, she was intelligent, she was charming, and she was rich. With all that, she was eager for things of the flesh, and if she disappointed him a little at the beginning, time would soon cure that. Once safe in Wildwood, there were ways to change her. Meanwhile, there was the never-ending delight in his possession of her and his pleasure in watching the coolly arrogant girl turn subject in his arms.

Even thinking about it excited him. He pressed the arm through his and with his free hand reached over to cup her breasts lightly. She started and tried to withdraw her arm, but he said, "Be still or you will have the coachman stopping to see what the matter can be."

"Joshua," she whispered, "'tis broad daylight on the king's highway and the guard soldiers are just ahead."

"They will not ride back to peep into our windows. Hush." He looked at her trembling lips and wide eyes, then felt her breast rising and falling beneath his hands, and he wondered if he could take her here and now in the rocking, swaying coach. It would be more than three hours until they would stop, and already he was in some discomfort.

He began to undo her bodice, ignoring her faint protests, seizing the warm flesh greedily, squeezing and nipping at it. Her traveling costume was far less cumbersome than ordinary clothing. He tugged at her knickers as she fought him silently, and all the while the coach swayed and careened. The horses' beating hooves filled his ears. The shouts of the driver and the clatter of the wheels of the coaches before and behind all seemed to be part of the hammering of his own excited blood. The seat was far too narrow, he thought, as he stroked and squeezed her thighs, reaching behind to grasp her small, silky buttocks.

At some point he realized she had ceased her struggles and was returning his embrace, clinging to him and making those incoherent sounds that fired him. He was sweating and panting and pulsing, and at last, with a mighty heave, he lifted her up and astride, his face buried between her breasts as he thrust himself into her. He felt her eager willingness, felt her squirming upon him. When he sought to move her, she clung until, clasping with hard hands at her waist, he succeeded in lifting her up and down with swift, impatient jerks until his own passion broke and he was spent. A moment later he had restored her, half-sobbing, to her seat.

As he rebuttoned his breeches and rearranged his clothing, he saw that she still lay sprawled, breasts exposed, skirts well up on her white thighs.

"Here," he said roughly, annoyed that she had remained so, "lace up your bodice." He drew her skirts down, and, seeing the knickers on the floor, he picked them up and stuffed them under his tunic. "And no one is the wiser." He laughed. "Come, Caroline. Tears? You were willing enough in maze and garden and on the divan before we wed. Now we are man and wife and you balk at the privacy of a coach."

She did not answer him. Her fingers shook as she relaced her bodice and brought order back to her costume.

After a time she said in a low voice, "I am not any woman of the world, Joshua. Such as this offends me."

"Offend and be damned," he replied. "I know a willing woman when I am with one." At her silence, he said, "But if the sport of love is too difficult, very well, we will leave desire to the bed in the future."

Any promise if it would bring peace, he thought, very tired now. He fell asleep to the sound of her quiet weeping.

Chapter Four

The *Princess Charlotte,* while not the largest of the Rowland ships, was nevertheless the pride of its fleet. Built with special accommodations for the exclusive use of Sir Bertram and those of his family and close friends whenever they might wish to journey to the Colonies, it had initially been christened the *Sea Nymph.* The original carving of a mermaid just below the bowsprit had been slightly altered to suit the new lettering along the side of the bow.

The ship rode low in the water now that she was fully laded. Her holds carried not only Caroline's many chests and furnishings, but goods for trading, as well: manufactured cotton goods; woolens from Exeter mills; rugs from the Orient; casks of wine and spirits; tea; coffee; olives; spices; guns; utensils; and seeds of various kinds, destined for the Indies islands, where there was not much in the way of natural vegetation. All this, together with provisions for the crew, the live chickens and pigs to extend the meat supply, crammed the holds and spilled over to an open deck, where casks of water were lashed to the sides.

Boarding the ship from the bobbing launch, Caroline's uneasiness turned to amusement as she saw the juxtaposition of the voluptuous mermaid to *Princess Charlotte's* name. Not the soon-to-be-queen's fondest friend or relation could claim so much for her. By London standards —if the reports of the king's ambassadors to Mecklenburg were true—Charlotte was plain and housewifely. Considered dull by the sophisticated coterie around the throne, she was rumored to show a devotion to king and to family matters in general. Both traits augured well for the royal marriage. Virtues such as domesticity and loyalty had been notably lacking in her Hanoverian predecessors.

Imagine marrying without seeing more than a painted miniature of one's future spouse. Yet, by all accounts, Charlotte was prepared to promise love when there was not even a bond of established affection. Such a bond was rare enough among arranged marriages and marriages of convenience. Caroline knew it was absent between her own parents and seldom to be observed among their circle. Thinking of that, she experienced a pang for something she dimly realized she would never know.

That moment in the coach when she had resolved to accept her fate, when she had bethought herself of what Joshua had promised and laid an affectionate hand upon him, was gone forever. What followed, however it had excited her at first, had driven any thought of true wifely devotion from her heart. It had been worse later in their room at Exeter. There, he had been angered by her withdrawal and she had been afraid of that wrath, for it had turned on her, hurting her, making her fight, and she knew now that such would be her fate were she ever again to hint at her personal distaste for his lovemaking.

Surveying the confining quarters they would share for the next months, her heart sank. Although they were richly furnished, they were only seagoing miniatures of the apartments at Abbey Hall. The quarters consisted of a bedplace built into the ship's timbers and separated from the grand salon by tasseled strips of cloth, and the salon itself, which contained bolted desk and chairs and table and divan.

In the center of the cabin floor, she spied one of her packing chests, and the sailor who had accompanied her said, " 'Twere lef' behind, Mistress, and only come late and 'twas no room in the hold. Where'm I to put it, Mistress?"

Caroline directed him to the space at the foot of the bed and had him place the other two chests between the writing table and the shelves, which were on either side of the porthole.

Wanting to freshen herself, she then sent the sailor to summon Dobbs. Half an hour later he had not returned, nor had Dobbs appeared. Caroline made a hasty toilet herself.

She was just finishing when Joshua came to lead her topside so they might see the ship leave the harbor. As they stepped onto the open deck, she saw that the main and foremasts were already rigged and that the mizzen was being set. Sailors lined the riggings or scurried from them to new tasks.

"Heave the capstan! Ho! Heave!" the boatswain called. The call was taken up smoothly, sending it on to the men, who replied to it in unison. The cadence was like a song.

"Yo! Heave! Ho!" they called as they bent back and upright and forward in perfect rhythm.

Onlookers ranged themselves along the quay, waving and calling, their voices faint on the wind that blew southwest.

As Caroline and Joshua leaned upon the railing of the veranda deck, the last of the sail was set and the anchor was raised. On the next incoming wave the *Charlotte* lifted, and as the tide receded it drew the *Charlotte* farther from the shore. A cheer rose from the men in the rigging and from those who ranged the yardarm, and it was joined by the watchers upon the shore.

"Set the topgallants," a voice called.

"Set the topgallants," echoed the boatswain.

"Larboard one-quarter," the voice sang out, and the command was echoed again.

This maneuvering brought the *Charlotte* full in front of the wind. "Steady as she goes," came the last call.

The land dropped away behind them, and those ashore became tinier and tinier, until at last they were only a blur. Still, Caroline and Joshua stood there, he looking to the right at the coastline, she ahead to the waters dividing under the *Charlotte*'s plunging bow.

The breeze that had touched the sails lightly while the ship still rode at anchor had stiffened. The sails bellied out and the *Charlotte* picked up speed, careering fast. In the rigging, the men reefed sail to accommodate to this new condition and the *Charlotte* continued on her course, west by southwest.

Ahead and to the right lay the Cornish cliffs that rose beyond Whitesend Bay. To the left lay the shore of France. Three decks below, under the command of the gunnery officer, Mr. Hardin, the gun crew manned their weapons against the possibility of French attack during this passage so close to her coastline.

"However," Joshua calmed Caroline, "it is more likely to have an engagement at sea than here, where other ships might sail to the rescue. Still, we are prepared for anything, save a man-of-war, and those are busily engaged near the Colonies, so we need have no fear. France is finished now. She is outnumbered in ships. Her crucial colonial lands are taken. Nothing much remains, save for New Orleans and a few islands in the south."

"But the Spanish . . . " Caroline began.

"They have yet to enter, in fact. I know they are more interested in preserving their colonies in Florida and Cuba and Hispaniola than they are in assisting the French with New France. There is little to fear, Caroline—not in the Indies and not from Georgia to Virginia."

He thought of the privateers sailing under letters of marque and of the pirates still haunting the Caribbean despite international agreements made twenty years before, but of this he said nothing.

"I shall be happy to see the land again!" Caroline exclaimed.

"Ah, but you have yet to lose sight of land," Joshua pointed out. "See yonder?" He waved his arm at the Cornish cliffs. "Presently, we shall raise Falmouth and then Penzance and then . . . " He broke off as a sailor approached to say that he was sorry to advise them that Dobbs had slipped ashore on the last launch and a letter had been left for Caroline.

At first Caroline could not believe it. "She was not forced to come with me," she said indignantly. "Had she refused, she knew I would give her fair recommendation. If she had but spoken as late as this morning, I . . . "

"I would have purchased you a bondswoman, my dear," Joshua said.

"As for a note . . . why, Dobbs could not sign her own name." She took the proffered paper, saying, "This is some foul trick."

The note was ill written and badly spelled, but in substance it said the writer was performing the service for one Mary Dobbs, who did not want to leave her family and friends for a strange land, after all. She was sorry to upset Caroline, but at the last moment she could not face going.

It was signed "a frend to Mery Dobz."

"I don't believe it," Caroline said again. "She never spoke of friends here."

" 'Twas a young man who brought the note to the deck

watch afore sailing. He be goin' back at once by launch. An' they, thinkin' it a farewell letter, be too busy to bring it at once," the sailor explained.

Joshua dismissed the man and said consolingly to Caroline, "A great pity. I had anticipated my own difficulties leaving one valet in England with another in Virginia. But for you, my dear, 'tis more than difficulty. It is a catastrophe. For, while I am willing, nay, eager to assist you in your robings and disrobings, I am not adept. I shall buy a black for you when we reach New Providence."

" 'Tis no matter," Caroline said, smarting under Dobbs' deception. " 'Twill not be the first time I have maided myself. When her mother was ill, I sent Dobbs home for a week and I managed. In any case, I will not be wearing hoops and silk gowns if this dipping and swaying is my lot aboard ship."

"You do not feel ill, I trust," Joshua said.

"Not at all, a bit topsy-turvy, but I expect I shall grow used to that."

"Admirable," he murmured. "I find my sealegs well into a journey, if at all. Shall we go below? I know I feel better when I am lying down."

Captain Ramsey, awaiting the arrival of the Welleses for the supper to be taken in the great cabin beyond his own bedplace, was still smarting under Joshua Welles' indignance over the loss of the bondswoman.

"Some sailor has helped her ashore, I'll be bound," he had accused. Ramsey had denied it, saying the woman had probably gone masquerading out as a maid to one of the shore ladies visiting the ship earlier, but privately he agreed. He thought he knew which sailor, for the matter of that. But he had no intention of beginning a voyage by charging the man and consigning him to ten lashes or chains. It was no way to begin any journey. As long as he pretended to believe the woman had acted on her own, he need not stir the crew unnecessarily. Let other captains please themselves. He had found fair treatment brought a good crew, except for the odd rogue now and again.

The crew he had now had sailed with him and willingly for more than two years. That was his good luck, just as it was his good fortune to meet and overcome dangers at sea. Despite the endless wars that raged between England and France, he had brought every cargo safely to port. Thrice he had engaged French frigates and once an old Spanish galleon manned by pirates, and each time he had been successful in fending off disaster, destroying one French ship, sending the galleon to the bottom with all hands, and routing the other Frenchman, which slipped away during the night, rigged fore and aft by tattered sails.

He had refused command of a slaver, saying he preferred cargo that did not require that he give it sustenance in order that it arrive as ordered. Privately, he deplored the slave traffic and admired the English Quakers' recent edict banning from membership any of those engaged in the buying or selling of slaves. It was not, however, politic to mention this, especially in view of his dealings with the Colonials and the fact that Sir Bertram's own slavers were part of the fleet.

Sir Bertram, he knew, suspected his leanings, but, save for the oblique reference from time to time, he did not engage him directly on the subject. Open disagreement with anyone who opposed him was not Sir Bertram's way, especially when that person was valuable to him. It was, however, Joshua Welles' approach to any problem.

Ramsey had little regard for Welles. He had disliked him instantly at Lloyd's, remembering him as a man he had seen at the Charleston slave market two years before. He had watched Welles as he appraised a powerfully built black man, punching at the man's bulging biceps and kicking at his calf muscles. The slave had not endured it for long. Bringing his arms up, he had slammed his chained fists into Welles' shoulder. Seconds later Welles had whipped out his pistol and shot the man dead and then coolly paid the slaver for the carcass, much as if he had accidentally butchered a neighbor's cow.

He was notorious in Virginia Colony for his ill treatment of his own slaves. Here he had kept a black mistress as housekeeper. Ramsey had never seen her, but she had been spoken of as "regal, the way one imagined Sheba." She had died in Charleston just before Welles sailed for England last year, leaving behind half a dozen mulatto children, all of whom remained in bondage to their natural father and, rumor had it, were no better treated for the blood relationship.

Ramsey would have preferred any passenger to Welles, but he gave no indication of this as he welcomed him that evening.

Caroline Welles struck him at once as an unlikely mate for the Virginian, and he could not help but wonder how Welles had captured such a prize.

During the amiable preliminaries of the evening, she remained subdued, but as they approached the dinner and wine, she relaxed and a sparkle came into her face.

They were six at the table. Aside from himself and the Welleses, there were his master, Mr. Bell, young Hardin, the gunnery officer, and Dr. Bascomb, the surgeon.

Caroline Welles blossomed under the attention of the five men, and Ramsey noticed that the fact that it was his wife who was admired set Welles into an expansive humor.

"I thought," said Caroline as the meal progressed, "that one supped on hardtack and bully beef aboard ship. Instead, I find hot breads and pheasant and beef and fresh vegetables, as well as delicious wine."

"Eat heartily, Mistress Welles," Captain Ramsey said. "We shall be out of most fresh food, save chickens, soon enough. You will be very bored with salted meats and herring and weeviled breads by the time we get to Nassau. The wine will be all that remains of this kind of feasting." He gestured politely in her direction with his glass, and as he did so the ship gave a mighty roll to starboard, and the contents of the beaker slopped upon the table.

"Ah, we are nearing Land's End," the captain remarked as the ship eased in the return and his cabin boy rushed to wipe up the wine. "We have been fortunate so far. The Channel has been as smooth as the sea around Cathay."

"Let us hope we may continue that good fortune," Joshua said. Looking at him, Ramsey saw he was a little pale.

He won't sail well, Ramsey decided with malice. He would not mind some rough weather himself if it confined Mr. Welles for part of the voyage.

"Let us hope Mistress Welles is a good sailor," he said aloud, noting with satisfaction that Caroline retained her high color and spirits against the increasing roll of the ship.

"I hope so, too." She smiled. "Or else Dr. Bascomb will be attending me the voyage."

"An honor, madam," the doctor said gallantly, "but for your sake I hope to forgo it."

Caroline blushed at the compliment, and, looking up, she met the frankly admiring gaze of Mr. Hardin, the gunnery officer. The youngest man at the table, he had the gentle fair looks of a county boy, and for a fleeting instant she was reminded of Geoffrey Lyons. His admiration added further color to her cheeks and she looked hastily away, hoping that the exchange had gone unnoticed by the others.

Ramsey, however, had noticed, and, added to his other observations of the evening, he concluded that whatever the reasons for the marriage, the heart of the lovely Mistress Welles was not directly involved. He made a mental note to warn Hardin off. Dearly as he himself might love to see Welles cuckolded, he did not wish to precipitate an ugly quarrel with Welles, nor lose his young officer. He'd an idea that Welles would shoot Hardin with no more distaste than he had shown in shooting the black.

Shortly after the meal ended, all but the doctor and the Welleses left to resume their duties. The ship, which had been rolling heavily for sometime now, began to pitch into the strong coastal swells. Joshua, full of wine, continued to help himself to more, and by the time the doctor excused himself Joshua was clearly half-inebriated. The doctor's delicate suggestion that too much wine might bring about *mal de mer* was met with indifference.

Caroline, feeling the fatigue of the long day and evening of their departure, longed for bed and yet dreaded the thought of it. She stifled her yawns with difficulty, but Joshua, steadily worsening, had ceased talking and did not appear to notice that she was there.

She rose at last, saying she would retire. He raised glazed eyes to her face, tried to get up, and fell back into the chair with a murmured incoherence that she took for agreement.

"Good night, then," she said, then left him in the great cabin. She had considerable difficulty navigating to her own quarters, but she soon instinctively picked up the seamen's trick of walking along the upward surge of the ship so that her body, no longer fighting the pitch and toss of the vessel, was stabilized.

It was strange to stand in the dark cabin, undressing herself. Braced against the bulkhead, as she wrestled with hoops and bodice, she resolved to wear plainer clothes minus the hoops for the rest of the voyage, or at least until they reached the smooth seas of the South.

For a time after she had climbed over the guardrail of the bed, she lay tense, half-expecting Joshua, but exhaustion finally overcame her and she was nearly asleep when she heard him stumble into the cabin. He careened from side to side of the room, finally fetching up against the guardrail with a muffled oath. Caroline, rolling away to the far side, heard the bed creak as he fell into it, clothes and all. He reeked of wine and sweat. She pressed farther from him, but he made no move to touch her and was soon snoring heavily. With a half-murmured prayer of thanksgiving, Caroline herself was asleep almost at once.

The first morning on the open sea dawned clear and brilliant. The choppy waters of the coastal swells had lengthened into long, rolling billows through which the *Charlotte* sailed in an easy side-to-side motion, her bow and stern almost steady.

Caroline awoke to find Joshua still snoring beside her, his mouth hanging slack, his face exceedingly flushed. He did not stir as she crept from the bed and robed herself in a thin woolen morning gown. The absence of the hoops made the gown too slender, and she added an extra petticoat to fill it out. She laced her bodice lightly, tying the stomacher more firmly to compensate.

She had washed her thick wheat-gold hair on the previous morning and had dried it in the sun. The ocean spray lent extra weight to it so that it curled in springing ringlets to her shoulders. Caroline bound it at the nape of her neck. After setting a frilled cap on her head, she went to the great cabin to partake of her morning meal.

She spent the rest of the forenoon walking to and fro upon the veranda deck, braced by the crisp air, watching the sailors below at their various tasks. She discovered that they were a cheerful lot who seemed congenial with each other and who appeared to enjoy their work.

Coming down the passage toward her cabin as the first meal call was piped, she met Captain Ramsey, who swept her a low bow and said, "I see, Mistress, you are a good sailor. Most of our lady passengers, including my own good wife, suffer for the first few days."

"Oh, I think it's glorious," Caroline answered. "But I am quite blown about and must first go to my cabin."

He stood aside to let her pass, saying, "Another good meal is waiting, Mistress. I hope you are of good appetite."

"Ravenous," Caroline assured him extravagantly.

When she reached the cabin, Joshua was in the act of buttoning up his waistcoat.

"Good morning," she greeted him sweetly, to which he grunted a sour reply.

"Lunch has just been called," she said, hurrying with her toilette. "I am as hungry as a hound after a hunt."

"I may never dine again," he answered. "My head is as large as a pumpkin and feels as if a hundred Indians were beating their drums within it."

"You must go up into the fresh air," Caroline advised. "It blows away all ailments."

"Um," he said, putting out a hand to brace himself against a sharp roll. "I will be happy to reach the southern waters. If you are ready, Caroline, we will go to lunch."

In spite of his disclaimer to hunger, Joshua ate well and afterward agreed to accompany Caroline to the main deck. The air did seem to restore him, and as the afternoon wore into early evening and the sun hung before the mast like a huge orange globe, he seemed almost himself again, saying, "This life appears to suit you, Caroline. You are very agreeable today, and you are more fetching than you have been of late."

The look on his face foretold his desire, and Caroline wished fervently she had left him to his own devices.

"Come, now," he added. "I would enjoy a rest before supper, and I fancy your company." They were alone on the deck, standing in the shadow of the longboat and thus invisible to the working crew. He reached out to pull her roughly against him, cupping her buttocks through the thin skirts and saying, "No hoops. How convenient."

Caroline suffered the embrace in silence, trying to give a good imitation of interest in the proceedings and wishing with all her heart that she could think of some way to distract him from his purpose, all the while knowing from her short experience with him that such was not possible. And then he said thickly, "Come below."

Just then a voice sang out high and clear from the crow's nest: "Sail, ho!"

There was an immediate scurrying as men went to their stations to prepare for the eventuality of an enemy encounter. Joshua, distracted at last, rushed at once to the side and peered out at the horizon. "I see nothing," he muttered. And then he yelled, "There she is!"

High above them the signal flags were hoisted aloft. Caroline stood, her hands gripping the mahogany rail. Save for the terse, shouted orders, the *Charlotte* sailed on to meet the other ship, bearing leeward to it.

The silence seemed to last an eternity. The other ship tacked steadily on its course. All at once the clear call came: "English, sir! I see her Great Union and . . ." There was a pause. " . . . the Cross of St. George." A loud cheer rose from the ranks. The *Charlotte*'s bell tolled in salute and was answered by the ship of the line.

"She's the *Southampton!*" the watchman called again. There was another cheer for this first of the English frigates. The *Southampton* had seen arduous duty since her launching in '57, and her exploits were well known. She was heading home now, covered with glory.

Her sails, stretched full, were as white as the foam beneath her bow. The rampant lion jutting out from the beakhead looked almost real. Its carved mane appeared to toss in the light and shadow of the sunset that turned it tawny gold.

At a signal from the *Southampton,* the *Charlotte* hove to. Sailors scrambled into the rigging to reef sail. Forward, the anchor was dropped to drag against the pull of the currents.

The *Southampton,* already lying to, had lowered its launch, which was even now, being rowed steadily across the small intervening space to board the *Charlotte.*

"I wonder what the matter can be," Joshua said, his face pale and anxious. "Go below," he added peremptorily. "I will see the captain."

She obeyed him silently, too troubled by his obvious anxiety to question his reasons. In her own quarters, she looked through the brass-bound porthole, but from that angle she could see nothing. Footsteps hurried endlessly in the passageway and on the deck above her, and after awhile she began to tidy up the cabin, more to ease her anxiety than because it was required. The cabin boy had already been in to make up the bed and put away discarded garments. She thought of her hoops and the casket sewn in them and went to look for them. She found the hoops stacked neatly behind one of the chests.

It was strange to have a man performing such services for her, and once again she regretted Dobbs' disappearance.

The cabin grew dark with evening, but Joshua did not return. Caroline lighted a lantern and began to disrobe. Dressing herself was difficult and time-consuming without help, but more so since she had to deal with the constant motion. Even now, with sails reefed and anchor dragging, the *Charlotte* rocked in the current.

Slipping her negligee on, Caroline reclined on the divan of the sitting room while she brushed her hair. The rocking motion was so soothing she stretched out to rest before dressing.

She fell into a light doze, waking up at once when Joshua finally returned. He stood with his back against the door and observed her as she sat erect.

He was, she could see, slightly flushed. "Nothing to worry about," he said in answer to her query about the *Southampton* boarding party. "It seems the rats got into the last of their meal, the bread's gone moldy, and one of the rum barrels broke during a skirmish. Captain Ramsey gave them provisions to last until they reached port in a few days, plus two caskets of rum. We sampled the rum with the first lieutenant. Pleasant chap."

"It will be supper time soon," Caroline said. "I was worried when you did not return sooner."

She rose and he said, "No, don't get up." Coming forward, he fell beside her. "What a sweet and obedient little wife," he said thickly. "She makes herself ready for her husband and waits as patiently as Penelope for Ulysses." He slipped his hands beneath her robe and caressed her breasts slowly. As always, the touch gave her a strange little thrill.

At least there is that, she thought as he began kneading her belly. It makes it easier to pretend in the beginning, and later—later he was too excited to notice how she felt. She gave an unconscious sigh and he took it for pleasure. Thereafter he wasted no time, pushing her back to lie atop her and release himself.

For the next few days their life fell into a pattern. Joshua would rise just before lunch, eat, take his exercise with Caroline beside him, and then bring her below to bed her and nap until supper, when he would drink liberal amounts of wine until he was drunk enough to sleep. It occurred to Caroline that this last might be his way of combatting what she perceived to be a disaffection for the sea. At the end of the week he was still unable to navigate smoothly, and any change in the ship's roll would invariably catch him unaware, and once or twice it caused him to fall before he could steady himself.

When they had been at sea a week, Caroline awoke one morning to discover that her benefit was upon her, and even as she felt a sweeping disappointment that she was not yet with child, it was followed by a sense of relief that at least for a few days she would be spared the afternoon ordeal. For, as the time had passed, even the small excitement of being caressed had disappeared and it was becoming more and more difficult to simulate a passion she was far from feeling.

Joshua took the news with an irritating smile and said meaningfully, "We shall have to see that it does not recur. I have been remiss in not paying you sufficient attention."

This remark created a small panic within her, and she longed to blurt out the truth that his attentions were far too plentiful as it was.

A sense of melancholy overcame her and it stayed with her as the next few days passed. The future looked bleak, and in the absence of anticipation she did not recover her spirits. This condition became apparent to her companions aboard the ship, and it served to diminish the usual sociability of the meals.

She dreaded each day that brought her closer to the benefit's conclusion. Toward the end, she drank rather more than was her custom at supper, and feeling tipsy, she retired at the earliest possible moment, leaving Joshua in his accustomed place in the great cabin, sprawled in a chair, brandy at his elbow.

She had fallen asleep at once and slept so deeply she was unaware of Joshua's return to their cabin. Toward the early hours of the morning, she awoke to feel the ship tossing violently from side to side and then pitching with the rearing, plunging motion of a newly broken stallion. She opened her eyes to find the room eerily lit by flashing lightning. There was a deafening clap of thunder, followed by another stab of light.

Beside her, Joshua moaned and stirred in his stuporous sleep. Waves slapped forcefully at the sides of the ship, covering the portholes. Above the noise of the storm and the ship's protesting timbers, Caroline could hear hoarse shouts, shouts that tore from the men's throats before they were half-finished and flung upon the howling wind.

Alarmed by the way the ship was heeling half over toward the ocean, she managed to struggle to her feet and claw her way along the walls to pull her robe and shawl around her.

It seemed incredible that Joshua still slept, that he could sleep amidst the roaring sea, the sizzling lightning, and the thunderclaps that overlapped each other to produce the effect of cannon fire.

She fought her way to the door and managed to pull it open and brace herself against the frame. In the passageway, she saw Mr. Hardin struggling by and called out to him.

"Mistress Welles!" he exclaimed. "You had better lie upon your couch. 'Tis a bad storm."

"Are we sinking?" she asked.

He shook his head as he came abreast of her. "We've ridden out worse than this. Nonetheless, it is bad. Stay here. You are safer in a hammock or berth. Where is your husband?"

She gestured mutely toward the cabin.

"Is he unwell?"

"Sleeping," she said.

"It is well for him," Hardin said with a grim laugh. He smiled at her and then quickly averted his gaze. Looking down, she saw that the shawl lay open and the outline of her body showed itself beneath the filmy material of her gown and negligee. Hurriedly, she pulled the shawl around her and said, "I . . . I . . . thank you, Mr. Hardin."

She watched a moment as he made his way up the passageway and through the hatch to the ladder, then closed the door. She pulled the heavy bolt into place before she staggered back to her still-unconscious husband.

Somewhat reassured by Hardin's remarks, she attempted to sleep. She dozed fitfully until morning, when the fury of the storm abated somewhat, leaving the *Charlotte* still pitching in the fierce swells that radiated from the storm center overhead. The sky was a dull, leaden gray; the day was as dark as late twilight; rain fell in thick sheets, as if the clouds had burst open to pour torrents of long-accumulated water down upon them.

It was easier to move now than it had been earlier. In spite of the ship's continued heeling, Caroline felt as hungry, as she normally did upon awakening. She had with great effort managed to dress herself and pull on her soft leather riding boots for better stability.

Someone knocked, and when she opened the door she found Tim, the cabin boy, standing there with two beakers of ale and some bread and cheese.

"Captain Ramsey says you had best remain in your quarters until we ride out the storm altogether. There is not hot food to be had, ma'am."

He thrust the provender at her and Caroline accepted it with thanks. She selected the table and chair as the most convenient spot to eat and was busy chewing bread and cheese when Joshua finally weaved into the sitting room.

He was greenish-white in color, his sparse hair blown about his face, his eyes bloodshot.

"We are in a storm," he said.

He made a comic figure to begin with, and the inadequacy of his remark made it worse. She managed not to laugh, saying only, "It was worse earlier, but Mr. Hardin says we will not sink."

"Hardin? Hardin? What was he doing here?"

"He wasn't here. I saw him in the passageway. See?" She held up her food. "They've brought us food. There will be no hot meals until the storm is over, and Captain Ramsey says that . . . " She broke off as Joshua clawed frantically for the slop basin. Too late. His fingers touched it and it slipped out of his grasp, clattering to the deck, where it lay overturned while he retched upon it.

Cleaning up after Joshua, Caroline came close to following his unfortunate example. She tried to think of more pleasant things: of clear waters in quiet pools; of snowy fields around Abbey Hall; of dark silent woods. At last she was in control again.

Joshua lay upon his bed, wretchedly ill, an empty slop basin beside him into which he now heaved without bringing up anything. He made sounds like that of a dying animal.

She stayed with him for the afternoon, keeping out of

his sight the cake and wine the captain's cabin boy brought to them. Inquiring after Tim, their own boy, she learned that he lay in his hammock below, as sick as his master.

Toward evening the ship settled into a more normal track. The sky cleared ahead of them; the waves, while still choppy, were less violent, and a stiff breeze filled the newly rigged sails. Pressing her cheek against the pane of the porthole, Caroline was able to observe that the sea ahead looked more tranquil.

However, taking the news to Joshua, she found him as ill as ever, and no amount of coaxing on her part would persuade him that the fresh air above would clear away the sickening effects of the storm.

Promising to fetch the doctor, she left the cabin and ran into Mr. Hardin at the hatch of the open deck.

"Careful, ma'am," he warned. "The decks are wet and slippery. 'Twould be well to remain here for your breath of air."

"My husband is very ill," she said. "I am looking for Dr. Bascomb."

"I'll carry your message. Will you remember not to go on deck? I assure you, even an experienced sailor has been known to fall and be swept overboard."

She smiled at him. "I am not foolish, Mr. Hardin. I will wait here."

She leaned against the frame, holding it with both her hands, and breathed deeply of the air. Despite her efforts at cleaning the cabin, it had retained the foul, sour odors of Joshua's illness. She was loath to return and waited gladly until it became necessary for her to do so.

Dr. Bascomb found her there sometime later. He looked a little pale himself and confessed to a slight attack of Joshua's complaint.

"However, I am well enough now," he added with a smile. "You, Mistress, are the best sailor of all. Your husband, I am afraid, will be ill for some time yet. I have given him a small dose of Indian opium. It is enough to quiet his stomach and induce rest."

"Opium!" Caroline exclaimed. "But that is dangerous to the mind, is it not?"

"Misused if it be, yes," the doctor said. "But I learned during a journey to India seven years ago that it can be used in very small quantities to soothe such ailments as the one presently besetting Mr. Welles. You may trust me not to disarrange his sensibilities. He was sleeping before I left him, a natural sleep. I suspect he will sleep through the night. If not, please send for me."

"Will there be a hot meal this evening?" Caroline asked, and the doctor made a mock face.

"There will be, but I shall rest my digestion. I must leave you to the company of the captain and Mr. Hardin. I believe that the master's mate is ill, and Mr. Bell takes his watch. I also understand that young Tim was unable to leave his hammock. After I have attended the sick, I shall attend to myself."

Joshua was sleeping. There was no need to hurry back. After the doctor left her, Caroline put her head out to catch the last glimpse of the world beyond the ship and made her way to the great cabin, where she found the captain and Mr. Hardin, looking fit if tired.

They greeted her with approving smiles.

"Very sensible, Mistress Welles," Captain Ramsey said. "Plain dress and boots. Had you been a boy, you'd be an ideal sailor. Come, come, sit down. Your appetite holds, I trust?"

Caroline said it had, indeed, and she was informed that she would have a taste of the Indies before she arrived there, since the *Southampton's* master had sent them plantains and coconuts as a gift, as well as some rice he had obtained in Charleston.

"Together with the last of the mutton, we shall have a meal fit for the governor of Nassau," the captain said. "Tell me, how did Dr. Bascomb find Mr. Welles?"

"Somewhat recovered," Caroline said. "But he thinks it will be days before he is able to be up again."

She sensed rather than saw that this news pleased the captain and Mr. Hardin. She knew that a normal wife would take umbrage at this, but she would not assume the role of hypocrite and chose to ignore the evident relief in her companions.

"The storm is ended now, is it not?" she asked.

"Aye. We are sailing into calm enough seas. The winds are good. If they keep up, we will reach Nassau sooner than expected," the captain said, "I reckon another six weeks, as we go."

Another six weeks! Caroline wondered if Joshua might be ill as long as that. After that, she did not care to speculate. It was too disturbing. Instead, she relaxed in her present freedom, and the meal was eaten with a return of the old gaiety.

At its conclusion she mentioned that she longed for a stroll around the veranda deck before retiring, and the captain, regretting the necessity for returning to the watch, said that Mr. Hardin would be glad to accompany her for a short while. He emphasized the "short" ever so slightly and parted with them at the door to the veranda deck.

For a time they strolled in silence, Caroline's hand resting on Mr. Hardin's proffered arm. She was conscious of his nearness, a bit confused by the fact that it was disturbing in a rather pleasant way—the way it used to be to stroll with a handsome man.

The breeze grew colder after a bit and the sea became choppier. Mr. Hardin cleared his throat and suggested it would be well now to go below. They had just turned when a sudden pitch made Caroline lose her grip on Hardin's arm, but it went swiftly around her, holding her steady. For a brief moment they were close, his cheek grazing her temple, her body pressed against him. A leaping of her pulses warned her and she drew away.

Mr. Hardin led her at once to the state cabin and left her there with a stiff bow and a mumbled "good evening."

Caroline, undressing in the dark, realized how swiftly she had been excited by yet another man and thought fiercely, and that is what has led me to this odious present. It was unfair. God was unfair. To tempt the flesh with half-realized dreams of pleasure, only to take them away in the act of uniting which, as far as she could tell, gave a man great happiness and left a woman disgusted. It was what everyone meant by men being the Lords of Creation. And so God made a man in his own image, and woman— ah, woman—was nothing more than a piece of his rib. "I wish," she said aloud, "I wish I were a man."

Joshua stirred at the sound and then was quiet again. As she got in beside him, she thought, and if I had been a man, I'd be a better man than this foul-smelling oaf who lies beside me.

Chapter Five

On the following morning the *Charlotte* sailed into the calm seas and the warm air Joshua had spoken of. In the days that followed, however, Joshua remained in bed, managing only broth and bread, and this under the sedating effects of Dr. Bascomb's Oriental remedy.

After one such dosing, the doctor said to Caroline, "He is becoming addicted, I fear. I am giving less and less of the medicine, yet he is requiring more frequent doses. I confess I am at a loss."

"He will be well enough once we are on land," Caroline said. "He is not suited to the sea. I am certain it is why he indulged so heavily in wine and spirits before the storm."

The doctor sighed. "Between the spirits and the medicine, it appears we have little choice. Still, I am tempted to tell him that the medicine is at an end."

Caroline, shuddering at the thought of a newly revived Joshua, protested, "But he will die from lack of food. It is only with the medicine that he is able to take broth."

Dr. Bascomb smiled. "He is well fleshed, Mistress Welles. I think it unlikely that another week of fasting will result in death by starvation."

Yet when he attempted to refuse the next request for the opium, Joshua raised a storm of protest that belied his insistence that he was too weak and ill to be considered cured.

His appearance, however, lent credence to his claims. He was considerably thinner, his color poor, and, when he spoke, perspiration beaded his face and his breath came shallowly.

Bascomb hesitated. His own supply was running short with this burden upon it. Belatedly, he cursed himself for having introduced Welles to it. The small amount he reserved for severe cases of seasickness or other stomach ailments had always been more than enough on other voyages. But Welles had taken to it, and it was having an effect upon him. Welles was not even putting the crushed leaves into a pipe and smoking it for its greatest effect, as the doctor often did.

"There is very little left, Mr. Welles, and there are others aboard," Bascomb temporized.

"Not the least of whom is yourself, Dr. Bascomb," Joshua said shrewdly.

"I? I have no need for remedies."

"But for pleasure, Doctor. Do you know I discovered only last week that it is possible to have better effects by using the stuff as if it were tobacco? You never told me that, Dr. Bascomb. 'Twas only my error. Reaching for my tobacco, I took the paper of opium instead and filled my pipe. Almost at once I saw why you were reluctant to part with much of it."

"To smoke it is harmful," Bascomb said, alarmed.

"Harmful to whom, Dr. Bascomb?"

"One becomes addicted. 'Tis more pleasant . . . " He stopped, realizing he had admitted his own attraction for the drug.

"More pleasant, indeed, Dr. Bascomb? Pray, how do you keep such stores of it?"

"I buy it in London. 'Tis brought in by Orient traders who know all its properties."

"Then you have a sufficiency for me," Joshua pointed out. "I will not be greedy, Bascomb, but you must share, or you must bear the consequences. Do you think the good captain or my esteemed father-in-law would relish knowing their surgeon spent most of his time in the land of pleasant dreams?"

Bascomb paled. "You surely will not bring about my downfall!" he protested.

"Not unless you force me, Doctor. The opium, please, and let us have no more falsehoods about its short supply."

Bascomb gave in. As he left the cabin, he resolved to secrete a good portion of the stuff. Whatever he had to share, he would now be forced to share. And it would be many months before he could hope to purchase more. The thought that he was now on shorter rations than usual made him sweat. The wine, the brandy, and the spirits were never as good. He had to drink so much of them to sleep, and they did not give rise to the comforting dreams he obtained through opium. In those dreams he was rich beyond belief, loved, famous, and the idol of a young and beautiful wife. In those dreams all that he desired was there and the realities of his existence vanished . . . apothecary calling himself doctor, poor, unknown, and despised by a shrewish wife on whom the years had laid a cruel and heavy hand.

Damn Welles! Damn himself for helping him. "I had better left him to retch his very bowels out," he said aloud. "He has bested me and even now he's gloating over his success."

Behind him in the cabin Joshua relaxed, drawing deeply on his pipe, wallowing in the soothing effects that stole over him, anticipating the dreams that would follow. In some ways they were more exciting than bedding a woman, for each of the women in his dreams were virgins, crying and shrieking beneath him, fighting him, making him feel powerful. In his dreams their thighs and breasts were large and soft and infinitely voluptuous, and he savored every part of these bodies.

As he drifted off, Caroline came into the room and tiptoed across it to lean over him and inquire solicitously if she could fetch anything before she went in to supper.

Her face loomed large, its outlines blurred, with her full red lips parting and closing in speech. His vision narrowed upon them so that all he could see was that mouth. In his fantasy, he felt those lips moving over his body, and the feeling was ecstatic. He reached out a hand to bring them to him, but lassitude prevented his grasping Caroline, and in a moment she had drawn back and was gone.

During the course of her husband's malaise, Caroline, freed of his demands, had regained her pert, independent air, as well as her vivacity. The suppers, even though they now consisted mainly of cold salted meats and fish, grew merrier.

"I vow, Mistress Welles," said Ramsey, laughing heartily at one of her sallies, "you are the most charming lady ever to grace me at a table. What say you, gentlemen?"

There was an enthusiastic agreement from Dr. Bascomb and a more constrained one from Mr. Hardin. Meeting his eyes, Caroline saw, with a surge of pleasure, that he looked love-smitten. She lowered her eyes, batted her eyelids briefly, and looked at him again. His color deepened at this blatant response, and in his eyes she saw a gleam of desire. She knew that he would, given any encouragement at all, cease his formal speech and manner the next time he escorted her around the deck on her pre-bedtime stroll.

The idea excited her, as the idea of his kissing and caressing her had for many days now. She knew that it was wrong to entertain such thoughts, much less put them into action; yet, deep inside, she knew that she would do just that.

I don't care, she thought recklessly. I like being kissed. More, she loved a man's touch upon her body, loved the sensations that made her grow weak and warm and wildly desirous. The idea that Hardin might touch her that way was fascinating. Her heart missed a beat as she thought about it.

Well, if it were wrong, so be it. After all, it wasn't as if she planned to bed with Hardin. She let her imagination flow unchecked, and all the while she kept her eyes demurely lowered as she was led from the great cabin.

Yet, once they were alone on the dark deck, she became nervous, and as they walked she found herself keeping stiffly away from him, her fingers touching lightly on his rigidly held forearm.

The silence between them grew. Beneath her fingers she felt a tremor, as though he kept the arm steady with effort. All at once the feeling of wanting him to hold her returned, and as they turned back she pretended to stumble and fetched herself up against him with a little gasp, so that her bosom pressed into his upper arm.

His other arm came around to steady her, but she turned as it did and found herself at last held in a strong, muscular embrace. She lifted her face at that moment, putting her free hand along his shoulder. With a muffled exclamation, he tightened his grip and found her lips.

Heaven, she thought, as she returned the kisses, with a

feeling she had not had since that long-ago day in the maze.

He drew her under the shadows of the deck above, and her arms slipped around his waist as she pressed closer.

His mouth moved over her brow, her cheeks, and down along her throat while she shivered with pleasure. She arched back, but even as his lips reached the line of her bodice he raised his head, pushing her away from him.

He was breathing heavily, and his words, when they came, were rough: "I forget myself, Mistress Welles. Please excuse me."

"I . . ." She couldn't think of what to say.

"I will take you to your quarters," he said after a moment.

But I don't want to go! she thought. I want to stay here! She nearly said it aloud and stopped, realizing how wanton he would think her.

She allowed herself to be led inside, but as they neared the state cabin she turned to him and said, "It was not you who forgot yourself, Mr. Hardin. It was I. And," she added, "you must not blame yourself that I did. I have no great love for my husband. The marriage was arranged."

"Still, it is a marriage," he said.

"Yes," she agreed.

"And I have my orders," he added.

She blushed. The captain! He had seen her flirtation and had warned his young officer away.

As if reading her mind, Hardin said, "The orders apply to all married ladies traveling with their husbands."

"Oh," she answered inadequately.

She had thought it was the end of her adventure and that it would be Dr. Bascomb or the captain who would take Hardin's place on those nightly walks. In this she was pleasantly surprised. For the next two nights Hardin was back at her side. However, he made no attempt at further intimacy. But he was talkative now, where before he had been silent. He told her stories of his home in Devon and tales of adventures at sea. There was a complacent expansiveness in him that she finally realized was based on her own capitulation and on her tacit admission that she preferred him to her husband. It nettled her, and on the third night she announced that she would retire early and forgo her walk. She took a perverse pleasure in Mr. Hardin's quickly concealed disappointment and went to her cabin to read until she should become sleepy.

They were only a few days out of Nassau when Joshua finally rose and dressed. The southern waters were so quiet that, despite the good wind that sped them on their course, the waves were mere lacy ripples on a turquoise sea.

Caroline, used to the constant rolling, felt as though she now stood on solid earth. Unfortunately for him, Joshua still felt the slightest movement, and while he looked more normal, he was still very pale and went paler as he left the cabin ahead of her to partake of his first solid meal.

Buoyed by the good weather, Caroline dressed with an elegance she had forgone during the crossing. She laced her white bodice tightly so that the concealed gold coins pressed into her flesh and her mounded breasts peeped well above the richly embroidered stomacher. Her hoops felt strange and cumbersome after such long disuse, but they were necessary to her present toilette. She selected a sky-blue silk gown embroidered with tiny gold leaves and draped it carefully over her lawn underskirt, which was thick with frothy lace.

Dressed, she regarded herself in the mirror and regretted the absence of Dobbs and thus the final effect of an elegant coiffure. She did not regret the powdering, however, noting with satisfaction that the gold leaves of her gown heightened the color of her curls, disarrayed though they might be. She struggled for some time trying to force the ringlets into the long finger curls that Dobbs had known so well how to induce. She succeeded well enough to be pleased with the effort.

Her appearance at supper in this fashionable garb produced gallant and extravagant compliments from the assembled company, and it elicited a beaming air of prideful ownership from Joshua.

Throughout the meal she made it a point to defer to her husband, directing her conversation toward him and flirting with him. Hardin, she saw, was let down by this display, and the smugness with which he had been regarding her faded. So much for you, Master Hardin,

Caroline thought with childish satisfaction as his brow darkened.

After supper she remained in the great cabin with Joshua and Dr. Bascomb. Joshua was back to his old form and helping himself liberally to the brandy that the captain had provided.

"The captain was right about this brandy," he said at one point. "Takes the stink of salt herring away. Sink me if it doesn't."

"Let us hope it doesn't sink you now, Joshua," Caroline teased, "or else we will be drowned, too."

This modest sally brought greater laughter than it deserved, and the laughter itself was contagious in their brandy-heightened mood. They were soon seized by hilarity, so that the feeblest joke became wit Dr. Johnson might envy. In the middle of this they heard the "Sail, ho!" cry, which added to their mirth.

"Brandy, ho!" cried Joshua foolishly, waving the bottle aloft.

"Pour, ho!" Dr. Bascomb took it up as he extended his beaker.

In the next moment a loud, shattering boom filled the cabin. They were struck dumb at the sound. Before they could comprehend the meaning of it, another boom followed.

Suddenly the night was alive with noise. Everywhere there was the sound of movement, of shouting, of oaths and curses. Another boom and then another, following each other so fast that it was impossible to formulate a thought before that thought was diffused and scattered by the reverberations in their brains.

The three in the great cabin acted out of blind instinct, running from the cabin, jamming up at the entrance, where Joshua pushed through and left Caroline at the narrow aperture, through which it was impossible for her to pass without turning sideways to accommodate the width of her hoops.

Dr. Bascomb, once more in some control, assisted her and led her quickly to her cabin.

"Stay here," he ordered. "Keep out of sight. I will return when this is over."

"Where are you going?" she cried out.

"I must attend to the wounded," he replied.

"Wounded?" she repeated stupidly.

"We are engaged in battle. A Frenchman is making war on a merchant ship," he said with some anger as he hurried forward.

Above, the captain, taken totally by surprise, was making a desperate effort to recover the ship's position. The *Charlotte*'s guns under Mr. Hardin were unable to fire with any effect. The Frenchman had come up on their stern and in the initial bombardment had split their mizzen. It lay half over, its sheets torn and dragging. This damage had lessened the maneuverability of the ship considerably.

Each time that Captain Ramsey managed to bring the *Charlotte* around, to level a broadside at the Frenchman, the latter circled with her so that, save for the moment of turning, the *Charlotte*'s guns were unable to inflict much damage on the enemy.

The sailor who had been in the crow's nest had scrambled down as the firing began in earnest and reported to the captain that the enemy was a French frigate carrying at least forty guns.

"They have signaled us to surrender again," he added.

"They can go to hell," Ramsey replied, his face red with rage. "I'll surrender to no one."

"Aye, sir," the sailor replied.

"They waste their shot," Ramsey said to his helmsman. "Save for the mast, they have not touched us. Trail me, will she? We'll outfox her, yet. Helmsman, half-port rudder. Easy. Now! Full starboard, hard starboard!" he bellowed.

The *Charlotte* heeled desperately at this maneuver, her timbers shrieking protest. "Fire!" the captain shouted, and the call was taken up.

"Fire!" Hardin repeated on the gun deck, and the *Charlotte*'s guns boomed across the water at the Frenchman, which at the second of the maneuver had faced up almost broadside. And yet when the smoke cleared, she was gone.

"Damn," said the captain, "she's a bleeding ghost ship! Helmsman, hard port!"

The *Charlotte* turned once more.

"Break out the small arms!" the captain thundered at Hardin. "Man the bowsprit, set foremast fore and aft. All hands prepare for boarding."

His orders came thick and fast, and as fast as the words left his lips, the crew hurried to obey.

The two ships finally faced each other. It was Ramsey's intention to secure the pirate ship with the bowlines and thus render the use of her big guns ineffective. Hand-to-hand combat. Take her by surprise while her men were still manning the cannon.

It was an admirable plan, but the French commander had anticipated him, and even as the *Charlotte* faced her, the Frenchman reefed sail and its lines were already securing the *Charlotte*'s bowsprit. The countermove was effected before the men on the *Charlotte* had time to carry out their own orders.

The Frenchman's crew was leaping along the bowsprit, slicing out with cutlass and dagger. The screams of those men who fell in the path of this onslaught split the air.

In seconds, they lined the *Charlotte*'s deck and rails, muskets held at the ready. From their midst a tall black-haired man called in English, "I am the captain of the *Mouette*. Surrender!"

"Surrender, hell!" shouted Ramsey, raising his sidearm.

A single shot rang out and Ramsey gazed in stunned surprise at the pistol, which leapt from his wounded hand.

"Surrender!" the French captain called again.

For a second, Ramsey wavered. He had never lost ship or cargo, nor was he afraid to risk death. But he admitted to himself that he was beaten. He had mustered his own men too late and less than half a dozen of them had received their muskets. Facing them were thirty men, their muskets aimed. If he sent his men into the breach, most would be slaughtered, and the cargo would be lost, in any event.

"Strike the colors," he called out in a steady voice.

"Captain!" shouted Hardin in protest, holding his wounded arm.

"Strike the colors," Ramsey repeated. He stood watching the Union slither down her ropes to follow the ship's ensign into ignominy, and the gall was bitter in his throat.

He raised his head and saw the French ship's flags: white ensign with the motto *"La Liberté"* fluttering in the breeze above the Jolly Roger.

His eyes came back to rest upon the French sailors.

Most of them wore head kerchiefs and were dressed in a motley array of shirts and jackets and breeches. Several had earrings swinging from their ears, and all of them bore the same cold and uncompromising expression their captain did.

"Pirates!" he ejaculated.

"Pirates," the pirate captain agreed pleasantly. He began at once to issue orders and his men leaped from their positions, pushing the *Charlotte*'s crew against the rails. Some pirates stood guard while others hurried below.

Then their captain himself leaped from the rail and made his way to Ramsey, his pistols still at the ready.

"My apologies, Captain." He nodded toward Ramsey's hand, where the shot from his pistol had grazed the flesh.

Ramsey said nothing, glaring stonily past the tall intruder.

"We will take no prisoners. We will impress no seamen. Please order all hands on deck, as well as any passengers."

Ramsey obeyed without answering him directly.

"We will take your cargo and your arms. We will leave you sufficient store for Nassau."

"How generous!" Ramsey sneered.

From the corner of his eye, he saw Hardin creeping up the side of the pirate ship. Blood poured from his arm, where a cutlass had laid open the upper portion from shoulder to elbow.

He is going to fire the ship, Ramsey thought. The fool, the young blithering fool—he will die for naught.

He tried to focus his attention on the pirate captain, who was saying, "More generous than you think, Captain Ramsey. Capturing the *Charlotte* and towing her to port would be a great feat. Oh, yes," he said in answer to Ramsey's startled look, "your reputation is well known. One frigate and a galleon so far, and two more frigates routed. You would have made a great commander of a man-of-war . . . or a privateer," he said with a flash of white teeth.

"You have me at a disadvantage," Ramsey countered. "I have not heard of the *Mouette* and I do not know her master."

"Ah, but today we have corrected that oversight," the pirate captain replied. "As for my name, I am Captain Domino."

There was a hiss from the deck where the pirates held the English at gunpoint, and without turning, Ramsey knew that Caroline Welles had come upon the open deck. He prayed that Domino meant it when he had said "no prisoners."

"A lady," Captain Domino said. "Is there more than one aboard?"

"No. I trust you will leave her unharmed."

"You have my word, Captain Ramsey. Even when we take prisoners, we never take ladies. It is the rule aboard my ship. We are not savages."

"You attacked a merchant ship," Ramsey accused.

"An armed merchant ship that resisted our signal to surrender. Very unwise. You see, we have been forced to fire."

"I suppose you expect me to believe you would not approach an unarmed vessel?"

"I prefer unarmed vessels." Domino smiled. "A shot across their bow and they heave to without offering resistance. We board them, take the cargo, and send them on their way."

"Leaving all hands on board?"

"All save those who wish to join us. And that reminds me, I must take care of that now."

He left Ramsey and approached the English sailors.

"Are there any men here who wish to join us? Any Frenchmen? Spanish? No? Then anyone longing for a richer reward for his duties? I have special need of gunners and carpenters."

There was a moment's silence. Almost to a man, the English sailors stood quietly, eyes straight ahead.

"I am a carpenter's mate, sir," said one man, then stepped forward.

"Are you French?"

"No, sir. At least, my father is an Englishman. My mother was French. I was born in New France."

"A compatriot," said Domino. "Come forward." As the man stepped out, he saw Captain Ramsey staring at him.

"Sorry, Captain," he called up cheerily. "But I've a mind for a better life."

"Anyone else?" Domino asked. The carpenter's mate had broken the English band. Three men, all gunners, stepped forward.

"Four in all. That makes up for our losses," Domino said. "Gather your articles," he ordered his new recruits. "Couvre, here, will show you aboard the *Mouette*."

"Excuse me, Captain, what's a mowit?"

"*Moo-ette*," Domino corrected. "It is French for sea gull."

Having collected the men, Domino turned his attention to Caroline, who stood between Dr. Bascomb and Joshua, close by the main mast. She held herself steadily erect, her eyes dark in her white face.

"My lady," Domino said and bowed low, "forgive the intrusion that has brought about your pallor. You have nothing to fear. You may return to your quarters."

Both Joshua and Dr. Bascomb made a slight movement forward.

"Only one of you gentlemen may escort her. Bigarde"—he raised his voice and one of his men hurried up—"see these people below. The gentleman will return."

With another bow, he walked away.

Caroline was so relieved that her knees went weak. Joshua steadied her with his arm and together they moved off, trailed by Bigarde, who carried his musket before him.

"Do not," said Bigarde, in heavily accented English laced with French infinitives, "make the movement to *courir*, or it will be of the necessity to *décharger mon mousket*."

"What the devil did he say?" Joshua asked.

"He said we mustn't run or he will have to shoot us."

"I have no intention whatsoever of running," Joshua said irritably. "I wish only to lie down. If your captain isn't taking prisoners, why must I return to the deck?" he asked Bigarde.

The man shrugged. "It is *le désir de mon capitaine*."

"But my wife will be alone," Joshua argued.

"Madame is not . . . uh . . . she . . ."

"I will be safe," Caroline interjected.

"*Oui*." Bigarde smiled at her.

As she closed the cabin door, Joshua and Bigarde were already on their way back to the deck.

The sitting room was empty and there was no sound from within the bedplace, and yet she had a curious presentiment that she was not alone in her quarters. She half-turned to go out again and call to Bigarde when a voice from behind her said, "Stay! Turn around."

Caroline went cold and then hot with fear. She moved slowly, and as she turned around she saw that the owner of the voice was a swarthy, dirty little man with a black, scraggly moustache. His hair was bound in a red kerchief, and gold hoops swung from his ears.

"*Andale!* José, Manuel."

The curtains to the bedplace opened and two other men slipped silently into the sitting room. They were not unlike the first, but they were taller, and, if possible, they looked dirtier.

They spoke a tongue that she did not understand.

"Who . . . who are you?" she managed to blurt out.

"I am El Loco," the swarthy man said. "We are your captors."

"The . . . your captain said there would be no prisoners, only prizes."

"Ah, our good captain . . . no prisoners, only prizes. Ah, but you *are* one of the prizes, you see!"

"No," Caroline said, and, opening her mouth, she drew breath to scream. In a moment, El Loco was beside her, one hand pressing her mouth, the other grabbing at her. She bit at the hand, and, giving a startled curse, he struck her a forceful blow along the side of her jaw, stunning her to silence. In a flash he had wrenched the kerchief from his head and stuffed the greasy rag into her mouth, tying it tightly behind her head.

She struggled madly but to no avail. The other two, rushing to El Loco's aid, bound her hands behind her. Before she could move again, she was seized and dragged into the bedplace. She heard them talking in their own tongue, heard her chests being dragged across the floor, and then she was lifted and flung into one of the chests. Her panniers remained caught on either side of the chest. El Loco tore at them, twisting them until they finally were pressed lengthwise between her body and the sides of the chest.

She watched, eyes wide with terror, as El Loco took his dagger out and moved toward her. No! her brain screamed silently. But the knife went past her and hacked a hole in the lid before it was closed over her, blotting out the last of the light.

The peak of her terror had been reached at the sight

of El Loco's dagger, and when it had only made a hole in the lid and she perceived that it was meant for her to breathe, the relief flooding so soon after rendered her half-conscious.

Dimly, she was aware of the chest being lifted and carried aloft. It was suffocatingly close inside despite the air hole, and the gag in her mouth made it almost impossible to breathe. Nausea welled up and she fought it down, desperately aware that were she to regurgitate, she would strangle to death in her own vomit.

"*Alors! Qu'est-ce que c'est ça?*" "What is that?" she heard the pirate captain call out.

"It is gold, *mon capitaine*," El Loco whined in awkward French. "Very heavy. I take it to your cabin, no?"

"Be careful," the captain warned. "I don't want it spilled into the sea."

"But, no. This is too precious a prize." Loco sniggered. He said something to his cohorts and they laughed.

As she felt herself lifted at an angle, Caroline realized that they must be handing her up over the railing to the waiting ship.

"I have left you a cask of rum, Captain Ramsey," she heard the pirate captain say. Then, as she was tilted once more, her head struck the end of the trunk and she fainted.

On the deck of the *Charlotte,* Ramsey said, "You have been very generous, Captain, for a . . . uh . . . a pirate. But, mark you, there will be many English ships after you when I report this in Nassau."

"There are always many English ships after me, Captain Ramsey. So far they have not caught me. With God's grace, they never will."

"You speak of God?" Ramsey said incredulously.

"And why not? Does the French captain of a pirate ship have less right than that of an English man-of-war? Or a slaver? Or even a shore merchant who plunders the poor to enrich himself?"

Ramsey was silent.

"Ah, Captain Ramsey, if only we had met under happier circumstances, what good conversation would be ours. But I, alas, must run for safe port, and you must run for Nassau. *A bientôt.*"

He made a mock salute and wheeled around with an order to his men.

While three of the pirates covered the crew of the *Charlotte,* the rest made an orderly march back to the *Mouette.* The bowline was cast off, the ships rolled apart, and with a mighty roar of the crew on the French ship as her sheets caught the wind, the *Mouette* sailed past the crippled *Charlotte* and was swallowed up in the dark.

Part
Two

Chapter Six

Inside the sea chest among the very linens and silks that were part of her dowry, Caroline had been too numb with terror to move. Regaining consciousness, she had lain, her face pressed against the hole in the lid to breathe what air she could as the jolting chest was carried down to the hold and slung on the deck.

She had prayed so long for deliverance from her confinement that when at last the chest was flung open and the dank air of the hold rushed into her parched nostrils, she gave a strangled sob of relief and struggled to pull herself erect. She could hear whispers and she felt hands groping through the silk to grasp her and lift her into the open.

Her legs, so long deprived of blood, were useless rags beneath her body, and she fell to the deck with a moan. In the light of a lantern held by El Loco, she saw the two men who had helped him kidnap her from her cabin.

They were arguing in their foreign tongue, but by the way they looked at her she realized that somehow her fate was being decided then and there. Her legs were tingling now as the blood coursed through her veins, and her heart began to pound so furiously it seemed to rise to her throat and cut off her shallow breath.

At last, with a snarl, El Loco turned to her and said, "So, it is to be now. And what a prize you are, Englishwoman. What a price you will fetch, no? But, first, we will sample you."

As he spoke he reached down and thrust his hand inside her stomacher, ripping it down the front. Seconds later one of her petticoats was shredded and the taller of

72

the other two pirates had bound her legs apart while his companion lashed her arms to hooks embedded in the timbers. She struggled and twisted, straining against the hands that held her, trying to get away from El Loco as he took the rest of her clothing from her body. As those hairy hands groped at her breasts, nausea rose in her throat once more and she thought: I will die here, yet I would rather be dead.

She was growing faint with the exertion and the terror and her eyes bulged above the cruel gag. El Loco stepped back, grinning as he looked at her. His eyes raked her naked body with relish, and his loose, wet mouth worked in excitement. With one hand he had opened his breeches and he fumbled inside them to produce his member. Caroline finally closed her eyes, shivering uncontrollably.

With a coarse cry, he flung himself upon her to the muted gasps of pleasure from the onlookers. The rank odor of his unwashed body and greasy hair filled her nostrils. His hands moved as he sought to thrust himself between her quivering thighs. Caroline's mind went blank with shock.

In the next instant she felt a rush of air and the reeking body was no longer upon her. There were feet pounding along the deck above, scrambling down the ladder. She opened her eyes to see the tall dark-haired captain, a pistol in each hand, standing just above her. His face was tight with cold, hard fury, and his eyes were intent on the targets of his aimed pistols. Behind her, she heard her assailants beginning to whine.

"You have disobeyed my orders," Domino said. "You know the rules—no hostages this time, and never a woman hostage at any time. I should kill you here and now for the mutinous scum you are. Instead, it will be twenty lashes."

At this they broke into renewed pleading, but he silenced them with a short cry.

"Christos," he called, and a stocky, dark man stepped forward. "Lash them to the foremast. I will be above shortly."

As the sailors were hustled away by Christos and two other crewmen, Caroline's rescuer moved to unbind her mouth and arms. He worked swiftly and efficiently without saying a word. When he had finished, she felt the soft silk of some of her own clothing covering her body.

Only then did he speak to her. "Have they harmed you?" he asked.

"No," she blurted out in a voice she barely recognized as her own.

"Thank God for that," he said. "I am Captain Domino. I can only offer you inadequate apologies, Madame. But I can promise you that you are safe now and will not be molested again. I will find some way to put you ashore so you may return to your own people."

"Thank you," she blurted out.

"Please, your clothes are in ruins. Wrap yourself up well and I will take you to my cabin." He reached down and drew her up, his voice softening at the sight of her pale, frightened face.

"Believe me," he said, "there is nothing more to be afraid of."

She was staring at him, still trembling and unable to think of what to say or do next. She met his eyes full on and suddenly the blood came up in his cheeks and he averted his face. "Cover yourself, my lady," he said in a strained voice. Looking down, she saw that the silk had slipped to one side, revealing the full curve of one white breast as far as its pink nipple.

Hastily, she wound the silk around herself. "There is rather a lot of it," she said stupidly. For answer he drew his dagger and whacked off a length of the cloth.

"Can you sew?" he asked with seeming irrelevance.

"Yes, yes, of course . . . I . . ."

"Good. I have needle and thread. You can repair your clothes where possible." He gathered her clothing and made a bundle of it. "Come, now." He took her hand and led her to the ladder.

"Up you go," he said.

"I . . . I can't climb in this wrapping," she protested.

Silently, he swung her up and over his shoulder so that her head was pressed downward against his broad back, her arms clutching him.

"Hold tight," he commanded. "I need both my hands." She strengthened her grip on him and he went swiftly up one ladder, then another, and through the hatchway into a small passage. There he swung her down. Her body grazed his and again she saw his face darken.

There was a moment's strained silence as they stood facing each other. Caroline experienced a little tremor along her nerves and her eyes fell before his dark, unreadable stare.

"I . . . oh . . . those men!" she said, suddenly anxious to break the spell, unable to think of anything to say.

"They will be punished. Twenty lashes will teach them to obey. Were I ready to let them die, 'twould be Moses' Law."

"What is Moses' Law?" she asked.

"Forty lashes minus one. You shall have the pleasure of watching them receive twenty."

"I . . . no . . . I . . ." she stammered.

"You will watch," he said inexorably. "Your presence will add to their punishment. You see, they will have to bear it in silence or suffer as well the humiliation of being unmanned in front of a woman."

She made no reply, her breast a conflict of emotions, her mind dazed by the swift succession of events. "Come, then," he said, "I will take you to my quarters." She followed meekly along behind him.

He left her as soon as she was safely inside the small but well-fitted cabin, instructing her as to where the sewing pouch was. "There is sea water in that large jug, fresh water in the small one," he said. "Please make yourself presentable as quickly as possible." He offered her food, but she refused it. He closed the door and she heard a key grate in the lock.

Alone, hysteria welled up and she knew that the screams so long suppressed were pressing for release. Her body shook in her effort to control herself, her heart fluttered wildly, and her eyes grew dim. If I scream now, she thought, I will never stop. I must not, I must not. She stumbled to the water jug and threw handfuls of water on her face and neck. The cold, briny liquid fell into the basin below. She repeated the motion over and over until her panic subsided. With shaking hands she opened the smaller jug and took a long, soothing drink of water.

She still quivered in the aftermath, but her breath was more even now and her mind had cleared. She proceeded mechanically, letting the long wrapping of cloth fall from her body as she washed herself thoroughly. Her mind shied desperately away from the memory of El Loco's groping hands and filthy body.

At last, tingling with cold, she dried herself on the silk and turned to unwrap the bundle of garments. Her corps and one petticoat were whole; her stomacher was beyond repair. Perhaps a bit of silk would serve, stitched into place under the bodice.

She took her gown in her hand and began to baste the sleeves. She worked swiftly, anxious to finish, the needle stabbing in and out of the cloth. It was careless work, but later she would sew it properly.

"You will watch," he had said, and from his voice she know she could not refuse. He had saved her. He had given her sanctuary. He had promised to put her safely ashore. He had behaved not like a pirate, but like a gentleman. She remembered his face and his delicacy in averting his eyes from her exposed flesh. It was as if he had not seen her lying naked and stretched upon the deck of that hold. She flushed at the memory, more acutely embarrassed by that single intimate instant when her breast had been bared before him than by the fact that her whole body had been subjected to his gaze and to that of the others in the hold.

When she was finally dressed, she took the comb that lay beside the basin. Looking at the porthole, she saw herself reflected dimly in the light cast by the ship's lantern. The *Mouette* glided through the southern waters and overhead a full moon rode in and out of soft clouds.

As Caroline tried to unravel the snarls in her thick hair, a curious sense of peacefulness overcame her. Her body grew heavy with a sweet lassitude. Sleep: oh, to sleep and wake up far from here in her own room at Abbey Hall with the lark pouring its heart out to a gentle dawn; oh, to wake up to the sounds of the stirring household and the tempting odors that wafted from the kitchen as the morning meal was prepared.

So lost was she in her dreams that she did not hear the door open or hear him step into the room. Catching her hair and knotting it, she turned away from her primitive mirror to find him standing at the door. She gave a little start and her heart beat more quickly, sending the blood coursing and clearing the mists from her brain.

"You are ready?" he inquired.

She nodded.

"Come, then," he said briefly, and once more, without a word, she followed.

A stiff breeze had sprung up, and as they came out on the deck it tugged at Caroline, pulling the tendrils from her loosely bound hair and whipping them across her eyes. With the breeze, the currents began to run stronger and the ship entered an easy roll. Ahead of them, the pirates had gathered on the foredeck, standing stiffly at attention, as if they were the legal seamen of a British frigate instead of pirates above whom flew the dreaded black flag with it grinning skull and crossed bones.

In the flaring light of torches held by silent crewmen, she saw El Loco lashed to the mast; the other two stood in chains. They were all bare to the waist. Caroline stopped at the sight, but Captain Domino put a firm hand on her elbow and walked with her until she was moving in a circle around El Loco. The man met her eyes with a look of such violent hatred in them that Caroline trembled. The hand beneath her elbow pressed more firmly. In a moment they were past the man and she was brought to stand at one side, where she could see El Loco in profile.

There was a moment's utter silence. Then, at a curt order from Captain Domino, Couvre, the boatswain, holding a leather thong, stepped forward. His arm moved up and out in a wide arc. Whip bit flesh and Loco stiffened but otherwise gave no indication that he had felt the sting. Again and again the whip swung while Christos counted. When it was over, blood stained the deck and Loco sagged against his bonds, semiconscious.

The effect on his conspirators was disastrous. They were white and shaking as their own turns came. As the first one felt the cut of the leather, he moaned. Long before he had borne his full punishment he began to scream, until Caroline, sickened by the sight and the sound, longed to cover her own ears and turn her face away.

"I can't," she whispered to the captain. "Please don't make me watch this last one."

He did not answer. Somehow, she found the courage to make no further plea, but as the last man's screams rose, high-pitched and desperate, she closed her eyes, swaying a little, whereupon she felt the captain's arm grip her around the shoulders, and, with a rush of giddiness, she leaned back against it.

"Now," he said at length. Opening her eyes, she saw that the last of the trio was being hauled away and that two of the crew were already scrubbing down the deck, removing the bloodstains.

"I . . . please," she managed to say.

"It's over," he answered. "Come."

Still leaning on his supporting arm, she allowed him to lead her back to the cabin, where she sank gratefully upon the bed. Her head was swimming, her eyes bright with unshed tears.

"Cruel," she half-whispered, "cruel."

"Cruel? Yes. As cruel as their treatment of you? I think not. And on my ship a man obeys the rules. This is a privateer, my lady—in service to the king of France. We are not beasts. If beasts are among us, they must be punished according to the rules of the sea. Disobedience unpunished brings mutiny, and mutiny is treason."

"But . . . treason . . . That man, El Loco . . . he isn't French. Christos . . . some of the others."

"I man my ship with the best crew I can find. Christos is Greek. Loco is Spanish, as are his two friends. Aside from the *Charlotte* crewmen, I have as well another English officer aboard, one who has sailed with me these two years—Christos' mate, Haywood."

"An English officer?" she asked.

"Ah, yes, English—Mr. Haywood. He was brought to court martial by a particularly savage captain who had many friends in the government. He was stripped of his rank and imprisoned. He escaped. And now he is one of the *Mouette*'s crew."

"I see . . . a privateer. So you intercept English ships and we . . . we are enemies," she finished, rising slowly and looking at him.

He made a small bow and smiled. "Enemies," he said softly, and something in his face and voice made her look more keenly at him. His black eyes were unfathomable despite the smile, and, looking into their depths, she was seized with an impulse to move closer. It was as if she drifted toward him without her own volition. There was a roaring sound in her ears. I must be going to faint, she thought, and yet she found her legs surprisingly steady beneath her. For a long moment they stood so, staring intently at each other. A sudden sharp roll of the ship sent her against him. His arms came out to steady her and for one split second they were pressed together. She had a fleeting impression of the length and hardness of his body, the warmth of his hands, and then on the return roll she was upright once more, leaning back, still supported.

It was over. She felt a surge of disappointment when he moved away.

"You had better sleep now, if you can," he said in a distant voice. "I will lock the cabin. There is a guard outside. I have the only key, but if anyone should attempt to enter, do not hesitate to call out. I will be sharing Christos' quarters, which are next to these. One of us will be there all night. You have only to call. Pleasant dreams, Madame." He bowed and left before she could utter a word.

She lay down upon the bed, fully clothed, her face turned to the door, her body tense. She had been ready to sleep, but now sleep eluded her. She lay there and the night grew black. High above, the moon sailed behind thick clouds.

After a time, she rose and removed her outer clothing before crawling beneath the coverlet, where she tossed and turned for some time. Her mind was an endless chain of pictures of the past hours, and between each picture the face of Captain Domino rose and fell, until at last it grew larger and larger, blotting out the rest, before it, too, disappeared and she slept at last.

Chapter Seven

Her ordeal made Caroline seasick for the first time. Captain Domino, arriving with the cook's boy, who carried her breakfast, saw her condition, took the food himself, and ordered the boy out.

"You must try to eat," he said as she turned her head away from the tankard of ale and the bread and cheese.

"I cannot," she answered.

"You suffer from *mal de mer?*" he inquired.

She shook her head. Try as she might, she could not stop the teeth-chattering ague that had begun on her awakening.

"Then you will eat," he said firmly. Setting the food down, he raised her to a sitting position, bringing the covers up around her for warmth.

Under his insistence, she dutifully swallowed sips of ale. At first the pungent bitterness made her stomach turn over, but as each mouthful found its way past her throat, a measure of calm descended. Her body slowly lessened its quivering and her stomach settled. After a while, she found she was able to consume some of the bread, although the sight of the well-aged cheese, which smelled stronger than any she had ever eaten, disgusted her. She finished the ale.

Domino said, "Rest now. You will be better able to eat a midday meal."

He helped her back to a reclining position and left her there. Presently she slept again, and when she awakened the second time the sun was high overhead.

She felt immeasurably better, although still somewhat weak. She rose and attempted to bring some semblance of order to her appearance. She splashed cold water on her sleep-grained eyes, ran damp hands over her hair, and then combed it.

Having completed these small tasks, she paced up and down the small space, occasionally stopping to look out of the porthole on the sea, which stretched smooth and empty before her.

On board the *Charlotte* they would probably be searching for land now. Thinking of that, a wave of loneliness swept over her and easy tears sprang into her eyes.

They must have missed her very soon after the *Mouette* sailed away. They could not give chase, of course. As of this moment, no one knew where she was or whether she was even alive. For all they knew, she might well have been swept overboard.

Captain Domino had promised to get her back to her people, but how long it would be before he could fulfill that promise she could not imagine.

In her present predicament, the idea of finding herself once more aboard the *Charlotte* and under the protection of Joshua struck her as the happiest possible outcome. From this distance Joshua loomed more like a savior than like a husband she had come to loathe, not only for the onerous duties he imposed on her, but for his weaknesses that led to excesses of food and drink, indeed, any and all sensual pleasures such that he had found from Dr. Bascomb's medicine.

Still, being with Joshua would be better than confinement to this narrow cabin, with nothing between her and the vicious Loco, save the captain's orders. She began to worry that there would be another battle with yet another ship and that Captain Domino would be the one to lose or perhaps be killed in the fight.

This line of reasoning made her shake again, and far back in her mind panic beat its deadly wings against her hard-won composure.

Hastily, she glanced around the cabin, making note of each and every object in an effort to distract herself. Piled upon one chest she found several books. Opening the first of these, she saw on the flyleaf the name André de Beaufort. Curious, she leafed through the others and on each found the name repeated. On one, a very old copy of Rousseau's *Origin of Inequality Among Men,* below the name were the words: *Liberté, Acadia,*

La Nouvelle France. "Liberty, Acadia, New France," she said aloud in English. Acadia. She had heard something about Acadia and the people there turning traitor to the English and siding with the French of their original homeland. They had been deported, she thought, for insurrection.

On the opposite page was the inscription: *"A mon fils, André, pour son treizième anniversaire, avec mes compliments. Affectueusement, Papa. 30 Octobre 1732."*

Looking at the books, it occurred to her that while they might well have been stolen from some hapless passenger aboard a ship seized for bounty by Domino as a French privateer, he would hardly attack French vessels, would he? Perhaps they were his own, and the name Domino was merely a false name, as indeed many pirates of history had so they might enjoy their ill-gotten gains upon their retirement in their own country.

Among the copies of Rousseau, Montesquieu, and Voltaire, she found one English translation of Rousseau and tried to read that, feeling that her French was not up to such serious endeavors. After a few moments, as her head grew heavy and her brain became irritated, she decided she was not up to any serious work, whatever the language. Looking further, she found a copy of Dr. Samuel Johnson's *Dictionary* and gave a little exclamation of delight. The book had been forbidden reading at home. Her mother had claimed it was "cynical, low, and vulgar in too many of its definitions," and her father had taken aim at Johnson's cruel satirical definitions as they pertained to the Scots. She had remembered him quoting something about oats being food for horses in England and for humans in Scotland. She had known of course, that it was her father's intimacy with Bute and with the Camerons that had prejudiced him. She did not think that personally he cared a bit for the Scots otherwise.

She settled herself comfortably upon the bed and began to read. The dictionary was precisely the cure for her tired mind and sensitive nerves. It occupied her, amused her, and made no demands on her. One word suggested another and she skipped around among them, absorbed.

Domino, coming in sometime later and bearing her food himself this time, said, "You are recovered, I see, Madame."

"Yes," she replied, smiling at him for the first time. "I have found Dr. Johnson's dictionary. I was not permitted to read it at home."

"So, there is at least one small mercy from your trial." At the sight of her sober face, he added quickly, "It will soon be at an end. We're bound for Martinique, but I will see you to Havana first. The Spanish are still neutral in spite of the compact. There, I can arrange passage on a ship for the American Colonies."

"How long?" she asked.

"A few days. We will sail windward of the Bahamas. Once we reach the end, I can run through the Florida Straits with less danger than I can through any other passage and then sail to Havana."

"But if we are near the Bahamas, there might be many English vessels there. I recollect my husband telling me that English men-of-war sail into the Bahamas."

"That is nothing for you to fear. If we are taken by an Englishman, you will be the sooner among your own people."

"That's true," she agreed reluctantly. How strange that a few hours before she longed for just that reassurance. Now, she actually felt a bit let down at the prospect.

"Well, then, I will leave you to your dinner."

"Captain Domino," she said as he opened the door, "how is it that you speak English so well?"

"My grandmother was English. She lived with us until . . ." He stopped, his face tightening.

"Until?" she prodded.

"Until she died," he said brusquely and closed the door.

While Caroline ate, she puzzled over Captain Domino. Pirates, she had been told, were low brutes without knowledge and without human kindness—in fact, very much like the men who had spirited her from her cabin. Yet, there was Domino: a man of some education, well spoken, conversant in French and English, and, from what little she had observed, other languages as well. His manners were elegant in all his addresses to her. Yet he was a pirate; for all, he called himself a privateer. Her father had often said that a privateer was no more than a pirate with his sovereign's blessing.

She had heard of other buccaneers who were able to move among landsmen with some grace, but none of them could have been called gentlemen, nor were they as educated as Domino.

He was a curious man. He had rescued her, had been gentle with her, and he had also ordered those cruel lashings and stood watching them with satisfaction, had even forced her to watch.

He was clearly educated, even learned, but he had seized and looted the *Charlotte* with consummate skill. He had spared food and drink to the *Charlotte*'s company and requested, rather than ordered, members of her crew to join him. At the same time, he was ready to shoot anyone who failed to surrender to him. He had crippled the *Charlotte* with his guns and yet left her to limp to port.

His cabin and his person both bespoke his liking for order and cleanliness. Still, he associated with the foul-smelling crew members without apparent disgust.

She had never known anyone like him, and the more she thought about him the more curious she became to learn when and how he had chosen such a life for himself.

She slept again after her meal. When she awoke she discovered that Domino had been in the cabin, removed the remainder of her meal, and left again.

The quiet, the food, and the sleep had begun to restore her, and now that the weak, sickly feeling was gone, she longed to be out in the fresh air. She stared through the porthole, watching the sea gulls swooping and diving as they followed their namesake's course.

Oh, to be as free as that; to wander where she pleased and when she pleased; to leave off the habit of civilized living and find herself unbound! Perhaps that was why Domino had taken to this life. He had a longing for freedom, too, like her own, a freedom where no one was master of her fate and only she herself could decide what course to take.

She turned away restlessly. Seized with a need for some activity, she picked up the cloth that had wrapped her the night before and attempted to fashion it into a loose sack gown. The clumsiness of her tools—a small knife, the large needle, and heavy thread—made a poor job of it, but slowly, as she worked, the pleats at the back began to give form to the cloth. She sewed until the light grew dim. There was only the partially finished back attached with basting to the front. The neck was raw, the sleeves not yet cut, but she lit the lantern and began to disrobe so she might try on the crude effort.

She was standing in the center of the cabin, turning this way and that, wishing she might catch a glimpse of herself in the porthole. But the sky was not dark as yet, and the lantern light diffused against the late-afternoon glow.

Hearing the key in the lock, she turned to see Domino enter.

"Very charming," he said approvingly, "and far more suitable than the furbelows of your other gown."

"I was weary just sitting here," she said. "I want to go above into the fresh air."

He shook his head. "Too dangerous. I noticed last night how the men stared. We have been too long at sea. They are longing for women. The sight of you would stir them more. Even your presence here has created some tension. If I could put you ashore at Nassau, I would. We are north-northeast of it now. If I dared change course, you would be dining at the governor's mansion in three days' time . . . or four, if the wind failed us."

"But you won't change course?" she asked.

He shook his head. "No, not for Nassau. I have thought, however, of running into the Virgins, instead of Martinique. They are English, but there are so many islands with available sheltering where we could beach the *Mouette* for her barnacling and I could take you to St. Thomas. The merchant ships call there regularly."

"I see. But if the islands are English . . . "

"It's safe enough. We'd sail in at night. There is an island windward of Tortola. We could beach there for months and never be found. For that matter, there is a cave in Tortola itself that is safe enough."

"But food and shelter?" she said.

"There are people there—a small town built by pirates long ago. We pay the townsmen well, with some of the booty supplied to us by such as the good Captain Ramsey." He laughed suddenly, as if the whole affair had become a huge joke. It was a gay, ringing laugh that brought a light to his dark face and made his black eyes dance.

She stared at him as he stood, arms akimbo, black hair springing in thick waves above the ribbon that bound it back. His rough white shirt was open at the throat, and at the vee made by the points she saw the feathery dark hairs of his upper chest. The image of him burned itself into her mind so that long afterward when she thought of him it was always that picture that came to mind first.

Under her penetrating look his laughter stopped, although his face and eyes were still lit up.

"Has my laughter offended you?" he asked.

Startled, she shook her head, looking down at her confusion.

"Then what is it?"

"Nothing at all," she said, "that is, I . . . I never heard you laugh before this." She ended lamely, thinking, what a stupid thing to say.

"Not surprising, considering the shortness of our acquaintance and the circumstances."

She looked up at him, met his gaze full on, and was unaccountably rendered light-headed. Her heart began to hammer unevenly and the room itself grew dim around him, as if all the light had been drawn to him, leaving the rest of the world in darkness.

"I . . . I feel faint," she said.

Instantly, he was beside her, urging her to lie down.

"No," she objected. "I must have air. Please, Captain, surely a few minutes in a secluded spot won't cause any harm."

He frowned thoughtfully for a moment and then said, "Very well, I'll take you to the quarterdeck, where Christos has the watch. He is my lieutenant. Christos is, in fact, the most indispensable man aboard. He can mend a sail, use a sextant, repair a broken spar, and even cook if necessary. More than anything, he is the best navigator on the seas."

"And you?" she asked.

"I? Ah, I am the lucky fellow who persuaded King Louis that a privateer could be of service to him and that it would cost him nothing to run. He liked that part best, Louis did. Wars are very costly, and when one has a mistress to consider, as well, one must think of savings and of new revenues. The marquessate of Pompadour did not come cheaply, and now that it is the duchy of Pompadour . . . oh, poor Louis!"

"Do you know him—King Louis, I mean?"

"We have met, through the kindness of the duchess of Pompadour."

"You know Madame Pompadour?" Caroline was fascinated. "I hear she has great influence on the French king and is very clever at domestic politics. Is it true that she bathes every day in ice-cold water?"

He laughed. "I do not know. I have never asked her. We met only through a cousin of my father, a Monsieur Quesnay, who is an old friend of Madame la Duchesse."

"Oh. Is she as beautiful and witty as they say?"

"More than they say—intelligent, too. If it were not for Madame la Duchesse, there would be no Austrian alliance, no Spanish compact—indeed, probably no war."

"You are happy about the war?" Caroline asked curiously.

At this, his face closed up and he said curtly, "Come, then, if you must have the air, it had better be now. The light is fading fast."

He was silent as they went up, but as they reached the open deck he grew amiable once more, asking her how it came about that she had an interest in subjects uninteresting to most women.

"From my brother's tutors," she said. "They taught me some things. The rest I learned by reading."

"And your father permitted the tutors to teach you as if you were a boy?"

"My father was very indulgent with me once," she said. Then, remembering her last words with Sir Bertram, she, too, grew serious.

"You will see him soon," Domino said, comforting her, mistaking her silence for sorrow.

"I hope never to see him again," Caroline said. "He . . . " She stopped. She had been about to tell Domino about Joshua and how she came to marry him, but she quickly thought better of it.

"I take it he ceased indulging you," Domino said with a hint of laughter in his voice.

"More than that!" she burst out, stung. "He . . . he tricked me!" How inadequate it sounded, as if she were nothing more than a frivolous maiden pouting because her father got the best of her.

"There is Christos just coming now," Domino said, changing the subject. "Hola! Christos! *Va-t'en, s'il vous plaît.*"

Christos hurried up.

"May I present Mr. Christos, Madame?" Domino said in English with an air of mock formality.

Christos bowed and murmured a conventional greeting, as if he had not seen her before. Then, turning to Domino, he began to speak rapidly in French.

Caroline observed them as they spoke, paying little attention to what they actually said. Domino was a head taller than Christos, but they were both of the same coloring. Domino's nose was more aquiline and she thought him by far the more handsome, but Christos was like him in a curious way. They could have been brothers, even though one was French and the other Greek.

She caught the name Hardin in the rapid exchange and started. Domino looked at her.

"Ah," he said, "you didn't know, of course. One of the *Charlotte*'s officers, a Mr. Hardin, came aboard while we were engaged in carrying off cargo. He tried to set fire to the powder cabin, to blow up the *Mouette*. One of my men caught him and there was a fight. He was badly wounded, and, although we tended him, I regret to say he died a few moments ago."

"Died?" She gasped. "Oh, but he was . . . "

"Was what?" Domino asked.

"Young," she said. And, remembering how she had enjoyed his kisses, had flirted with him and teased him and at last wounded him with her cool indifference, she felt quick tears of sympathy form beneath her lids.

"Young, yes," Domino agreed, "and very foolish."

"He was brave," she snapped.

"Foolishly brave, then," Domino said. "I dare say his own captain would agree. You are very distressed, Madame. Was Mr. Hardin an old friend?"

"I knew him only aboard," she answered, turning away.

"Perhaps, then, you will arrange to notify his captain, once you are among your own people, so that he may write to Mr. Hardin's family. He was, as you say, a brave man."

She did not answer, and presently the two men returned to their conversation in French.

Hardin, poor Hardin. Such a short time ago she had leaned upon his sturdy arm, had laughed with him, had felt his warm lips pressed upon her own, and now . . . ! Oh, it was cruel; life was cruel—so short a time to know the joys of youth, so long a time to suffer, and with death at the end. Had she only known, she would have gone to him, tried to ease his last hours.

She turned to say as much and heard Christos say, "There is some unrest. The men talk of nothing but the Englishwoman. Loco and the others are besieged with questions. I don't like it. If she were old and ugly or one or the other . . . even then. . . ." He sighed. "Instead, she is young and very beautiful. I think we would be wise to head west into New Orleans. There are women there."

"No. It is too much of a risk just now. We are going to the Virgins . . . Tortola."

"There are few women on Tortola, and the ones who are there are not friendly at all. Or if they are amiable, their husbands and fathers are not."

"I don't want to take chances with this cargo," Domino said. "Remind the men that there is a goodly share of treasure for them and that little more than a fortnight will see us in Martinique."

"I will try. But Loco, José, and Manuel . . . they . . . " He caught Caroline's sudden start and stopped, saying rapidly, "The Englishwoman understands French."

They both turned to her and Caroline said, "I understand French fairly well, yes. I have some knowledge of Latin and Greek, as well. I know only a few words of German, though, and no Spanish at all."

Domino laughed. "Unfortunately, Christos knows none, either, and I . . . I am very deficient. It doesn't matter. You heard?"

"Yes," she said, "I heard."

"Then it is down to the cabin for you until we reach Tortola."

"I beg your pardon, Captain," Christos interjected, "but what will we do with Madame in Tortola? It will be worse then."

"We shall take her to St. Thomas. It will be possible to hire a boat from Etienne Goulème in Tortola. Meanwhile, the ship will be cleaned and we will be on our way to Martinique as soon as possible."

Christos looked doubtful. "I am afraid . . . " he began, but Domino cut him off.

"We will manage. There are not many men who would prefer to lose their share of the treasure or to be lashed and fined, as Loco was. If there are others, well, there is a guard at Madame's door, and I"——he patted his belt——

"have the only key. Come, Madame." He took Caroline by the elbow. "We will go below."

Captain Domino had been friendly and conversational on that first day, but the next morning his courtesy was thinly overlaid with cool withdrawal. If she were going to be confined until they reached Tortola, Caroline had thought to brighten her days with some social intercourse. When it became apparent that, beyond a formal inquiry as to her health and the usual greetings when he brought her meals, she could expect no further contact, the next few days dragged on interminably.

One evening, unable to bear the silence of her own thoughts any longer, feeling woolly headed and cross from her self-imposed task of reading the one English copy of Rousseau, she became determined to engage Domino in some sort of conversation.

She had finished the sack dress and had been wearing it over her single petticoat and without her hoops, indifferent to her appearance. All that mattered was that it was loose and comfortable; she frequently wore it without bothering to don her underbodice first.

Feeling that she would be better armed to approach the now-unapproachable Domino if she were formally arrayed, she dressed for the occasion. As she looked down at the blue-and-gold gown, she remembered that last evening aboard the *Charlotte* and the gaiety that had preceded the stunning roar of shot. It was like another world now, something that happened long, long ago. In spite of her daily ablutions and her attempt to wash her hair in the briny water, she felt sticky and uncomfortable. The comb could scarcely get through the salt-stiffened locks of hair. They resisted her best efforts, and her scalp was sore and irritable before she finally abandoned hope of bringing the snarls into order.

As the hour approached when Domino would enter with her evening meal, she stood, her back against the wall, bracing herself for his entrance. Yet when he arrived with his customary greeting, she found herself unable to speak.

"Is something wrong, Madame?" he asked.

"No . . . that is, yes," she stammered. Then she said rapidly, "I cannot bear this cabin any longer. I cannot bear the solitude. You must talk to me, at the very least."

As she spoke the dreariness of the past days welled up and she felt tears sting her eyes. Her mouth shook with her effort to suppress her emotions and she swallowed hard. "I am worse than a prisoner," she said, and at that the tears spilled over. In a moment, she was sobbing helplessly, unable to stop, a feverish hysteria manifesting itself in noisy gulps.

With a sharp exclamation he came to her, patting her shoulder clumsily, urging her to be quiet, promising her it would be over in a very short time now.

"We are due east of Nassau," he said. "We will be through the passage and into Tortola by early Friday morning."

His efforts to comfort her made her sob harder, and she reached out a hand to clutch at his shirtsleeves.

"Days, yet! I can't!" she kept repeating between her tears. "I can't! I was so frightened, and then when it seemed I would be safe, this dreadful loneliness began. I want . . . I want . . . " She floundered, unable to think what it was she wanted, only knowing that the solitude had broken her, as all the terror had not succeeded in doing.

His arms went around her gently and he pressed her head to his shoulder, as if she were a child, and, as a child, she leaned there. His hands smoothed her elf locks and he murmured wordless sounds of comfort.

After a time her crying grew less noisy and her tears began to stop. Still, she remained as she was, feeling that, were she to leave the supporting arms, she would once again be seized with weeping.

It was he who finally moved her so that he could look down into her tear-stained face. "Poor child," he said, smiling at her. "So brave. I admired that. Many another would have gone mad with fear, and, even recovered, would have remained silly and fretful."

The compliments, like the comforting arms, were balm to her sore spirit. "Please," she whispered, trying to smile.

She saw his own smile fade, saw his eyes deepen, and then felt the arms holding her grow rigid. A sudden tensing of his facial muscles made the line of his jaw grow white. In another moment he had put her roughly to one side. Turning, he went to rearrange the utensils on her tray, his back to her.

She stood, swaying a little at the abruptness of his departure. "Please," she said again, this time in her normal voice, "I need to talk to someone, if only for a little while."

"Very well," he answered, turning around. "We will talk. Come, sit down and eat your supper. I will stay with you until you have finished."

She was not the least bit hungry. Her eyes were sore and swollen from her tears and her body felt empty in the aftermath of her stormy grief. Nevertheless, she went dutifully and took her usual chair at the table while Domino seated himself opposite her.

"You must not think me harsh," he began. "If I have been aloof, it is only . . . " He stopped as she looked at him. "Well, if I spend time with you, it only increases the tension among the crew," he went on.

She said nothing, still gazing steadily at him, and he looked away.

"I am, after all, no different from them," he said at length. "I wish you no harm, Madame. And to make certain you are not harmed, I do not expose myself to temptation. You understand?"

He looked back at her, half-smiling, and she saw that he was once more in control of himself, that he was even mocking himself.

She could think of no adequate answer and hastily cast about in her mind for something to say, something normal, something that would start up the conversation she had begged for.

"Tell me about Canada," she said at length. "I know your name. André de Beaufort, isn't it? Tell me about your home in Acadia."

"I can't think of anything duller," he said in a tone that belied his words. "Tell me about your home."

"Equally dull," she said lightly, and she was rewarded by his smile.

"Dull homes. Then what of your life in London? And what made you demand learning?"

"I wanted to learn. The things I was supposed to do that my sisters loved doing were dull. Oh, I learned to sew and I learned how to run an establishment. I took lessons on the harpsichord and singing lessons. I enjoyed it well enough. But once my own education was considered finished . . . once I had learned deportment and letters and simple figures, I was bored. What history I was taught was little and mostly about the kings of England. I had done well in French, so when I begged for lessons with George William's tutors, my father did not greatly struggle against me."

She bit into the salted fish and chewed on it thoughtfully.

"And then?" he asked.

"And then I was doing so much better than George William that my father was annoyed. In any event, it was time for George to go away to school. My father had always wanted to go to Eton himself, and now, with the king's influence, George is there instead of at Harrow."

"Is that not a good school?"

"Oh, yes, of course, but Eton is older, and my father is a snob."

Domino laughed. "And you?"

"I don't know," she said slowly, "I never thought about it. I know I don't like people of vulgar manners. I like my maid, Dobbs. Yet I wouldn't have a brother of Dobbs for my husband. I suppose that means I am a snob."

"Or that you have no fancy for Dobbs' brother," he joked.

"Dobbs' brother is not twelve," she replied with a grin. "And I have seen him only once. He walked all the way from Tunbridge Wells to bring Dobbs a message that their mother was ill. I made Papa send them home together in the carriage and maided myself for the week Dobbs was gone."

"How very gallant," he said with faint irony, and she blushed.

"I did not mean it that way," she said defensively. "As it turned out, it was as well that I had the practice, because Dobbs ran away before we sailed. So, you see, my little act of mercy proved a blessing," she finished sarcastically.

He bowed in silent acknowledgment of the retort.

"And you?" Caroline asked. "Where did you learn all the languages? You are an educated man with the manners of a gentleman, and yet you are a pi—— . . . a privateer."

"A pirate, if you like," he replied. "It is as decent a business as that of your father, or your husband. Or do they merely live from the work of others on their own land and from the revenues of their tenants?"

There was no mistaking the insult in his voice, and Caroline's temper flared.

"My father is a merchant, an importer. The *Charlotte* is one of his ships. As for my husband, he is a tobacco planter in Virginia."

"Where he uses the slaves other merchantmen buy along the African coast, I presume."

"You sound like a Quaker," she said.

"I am a French Huguenot, at least by birth," he answered. "One needn't be a Quaker to despise the buying and selling of human beings."

"But they are only ignorant savages who cannot fend for themselves." She quoted from her father's teachings.

"On the contrary. In their own homelands, they are better able to care for themselves than you, my pretty daughter of a rich merchant who has only lately learned to robe herself."

"That is an insult!" she cried.

"But true. If you must support slavery, see it for what it is—a convenience to those who need much labor and have not a peasantry from which to extract it."

She stared at him. "What strange things you say. You speak worse than your Monsieur Rousseau." She nodded unconsciously toward the stack of books.

"So, you have whiled away your time by reading Rousseau—another small mercy in your long ordeal."

"It is difficult to read. I dared not attempt any of the French, and I understand very little of it even in English."

"New thoughts are always difficult to absorb, not that Rousseau is new. I recommend the Montesquieu to you, as well. Since you are still anxious to learn, you might also try others: the Greeks, Plato for one; your own Englishmen, Locke and Newton, if only for instruction. I will, if you like, supply you with a list before we part."

"And help me to speak against slavery on my husband's plantation in Virginia?"

"I would not advise that," he said dryly, "certainly not if your husband approves of it."

"Then to what end?"

"For your own information," he said. "And now I see you are finished and quite yourself again, more yourself, I fancy. There is a spark of annoyance and of stubbornness, a suggestion of a sharp wit and a willingness to sting with words. It's not the usual fare of a young girl . . . or, I should say, a young matron."

"You are odious," she said, rising.

"You have uncovered my character," he replied imperviously, moving toward the door.

"I have uncovered more than that, Monsieur André de Beaufort Captain Domino. You boast of your piracy and hide behind letters of marque, but you are a brigand just the same, and like any other highwayman, only you rob and plunder on the seas and sink ships and . . . privateer, indeed! How like the French, always to deny they employ such when they do!"

"How like the English," he answered quietly, "to imagine that people will believe them when they pledge they use no privateers and yet do, and more—reward them. What of Captain Morgan, who was retired with full honors and knighted?"

"That was years ago, and . . . "

"And nothing has changed. There are English privateers, as well as French . . . and Spanish. You delude yourself, Madame. The English are as savage as any other warlike race . . . more savage. Without provocation they turned six thousand Acadians from their homes, burned their settlements, drove them into the wilderness to die of starvation, or deported them, rending families and lovers apart to die of broken hearts."

"The Acadians betrayed . . . "

"Betrayed whom, Madame? They were French."

"They lived on British soil."

"Seized by the British, ceded under the Treaty of Utrecht at the end of a previous bloody war."

"And what of Fort Necessity? What of the slaughter of women and children by the Indians you French roused?"

"What of the Indian women and children slaughtered by the soldiers your king roused?"

"You twist words. You speak ill of us and yet . . . "

"It was not I who first spoke ill, Madame."

"You insulted me first," she said childishly.

"My apologies, Madame." He bowed and opened the door.

"Oh!" she exclaimed, wishing to prolong the scene, yet unable to think of a suitable rejoinder.

"I shall return later for your tray, Madame," he said.

"I prefer the cook's boy," she answered.

"I prefer to send him, but even he I dare not trust to your charms, Madame. In fact, I seem to be the only man aboard who is able to wait for better days."

He closed the door even as hot words sprang to her lips. Balked, she flung herself on the bed and in a fit of childishness drummed her heels and fists in impotent rage.

Almost as soon as he had left, Domino returned to the cabin. She heard him and sprang to her feet, her face flushed, her bosom heaving.

"You," she began, then cowered back as she saw his face, stiff, angry, and with something in it she had not seen before.

He crossed the room in a few long strides and seized her by the arms, half-lifting her, bringing her face close to his own. She could feel his breath warm upon her face, and his eyes, large with emotion, blotted out the room.

A wave of weakness swept over her and her heart pounded, as if in overpowering fear. As his face touched hers, she went limp, clinging to him to keep from falling.

She could not fight her surging emotions, and with a stabbing joy she knew she did not want to. She parted her lips and closed her eyes to shut out the burning intensity of his gaze, felt his lips reach hers, and then the door burst open and Christos was whispering so low she could not hear him.

Domino loosed his grip upon her and she sank back, feeling for the bed.

"What . . . ?" began Domino, frowning, but Christos put a silencing finger to his lips. He began to speak in low and rapid French. Caroline, straining to hear, caught only certain words, but those words were enough to turn her prescient alarm into active fear.

Mutiny and El Loco and arms. Dazed, she pieced together what she could. The three Spaniards had seized the ship with a handful of others.

"Tell me," she said suddenly and in a loud voice. They turned as one to urge her silence. "El Loco," she went on in a lower voice, "has seized the ship."

"Yes," Christos answered tersely. "Listen carefully, Domino. I have pretended to join in. They have every arm, save the weapons you carry. They have already knifed to death the few who opposed them with daggers: the carpenter is gone; the sailmaker; three of the gunners; the cook's help; the cook himself is bleeding from his wounds. I came upon him first and it was he who told me. I went to Loco, and when he saw me he charged me with a cutlass. Look." He held up his left arm, which bore a long slash now oozing blood despite the cloth that bound it at the elbow. "I knew we were outnumbered, outfought." He chewed furiously at his lip.

"And you joined them."

"Yes. Yes, that is what I told them. So did Haywood and some of the others. Loco sent me to bind my wound, but he has not given me a weapon yet. They are coming for you and for the Englishwoman. For you, it is death. Loco bears his name well. He is a madman. A lashing first and castration, and then hanging from the yardarm is what he proposes for you. The woman . . . "

"They will have to kill me first," Domino said. He went to his chest, pushing the books aside and lifting the lid. From it he withdrew a pair of pistols and another dagger.

"They will kill me and you, too," Christos said, refusing one of the proffered pistols, but taking the dagger and securing it in his waistband. "Every man alive is behind Loco now. No more treasure to the king of France; all is to be equally divided. The men who remained loyal are dead or in chains. If we die, who will put the pistol to Madame Welles?"

Domino swore violently. "I cannot permit myself and my ship to be taken without a fight."

"Domino, heed me. If they believe I am one of them . . . and they want to believe it . . . who else will navigate? All that could take my place are no more. Even Haywood has not my knowledge with a sextant. I can stay with the *Mouette* and we can rendezvous later."

"Rendezvous? Where? In heaven or hell, Christos?"

Christos shook his head, as if to clear it. "I am going too fast," he muttered. "The launch—it has some provisions in it. If you come with me now, you can get into it and I will lower away."

"Where are they now?" Domino asked after a lengthy moment.

"At this moment Loco is preparing to issue orders. There is only José up with the helmsman. The rest are mustered on the afterdeck. Soon a party will come for you. I am to lead it so that you will not resist. They believe you are below. That is what I told them, and that is where you were last seen by Manuel. We have only a little time. Come, now."

"What is our position?" Domino asked.

"Close by the outlying Bahamas. The sea is smooth. The tide is running in. You can reach land. It is the only chance. From there, you can make your way to Nassau or Eleuthera."

Domino stretched his lips in a wry grimace.

"You planned so well, one would think you knew beforehand."

"Domino!" Christos protested.

"Never mind. Let me think."

"There is no time. You must come with me now or all three of us are lost. Please, I will persuade Loco to head for Martinique at once. It is where he wants to go, anyway. The men were angry over the stop in Tortola. They are crazy for women."

Domino frowned. "Very well," he said abruptly. He handed one pistol to Caroline, saying, "If Christos and I are taken or slain, do not hesitate. Put the muzzle in your mouth and squeeze like so." He demonstrated in pantomime.

"I . . . I . . . " she stuttered.

"I hope you can do it," he said. "For if we are killed and you remain alive, you will wish for death in a matter of minutes after they take you. There are still thirty-odd men aboard. You will die from their combined attentions, die horribly."

A cold blanket seemed to descend over her then, as if she had no feelings to respond to her brain's urgent message of danger.

"I am ready," she said to him.

He gave her a keen look, and, apparently satisfied by what he saw in her face, he nodded. Swiftly, he gathered up some things from his chest, the rest of the silk material, and, almost as an afterthought, he pulled the gown she had made from its peg and added it to his bundle, securing the lot on his back with a rope.

"If there is anything you must have," he said, "take it now." But she could think of nothing.

Christos opened the door and stepped out first, the dagger in his hand. He motioned to the others, and when they were in the passageway Domino turned the key in the lock.

The passageway was dark and empty and there was only the faintest rumble of voices from the stern. With Domino leading and Christos behind Caroline, they moved slowly forward. The heels of Caroline's shoes clicked along the planking and Christos whispered for her to remove them. She did so, stuffing them into her bodice, where they protruded by the heels. At the ladderway, they paused and Domino motioned Christos to go ahead.

"If they see you, call out to them and we will secrete ourselves in the galley until you come," Domino whispered.

Christos scrambled up the ladder and in a few seconds looked down to motion them up. They gained the half-deck unobserved and were halfway up the ladderway to the quarterdeck when they heard Christos, above them on the deck, say, "The Englishwoman is not in her cabin. Domino must have removed her. I have searched everywhere on the forward deck. He must have taken her to the afterhold. Quick, look in the launch."

Footsteps and cries broke out overhead. They shrank against the ladderway. Presently they heard Christos call, "Not here. Come on, José. Helmsman, hold steady as she goes."

The footsteps ran toward the stern, and then all was silent. Caroline longed to ask Domino why Christos had left them, but she was afraid to make a sound.

Behind her, Domino tugged gently at her skirts and she moved down. As she reached the bottom, he put his mouth close to her ear and barely breathed his instructions. Nodding to let him know she understood, she stepped back into the shadows. He began to creep up as stealthily as a cat. Nearing the top, she saw him move his arm. A sharp clatter rose from the deck.

"*Qui est là?*" she heard the helmsman call. Domino was instantly on deck. There was a choked cry, a low rattling gurgle, and then all was silent again.

"Psst!" Domino called for her. Gathering her skirts against her swaying hoops, she crept upward. He reached out his hands as she emerged and caught her under the arms to bring her the rest of the way. She saw the helmsman lashed upright to the wheel, his head twisted to the side, and she knew his neck was broken. She barely had time to realize Domino had killed him when he signaled her to follow to the launch. He helped her into it, pulling the canvas covering back over her prostrate form to conceal her from view.

She lay there in the darkness, waiting for him to follow. Presently she heard Christos call loudly, "Helmsman, has anyone come near? No? Good."

There was silence again and then the sound of a mighty splash.

The boat she lay in began to rock and then descend partway before it stopped. Still she did not move. The coldness that had overcome her in the cabin had become a frozen shield between herself and the circumstances surrounding her.

She clutched the pistol tightly, taking comfort from its metallic hardness. The boat was agitated again, more violently now. There was a pull on it and a heaviness just forward of where she lay. A soft thud, a violent rocking, and Domino was in the launch. He threw back the canvas, urging her to sit erect. His dagger was in his hand and, looking upward, he waved it. She could see the moonlight glitter against its blade. The boat began to descend noiselessly. As the first fine spray hit them, Domino sawed at the forward rope and then they were in the water. The rope broke free and he moved swiftly to cut the sternline.

He then settled himself in the center opposite her and, taking up the oars, began to row with powerful strokes.

Still he said nothing. Looking astern, Caroline saw the ship moving away from them, all sheets to the wind. She watched its receding shape until it was well out of the path of moonlight and growing smaller. They themselves seemed to be edging away from the shimmering line of silver, not realizing they were in the troughs of the waves and out of sight of anyone aboard the *Mouette*.

Still she stared, expecting at any moment they would be discovered. When the first shots came, she cowered, her face in her hands.

"Do not be afraid. They cannot see us," Domino said. "They have discovered our absence. That is Christos. He has claimed he spies us. It is his signal that all is well with him."

"Where are we now?" she asked.

He squinted up at the heavens. "Off our course," he said. He began to turn the small launch around. "Over there"—he nodded—"there are islands. I can only hope we find one that offers some shelter and water."

"How long?" she asked faintly.

"I don't know," he answered briefly. "If Christos' calculations are right, it will be a matter of a few hours. If he is wrong . . . " He paused and she saw his shoulders move. "If he is wrong," he finished, "it will be the first time. Try to remain calm. You will need all of your strength when we reach the breakers."

Part
Three

Chapter Eight

Caroline's first sight of the island was through sleep-laden eyes. Incredibly, she had slept during part of the long night while Domino rowed. She had remembered burrowing down upon the bundle he had carried from the cabin, shivering in her sea-dampened clothes. She had lain there, watching him through half-closed eyes. The waves that broke over them from time to time soaked through his shirt. Beneath it his muscles rippled as he moved his arms back and forth in long, even strokes. The steady, rhythmic motion hypnotized her and, against her will, her eyes had closed at last.

She had not slept truly, but in a weird, half-dreaming state that rendered her aware of the boat's motion and of the waves against the sides in a distorted fashion. She had lost the sense of time and place, sometimes fancying she was wide awake on a punt on the Thames, sometimes dreaming that she was once again in the *Charlotte*'s state cabin with Joshua snoring beside her. And yet somehow she knew that it was the launch that moved, the shore-borne currents that sent the spume over them, and that it was Domino who rowed so silently.

His voice calling her name finally awoke her, and for a second or two she could not break through to the reality of the present.

The boat was riding high now, swooping up and down the long waves. A faint pink dawn flooded the sky before her and Domino said, "Look behind you." She turned and saw the low-lying coast etched against the horizon, a thin, undulating line. Huge foaming breakers raced toward it to scatter themselves along the sand.

The western sky had yet to receive the full benefit of the rising sun and hung deeply blue over the beach and the slender, curved outlines of the trees beyond it.

As she stared, hardly grasping the significance of landfall, a swooping wave, higher than the rest, bore them along its crest before Domino, struggling against it, managed to bring them backward so that the wave, when it broke, would not hurl them headlong into the water.

"Can you swim well?" he called above the roar of the breaking surf.

"Yes," she called back.

"Then take off your clothes. I don't think I can bring her into shallow water without capsizing. There is a strong undertow."

She made no effort to obey him, and he said again, "Take off your clothes. You will be swamped."

He was pulling mightily at the oars now, his face glistening with spray and sweat.

"Roll them up and put them under the canvas. Put the bundle there, too—after you have taken your clothes off. Hurry!"

The note of urgency in his voice galvanized her. The gown, the stomacher, the underskirt, and petticoat came off easily enough. She rolled them all into a ball. The hoops, soaked with water, their ribbons knotted wetly, were more difficult. She ripped at them until they came apart, spotted with droplets of blood oozing from her torn nails.

She nearly threw the hoops overboard, remembering only at the last moment that they contained the small pirate chest and some of the gold coins. The incongruity of this struck her even as she stuffed the hoops away and her shoulders shook with silent, hysterical mirth.

She had finished stowing away the rest of the clothes and the bundle when Domino said, "That corps, as well. You may keep the drawers."

Startled and embarrassed, she darted a quick look at him, but his head was once again bent to his task. She saw that as she had busied herself, he had managed to get rid of his own shoes and breeches and shirt so that he sat naked, save for his underclothes.

Mechanically, she undid her lacings and struggled out of the heavy bodice. This article, able to stand by itself, she tied by its lacings to the gunwales near the canvas cover. It looked ludicrous standing there, and once again she was shaken with unexpressed laughter.

I must be going mad, she thought dispassionately. She sat with her arms crossed against her bare breasts, but as far as Domino was concerned, she might be nothing more than the empty corps lashed to the gunwales.

He was pulling the boat crosswise to the shore now. One oar he finally rested, and with his freed hand he reached behind himself for a coil of rope. This he lashed to his waist, holding the second oar firmly under his arm all the while.

When he had finished, he uncoiled it and threw Caroline the other end. "Tie it to the prow, there," he said.

She followed his gaze, saw the small projection, and slipped the heavy rope around it, tying it loosely in a clumsy knot.

"Here," he said. "Come beside me. No, don't stand up, crawl. There, that's it," he said as she dropped to all fours and began to worm her way across the small space.

"Now," he said as she sat beside him, "hold these oars. Just hold them, like so. Feel the pull?"

She nodded.

"Good. Push against it, easy, now. Just push against it. I'll be back quickly."

He dropped down and edged his way to the rope. He bent over for a few seconds and then was back beside her.

"Good, very good," he said approvingly as she handed back the oars. He reached across her to grasp the starboard one, raising his arm to let her under it. "Go back now. When I say jump, dive clear of the boat and start for shore. I will be beside you. Don't fight the undertow. Push against it easily, as you did with the oars. Understand?"

She nodded.

"If it's too much for you, float. But don't fight."

She reached her own place and sat tensed against the order. When it came, she rose in one fluid movement and, springing high, flung herself into the water.

Surfacing, she raised her head to locate the shoreline and was surprised to see how close it appeared. At first there was no hint of an undertow. As she stretched out toward the beach, a rolling wave lifted her and she rode with it, thinking it must carry her to the land. It broke short and she was once again underwater. Now she felt the undertow like a giant hand tugging her backward. At that she panicked and began to claw upward and forward. The futility of it recalled Domino's words and she relaxed, stiffening firmly against the current until the next wave caught her again in a forward motion. Again it broke short, and again she was engulfed and pulled backward relentlessly before the next wave lifted her.

It became a silent struggle. She could not tell whether she was any closer to shore or not, and during the next crest she lifted her head and was stricken to see that the strand had receded. Almost at the same moment she heard Domino shout, "Don't worry! It will be all right!"

He was beside her then, giving her instructions. His nearness reduced her fear and she began to make headway. "Watch this last one!" he shouted. The words were hardly spoken when she was borne higher than before, higher and higher on a madly racing breaker that broke upon the shallow waters of the strand and dashed her to land. The water rained over her and the sand stuffed itself against her nose and mouth.

She longed to breathe. She attempted to raise her head up through the last of the wave which, now that it was being drawn back to the sea, drew hungrily at her exhausted limbs.

With herculean effort she staggered to her feet and stumbled the rest of the way while the water tugged backward and the wet sand pulled her ankles down.

At last, safe from the reaches of the waves, she fell upon dry land, spitting the sand from her mouth and sneezing violently. She lay there for a long time, gasping in breaths of clear air, her heart racing furiously. When at last her lungs had eased and her heart slowed its beat, she remembered Domino. She had not heard him, had not seen him since that last shout. Had he . . . " She couldn't bring herself to think the word that fit the picture in her mind of Domino, lying motionless upon the waves, drowned.

She shuddered and closed her eyes, unwilling to learn the truth. At last, unable to bear the uncertainty, she pulled herself erect and scanned the sea directly ahead. Nothing. She turned to look first to the left and then the right. There the boat bobbed in the water, moving toward the shore on a long breaker, as if rowed by invisible hands. And then she saw Domino, high on the beach, pulling on the rope that still circled his waist, hand over hand, pulling the boat toward the land against the sea that sought to claim it.

A spasm of relief overwhelmed her and she lay down on her side, curling up into a ball, her face half-buried in her cupped hands.

She was aware of neither the gentle warmth of the rising sun nor of the cool wind that played along her wet flesh. Her tired brain could receive no further messages and, like an exhausted child, she fell into a deep slumber.

She awoke to find that while she had slept, the sun had climbed and descended again to hover on the western rim. The silky stuff of the cloth Domino had snatched up lay over her, and above her head, secured by four thin poles, stretched the canvas covering from the launch. She was instantly aware of her surroundings, and clutching the cloth to her she edged from beneath the crude shelter. Domino was nowhere in sight. The boat lay on the beach. An indentation in the sand nearby indicated that Domino had lain there at least for some time.

Wrapping the cloth around her, she made her way to the boat. Her clothes, including the sack dress, were draped over the sides and had dried in the sun. The corps stood as it had the night before, stiffly at attention, secured to the gunwales.

With a quick look around, as if she expected to be observed, Caroline donned her petticoat and gown. She folded the cloth that had covered her and laid it beneath Domino's stretch of canvas.

Her mouth was burning and dry and her stomach rumbled. She searched through the rest of the boat, locating a small cask of water, already opened, from which she drank greedily, scooping the liquid into her palms and finally tilting the rim against her lips to let the water flow free.

There was a piece of hardtack lying on the seat. She dipped it into the cask and bit into the moistened biscuit. She was thus busily engaged when Domino hailed her at the high ridge of wild grass that began at the end of the beach and sloped upward to the scattered trees along the low crest of the land.

"We are fortunate," he said, coming up to her. "More than I dared hope. At one time there must have been habitation here, settlers. There is a cave made from the quarrying of pink sandstone. It is shallow, but it will suffice as a shelter while I construct a mast and sail."

"A mast?" she queried.

"We can't stay here," he said. "I need a sail for the wind, and the sail needs a mast of sorts. The canvas makes the sail. We can't row to Nassau."

So easy and confident was his manner that they might have been aboard the *Mouette* instead of stranded on this deserted island.

"I am hungry," she said, her mind more occupied with immediate survival than with the means of ultimate deliverance.

"Well, I can promise you better fare than hardtack and water. There are plantains not far from the cave. Those trees are coconut palms." He gestured to the rim. "And tomorrow I will try my hand at catching fish. There is a lagoon farther in—good for use as drinking water."

"Have you not slept?" she asked.

"I slept until midday. Come, now. We must move the boat to the tree line and lash it and then carry the rest of these articles to the cave before dark."

She started to ask if they mightn't eat first. She remembered the taste of plantains and her mouth watered at the idea of one. But he was already untying his own canvas, so she said nothing, stuffing the last bit of soggy hardtack into her mouth.

They worked with few words between them. Dragging the launch by its rope was arduous, especially when they reached the grassy incline. The shoots were rough and the coarse pebbles strewn beneath them cut her bare feet.

She was panting by the time the boat was secured, but she made no protest as they started back to collect those articles left on the beach. The tide was coming in again, and from the vantage point of safety, the crashing of the breakers and the sight of the high white spume rising out of the glittering water were no longer threatening.

Domino, surveying the beach to make certain they had left nothing, said, "Look. There's something at the edge of the water." She saw nothing and stood holding her bundles while he ran lightly down to the shore and picked it up. He looked at it for a moment, then slung it over his back. He came back to her, a wide smile on his face.

"Part of your attire, Madame." He laughed as he held

out her hoops. "I dare say **we** **c**an find some use for them."

It was suddenly more ridiculous than the night before. Peal upon peal of laughter broke from her, and she gasped out the significance of the hoops before she thought.

"You . . . you see how foolish . . . how utterly . . . " She broke down again. "Gold," she finally managed to say, "and some jewelry, and . . . and . . . " She gave a final gasp, then finished: "Nowhere to spend it." Here she went into fresh merriment so contagious that he began to laugh, too.

When they had finally spent themselves, he said, "It is good fortune, all the same. It can be well spent in Nassau. You will be able to purchase clothing, and I . . . "

"You?" she said, remembering too late that if Domino were her rescuer, he was also a pirate.

"I must rendezvous with Christos in Martinique," he reminded her. "You don't imagine I intend to let the *Mouette* remain in the hands of mutineers, do you?"

"Yes, I see," she said slowly. "Yes, I should have realized."

"In which case you would have found the situation less amusing," he finished.

"No," she replied with a faint smile. "It will always amuse me—a tiny pirate's chest finding its way to a real pirate."

He did not answer, saying only, "Come, then. It is a long walk to the cave."

As they made their way past the coconut palms and along a narrow, worn path that snaked through the wild, sparse vegetation toward the highest crest on which a lone eucalyptus stood, he said, "I found some berry bushes and a few apple trees no longer bearing fruit, save for a pair whose fruit is small and withered. There is other evidence of settlement, as well, although abandoned some time ago. The path from here to the cave and to the lagoon goes through a jungle of sorts. There I spied a wild turkey."

"But why does that mean that there were people here?"

"Because none of the trees, nor, indeed, the turkey, is native to these islands."

"Could the people have moved to another part?"

He shook his head. "Beyond the lagoon is more jungle

growth and another steeper beach leading down to the
leeward side. I have reckoned the island to be less than a
mile long, perhaps half as wide. All but the jungle and
the cave and lagoon sites are wild grass and sand. No, we
are alone."

The word gave her a devastating sensation of abandonment. "Wild beasts . . . " she began.

"I don't think so. There isn't enough to feed wild
beasts. I saw very little small game. There are birds,
especially in the jungle. And near the lagoon there was a
whole flock of flamingos. Beautiful. I will show them to
you tomorrow."

They entered the thick, viny growth of the jungle as he
spoke. "Follow closely," he said. "I will move the
branches aside." She bent her head and followed.

The flutter of wings and then the bird calls began almost as soon as the first of the branches closed behind
them. A sudden flash of scarlet streaked ahead of them
and was followed by another. There was a rustling in the
grass, the snapping of twigs, and the unexpected swaying
of branches. Each sound was loud in her ears, and this
sensation of hidden life pulsing, soaring, and scurrying
around them made the luxuriant growth eerie, even menacing. God knows what might suddenly appear, she
thought, and prayed that it was not a wild turkey. Did
wild turkeys attack the way geese did? The domestic
turkeys at Abbey Hall's farm didn't. Fat and self-
important, they waddled witlessly about, squawking in fear
when anyone approached too suddenly.

Domino veered right and she followed. "We are nearly
at the cave," he said. "To the left, if you follow that
track, you will reach the lagoon." She peered left but
could make out no path and said so.

"You must know what to look for," he told her. "I
will show you in the morning. Perhaps I can clear some
of it."

Show her? Did he mean that she would be able to come
through this jungle alone? Never! She started to tell him
that but decided it would be time enough when he suggested it.

Shortly thereafter they stepped out of the jungle and
into a clearing. There was the cave, hollowed out of the
stony hillock. Trees surrounded it, almost like the trees at
home. She could see that here the jungle section ended,

however, for through the trees stretched long, sloping levels of marshy grasses.

"It's strange that there should be a jungle in the midst of all this," she said.

"Mostly man-made. I told you, whoever planted it left the plantings to the wilderness that grew here to begin with, and the wilderness has taken it back. Come, I have started a fire."

She saw a pit dug a little distance from the cave entrance, with smoke curling up from it. Beside it was a cask filled with water into which he now placed a collection of wild root vegetables and a bit of salt pork from the boat's provisions. This he set over the fire on stones pyramided to form an opening at the top.

Taking up several large, green, rounded, oblong items, he thrust them into the ashes. "Plantains," he said briefly. "Not even as elegant as salted beef and hardtack, is it? But it is really better. The broth will be tasty, the plantains filling. We can drink coconut milk and eat the plantains from their skins." He gave her a mocking smile. "Poor Madame—from the soft bed of luxury to the life of a savage."

"Not for long," she answered sharply, stung by his sarcastic attitude.

"No, not for long," he agreed. "You watch the food. I have other work to do."

She crouched by the fire, staring at the primitive meal with no idea of when or how she could tell that it was cooked sufficiently.

Whistling, Domino set to stretching some canvas on poles in front of the cave and to arranging their articles inside it. He came out of the cave with an armload of rushes, which he heaped into a rough form of a mattress under the tent.

"You will sleep inside," he said, "I outside. I have made you a bed like this . . . not feathers, but better than hard ground."

She looked away. Occupied with her basic needs for food and water and shelter, she had not considered that the shelter would be for two. Outside and inside hardly seemed to matter, considering the intimacy of all the living arrangements. And for how long? She wanted to ask, but, fearing the answer, she said nothing.

As the food began to cook, the odors wafted to her

nostrils and activated her already voracious appetite. When it was finally finished, Domino ladled the broth into hollowed-out coconut shells and placed the steaming plantains upon two broad palm leaves.

Caroline ate all of it and then, still hungry, consumed plantains until she was full at last. "No supper was ever so good," she sighed as she leaned back on her elbows.

"Not even those of beef and pork and fish and puddings and cakes?"

"I am so full that all the cakes in the world would not tempt me now."

He did not answer, and, looking up, she saw that he was regarding her with a sober reflection that bespoke concern.

"What is it?" she asked, coming upright in alarm.

"I was wondering how you will feel in the days ahead. Making the sail is one thing; fashioning the mast and securing it are quite different. With luck and good weather and tides, it will be a week before we can sail. And we are coming to the stormy season."

"You mean . . . " Her mouth was dry.

"I mean that we could be here far longer than a week. Prepare for that possibility, Madame."

"Madame," she repeated. "That sounds so idiotic now. Madame . . . as if I were still gowned and elegant and enjoying the luxury of your cabin, at the very least."

"Yes. You remember how boring those days were? You would exchange this for that now readily enough."

"Of course," she replied, but unbidden came the thought that she would not, which was very curious, indeed.

They sat talking in a casual fashion after they had cleaned away the remains of the food. The moon rose, lighting their glen palely. Domino brought more brush to the fire and the flames leaped high.

"We must keep the fire going," he explained. "First, it is difficult to make, and the tinder was lost during the landing. Second, it will serve to keep away your wild turkey or any other small animals."

She thought at once of rodents and shuddered visibly. He gave a short laugh. "Never fear. I am stretched before your door." He squinted at the sky. "It is growing late," he said. "I must rise early tomorrow, and so must you."

She rose and went into the cave. Inside there was a

high pile of rushes over which he had spread the silk cloth.

"I cannot spare canvas," he said briefly. "But the nights are never very cold. I will awaken you at dawn." He left her there and she heard him moving around the fire, adding more fuel and then damping it down to burn throughout the night.

When he had finished, he came back. He made himself comfortable on his own bed, stretching out his length with a sigh. Presently, by the sound of his even breathing, she knew that he slept.

She could not sleep. The shock of the mutiny and the hurried escape from the ship rose before her like remnants of an old nightmare. It was peculiarly unreal to find herself lying staring up at this cave ceiling, her skin prickling from the grasses that pushed up through the silk of the cover.

As if in some distant past, she remembered Domino in those minutes before Christos broke through the door of the cabin with the news of the uprising. And that, too, was as if it had happened to someone else, some other Caroline, shivering and limp and surrendering to a man half in fear, half in joy.

The kiss he had been in the act of pressing upon her still hovered over her mouth, the physical memory acute. Yet that same man now lay a few feet from her, as indifferent to her presence as though the moment in the cabin had never existed.

She tossed and turned for a long time, her senses alert to every tiny sound: the hiss of the fire against its barrier; the soft sighing of the winds among the branches; even a change in Domino's breathing or a shift in his position. She never remembered falling asleep, and when dawn broke she awakened to find that she was still tired.

Chapter Nine

For the first few days on the island, Caroline was too timid to venture far from the cave or from the fire, which she spent most of her time tending. Domino was gone from dawn until sunset.

Sometimes, on his return, he would have a small fish or bird to vary the daily diet of plantains and coconuts. Once he caught a large young bass, which, separated from its school, swam too close to shore. She ate so much that night that she was bilious. He showed her how to dry the coconut meat and add it to whatever vegetables he had been able to find to flavor them.

Domino had adapted himself thoroughly to his new environment, working all day in his underclothes and a toga-like garment he had fashioned by tying the sleeves of his badly torn shirt around his waist. He grew brown and, in the absence of razor, black-bearded.

Caroline, remaining under the canvas shade most of the day, retained her pale color, save for a mild sunburn across her nose and cheeks.

On their first morning Domino had marked the day and the date on the sandstone walls of the cave, and each morning thereafter he slashed another line with his dagger.

Sometimes Caroline would stare at the markings, counting forward from the first and trying to imagine how many more would mark the passage of the days until the mast and sail would be ready and they could set sail for Nassau.

The lack of activity and the long hours until Domino returned for the evening meal made her fretful and nervous. Once, unable to bear it any longer, she summoned her courage and went off through the undergrowth and down the path to the beach.

Emerging from the green shadows, she found the strand deserted. The boat lay where it had been tied, and near it was the piece of wood that Domino had been whittling at with his dagger. She examined it curiously, having no idea of how close he was to finishing.

Shading her eyes, she scanned the area, hoping to catch a glimpse of him fishing, but the sands stretched smooth and bare, as did the foamy blue-green sea.

She waited there for what seemed hours, and when he didn't return the emptiness of the area drove her back to the more sheltered glen.

That evening, when the meal was finished and Domino began his silent preparations for sleep, she said, "I went to the beach today, but you weren't there."

"I was trying to catch the turkey," he said. "It was too clever for me. So I set a trap at the lagoon where it goes to drink. Perhaps tomorrow we can have some meat for a change."

"Will you take me to the lagoon tomorrow?" she asked.

"To see the turkey?"

"No. I . . . I grow very restless sitting here each day. If I could help, or if . . ."

"You can help by preparing meals," he answered. "But I will show you the lagoon." He yawned and stretched. "We will be ready in another day or two," he added, then lay down upon his pallet.

Caroline busied herself at the fire, scraping the remains of the meal into the cask and adding water for the morning. She was far from sleepy herself, and yet, with the night closing in and Domino silent upon his bed, she had no reason to remain awake. Sighing, she went to lie down on her own bed. Her body was sticky, her hair snarled, and her sack stiff from its immersion in the briny waters of the ocean.

As she lay there she heard Domino's deep and even breathing. It was the same each night. Once she had been afraid that Domino would use her as El Loco and his companions had meant to . . . been afraid, and yet . . . She thrust the thought away.

He was like no man she had ever met. He had saved her from her abductors and had risked his own life to protect her from the mutiny. He provided for her on this island with cool courtesy. Not again had he permitted the intimacy of personal conversation or touch. That day aboard the *Mouette,* when she had initiated the quarrel, was the last time that he had spoken to her in any personal way.

Domino had broken a man's neck without distaste, and yet he had discoursed upon the inhumanity of civilization.

He fought and looted and plundered, yet he saved lives —even the lives of enemies. He lived like an animal and read books too ponderous for her to fully understand. He had confessed to wanting a woman—any woman—and yet each morning found him stalking off to his self-imposed tasks, and each evening found him sleeping the sleep of utter weariness.

As much as she feared him breaking through the cool exterior, she longed to see him rattled and out of command. He was an adventurer, pirate, scholar, philosopher, cruel master, murderer, the enemy . . . her enemy, who was also her savior. And yet, aside from his admission that he was no different from other men who had been away too long from the comforts of a woman's body, he showed no more interest in her than he did in the sunset—less.

It was a new experience for Caroline. Men had always paid her the compliment of an admiring look. And there had been an endless parade of suitors. She had made many a conquest, even conquests she had not sought to make. In Domino she had found a man who, except for one moment, was impervious to her looks, her charms; he was a man who was actually faintly contemptuous of her. It irked her vanity even as she told herself she was grateful for his indifference.

In another day or two they would leave. It would be two days in that open boat before they could hope to reach Nassau. And then . . . and then there would be yet another ship that would take her to her new home—to Joshua. She thought of him: he was suddenly vividly before her, advancing to her bed, his face flushed, his breathing heavy, his hands upon her, his body . . . She shivered and curled herself up into a ball.

Between this island and Joshua, there was little choice. Escape from the island meant captivity of a different sort.

She knew that she had brought about her own misery. If long ago she had accepted one of her parents' choices for her, she would now be safely in England. Carteret or Redleigh, or even Fortescue. What did it matter? At least she would have been spared all that had followed her departure for the Colonies. Surely no man could be worse than Joshua.

All at once she longed for her old home with a terrible sadness. It was nearing the end of September. George would be back at Eton, and her mother and sisters would be preparing to move back to the London house. Jane's engagement would have been announced, and Anne's birthday was but weeks away. At home there was sociability, visiting, and parties. There were dinners of a plentitude that made her mouth water at the memory: great joints of meat and hot breads and crumbling, savory tartlets filled with melted cheese; ruby-red wines and fragrant coffee thick with cream; pastries stuffed with custard and little cakes smothered in chocolate; almonds and raisins and soft pink bonbons crowned with nutmeats.

There was gay laughter and conversation, and men in velvet jackets and snowy lace jabots were vying for her attention. And when it was over, Dobbs was waiting to hear the gossip, to remove her finery, and brush her hair. Then there was the softness of her feather bed, with its cozy quilts, and a hot flannel-covered brick to warm her feet. And there was nothing to follow but mornings filled with bright promise and evenings filled with amusement.

Remembering that and thinking of the bleak future stretched before her, Caroline burrowed her face down into the dry rushes and wept herself into an uneasy sleep.

The way to the lagoon was not difficult to follow. That next morning Domino stalked ahead without speaking and Caroline followed at his heels. The path from the cave led to a worn circular spot off which branched the twisting path to the beach on one side and the nearly trackless way to the leeward strand.

Straight ahead lay the narrow but, she now perceived, well-marked lane to the lagoon. "You cannot get lost," Domino said over his shoulder. "There is no other way into the lagoon. The trees surround it on all other sides, and at the end is the waterfall. The rocks are steep there and jagged. A goat might find its way, but, unfortunately, there are no goats."

"Unfortunately?" she echoed.

"Meat," he said briefly. "Ah, here we are." He pushed aside a curtain of vines and motioned her ahead of him.

Grassy banks sloped gently down to a deep-blue pool. Flat, shelf-like rocks jutted from the far end below the rocky prominence of the waterfall, which flung itself from the crest to splash its glory from level to level and cascade into the lagoon. On the other sides the jungle closed in, deeply green and hushed.

Upon their entrance a flock of pink flamingos soared swiftly skyward, circling and swooping before disappearing across the cloudless heavens.

"It's beautiful," Caroline breathed.

"Yes, but not so beautiful as that turkey." He gestured and she saw a large clump of feathers beating feebly against the snare that had broken its wing.

"Oh, the poor bird!" Caroline exclaimed.

"Yes. I shall put it out of its misery," he answered. Striding along the banks, he drew his dagger and bent over the bird. There was a quick, feeble squawk and then silence.

Caroline turned away, revolted.

"A fine bird," Domino called. "Tough, I am sure, but tasty, I'll bet. Have a look."

"No." Caroline shuddered. "I . . . I can never eat that."

"No? Ah, well, you can dine on coconuts while I gorge myself on meat, then. I presume Madame Welles is too dainty to pluck and clean a fowl . . . or cook it."

She said nothing, keeping her head averted.

"Too delicate to look, eh? But not too delicate to partake of food that has been prepared. Tell me, Madame, do you not know the look of the dying quarry? Of the lamb led to slaughter? Of the porker suddenly stabbed? Of the butchered calf that graces your table as breast of veal?"

"Don't," she said faintly, "or I shall never eat again."

"You will eat again. Calf and pig and lamb . . . and turkey, for that matter, when you have grown weary of legumes and fruits."

Without looking at him, she turned back to the jungle,

running and stumbling over the path to the clearing. She heard him coming after her, heard him laughing, and was filled with loathing for him.

Uppermost in her mind was how to avoid any contact with the dead bird. Surely he would not leave it at the cave for her to attend to. Well, if he did, he would have no supper of it. She would leave it wherever he put it and . . . and what?

So intent was she on her own thoughts that she was in the clearing before she realized he no longer followed her but had taken himself and his burden down to the beach.

As the morning wore on, the incident at the lagoon faded and the thought of the lagoon itself rose temptingly before her. She ate the leftover breakfast, stale and tasteless after its morning in the heat.

When the sun was directly overhead, she gathered her bedcovering and torn gown and went back to the lagoon. The flamingos were once more at the water, and she tried to enter softly so that they would not fly away, but the moment she stepped along the bank they fled as before.

Here in the lagoon the overhead sun warmed the water and sparkled on the waterfall, but the trees and underbrush offered shady spots, and a cooling dampness pervaded the grove.

Caroline knelt by the water and immersed her gown and bedcovering, wringing them out and laying them along the far side to dry. She surveyed her sack dress, now stained with grass and the bits of food from their meals, and rustled out of it, adding to it her petticoat and knickers. Naked now, she applied herself to washing these garments, as well, then put them to dry beside the others.

Her bare skin burned in the sun and she dove into the lagoon, alternately floating and swimming, trying to wash the sea water out of her hair, using her fingers to tug at the sandy tangles until most of them floated free in the water.

She swam until she was tired and then stretched out in the dappled shade to let the soft Caribbean winds dry her tingling body. She rolled from one side to the other like a young animal until her body was warm and dry, and then she turned over, pillowing her face on her arms while her long, wet locks spread over her back and shoulders—a cool barrier to the shafts of sunlight.

The cold water and the heat acted upon her body like a sleeping potion, and she presently fell into a deep and dreamless slumber. She awoke when the sun was hovering below the trees to the west. Stretching and yawning, she rolled over and lay for several moments with her face upturned to the sky.

It was so peaceful and comfortable now. She dreaded the idea of returning to the cave and to the dreary evening that loomed ahead. Sighing a little, she sat up and ran her fingers through her hair. It was dry. There were still tangles, but it was soft and free of the grainy sand that had itched her scalp. She tugged at the remaining elf locks, gathering the whole into one long length and binding it with two of its own strands. Her clothes, too, were softer and smelled sweet from their long drying in the soft air.

The lagoon still beckoned invitingly, the music of the waterfall rising above the gentle sighing of the wind in the leaves. On impulse, she threw down the sack and knickers and plunged back into the water for one last swim. She went the length to the waterfall and clung to its lowest ledge while the waters sprayed over her. Holding her face up, she caught the cold water in her mouth.

At last, reluctantly, she swam back to the far bank and climbed out. Her hair, soaking again, had slipped from its light bonds and she shook it back, gathering the wet strands and pressing the water from them. She turned to pick up her recently discarded clothes and a movement ahead startled her. She looked up in fear. Domino stood just at the entrance to the lagoon, his eyes intent upon her.

For a moment their eyes locked, hers wide with apprehension, his dark and glittering. How long had he been there? The thought flashing through her brain broke the spell. She darted toward her clothes, and as she did, he moved suddenly, striding like a tiger through the grass. Abandoning the garments, she turned and fled down the length of the lagoon. She heard him coming behind her, saw that she was trapped by the waterfall, and, unthinking, turned and dove into the water. She surfaced on the opposite bank, her eyes darting frantically about for escape.

He stood opposite her, his own brief garments discarded, and even as she looked he came in after her. She dove down again, through the clear depths of the water, twisting this way and that like a trout escaping the cruel hook of the fisherman.

He followed her without haste, and yet in a few moments she was caught beneath the surface, and with powerful thrusts he brought them both to the top. They broke through the water into the clear air. She was gasping, wiggling, trying once more to free herself. She could feel her body slippery in his hands, hands that held her firmly, bending her back until she was neatly floating while he propelled her inexorably to the shore.

In the shallow waters near the bank, his arms went around her and he brought her upright to fasten his mouth upon hers.

"Don't, don't," she begged against his lips, but in answer he pressed her more closely to him and, half-dragging, half-carrying her, laid her upon the bank. She rolled away, but he was quickly beside her, turning her to him with overpowering strength. Once again his mouth covered her broken pleadings and his hands moved over her body with rough insistence.

Silently she fought him, writhing and gasping. He lifted his head briefly and looked down at her, his eyes blazing with a furious passion, and then he bent his head again. He parted her lips to explore her mouth while his hands explored her body. She felt the soft, sweet taste of his tongue upon her own and moaned. He gathered her to him in a vise-like grip and they rolled together as she resisted him. He was too strong for her, and she was weak from her struggles. For a moment she ceased fighting, and in that moment she became fully aware of his body, hard, hot, unyielding. His mouth, drinking from hers, was soft and sensuous. A swift tingling headiness shot through her, and in the next moment she was returning those kisses, pressing her body eagerly against his. He made a muffled sound of surprise and his urgency gentled. Caroline, no longer thinking, no longer aware of anything except the wild sensations coursing through her, gave herself over voluptuously to his caresses, crying out when she felt his hands slipping sinuously between her thighs. For timeless moments she reveled in his touch,

and then he was over her, pressing her down, down on
the grassy bank.

The knowledge of his intent came over her and she
twisted away, her swift resistance taking him unaware.
She stumbled to her feet and he was up, after her, seizing her from behind and throwing her to the ground. This
time he was with her almost as soon, and this time he
made no soft signs of affection but thrust himself upon
her, spreading her thighs to effect entry. When she stiffened in resistance, he cupped her buttocks, bringing her
up and, despite her resistance, moving astride her. Over
and over and over she cried out in protest. He covered
her mouth with his and she bit fiercely at him, tasting
his blood with a throb of primitive delight. Then, with
his blood on her lips, his hands like steel bands holding
her, moving her back and forth at his pleasure, a thrill
shot through her. Somehow her arms were around his
neck, her body moving beneath his and of its own volition.
"Now, now," she heard him murmur. She felt his body
shake, and in the next instant a piercing ecstasy suffused
her and from a great distance she heard her voice burst
from her in a low, long wailing cry of intense pleasure.

It was over. He fell for an instant against her and then
rolled away. She heard him breathing deeply and unevenly. Her body felt light and floating and curiously
alone. She made an unconscious move toward him, but
he had risen and was standing over her.

"You are married," he said, "a matron, not a young
virgin. You know men. You should have expected this."

His eyes were stormy. She tried to answer him, but
words wouldn't come. He left her there. She heard the
water splash as he dove in, heard him surface on the opposite bank. Then, even as she raised herself up, he was
striding through the path, his clothes slung over his shoulder.

She made haste to follow him, snatching up her own
things, throwing the sack over her head and bundling the
rest under her arm. The waning light of the lagoon was
deep twilight within the jungle and she ran swiftly, afraid
that the night would close in and find her alone on paths
she could no longer see.

When at last she reached the clearing, Domino was
not there. The fire burned brightly, and, buried in its

ashes, the turkey roasted, filling the air with a mouth-watering aroma.

He had done this and come to find her and . . . The memory of those moments at the lagoon, of the fierceness of their encounter, and of the thrilling spasms suffusing her body swept over her. She had fought him, feared him, surrendered to him—been forced to surrender to him—and she had reveled in it. Her body still burned with pleasure, and her mind raced in a conflict of thoughts, but rising over it was the realization that she would welcome it all again.

She had succumbed not only to the enemy, but to another than her husband. She had committed adultery, yet, somehow it had felt less sinful than those nights of marital duty she had spent with Joshua. Shivering, she pulled the sack dress on.

She looked up at the sky. She saw that it was darkening more rapidly than was usual and that there were no stars between the dark clouds that sailed toward each other like lovers bent on meeting.

She heard a far-off clap of thunder and then another. Huge drops of rain splashed down: one and two and three—scattered droplets on the fringes of a storm. The fire sizzled angrily and Caroline hurried to it, dragging stones closer and pulling the cooked turkey free.

As she worked the rain began to pelt down. There was a thunderclap close by and an almost simultaneous flood of lightning. Catching the turkey in her recently washed gown, she raced for the cave with it. She hurried back to the fire and gathered all that she could carry: plantains, coconuts, and gourds.

She was seated near the opening of the cave when he came back, bearing the pole mast over his shoulders. He came directly to the cave and she moved back to let him enter.

"Storm," he said shortly. "I hope it is only the outriding winds." He went back to the fire and thrust a bundle of twigs into the dying embers. Shielding it with his hands, he managed to keep its feeble flame alive. He stuck the lighted sticks into the dirt floor of the cave and began to pile the rushes that formed his own bed against the opening. Against these be braced the mast pole.

"You saved the meal," he said without emotion.

"Yes," she answered in a like manner.

He stood peering through the rushes at the driving rain. "If we get the full force, there will be no boat left."

"And will we?" she asked, surprised at the tranquility of her voice.

"At the moment the winds are south by southeast. No. A shift . . . " He shrugged. "Hurricanes are unpredictable. I would say this one has come up from Martinique or farther south. If it continues on its course, it will pass us and spend itself at sea or over Bermuda."

"How do you know?"

"It is my business to know. The *Mouette* would long since lie on the bottom of the ocean were I unable to out-maneuver storms or outride them."

"And shall you find the *Mouette* again?"

"Yes. If she still sails, I'll find her. If not . . . I will find Loco, in any case," he finished roughly.

"How will you go from Nassau?"

"I will find a way."

"But if you're caught by . . . "

"By your English soldiers? I won't be."

"But . . . "

"I won't be," he interrupted. "Let's eat." He squatted down at the turkey and, taking his dagger, cut off a leg, which he offered her. She shook her head.

"Don't be a fool," he said. "The storm may last two or three days. The turkey will not be very good to eat by then."

Reluctantly, she accepted the meat and chewed at it half-heartedly.

Domino ate with obvious relish. When he had finished the turkey, he broke open a coconut and drank from it before cutting the meat out. When he was done, he broke open another and offered it to her. She drank greedily, glad to abandon the meat.

He cleaned up after that and wiped his hands on the edge of the gown that had wrapped the turkey.

In the wavering light of the fire, she watched him yawn and stretch out on the floor of the cave.

"You had better sleep," he said to her. "It will pass the time."

Obediently, she lay down upon her pallet, her face turned toward him. Outside, the storm increased its furious assault and, despite the barrier, gusts of wind blew raindrops into the cave, spattering them both.

Her hair was still wet from the lagoon, and the driving dampness of the wind and rain made her shiver from the cold. She lay huddled alone and wished with intense ardor that Domino would come to her now.

She wanted to call to him, yet those words flung at her at the lagoon—"not a young virgin . . . you know men . . . should have expected this . . ."—came back to her and she forbore speaking.

She moved restlessly on the bed and the rushes whispered as they rubbed together.

"You are awake?" his voice came through the dark.

"Yes," she answered.

"If this does not stop, if the wind grows stronger, we will be here a long time."

"I am cold," she said. He did not answer her. She waited, feeling her heartbeats. She counted them. Then, losing count, she said, "Domino?"

"What is it?"

"I . . . nothing," she replied, feeling foolish.

There was another silence and then he got up and went to look out into the night. "I think the winds are dying down," he said. "I am going outside."

"Why?" She rose in alarm. "It's raining in torrents."

"I want you again," he said evenly. "I don't fancy chasing you through the night."

Her breath caught in her throat so that at first she could not find her voice. She saw him tugging at the mast-pole and whispered through dry lips, "I won't run away again."

She thought he had not heard her. Rising, she went to him. "I won't run away again," she repeated, reaching out one hand to touch his broad back.

He turned slowly and looked down at her.

"I can't see you well," she said, "just a little." She moved closer and, reaching up, put her arms around his neck. "Please," she said even as he seized her.

At the first touch of his lips, she began to tremble, and by the time she was free of clothing, her knees were hollow and she pressed feverishly within the circle of his supporting arms lest she fall.

He moved her slowly backward to the pallet and came to rest beside her. He had been harsh in the lagoon, but now he was so gentle that she was torn between desperate passion and overpowering tenderness. She lay in a half-delirium as he kissed her body with slow, burning lips. He was stirring feelings she had never imagined, and desire shook her so that she pulled at him, wanting him with heightened intensity. She heard herself whimpering, making little incoherent cries.

"Now you want me," he whispered above her. "Say it!"

"I want you—now!" she cried. "Now!" And for the first time she surrendered gladly, caught at last, riding the crest, higher and higher until she drowned in the overpowering force of its current.

The storm lasted for three days, as Domino had predicted, abating for short periods only to renew its howling with increased fury.

Of those days Caroline was to remember most of all the desire between them rising and rising and then, like the storm itself, abating for a time, only to rise once more with greater force.

During the storm's lulls, Domino would forage for fruit and bring it back to the cave, where they would eat with voluptuous enjoyment. It seemed to Caroline that as her body rounded and softened under his touch, the texture of food, of the silk of her gown, of the rough leaves and brush, even the smoothed edges of the mastpole were increasingly pleasurable to her senses.

During those days she studied Domino's body, the quality of his skin, and the way he moved. She knew the way his eyes changed with different emotions and the difference between the thick smoothness of his head hair and the wiry harshness of his beard.

Of his past she learned little. She knew only that he had the education of a gentleman and lived the life of a rogue. Questions about his family he turned aside.

Once he said brusquely, "They are dead—all of them. I told you that. I told you how. I don't want to talk about it anymore."

Only on the last night before the storm broke did he reveal anything more.

"One day," he said, "I will own an island not too different from this. And I will have people on it—free people, no masters and poor servants. *La liberté.*" He stopped. When she pursued it, he laughed and said, "It is still but a dream. And you, will you come to that island with me?"

"Yes," she answered quietly, "anywhere with you."

"Another dream, less real than the first. At least I have the promise of *liberté*. You . . . " He turned away from her.

"I cannot go back to Joshua now," she said. "It was hard enough before. I was in despair. I hated him. I hated my father for withdrawing his support, for making me see that he would not stand with me against my husband. I was bound as much as any bondswoman . . . worse. You could free one of them, but you will take me back to prison."

He made a low sound and abruptly left the cave to walk in the abating storm, not returning for a long time.

When he came back, he could not meet her eyes.

"You needn't say it," she told him. "I know I must go. I know you will leave me in Nassau. But I won't go to Joshua. I will take the first of my father's ships to call and return to England."

"I can't take you with me," he said. "I have something I must do . . . will do . . . not just find the *Mouette*—more."

"And you won't tell me? Just as you tell me nothing of yourself . . . not a word about your family. Are you more indifferent to them than I am to mine?"

"Indifferent." He met her glance. "They are dead, all of them—my mother, my father, my . . . " His jaw tensed. "You want to know? They lived among the Acadians. My father liked them. He built his house just above their village settlement. When the English came to drive them out, he refused to go. A fight ensued, and they killed him. They cared nothing for the fact that he was as neutral as a man can be.

"I . . . I came home a month later. I had just bought the *Mouette*. I spent five years at sea, saving everything, taking the money my father gave me as my patrimony when first I went to sea. I was proud. I couldn't wait to bring them down to view my pride.

"Christos was with me. We met, Christos and I, in school in France. We went to sea together. My family had never met him. That was something else. I wanted to show my family to my best friend, who had no family of his own any longer.

"The house was burned." He took a deep breath, and when he went on the words seemed torn from him.

"The settlement was leveled. I saw it first. I knew. I went on. I had to know. The house. The graves. My grandmother. She . . . she and my sisters were hiding when the soldiers came.

"Only my mother . . . my older brother . . . my father—all were shot. My older sister heard the shots and she ran screaming to my parents, and the soldiers . . . they shot her too—seventeen . . . Marietta was seventeen."

He balled his fist and drove it into the wall of the cave. He seemed not to feel the pain. His eyes stared ahead, not seeing Caroline, just seeing the long-ago memory, instead.

"My grandmother lay in the filth of the old pigsty, with the stinking carcasses of the animals around her. My youngest sister was dead beside her . . . not long . . . her body was still warm. My grandmother . . . she died some hours later . . . starved, the last of the water gone. Too late. I was too late. We buried them beside the rest."

He rested one arm against the wall of the cave and pressed his forehead against it. The silence after that torrent of words vibrated in Caroline's eardrums.

Her immediate horror at so brutal a tale, plus her aching sympathy for his anguish, made her leap up to go to him; yet, even as she neared him, she stopped. What words of hers could comfort him?

"Now you know," he said in a more normal voice, straightening up and facing her. "Now you are satisfied at last."

"I . . . I never meant to make you live through it again," she said. "Forgive me for that."

"It . . . ." He stopped. "There is no past, he said. "Tomorrow . . . who knows tomorrow? There is only now —today and whatever it offers.

He pulled her roughly against him and began to kiss her with desperate urgency, as if to blot out all else.

The following morning broke clear and warm. The havoc of the storm would have been mere memory, save for the uprooted trees, the smashed coconuts, and the bodies of small birds and animals.

Domino cleaned away the worst from the clearing before he went down to the beach to check the boat. He had

filled it with sand before the storm and lashed it between
two trees on the high ground. It was no longer intact. One
side was smashed apart and the stern was cracked.

"Days of work lie ahead," he said to Caroline when he
returned. "Oars and canvas are safe enough, and so is this
mastpole. But they are useless without the boat, of course.
I wonder . . . " He mused, looking around him. "It might
be easier to construct a raft." He shook himself. "No. It is
better to try to make the repairs. One blessing came from
the storm though." He smiled at her. "I found a beached
turtle—a giant, a beauty. So we have food at last. Don't
worry," he added, "we will yet reach civilization."

She did not tell him that the news of their delay was
merely a relief. As much as she realized that it was only
a matter of time before they parted, she welcomed the idea
that they would be together yet a little longer.

Their days fell into the old pattern, except that now
they were together, and, between the work and the shared
meals, the evenings of love and the nights when they would
lie in each other's arms talking quietly, a newer and
deeper intimacy grew between them.

Each day as he returned and reported on his progress,
she smiled and encouraged him, as if it did not mean a
day closer to parting. Once, lying together on the bank
of the lagoon, he said, "Remember that first day here?"

"I will never forget," she answered quietly.

"I was angry that day, angry with you . . . but most of
all with myself."

"And now?" she asked.

"Now . . . too much has happened," he muttered and
held her tightly to him. For a moment she thought he was
going to say more, but then he moved her away and rose,
pulling her up beside him. "You are too great a temptation," he said lightly. "I spend time with you that is better
spent working on the boat."

"Better spent?"

"If we are ever to leave here, yes. Come, it is time to
go to work again."

"But it is nearly evening," she protested.

"Two hours of light are left. Tell me, what is the menu
tonight?" he asked teasingly.

"The last of the turtle roast, wizened apples, and, for a
change, plantains."

"What? No coconuts?"

"If you insist," she said.

"There are only a few short days left now," he told her. "I reckon the boat to be finished tomorrow. We will leave the following day. Two . . . three days at most and you will be tucked into a warm bed after a huge dinner."

"I would rather have my pallet in the cave and dried apples than the governor's mansion in Nassau," she said, looking at him directly.

"You're a fool, then," he said brusquely, then pushed past her roughly as he had done once before, leaving her to follow him through the jungle, parting at the turn to the beach without speaking again.

As he had promised, they were ready to leave on the second morning. Caroline, who had removed the coins from their hiding places, discarded the old hoops. The coins and chest she secured in the small nail cask. Wearing the tattered sack dress she had fashioned, she carried the petticoat and dress wrapped together and stowed them on the boat, the bodice around them.

They pushed off from the island, Domino wading out with the boat in front of him, then climbing in as it floated free of the bottom. The mast loomed above, and the sail furled until they reached the end of the island and the open sea.

As they rowed away, Caroline watched the island receding with a pang of foreboding. Well out beyond the shallows, Domino brought the boat around and began to row parallel to the beach so that the island remained in view for a long time.

When they reached the end and began the wide sweep around to leeward, Domino hoisted sail. The wind caught it and, using the oars as rudder and tiller, he headed toward Nassau.

The wind at their back sent the light craft skimming over the waves, and in a short time the island disappeared altogether.

"Domino," Caroline said, "I can't really leave you. Take me with you."

"Impossible," he answered. "You know well enough why."

He scowled and bent to the oar, and she, not wanting him to see her weep, turned her face to the bow.

On the night of the second day they came ashore at a

sheltered cove some half a league from the outer reaches of the Nassau waterfront.

Domino beached the boat. Taking Caroline's arm he led her up the strand to the coiled grasses that grew beneath the shelter of palms.

They were both well soaked from the journey and, although tired, too hungry to sleep. They sat, their backs to the trees, staring out at the water.

"I have a notion to take you to the governor's house tonight," Domino said at length.

"But you said . . ." she began.

"I know, I know. But we need food and drink, and I must find clothing to look like the sailor I will pretend to be. I can't very well haunt the governor's palace in this." He looked down at his torn breeches and bare chest.

"The money," she said, "I have money—the gold. It is in the empty cask. I nearly forgot it."

He went back to the boat and returned with the cask, from which he extracted the little pirate's chest.

"A boon." He smiled a little. I will take some and go into town. You will be all right here. There is no one around, nor likely to be."

"I don't want you to leave me behind," she said.

"I must. If you are seen with me while I purchase food and clothing, someone will be sure to remember, and then . . . No. You stay. I will go alone. Otherwise, I will be suspect, and you . . . well, you know what they will believe."

"What is true," she answered.

"But bad for you were it known. They would despise you for a . . . well . . . For myself, I cannot have all the king's men looking for me until I am under sail."

"How will you find a ship to sail on?"

"I will hire on a merchantman bound for the South . . . Barbados, Guadeloupe—it doesn't matter. There I will have word of the *Mouette*."

"All right," she capitulated suddenly. "I will wait here until you come back. It is better I do that."

"You are not afraid?"

"I am only afraid of what will happen when you leave me at the governor's house and go away."

He stood up abruptly. "I will go for the food," he said. "It may be some time before I return. Try to sleep."

She lay down on the grasses after he left, thinking that

sleep was the last thing she could do. On the island, even leaving it, the full truth of what she could expect had been less frightening. Here, knowing that there were people only a short distance away, knowing that an hour's walk would bring her to the luxury of the governor's mansion, she was overwhelmed. Domino would hear of nothing but parting.

Lying on this strange shore waiting for Domino to return, as she had done for weeks on their island, she knew it would be the last time for them. Nothing she could say would deter him from his plans; nothing would induce him to take her with him. That time on the island was all the time they would have. Tomorrow evening she would be safe in a comfortable bed and he would be on his way to whatever rendezvous fate had in store for him.

I will never see him again, she thought. The pain in her heart told her more than anything that she loved him. "I love him," she said aloud, "and he does not love me." How cruel the tricks of fate were. With clarity, she saw that it was always she who had been loved while others did the loving, if there was ever love between herself and anyone else at all, save for Joshua. But, then, there had been little love between them, desire, perhaps, and her own rebellious nature that wanted most of all what she was being denied.

Perhaps that was the way it was with Domino. He eluded her. She considered the thought and rejected it. Were he to come back to her now and offer to bring her with him, she would go gladly if sea-stained clothes and plantains were all she could expect.

After Domino, how could she endure a return to Joshua's clumsy, crude embraces? She could not, would not. She would not wait for a ship bound for Virginia Colony, but would take the first one for England. She would go home. It would be a long time before a message could be sent to Joshua. She would have months, perhaps a year, and in that time she would surely think of something, some way to extricate herself from a life that had once been promising and the thought of which was now utterly hideous.

Smiling a little, somewhat comforted by making her own decision to fight what she had once accepted as inevitable, she lay back down. Who knew what the outcome might be? Perhaps one day she might even find

Domino again . . . when the war was over. And if not? She would not pursue that possibility.

Domino returned sometime later, wearing a shirt and trousers of rough cut and bearing cold meat, ale, and bread. After they had eaten, they slept. In the early hours of the morning, Caroline awoke to see an edge of pink lining the northeastern horizon.

She shifted around so that she lay facing Domino. "I love this part of the morning," she said, "with the sky lightening there and still black above us."

He did not answer her but continued to look at her, his eyes black pools whose depths she could not fathom. She returned the look steadily, watching as the light flickered in those brooding eyes, and, sighing, she moved toward him even as he reached out for her.

Even in the lovemaking there was a sadness, like a threnody whose music squeezes the heart until it aches. It grew and grew so that it filled her body and mind, and at the highest peak of ecstasy tears dampened her cheeks.

Afterward, lying still within his arms, she sensed that the pain had touched him, too, but when she tried to seize this advantage to swerve him from his stated purpose, he withdrew into himself again and the moment was gone.

All day he catechized her, over and over. "Remember, we were mutinied but a week ago and the captain was taken. Do not say killed. I will be heard of again and you will be known to have lied. Your English seaman saved you. I am Hardin. Remember that. Now, what became of Hardin?"

"He drowned as we reached this island."

"And what did you do?"

"He had told me to swim ashore, but as he was preparing to jump I think the boat capsized."

"Did you know where you were?"

"No. He had only said the Bahamas. I thought at first it might be a deserted island."

"And then?" he prodded.

"I began to walk, and after a day I saw houses and found the town."

"And then?"

"You . . . I met you on the waterfront and . . . "

"Yes."

"I was fainting from hunger and you fed me and brought me to the governor."

"How did you live in that boat so many days?"

"We . . . there were stores aboard and we caught fish and once . . . er . . . Hardin caught a sea gull."

"And why did the men mutiny?"

"Because the captain would not let them . . . have me."

"Good." He gave her a brief smile.

"Domino," she said.

Meeting her eyes, seeing the question form, he answered, "No!"

She did not persist. When he was satisfied that she knew all the answers to any questions that might arise, he said, "Wherever possible, tell the truth. If you recite everything up to your rescue from El Loco precisely as it happened, you will be better believed for what follows. And in the end, describe the boat disappearing as you actually saw it disappear. The more truth, the more the lies will sound true."

She gave a faint smile. "'Tis hardly a believable story, even the truth of it."

It was dark as they entered the town by skirting the waterfront and cutting inland. The grass was cool and comforting to her bare feet after the sharp stones of the dusty roads. She had the impression of avenues, of the dark shapes of dimly lit houses, and of wide fields between.

A deep and melancholy singing drifted to her ears . . . hauntingly beautiful, so accurately describing her own pain at this parting that she said, "Who sings with such sorrow?"

"Blacks," he answered shortly. "Slaves."

"Are they so miserable, then?"

"What do you imagine? That they enjoy bondage? That they toil all day under the broiling sun for pleasure? That they enjoy the whip?"

"No, no, of course not. Only . . . "

"There will be no slaves on my island," he said in a tight voice.

"And where is that island?"

"Not far from Martinique. They call it Devil Trap

Island because of the waters that swirl around it and the ships that dash on its reef. But if one knows the way through the reefs, it is a paradise."

"Shall I . . . " She had no chance to finish the sentence, for all at once he took her arm and drew her to the left.

"The governor's mansion," he whispered. "It is just here." Looking up, she saw a high wall ahead, a dim light outlining its iron gates.

He drew her into the shadow of the wall a little distance from the gates.

"And here we say good-bye, Caroline. I will rouse the governor's guards and ask them to take you to the house and I . . . I will wait outside the gates. When you are safely inside, I will be gone."

He kissed her lightly, and she clung to him. "I can't," she said, "I can't."

"You must," he said sternly.

"Never to see you again . . . never." The word loomed large and menacing.

"Never is a long time," he answered cryptically.

"I can never go to Joshua now. I will . . . I will run away, go to England. Only say you will come for me."

"I can make you no promises," he answered.

"Please," she begged, tears coursing down her cheeks.

"Don't do this," he said roughly. "Don't you understand anything? I am the enemy, remember. I have my own course to follow. What happened, it was . . . " He began to fumble for words and she took hope.

"Shall you like to think of me with another man now?" she asked.

She felt him stiffen and he said coldly, "That, by all rights, is of less importance to me than to your husband."

"I hate Joshua!" she burst out passionately. "I told you 'twas no marriage of my choosing. My father tricked me . . . he . . . oh, Domino, say that you will take me with you." She flung herself into his arms, her own tight around his neck. "I love you!" she cried despairingly.

He pulled her arms loose, holding them crossed in front of her.

"No," he said in a low voice. "No, and no again. I know what I must do. You know what you must do. Never? You don't like never; then say not never, but perhaps. You are going inside now."

She looked into his face and saw that it was set. There was no appeal to his determination and the realization left her drained and apathetic.

He saw her resignation and loosened his hold. "Good," he said, and he stopped her from wiping away the tears in her eyes. "They will lend more credence to your story," he explained.

"Yes, they will believe me," she answered. "Don't worry," she added. "I will not play you for the fool or betray you. You are safe, Captain Domino."

She turned away and walked ahead of him to the gates. She stood stiffly, feeling that she would fall were she to speak or move or relax the muscles that held her trembling body erect.

Domino's call to the guards was answered at once. As if in a dream she heard his explanation, uttered in the accents of an ordinary British sailor. She heard, too, a whining servility in his voice, saw that he had seemed to shrink from his height, and realized he was stooping a little.

"Wait here," said the guard. "I will see if His Excellency has not some reward."

"Aye, sir, and thank-ee," Domino said.

At a touch from the guard's hand, Caroline was propelled forward and passed like a sleepwalker through the gates. She turned as they closed behind her and looked at Domino. In that flash she saw his face twisted, as if in pain. Then, meeting her eyes, he stepped back, melting away into the darkness.

Too dazed to comprehend at first, she followed the guard up the long path to the house. It was only when she was finally inside, hearing the guard explain, seeing people come forward, that Domino's face rose before her as it had been at that last moment.

There was a sudden singing hope within her, and rising with it was the enormity of her pain. Caught between the two, the feelings and events of the past weeks whirled like a kaleidoscope before her. As the guard said, "Now, Mistress, here is Sir Arthur Ormonton and Lady Susan," her bewildered brain could accept no more and she fell half-conscious against the guard's arm.

Chapter Ten

Caroline awoke to find herself in a large chamber whose windows were opened to the early morning breeze. She lay on a soft bed and over her was stretched a netting secured to each of the four posts. A light coverlet was draped over her. Looking down, she saw that someone had removed her stained gown and bodice and had put on a soft nightdress.

She looked around the room at the elegant furnishings: the narrow highboy; the dressing table; the broad wash-stand on which reposed an alabaster pitcher and basin; and indienne cloth printed in soft blues and greens was looped back from the windows.

Slowly, the night before came back: Domino going away, herself collapsing, and questions—so many questions. She could remember little of what she said and hoped that she had told her story as Domino had instructed. Of him she could not bear to think without pain.

She sat up and pushed aside the netting. The floor was cool beneath her feet as she walked to the windows. Below them, lawns rolled away to a pink brick wall and beyond it she could see rows and rows of cultivated growth through which dozens of half-naked blacks moved, bending, straightening, and bending. A man on horseback rode up and down and now and again his whip would flash out and one of the workers would move quickly down the row.

So these were the slaves of the New World. She had never really seen slaves before. Mrs. James had once kept a little blackamoor pageboy, but one day he had run off. "Disappeared," she remembered Mrs. James saying. "And

I had made such a pet of him." As if he had been a lap-dog. Though, in truth, Mrs. James had spoiled him and allowed him to study letters with her own son.

But this was different. These were not pampered pets. Caroline had heard tales of how the slaves were capable of revolt. There had been one such in Hispaniola, near a place called Cape Haitien. The revolt was quickly put down, but not before many had died.

The sun climbed as she leaned against the windowsill observing. The man on horseback was coming back within her line of vision, and again she saw the whip fly out, then saw a slave hurry out of its reach. No wonder they revolt, she thought. If I were being struck with a whip . . . It brought the flogging aboard the *Mouette* to mind. And El Loco had rebelled. And that brought Domino to mind too vividly to bear.

She began to search the room for a possible way to summon a servant. There was a long braided rope near the bed. She pulled it experimentally and at once the door opened and a young black girl entered.

"You call me, Miss?" she inquired.

"You came so quickly," Caroline said.

"Yas. I be beside you door all de morning. I sleep dere, too. Outside, de little bell tinkle, so I come here."

"I see. I want to dress," she said.

"Yas. I tell Lady Susan. I bring food, yas?"

"Please," Caroline said. The girl went away at once. She was a curious girl, not more than sixteen, she would judge, tall and slender with huge black eyes. She had a nice face, but . . . Of course, that was it—the girl's face had remained impassive, her voice was low, and her words were scarcely accented so that she spoke in a near monotone.

Lady Susan arrived a few moments later, breathless, as if she had been running. She burst into excited speech before she was quite in the room.

"My dear Caroline—I may call you Caroline, may I not? You are Joshua's wife. An old friend, Joshua. Why, he was a friend of my brother's when I was . . . well, but never mind my digressing. What a woeful end to your voyage! How did you survive it, my dear? Pirates! And one has heard of Captain Domino, a true crackrope. Mark my words, one day he will hang. How did you survive? I . . . oh . . . I would have fainted to be among such cut-throats. Why, the very idea of it. . . ." Lady Susan rattled on, repeating herself without apparent intent. Her prattle, her high, girlish voice, and the little giggles that skipped between her phrases were at odds with her matronly figure and long face.

Caroline, taken aback and unable to interrupt this steady flow, soon perceived that behind it Lady Susan was anxious to hear that she had been violated, at the very least.

" . . . and to think Hardin, poor man, died to save you," Lady Susan said, finishing up.

"Yes," Caroline finally spoke, "although not, I assure you, to save me. He was a prisoner, too. But he was noble to bring me with him. I was a hindrance."

"But I thought he drowned . . . " Lady Susan said.

"Just off Nassau itself," Caroline said smoothly. And then, thinking she sounded rather a bit casual in reporting the death, she dropped her face into her hands and managed a shudder. "Awful!" she said, her voice muffled. "There I was, free of the boat, riding the waves, and he, poor, poor man . . . "

"Why could he not swim if you could?" Lady Susan asked.

"I don't know," Caroline answered with another shudder. "The sailor who brought me here . . . he said it was likely that poor Hardin was struck in the head when the boat capsized and that he was caught beneath it. But I, I cannot tell you just what happened. I was swimming and swimming, and when I reached shore he was gone and the boat was well out on the tide."

Lady Susan made sounds of sympathy. " 'Tis amazing that the mutineers did not seize you at the very moment of their rising."

Caroline raised her head with a breath of relief. This would be easier, since she would be telling the truth.

"You see," she said, "Captain Domino does not permit the taking of lady prisoners. Some of his men disobeyed him, and when he found me in the chest, he had them flogged. He put me into his cabin and locked me in.

"When the men rebelled, the first person they came for was the captain. He was at their mercy, I suppose."

"But how did you get out of the cabin?" Lady Susan pried.

"I . . . " Caroline faltered. "Oh, it was terrible," she said, "terrible." She tried to think of a reasonable answer.

It was not a question of her catechism, or if it was, she did not remember it.

"How Mr. Hardin managed it I will never know," she extemporized. "But the door burst open and there he was. I scarcely remember what he said. The next thing I knew I was being pulled along a passageway and up a ladder and into the small boat. He . . . he hacked at the ropes and we nearly capsized, falling into the sea. Terrible," she repeated again. "After that . . . oh, Lady Susan, the sea and the lack of food and . . . please, if you don't mind, I can bear no longer to speak of it." She saw a look of disappointment, coupled with annoyance, pass over Lady Susan's face.

But her hostess said, "I understand, my dear. How thoughtless of me. I will not speak of it now, nor ever again."

"Thank you." Caroline summoned a grateful smile.

"Oh, and I am a fool!" Lady Susan cried. "You poor child. Not a stitch of clothing, save your torn gown. I fear nothing of mine will fit you, but I do have some of my daughter's old gowns. I think they will suit you. Sarah left them here when she sailed for England last June. Such a pity we could not sail with her. I should like to have seen her presented at court. But I know that my sister will do the best she can for Sarah. We are so isolated here. Ah, you must find us very provincial after London."

"Not at all," Caroline murmured politely. "Quite the contrary. Were it not for the climate, your conversation would make me believe I was in London itself."

"You're too kind. Now, I must see to your garments." She bustled away to the wardrobe chest. "You are in Sarah's room, you see. Ah, here we are—not fashionable, but quite neat and clean. We shall soon have you looking right. Oh," she broke off as the black girl entered, bearing a tray.

"There you are, Rosa. Will you help Mistress Welles with her toilet?" And to Caroline, she said, "Rosa is very efficient. She will maid you while you are with us. I expect that Joshua will be returning before the week is over."

"Joshua?" Caroline repeated stupidly.

"Yes, dear. He sailed again with Captain Ramsey to call at Barbados. He thought perhaps he might have news of you there. Poor man, he was distraught. We tried to persuade him to rest here. He looked quite ill, but he would have none of it. Poor Joshua . . . such a trying time . . . losing one's bride to a pirate . . . " Again that quick, furtive look of avid curiosity came over her.

"He has not lost me, as you see," Caroline returned, with a calm she was far from feeling. Joshua had not sailed on to Virginia. Joshua was returning. She was trapped. Would the woman never leave!

"No, not lost you, but—there! I promised we wouldn't speak of it. When you are ready, we are on the veranda. Rosa will show you the way and . . . " Here she paused and cocked a roguish eye at Caroline. "We have a surprise for you, a visitor from England—quite an old friend of yours." She gave a little giggle and hurried away, as if afraid to reveal her secret.

Caroline did not hasten her toilet. Rosa, silent and obedient, fetched water for her to bathe and wash her hair. She entered and left the room as Caroline required it.

Shortly before noon, arrayed in a green muslin frock over snowy petticoats, her still-damp hair contained beneath a white cap, Caroline made her way to the veranda.

The everyday tasks of normal life had done much to ease her sense of isolation and abandonment, even to soothe her misery at the thought of Joshua's return.

Someone from home, Lady Susan had said. An old friend. She could not imagine who it might be. Who would come all the way to Nassau? And for what purpose? Such friends as she could think of were in England when she left, and with no announced plans for a voyage to the Colonies.

She entered the veranda and discovered it was a long, shaded terrace enclosed by slatted wooden blinds all now opened to permit the breezes to sweep through and mitigate the crushing heat of the noon sun.

The brightness dimmed her vision at first, and then she saw Lady Susan reclining on a chair that seemed to be made of wooden lace. Stepping from behind that chair and coming toward her with a wide and mocking smile was Redleigh.

"My dear Mistress Welles," he was saying, "your adventures will be the talk of London for the seasons to come."

He bowed, and Caroline, stunned by his appearance, scarcely remembered to sweep him a curtsy.

"Lord Redleigh, I cannot believe my eyes. How is it you are here? I took you to be in England."

"I sailed a few days after your wedding—to heal my broken heart." He laughed lightly.

She tossed her head, denying the pleasantry, and said, "What of your boon companion, Fortescue? Shall I find him here, as well?"

"No. You are spared that. Fortescue would no more dream of venturing far from his tailor than he would canary with garlic-eaters. In truth, he would prefer reveling with peasants."

"How is it at home?" she asked.

"You know as much as I and more, for you sailed from England later. I see your misfortunes have bewildered you. You left England after I did."

"And what brings you here?"

"Why, to visit my aunt, Lady Susan, and to look over some land with my uncle."

"But what of Redleigh Castle and . . . "

"My dear Caroline, I mean only to take the land that is available and hire an overseer and return to London before the season is over. Slaves will work the land, the overseer will work the slaves, and my uncle will send me the profits."

"I am surprised that you have given thought to profits," she said.

"Ah, but I fancy the taking of a wife of not such extravagant a dower as yourself. For her I must think of profits."

The slight implicitness in his words brought a flush to Caroline's cheeks. "Indeed," she said coolly, "the lady must be a paragon of all the virtues if you would overlook her poverty for the sake of her love."

"It has been the uplifting of me," he said with feigned sobriety, "and so much more relaxing than pursuing well-dowered ladies of otherwise little worth."

This time his mouth turned into a sneer, as if to emphasize his insult to her. She felt her anger stir, but she would not give him the satisfaction of seeing that he had riled her.

"The wonder to me," she said softly, "is that her family would not take greater care of such a feeble-minded daughter."

A dull red mounted Redleigh's cheekbones, and Caroline moved away without giving him the chance for yet another discourtesy.

"What were you two whispering about?" Lady Susan greeted her. "The latest London gossip, I'm sure."

"Yes. Lord Redleigh wanted to know if his betrothed still pined for him, but, alas, I do not know the lady."

Sir Arthur rose from his own place, a smile of welcome creasing his plump cheeks. "My dear Mistress Welles," he said, "how very good to have you with us. Please be seated." He waved her to a chair similar to Lady Susan's.

Seeing the curiosity in his face, Caroline said hastily, "I have never seen such furnishings."

"A design for the heat," Lady Susan told her. "One of our slaves has a gift for making furniture most elegantly. Quite odd for a savage."

"You know, my dear Mistress Welles, your man at the gate was gone when I sent someone to reward him," Sir Arthur said.

"He spoke of no reward," Caroline answered steadily enough. "He was the first person I saw, and I was half-sick with hunger. I did not know where to go. 'Twas he who thought to take me to the governor's mansion."

"You are yet again fortunate," Lady Susan interposed, "to remain protected on a pirate ship, to have poor Hardin give his life to save yours, and then to meet a low person in the worst streets of town who, far from harming you, gives you food and brings you to safety. Oh, many a man would have fared less well."

"Many a man lacks Caroline's charm," Redleigh said, coming up in time to hear the last remark, "or her cleverness. Do you know she was not satisfied to learn her letters? She also had to learn French and Latin and mathematics with her brother. And she is very good at puzzles, I am told."

"Lord Redleigh pays me too great a compliment," Caroline said sweetly. "The only puzzle I have ever solved was that of my father's boxwood maze, and I was nearly twelve before I accomplished that." She turned her face up and smiled brilliantly at Redleigh.

At that moment luncheon was announced, and she rose with the rest. Laying light fingers on Redleigh's proffered arm, she followed the Ormontons into the dining hall.

The Ormontons, while expressing concern that she should rest after her long ordeal, were also anxious to give entertainments and to introduce her to the general society.

Caroline, longing to be left alone, dreading the interminable repetitions of her story she knew social gatherings would force upon her, pleaded for a few days' rest to be fully restored.

There was a good deal of truth in her insistence that she was unduly weary even after hours of sleep. The first day or so found her sleeping more often and longer than she could ever remember doing.

She rose each morning famished for her breakfast, and despite the heat, she was filled with energy. She walked on the grounds and once or twice ventured beyond the immediate lawns and gardens to the edge of the fields, there to observe the blacks at close range.

When the afternoon wore on, they appeared to work with greater energy and sang as they toiled. The tunes were different from any she was familiar with and the words were strange. Yet there was an exciting cadence to them and the blacks' bodies beat out the rhythm as they bent and swayed through the fields, sweat glistening on the naked backs of the men and soaking the thin cloth of the women's dresses.

The curiosity she had for this alien land did much to occupy her mind and keep at bay the problems before her.

The house was unlike English homes, its common rooms not truly partitioned, so that the air flowed through them and cooled the interior. Only the bedchambers off the upper gallery were enclosed, and these had doors made of wooden slats like those of the veranda.

From the outside, the house was an unpretentious building of clean lines with white-painted windowframes and doors, its bricks mellowed to a soft pink. Brilliant flowers grew everywhere; the passion flower, with its deep purple throat; the climbing tiny flowers of the bougainvillaea; the sweet scents of white hibiscus. Palms were everywhere: some tall, skinny brown shafts crowned with leaves and coconuts; others wide and rough-trunked with irregular prickly leaves growing out of knobbed and dwarfed branches. There were thick, pungent eucalyptus trees and one tree Sir Arthur called a gum tree. "Imported from the East," he said. "And when you bore a hole in its bark, it bleeds a sticky white liquid."

The first few days of good food and sleep should have restored Caroline to her self, yet, evenings, when supper was over, she was hard put to keep her eyes open.

On the fifth day the Ormontons told her they would have a gathering that evening "to wake us all up," Lady Susan said. "Oh, I fancy I grow as sleepy as you with these long, dull evenings."

That night Caroline committed the unpardonable breach of nearly dropping off to sleep while seated in a chair listening to one old gentleman tell her of the early days in Nassau when John Woodes leased the island from the king and was governor.

She was excused because she had, after all, suffered an excruciating time of terror and danger.

She managed to get through the rest of the evening in an agony of exhaustion. When at last she was able to make her escape, she sank upon her bed without removing her clothing or bothering to secure the netting.

Waking up in the quiet dark some hours later, she found an insect feeding on her bare forearm and slapped it away. She got up and went to the door, expecting to find Rosa stretched upon her pallet, but the girl was not there. Caroline left the room and went down the hall toward the stairs in search of water.

Just as she reached them, a door behind her opened and, startled, she shrank back against the wall into the shadows. Redleigh's door. She trembled, inexplicably frightened. But it was not Redleigh who stepped out; it was Rosa.

The girl stood, her back against the door for several minutes. Her breath was ragged, as if she fought off sobs. When she finally crept down toward her pallet, she wobbled as if she were ill.

Redleigh's room. Rosa in Redleigh's darkened room. But that meant he had bedded her!

She saw Rosa sink to her pallet and left her own place in the shadows. Coming up to the pallet, as she had, her sudden appearance startled Rosa, who sat up, clutching her arms around her body, looking up with a harshly drawn breath.

"It is only I, Rosa," Caroline whispered. "I . . . please come into my room."

Rosa followed her obediently enough, but when Caroline had lighted a taper and held it up, she saw the girl staring with a sullen look of hatred.

"W—— . . . what is it?" she asked.

"Nothing," Rosa said, her face smoothing to blankness.

"There was no water," Caroline said. "I went to find you and saw . . . "

"I am for lordship, too," Rosa answered in her regular monotone. "Sleep on pallet by door for lordship and Miss. I fetch water."

"No, wait," Caroline said. "Has Lord Redleigh harmed you?"

A flash of fear crossed the girl's face. "No, no," she said. "No, he not hurt. He . . . You say to Lady Susan he hurt and I be beat."

"He *has* hurt you!" Caroline exclaimed.

"No hurt . . . no hurt me," Rosa repeated. "Please, Miss, you do not say it."

"Does Lady Susan know?"

"She know. Maybe she say not know it if you speak, but she know it. She de one make me to sleep in hall to take care for lordship when you have not come here yet. She know."

"But . . . why, that is . . . " Caroline floundered.

"I tell my mother," Rosa said suddenly. "My mother say Lady Susan know. Same for her when she is young. Only no white baby. She for de lucky one. Say she hope I be for de lucky one, too. Say do not speak it. Dey beat you for lie when you do tell truth. Dey do not like. So say my mother." She finished on a dry sob and then, looking full at Caroline, she added in a stronger voice, "You say it and dey beat me. I don' mind to be kill. Not to beat me. If white baby will come to me, I kill me. I don' mind to kill me, only not to beat me." She drew a breath. "I fetch water now, Miss."

Caroline could think of nothing more to say. It struck her that she was as helpless as the slave girl. She could not save her from Redleigh any more than she could save herself from Joshua.

Except, she thought, I could run away. And Rosa cannot even do that. Her mind began to turn over ways in which she might yet leave Nassau before Joshua's return. If only she had remembered to take her share of the gold coins, she could purchase passage to England. But no one would let her sail without money, save a captain from one

of her father's ships. And such a captain, like Ramsey,
would surely notify her husband, unless she stowed away
until . . .

Rosa returned then and silently began to help Caroline
disrobe. Oh, the loosening of the bodice was a relief. Air
rushed into her lungs and she breathed deeply.

"Too small, dis here," Rosa said of the bodice. "Must
have bigger one, Miss."

It was true. Everything was too tight. She had thought
merely that Sarah Ormonton was smaller, but now it occurred to her that she was gaining weight. Even her old
bodice had been too tight, and once it had been . . . She
stopped in the middle of the thought. Half-remembered
bits of women's conversation came back to her. She had
not had her benefit since . . . since a few days before the
pirates came aboard the *Charlotte*. How long ago was
that? Feverishly, she calculated. Nearly six weeks. And
the sleepiness, the hunger, the . . . She gave a quick look
down at her body and saw that the flatness had disappeared into a soft mounding of flesh over her abdomen.

She was with child—not Joshua's child, but Domino's
. . . Domino's. There was a sensation of wild delight, and,
immediately following it, despair.

"You be pale, Miss," Rosa said. "You be sick?"

"Yes . . . no, I . . . I am a little tired, Rosa. I will
see you in the morning. Rosa?"

"Yes, Miss."

"Bring your pallet in here to sleep."

"I cannot, Miss. Lady say in hall. So must I do."

"Good night, Rosa," Caroline said gently.

"Good night, Miss," the girl replied, and for an instant
her features softened, as if she might have smiled.

Caroline slept fitfully the rest of the night, her sleep
broken by terrible dreams that upon awakening eluded
her. At dawn, however, she awoke calling Domino's name
and found Rosa leaning over her, saying, "Wake, Miss,
wake. You dream."

Afterward, she went into a deep sleep from which she
emerged only when her room became unbearably warm.
She lay looking up at the netting, on which a fly was busily engaged in rubbing its hind feelers together. She
watched it lethargically, her eyes grainy, her brain tired.

She was conscious of a weary sense of futility, and yet

beneath it something stirred, some sense of anticipation that tried to rise through the clouds of her despair.

Poor Rosa, but a babe herself. Redleigh was a beast, a filthy, degraded beast. Why did he not take his appetites to a woman who would welcome them, either for money or because she fancied him? Why this black child who bore his attentions only under the threat of being flogged?

"If a white baby will come to me, I will kill me," Rosa had said. How long had Redleigh been at her? Since he arrived, from what Caroline could gather. A month or two, anyway. Poor Rosa.

She got up and went to the door and found Rosa waiting.

"You wish food now, Miss?" the girl asked.

"Just coffee, Rosa, please, and perhaps some fruit."

"I bring you melon—nice melon, cool and sweet."

Caroline nodded, smiling, and was rewarded by seeing Rosa's mouth stretch into a grin. An unspoken bond flashed between them for a moment and Rosa went off with a lighter step than usual.

As she wandered about the lawns before lunch, Caroline found herself beginning to feel less despondent and more content.

That nameless anticipation that had beat beneath her earlier despair she finally recognized as arising from the fact that, if Domino was gone, at least she had his child. It was like a talisman against fate, something to plan for, something of joy and beauty and tenderness to lighten whatever burdens she must bear. She fell to dreaming that one day she would be with Domino again, she and the child that had been conceived in those days and nights together.

It lent a sparkle to her face and eyes and roused some of her old gaiety, so that even Redleigh remarked that the sojourn in Nassau seemed to have swept the effects of her misadventures away at last.

In her newly found contentment, a certain strength of purpose also began to reassert itself. Her fancies of the future took more concrete form, so that for as much as she dreamed on how it would be, she also began to plan ways in which those dreams would become a reality.

At supper that evening, hearing Sir Ormonton mention that the *Marigold* was in port, Caroline was elated. The

Marigold was one of her father's ships. There was no question that she might board her. Once at sea . . .

"You are dreaming, Mistress Welles," Redleigh said, "of your husband's return, I presume."

"What . . . oh . . . yes. I am sorry. I was thinking how exciting it will be to see my new home. I expect it will be soon. Tell me, Dr. Austin"—she turned to the gentleman on her left—"have you been to Virginia Colony?"

I must be careful, she thought, scarcely hearing Austin's answer. Redleigh is sharp-witted. Were he to fathom my intent, he would surely raise a fuss.

"Do you know," Redleigh said, engaging her attention, then speaking softly, "that Fortescue and I had laid wager it was young Geoffrey Lyons who would win your hand? I, of course, wagered on Mr. Welles."

"How you go on and on, Lord Redleigh," she replied. "You could scarcely have known my intent, since I myself had no thoughts on the matter of Mr. Welles until the very last moment before I accepted him. As for Lyons, he did not amuse me."

"Then, pray, why did you fly to meet him after the musicale last spring?"

The question took her so by surprise that she started, giving herself away.

"I overheard," he went on, answering her silent question. "Others may have. I was given to understand your father was among them."

"My father was . . . " She paused. Redleigh had heard and had gone to her father. Why? For spite, she supposed, or to win his wager with Fortescue. It mattered not at all since either reason was low.

"You are kind to tell me," she murmured. "The next time I wish to speak under the rose, I shall take care that no other unaccountable muskins are about."

She bent a cool look at him and saw him smile thinly at the insult.

"I would rather be a muskin than a bedswerver, such as you. Your husband was not the first, I think, nor will he be the last," he charged in that same low murmur.

Anger made her voice tremble. "Did you know it was I who warned my father against your suit? He has small use for candle wasters, and the Redleighs squander so readily that it was not hard to persuade him to send you packing. Bedswerver you may think me, but remember, I came not near yours, nor would I ever—oh, not because you are not handsome, Redleigh, but because you are such a dreadful bore."

"What did you say?" the gentleman on her left broke in. "You spoke of war, Mistress Welles?"

"Yes. I was just saying to Lord Redleigh that it seems, after all, England will win the Indian war."

"Will win . . . *has* won, my dear lady. Louisburg has fallen, Cape Breton is ours; North America belongs to England, and much of the Indies. Mark my words, in less than a year France will be on her knees, suing for peace."

"The Spanish . . . " Caroline began.

"Oh, the Spanish! They will fall, as well, if they are foolish enough to come to France's aid. Britain rules the seas, dear lady. Never fear. Do you know that . . . " He launched into a long explanation of the English strategy and Caroline feigned interest.

She cared not at all who won, a fact that would have stunned those present had they known. The sooner it was over, the sooner Domino would have his island. *Liberté.* A little way from Martinique, three miles long and half again as wide. When this war was over, she would find some way to it.

The idea sustained her through the evening and sent her to bed happier than she had been since she left the island.

Rosa seemed more than usually withdrawn, and again Caroline urged her to bring her pallet in, but Rosa repeated her statement that she must stay in the hall, as ordered.

"I will think of some way to help you," Caroline said. "Perhaps I can buy you from Sir Arthur and take you with me. There no one will hurt you. You shall be my maid."

"Yas," said Rosa with the same lack of enthusiasm Dobbs had shown at a similar offer. "Maybe Lady Susan will give you me. She can give me when she like."

"We . . . we'll talk of this in the morning," Caroline promised.

"Yas, Miss," Rosa answered, her eyes downcast.

But they did not speak of it in the morning, for that night Rosa slipped away and the next day the hounds were out baying after her scent. They followed it all the way down the cobblestoned streets that led to the water-front, and there at the edge they lost the scent forever.

Rosa's body was borne on the incoming tide late that day. "If white baby will come to me, I will kill me." The words, like Rosa's face, haunted Caroline.

"Stupid girl," Redleigh said. "She must have known she could not run from the hounds."

"She killed herself," Caroline said.

"Nonsense," Lady Susan said. "She was a stubborn rebel and got just what she deserved. She broke the law."

Caroline said nothing, and Lady Susan went on: "We will send up another to maid you, dear Caroline."

"Thank you, Lady Susan, but if I may beg a boon?"

"Certainly."

"May she sleep in my chamber? I have been fretful of late. Night terrors of my abduction, and now . . . well, it would comfort me to have her there. She can sleep at the foot of my bed on her pallet."

"A black in your bedchamber?" Lady Susan looked shocked.

"I would be pleased, Lady Susan, if you would oblige me."

"Very well," she said with a small frown of annoyance.

Redleigh, coming upon Caroline shortly before supper, said with a sneer, "Delicate Mistress Welles, who would rather have a foul-smelling slave than be alone."

"I, at least, do not bed with them," Caroline returned heatedly. "Rosa told me, yes. You can't have her flogged now, Redleigh. She is beyond your reach. How do you like knowing that even a black slave girl would prefer death to your bed or your child?"

He said nothing, his face white, his eyes smoldering. Looking at him, Caroline saw that she had made of a spiteful, rejected suitor an implacable foe.

Chapter Eleven

The *Marigold* lay at anchor off the town, and between it and the shore boats rowed all day, delivering sugar and rum and cotton and returning with stores and slaves.

The ship's captain, Oliver Hacket, spent his mornings at Prince's Tavern, where he met with planters and bargained costs. The sugar planters were an aggrieved lot.

"It cannot be helped as long as Guadeloupe sugar floods the market," said one man to Hacket. "But there must be some way to protect His Majesty's own people. The damned Spaniards and French on Guadeloupe! They will turn any way to make a profit. Should France offer more, they will as soon switch allegiance, while we . . . "

"My sympathies, sir," Captain Hacket growled, "but I have my orders from the company. Sugar is so plentiful in London that the poorest goody grows fat with eating it."

"We would have done better to plant cotton, as the governor did. But, then, Ormonton has the advantage of foreknowledge."

"Think, sir," soothed Hacket. "The war is drawing to a close. That means trade with France once more, and France needs sugar. You will find a ready market there, I think next year, at prices far higher than before."

" 'Tis done, then," another planter said in sour resignation. "But next year's prices will need to be markedly higher to compensate me for today. I will have my pence then, Captain, if it please you."

He watched silently as Hacket counted out the paper scrip and shoved it to him.

"And we will have coin for it next year, I trust," the man said as he stuffed the despised paper into his pocket.

"Or else how will we purchase from the French? They'll want no pretty pieces of paper marked five shillings to part with their own goods."

"Sir," said Hacket, "as to that, am I not paid with paper myself?"

The man turned away without answering, and the others taking payment soon followed. Hacket sighed and stretched. The journey from Africa had been long and tedious, with time wasted as they hit the doldrums and lay still for days at a stretch. The food had rotted and the men had growled over the scanty provisions and brackish water.

Now at last there were fresh provisions and would be more when they reached Charleston. Then home. It had been over eight months since they had left Spithead, and it would be three more until they could hope to raise the English coast, four, if the rest of the slaves were not sold in Charleston.

Once, delayed because of the slave sales falling off, he had thrown the rest of them into the sea. But Rowland took exception to the number reported sick and dead, and, since then Hacket had taken care to give a good accounting. Rowland paid his captains well, but he also kept a sharp watch so that none could line their own pockets at his expense. Well, Hacket smiled to himself, not line them too well.

He had devised a fair rule that so far had kept Rowland satisfied: three slaves sold but added to the list as dead on one voyage; seven on an unlucky voyage; none added and called a good voyage; and a few stores added on his own account for sale in the Colonies, crying for articles from England.

He finished the last of his ale and left the tavern. The day was brilliant, the sea smooth, and the winds fair. It was a splendid day for sailing. In a few hours, with the tide, they would leave Nassau for Savannah. It was only a matter of sending back the slaves who had not been sold at the New Providence auction and loading the last of the cargo.

As he walked along the waterfront, he saw his own launch still waiting for him, and standing near it, in conversation with the sailor on watch, he saw a young woman, a fine-looking woman—tall and slender, with wheat-gold curls rioting from beneath her wide-brimmed hat.

He swerved from his path to the auction shed. As he neared the launch, he saw the sailor gesture and the woman turned to greet him.

"Captain Hacket," she said with an imperious note in her pleasant voice, "I am Caroline Welles, Sir Bertram's daughter. I would like to pay a visit aboard the *Marigold*."

"Your servant, ma'am," he said with a clumsy bow. "I had heard you were recovered from the pirates. Mr. Welles will be happy to find you. He was very troubled when we saw him in Barbados."

"You saw my husband?" she said, and he noticed that her face paled.

"Aye, and Captain Ramsey. They are not more than a few days behind us."

"How wonderful!" she cried, and for some reason it struck him that her eyes were not as happy as her voice. "Then you must tell me all about Mr. Welles while I am aboard the *Marigold*. He is well, I trust, and still with some hope."

"Languishing for you, ma'am, yes, indeed," the captain said. "But I am afraid I can tell you no more, for I must be finished with business here. We sail within a few hours. I cannot, alas, invite you aboard."

She made a gesture of disappointment and said, "Then you are all loaded?"

"Nearly. Yonder"—he gestured to a boat that was drawing into the dock—"is the last boat. It fills once more and then comes back and we are ready."

"Then I must not delay you," she said. "I cherish your news, Captain Hacket, and I bid you a safe voyage." She moved off gracefully, turning her steps to the carriage that waited for her. He watched a moment and then went on his way.

Had he looked back he might have seen Caroline following his progress from the seat in her carriage. As he passed into the auction sheds she leaned forward and said, "Drive me to the Austins', William. I shall walk home from there."

The carriage moved off and Caroline sat well back, raising her parasol and giving every indication of indolent ease while inwardly she chafed at the slow-moving horses.

It was only a few minutes, but it seemed like hours before the Austins' home was reached. She clambered down without William's assistance and sent him on.

Ten minutes later she was back at the waterfront, panting in her haste, making an effort to appear cool as she reached the boat Captain Hacket had pointed out. She was scarcely in time. The oarsmen were in place and the order to cast off had been given.

The local man in charge was startled at her sudden appearance and by her breathless request to be taken out to the ship. But, having no reason to suspect her tale of traveling aboard the *Marigold,* he made room for her among the high-piled bales of cotton. Into this hastily improvised seat she sank gratefully from sight.

The sailor on watch at the ladder was more astonished than the boatman had been, and far more skeptical of her story that she had been invited aboard by the captain. He sent another man for the mate, Mr. White.

Caroline, nervous over the delay, kept darting glances back to the docks to reassure herself that the launch still awaited its captain.

Oh, suppose the mate refused to let her remain until Captain Hacket returned. Her heart pounded, her cheeks were flushed, and her breath was caught in her chest. With an effort she calmed her tingling nerves and composed herself, summoning a smile as she saw Mr. White approaching, girding herself to flirt her way into the great cabin.

As it turned out, Mr. White was entirely credulous, and in a few moments he had led her to the great cabin and hurried away upon her assurance that she required neither company nor refreshment.

Caroline sank gratefully upon a chair once the door closed behind Mr. White. Her heart was beating fast, her breath was uneven, and the stiff bodice pinched cruelly at her ribs. Oh, to cast it off and be free of such restraint, free as she had been when . . . No, no, she must not think of that.

This was the most difficult part. It had been easy to ascertain that the captain dined each day with different planters. It had been a simple matter to absent herself each afternoon from the plantation, always returning before the supper hour. It had not been too troublesome to persuade the sailor in the longboat to take her to the

Marigold or to mislead the sailors on watch. Now, without a clear idea of when Hacket would return, she must wait half an hour or more and then slip away and secrete herself. When they found her gone, it would be assumed she had gone ashore in one of the many boats plying between the pier and the *Marigold*.

At the Ormontons, there would not be a big fuss for several hours, and by the time they had exhausted the search the *Marigold* would be sailing out of the harbor.

There was no reason for anyone to search for her along the waterfront. And if they did . . . well, they would not find her aboard the *Marigold*. She would be hidden even if they were to imagine she might be there.

From her present position at the stern of the ship, she could see only the farthest point of the harbor, beyond which the bare coast curved out and around toward the tip of the island. She could hear the shouts of the men loading and the sounds of cargo being dumped upon the deck. A door at the end of the cabin led to the small promenade deck, very like the one she used to walk upon with Mr. Hardin. How long ago that was. She tried the handle and found the door unlocked. Stepping out on the deck, she saw she had a better view of the harbor and, in fact, could make out the lines of Prince's Tavern, below which the captain's launch would be waiting.

Caroline closed the cabin door and, leaning on the rail, settled herself to wait. Sometime later she saw the boat that had brought her pull away from the side, and shortly afterward another boat followed. Watching them glide through the harbor waters to shore, she noticed a third boat approaching. She could not be certain at this distance, but it seemed to her that it must be the launch.

It was now or never. She moved aft, searching for a ladder from the enclosed promenade, one such as that aboard the *Charlotte*. In her haste she nearly overlooked it, blocked from immediate view as it was by the curved planking of the cabin wall.

The deck below appeared deserted and Caroline quickly descended. Her destination was the hold of the ship. As she crept along the deck, hugging close to the sides, she tried to remember the features of the *Charlotte*. The *Marigold* was not a first rate, and she knew that it was thus shorter in length than the *Charlotte*.

Behind the closed ports she saw the muzzle of the

cannon and knew that the orlop must be below the gun deck. Accordingly, she went down the next ladder she came upon and stepped through an open hatch.

Large piles of rope and canvas lay along one wall and jutted out from the far corner. In the center there was a closed floor hatch. She had seen one like it aboard the *Charlotte*. It opened up to reveal a ladder going straight down into the hold. And there had been one like it on the *Mouette*, too. But the *Charlotte's* hold contained casks and chests of goods, while the *Mouette*'s was filled with booty. The *Marigold* would be similar to the *Charlotte*, and she could hide there among the storage and never be found until long after they sailed.

She hurried to the hatch and, seizing the ring, tried to lift the top. It did not budge. An iron bolt had been thrust through the ring, and chains on either end were lashed to iron posts embedded in the deck itself. "As if the bread might fly up and mutiny," she muttered in exasperation.

She was trying to decide whether to settle for hiding behind the canvas in the far corner or seeking another entrance to the ship's hold when she heard the sounds of commotion on the gun deck above her and the tramping of heavy feet moving toward the ladder to the orlop.

Hastily, she made for the canvas and burrowed behind it, taking care to pull her skirts in and wrap them around her drawn-up feet.

So many feet were descending the ladder, some footsteps soft, as if the men wore no shoes, others sharp and ringing. There was a scuffling sound, a shouted curse, and then a volley of curses. A hissing and crackling and a tortured scream followed.

Without thinking, Caroline raised her head and peered over her barricade. Five black men and one woman, chained together—all of them dirty, ragged, half-naked—stood at the hatch. The first man in line sagged forward, a wide red gash across his back where the whip had laid bare his flesh. Three sailors, one with a whip at the ready, stood with them.

"Open the hatch," bellowed Mr. White from his position at the foot of the ladder. "Look lively. Boatswain, lay him another lash should he move."

"Aye, Mr. White," came the reply.

Caroline, her own peril forgotten, stared at the scene in astonishment.

With the opening of the hatch, a foul and rank smell rose. A stink of sweat and fetid air, of vomit and human excrement, permeated the air and Caroline buried her face in her hands to escape its noxious odor.

From below, a low, anguished moaning began, as of souls in torment.

There was another scuffle. "Move, damn your eyes!" a voice shouted. A second later cries were added to the moaning as the foremost of the blacks was shoved down the ladder so that he fell, dragging with him his chained companions. Bodies thudded and cracked against wood and a loud, piercing scream announced a broken limb.

The moaning rose and the cries increased, only to be muffled at last with the slamming of the hatch.

"Secure it well or that black bastard will surely raise it!"

"They must have water and bread now, sir," one of the sailors said.

"Aye. I near forgot. Rowland counts his slaves sold like he counts his yellowbags. Pretties for his fine daughters from each."

"Will I give it to them now?" the sailor asked.

"No. Wait until they are more eager for it. That way they will not rush the hatch. Throw it down to them within the hour. Secure the hatch."

"Aye, aye, sir."

With the sound of the bolt driven home, the muffled moans and cries reached a higher pitch. One of the sailors rattled the hatch cover and the noise subsided.

"Begging your pardon, Mr. White," said the boatswain, "but there's one with a broken leg, I think. We've lost a good number on this voyage. It might do well were the surgeon to splint it."

"And, pray, why?" asked White. "Do you think anyone will buy a black with a splinted leg and likely to be lame? Would you buy a horse that way?"

"No, sir, not I."

"Nor will anyone buy him. I'll report to the captain. It's likely he'll have him shot out of his misery . . . or drowned when we're at sea. Look lively now, lads. The day's work is not done."

The feet ascended the ladder and strode off down the

deck. Silence flowed back into the orlop and Caroline clambered painfully from her hiding place.

"Pretties for his fine daughters." Oh, surely her father could not know of this: slaves bought and sold but not laid to the whip or shot when they were injured like animals, or kept in that pestilent hole. But as soon as she thought of it, she knew it was not so. Her father must know, if not the whole truth, at least some part of it.

Blacks in chains. Rosa and Redleigh. And the Ormontons, so solicitous of her own welfare, turning bland faces to Rosa's ill use. This was what slavery meant, not Mrs. James' little blackamoor, dressed in clothes like his master and, like his master, well fed and schooled.

"No slaves on my island," Domino had said. She gave a half-sob. With every fiber of her body she wished passionately she were once again on that other island with the sound of surf and of birdsong, to see again the quiet waters of the lagoon, the foaming waterfall, and the pink cave with her crude pallet and Domino beside her. It had been heaven, a heaven she must find again.

She smoothed her hair and skirts absently. The hold was no hiding place. Never would she descend into that hell of human misery. Were there slaves in every hold? Surely some must contain the sugar and cotton and rum being brought aboard.

She started for the ladder, but as she neared the hatch she saw that the bar through the loops had been drawn back. Even as she stopped, staring, it fell to the deck and the hatch itself slowly opened.

Panicked, she darted back to her hiding place, stumbling, her lips pressed tightly together to hold back her inarticulate murmur of fear. Once she reached the canvas, she dared to take a look toward the hatch.

They came quietly, some twenty of them, crowding the deck, blinking at the light like animals just out from hibernation. There were more than those who had been shoved roughly back into the hold. Some were chained together still, and one carried in his hand the iron pike to which the chain was attached.

The last of them, filthy with bits of food and dried excrement clinging to their nearly naked bodies, were more sickly looking than the first. One woman carried an infant of not more than two months of age, a silent, swollen-bellied, naked boy who clutched at his mother's skinny breasts with claw-like fingers.

Oh, Lord, Caroline almost cried aloud, realizing the woman had been pregnant when captured and that the child had been born in the foulness of the hold.

They came quietly now, nearly fifty of them, crowding the deck, blinking incessantly, unaccustomed as they were to the strong sunlight. The lead man, his back wound still dripping blood, went first and the others followed closely. Bringing up the rear came a man on one leg, his mouth compressed grimly, his face gray with pain as he dragged his broken and useless leg.

At last, when even the sound of their soft, padding feet had died away, Caroline stirred herself and with shaking knees began her own ascent.

Once aloft, she moved as swiftly as she could, hardly pausing to make certain that there was no one about. Nearing the ladder that led down along the casing of the main mast into the next hold, she stopped.

Outside, there was a shrill piping of the boatswain's whistle and a cry: "Company muster aft!" Feet pounded along the deck, shaking the very timbers where she stood. There was the crack of a musket and then terrified screams and cries. Another crack followed, then another.

"Oh, God," she prayed, "help them." Sobbing, she began her long descent to the hold.

It was quiet in the hold, save for the slapping of the waves against the hull. The gentle movement of the ship as it rode lightly at anchor was soothing, and the salty damp of the hold filled her nostrils like perfume after the rankness of the afterhold.

Presently, she pulled herself erect and wedged herself between the lashed casks of rum and sacks of sugarcane. This was her place until the *Marigold* sailed. How much time had elapsed she could only guess. She had left the Ormontons' at four . . . more than an hour to the *Marigold* . . . more than an hour aboard.

It must be well past seven. According to the captain, they would sail on the tide in the morning, sometime between midnight and noon, five to seventeen hours. Her mouth was dry and her stomach was empty, yet she would manage. She had managed on that long night when Domino had rowed them from the *Mouette* to the island. Vividly, she recalled waking up with her mouth feeling like cotton. But then she had been twenty-four hours or more without food or drink. If she could do that, she could do this.

All she need fear was discovery before the ship sailed. A hundred pictures and thoughts swirled in her mind as she lay there, and to ease her brain she began to count and then add long numbers together, and finally to multiply. The boredom of it drove her to short naps, from which she awakened to resume her mental exercise and fall again into light dozing.

Chapter Twelve

It was shortly after sunset before Caroline's absence aroused any concern in the Ormonton household.

"I hope she has come to no harm," said Lady Susan. "Arthur, we must send a search party for her at once. It is nearly dark. Suppose she has fallen or . . . "

"Or some slave has her securely tied in his cabin," Redleight interposed. "Poor Mistress Welles."

"Edward, that is unseemly," his aunt reproved.

"Caroline is new to Nassau and to the plantation. She might easily wander too far and be lost."

"You misunderstand me, Aunt," Redleigh answered. "I was making a feeble joke to lighten gloomy speculation. No doubt she has walked farther than usual and thus is later in returning."

"Nevertheless, Arthur," Lady Susan said to her husband, "I believe we must look for her."

"I agree, my dear, I quite agree, quite. Apart from not wishing to see her harmed, it would not do to have Rowland's daughter fall into peril while she is under our protection."

"Yes," Redleigh drawled. "There is your lease from the Crown, Uncle—shortly to come up for inspection, is it not?"

His uncle flushed with irritation. He would be glad when Redleigh sailed for England again. He was a foppish, wasp-tongued dandy whose arrogance and calm assumption of superiority were visited as often upon his family as they were on acquaintances.

"My lease is not of paramount importance," he answered shortly. "Still, it helps to have a friend at court, old boy, as you must know. Or else why sue for the hand of a lady you like as little as Caroline Welles?"

"Really, Arthur," Lady Susan said with some asperity, "this is hardly the time to argue with Edward. And you, Edward, you forget yourself."

"My apologies, Aunt." He bowed. " 'Tis true I sued for the lady's hand, but that was before I knew what she was really like. Delicacy forbids my saying more."

"I will send a search party," Sir Arthur said stiffly. "She cannot have left the island, and it is hardly likely that she would go for a swim in the sea."

When he had gone, Lady Susan said, "Edward, I do wish you would be more careful. Arthur frowns on gossip."

"I disagree," her nephew said. "He was as eager as any of us to learn whether or not she had been seduced by the notorious Captain Domino or possibly by Mr. Hardin."

"Oh," his aunt rejoined, "that is uncivil."

"Uncivil, perhaps, but true. You know as well as I that she is not the innocent babe she pretends to be. Did not Amelia's letter give you the latest London talk? You told me so yourself."

"Well," said Lady Susan, torn between wanting to hear more and yet anxious to preserve a modest front, " 'tis true that I understand her family was much relieved when she married, and that the haste of it created some talk. But you can see for yourself that the marriage could not have been forced."

"True. Still, mark my words, were Caroline Rowland born in some farmer's cottage, she would be a fully fledged Bona Rona at this point."

"A . . . a what?"

"A whore."

"Oh, Edward! You must be careful, really. She is the late Prince of Wales' own godchild, and her father . . . "

"Soon to be an earl, I know, sitting in the House of Lords. Fortescue swears he will shun the place even more than his father has once he is seated. And the earl of Oxnard has not answered in the Lords for twenty years."

Lady Susan tittered. "You must tell me someday how it is that you came to despise Caroline."

"It is not fit for your ears, dear Aunt." Redleigh laughed.

"Edward!"

"Well, perhaps one day," he soothed, "seeing your disappointment."

How he had come to despise Caroline, eh? He himself had no single answer to that. The ignominy of being rejected by the daughter of a tradesman so newly come to wealth and power and title was bad enough. But she had made a pointsticking of him with her tricks and quick tongue. Worse, she had charged him with the black wench's suicide. Were she to tell that in London, he would be more than a fool.

"Oh, and here is Uncle Arthur. Well, Uncle, has she been found? You look quite pale."

"Found? Eh? No, no. But word has just come that the *Charlotte* dropped anchor less than an hour ago and that Mr. Welles is on his way here. One hopes she will be found. This is unsettling, quite unsettling. We should have kept her under better watch." Sir Arthur mopped his brow nervously.

Redleigh sauntered to the door. "While you greet the anxious groom, I think I shall aid in the search for his bride," he said.

Coming out into the night air, he saw the torches of the search party moving through the fields. A waste of time, he thought. As he talked with his aunt it had occurred to him that Caroline was not missing by accident.

For the past few days she had set out each afternoon with a rigid adherence to routine that was quite foreign to her. He had followed her at a discreet distance twice, thinking to catch her unaware with some low fellow and thus compromise her. But she merely walked with apparent aimlessness, sometimes partway to the town, other times in quite the opposite direction. And she walked not with enjoyment, but as if she must do so. It made no sense, and whatever else Caroline Rowland was or had been, she always had method in her most outrageous behavior.

Ergo, it must make sense, perhaps the very sense it was making now. Were this not a newly acquired habit, her absence would long since have been noted.

It was the merest chance, but he thought it worth following. He made his way to the stables and roused a boy to saddle his horse for the ride into town.

As he galloped over the cobblestones, he passed a sedan chair. He reined in as the chair came to a halt, and

Joshua Welles' head and shoulders emerged from the top.

"Good evening to you, Mr. Welles. My aunt awaits you."

"Eh? Is that you, Redleigh? Where is Caroline?"

"'Awaiting you, too, I would hope," Redleigh answered smoothly. "I shall join you soon." He dug his heels into his horse and galloped off, leaving Joshua to stare after him.

"The devil," Joshua muttered to himself. Then settling himself inside again, he ordered the bearers to go on.

"Awaiting you, too, I would hope." What did he mean by that? Drat. He would like to have more information. What Ramsey had gleaned from the men boarding to carry off the last of the cargo had been scant, indeed, even preposterous. Mutiny on the *Mouette.* Saved by an English sailor who was also imprisoned. A sailor who drowned later, somehow. Preposterous. He grunted and bit his lower lip. And what else? Ah, yes, protected from molestation by the very pirate who kidnapped her. A likely story. Were it not for appearances, he would have gone straight to Virginia from Nassau instead of badgering Ramsey to try Barbados in the hope of learning something of her whereabouts.

There was Rowland to consider. He could imagine himself attempting to explain why he had not searched for Caroline, or why he waited in Nassau for word of ransoming her.

There was still no effort to ransom her. And she had unaccountably turned up just as he had been satisfied that she was dead or permanently at the disposal of the pirate.

Damn. He did not fancy a wife who had been despoiled by God only knew how many low men. However, he would not intimate this to Caroline. He would extract the truth from her and deal with her after that.

A month with a man who abducted her. A man who had not touched her? Pshaw! Impossible for any man— for he remembered her as voluptuous and seductive— especially a sailor long at sea.

They were entering the gates, and up ahead he saw the doors opened and Susan Ormonton standing there. He smiled. How fortunate, indeed, that old Lord Redleigh had denied his suit. Otherwise, now he would be saddled with a plump, giggling woman of dull mind and little attraction who used so much of the new London argot that her speech itself was boring.

It had pleased him to flirt slyly with Susan during his first visit and to see her arch coyness and meaningful glances. Time had given him his vengeance on the Redleighs, as it had given him land and slaves and a ripe virgin for a bride. And time would take care of that bride, as well, unless this very preposterous story turned out to be true, after all.

"My very dear Susan," he said on alighting, "I am forever in your debt. Is Caroline with you?"

But Susan was not bridling and simpering this time. With an anxious face and wringing hands, she said, "Oh, Joshua, I am sorry, but . . . well, Caroline seems to have gotten lost."

"Lost?" Joshua said. "Lost? You are jesting."

"Arthur and Edward have gone in search of her, the slaves, too—indeed, every man on the plantation. We are sure to find her, but . . . "

"How is it she wandered off knowing of my arrival? Did you not receive my message?"

"Yes, yes. But Caroline was already lost. Oh, dear, if only you had come sooner, she would not have gone. She was quite anxious to return home to Virginia. Why, she had even hoped to find a ship bound for Virginia, thinking you would go home and she would find you there."

"I see," he said, somewhat mollified. If Caroline had tried to find a ship bound for Virginia, she could scarcely have much to conceal. He began to feel better. The story was preposterous, but then the entire adventure was preposterous. Storms and pirates and abductions. He felt cold in spite of the warm evening. Drat Bascomb and his damned Oriental remedies. He shouldn't give them to a man unless there was a sufficiency.

"You are shaking, Joshua," Susan said.

"A touch of the March ague in the middle of a tropical October, dear Susan."

"Do come in, Joshua. I'll give you some brandy. There, don't worry. I'm sure we will find Caroline soon."

The men were still out in the fields when Edward Redleigh returned, bearing the news that Caroline had been taken out to the *Marigold* to visit the captain and had not been seen since. Apparently she was still aboard.

There had been an attempt by the unsold slaves to escape. "And," he finished languidly, "I bethought myself to go aboard and then said, 'No, surely Mr. Welles will want to fetch his bride himself.' " He smiled.

"Aboard the *Marigold?*" Joshua repeated, stunned. "Why, that's preposterous!" There was that word again. He felt himself flush with anger, the more so because Redleigh stood there, giving every appearance of solicitude but with a look in his eyes that bespoke his pleasure at the turn of events.

"We will go at once," Lady Susan said. "I will send for Arthur and the coach."

"The coach first, please," Joshua begged. "I have no wish to tarry. We had it from the captain of the *Marigold* that she sails within the hour."

"I will ride ahead," Redleigh offered, "and send word to the *Marigold* by boat. I will wait at the shore for you with a boat all ready to speed you across the water."

The man who carried Redleigh's message to the *Marigold* found its captain in a bad mood.

"What? Aboard my ship? Stowed away?" Hacket shouted. "Blast it! Held back again! Do you not see that we make ready to sail? Why the sheets are being set this very moment! We cast off before half an hour has passed! Wait? I will not wait!"

"No, sir," said the man. "I will tell his lordship."

Hacket cleared his throat noisily. Tell his lordship he meant to carry Rowland's daughter off? Blast! Damn! Curse them all!

"Get out!" he shouted, and the man scurried away gladly. "Mr. White!" Hacket bellowed. "I want you!"

"I am here, Captain," White said quietly at his elbow.

"Eh? Ah, so you are. Damnable business, White, damnable. Order the sails reefed. Order the company to stand by. Muster a search party. I want the lady found before Welles boards this ship. Found! Search everywhere! Even the hold where the blacks are!"

"Sir, do you think she would descend into such a foul-smelling place?"

"Everywhere!" Hacket bellowed again, his face purple. "Everywhere, Mr. White!"

"Aye, aye, sir. Boatswain!" he shouted in his turn. "Reef sail! Company stand by! Mr. Blount!" he roared to his mate. "Muster a search party on the poopdeck!"

A chorus of voices rose at this change in orders.

"Belay that!" called the boatswain. "Stand by!" He hurried up to the captain as White marched off to the poopdeck to lead his party.

"Captain," he said, "shall I pipe the visitors aboard?"

"Pipe them? Pipe them?" Hacket growled. "Pipe them to hell! I'll do no honor to a damned cub who can't keep track of his own wife! You saw her, Bosun. Are you certain you did not see her leave?"

"No, sir. She said she'd go back in another boat. I thought . . ."

"Thought? Thought be damned! You should have *known*," he muttered. "Odd. Visit the *Marigold*. Should have known then."

"I beg your pardon, sir?" the boatswain said.

"Nothing, nothing. I will be in my cabin. You may send Mr. Welles to me there."

Hacket's rage was in direct proportion to his fear. If the woman was not found, there would always be some suspicion that he had had a hand in her disappearance. He knew full well that he was not Rowland's favored captain. Were it possible to hire good captains for slavers easily, Rowland would long since have seized any excuse to relieve him of the *Marigold*'s command.

It did no good to remember that the Welles woman had come aboard in his absence. He thought about the very way she had gone about it: sending a message with his launch oarsman and then going off on another boat shortly thereafter. Had he not been such a fool, he'd have realized that was proof she intended to run away from her husband. She would not admit that. Women were sly. No, he would be held responsible if any evil had befallen her. Indeed, if she had met with foul play aboard his ship, he would be cashiered once they berthed in England.

The minutes dragged on as he paced the great cabin. What to say to Welles, first of all? *I am sorry, sir, but your lady came aboard without my consent and I have no idea where she might be.* He snorted.

The tap on his door some minutes later found him no nearer to a solution than before. Straightening his jacket, he put his tricorne on. "Come in," he called gruffly.

He had been certain that the boatswain would be standing there to usher in the party from the governor's mansion. But upon seeing White and behind him two sailors bearing Mistress Welles between them on crossed arms, he goggled.

"We found her in the forward hold, Captain," Mr. White said. "Mistress Welles was walking on deck when she saw the slaves attempting to escape. They frightened her and she ran. She saw the midships ladderway and went down it and fell into the hold."

Hacket found his voice. "And pray, Mistress, why did you not then return?"

"Sir," interposed White, "she suffered an injury to her ankle."

"Nothing serious, Captain Hacket," Caroline spoke faintly. "A sprain, I think, but it's very tender."

"Put her down," the captain said testily. Then: "No, no, not on her feet, you assheads, on the chair! Mr. White, will you ask the surgeon to come here, please?"

When the men had left, Hacket turned to Caroline. The relief of finding her not appreciably damaged and before the arrival of Welles emptied him of wrath. Still, for appearance's sake, he assumed a stern tone.

"Mistress Welles, it was unwise of you not to wait in the cabin. You might have come to far worse harm had one of the blacks caught you."

"I know, Captain," she said meekly, "but I thought the *Marigold* would be like the *Charlotte*. I didn't realize you carried blacks as cargo."

"They are the main cargo, Mistress—valuable cargo."

"I see," she answered calmly, but her thoughts were swimming. Valuable? Whipped and shot and left in a hole that would rot any other commodity?

"You must have had quite a fright," he went on.

"Dreadful," she agreed with downcast eyes. The lies sat lightly on her conscience. It was bad enough to hear Mr. White and his search party and know that she had been found out; it was worse to learn that Joshua was at this very moment hurrying to the *Marigold*. She had sought frantically for some plausible excuse, and in reply to Mr. White's questions she had seized on the first thought that occurred to her.

"Well, we will say no more of the matter," the captain said briskly. "The adventure has turned out well, after all—and happily, for Mr. Welles is here in Nassau, hurrying to the ship, anxious over your new disappearance."

"I know," she said. Her heart, lurching with disappointment and dread, made the color rise in her face.

"Blushing, ma'am?" the captain said.

"I . . . I am very warm," Caroline murmured. "Could you please send for some water?"

"Water . . . water, of course, and I fancy a touch of brandy. Ah, here is Dr. Kellims, our surgeon. Another injured limb, Dr. Kellims, but fortunately we need not put the victim out of misery this time."

Caroline could barely repress her shudder of revulsion at this reference to the killing of a slave.

"I shall send water and brandy, Mistress Welles. And you will await your husband. We will pipe him aboard in honor of your happy reunion." He smiled ironically.

As the surgeon came forward to examine her ankle, Caroline said, "It is sore and makes me feel faint when I stand, but I do not think it is broken."

"You must leave that decision to me," Dr. Kellims said. Then, bending his tall, skinny frame, he lifted the foot she indicated. "No real swelling," he murmured. "You are fortunate. We shall soon have you bandaged."

He had finished his task and had handed her the water and then the brandy that the cabin boy brought when they heard the shrill piping of the boatswain's whistle.

Caroline took a deep sip of the brandy. The liquid burned her throat and brought tears to her eyes. With the feel of them, she realized her hope of freedom had disappeared, and as she put down the beaker the tears welled and spilled down her cheeks.

"I say!" exclaimed the surgeon in some embarrassment. Joshua, on entering at that moment, found her bandaged foot resting upon a low stool, tears wet on her cheeks, and the surgeon patting her hand awkwardly.

"Caroline!" he exclaimed.

Coming in behind him, Redleigh said, "My dear Mistress Welles, you are surely fate's pawn. Misadventure follows misadventure." His face was grave, but his eyes danced with malice.

"Oh, Joshua!" Caroline said and stood up before she remembered she was supposed to be injured. There was a split second of astonishment on the faces of the men regarding her, and with a flash of inspiration she started forward toward her husband, then turned her foot under and would have fallen had Joshua not reached out to catch her.

"My ankle," she said, the tears still falling, and she suffered herself to be embraced.

Joshua, holding her as she wept noisily, felt some of his doubts laid to rest.

"There," he soothed, "you must thank Lord Redleigh. It was he who thought you might be aboard the *Marigold.*"

"Not at all," Redleigh disclaimed. "Knowing your spirit and curiosity, ma'am, I simply took myself into town, and it was there I learned of your voyage to the *Marigold.* The rest . . . well . . . that was mere luck."

Looking over Joshua's shoulder, Caroline met Redleigh's eyes. Malice had given way to triumph.

"Come, my dear," Joshua said, "we must make haste. Captain Hacket is anxious to sail. We sail ourselves within the day. Captain Ramsey, too, has been delayed, remember? The damage to the ship, the search for you in the southern isles. Here, lean on me."

"She should be carried," Dr. Kellims interposed. "If I may assist you?"

Joshua released his hold, and Redleigh, in an amused voice, said, "Careful, Welles, were I you, I would keep a close eye on her until she is safely aboard the *Charlotte* again. Who knows what fresh misadventure awaits?"

With the sound of his mocking laugh in her ears, Caroline was lifted easily in the surgeon's arms and borne from the cabin.

It was difficult to take her off the ship, and they made slow progress. Even as they were descending into the longboat, the very same one that had brought her out to the *Marigold,* the ship's company prepared to cast off.

"Set the mizzen!" rang the order, and the small sheet was secured.

As the longboat pulled away from the side, the boatswain took up the master's call: "Weigh anchor!"

Then came the men's response: "Yo, heave! Yo, heave! Yo, heave!"

With her anchor atrip and the sails full, the *Marigold* slipped forward on the tide.

"Top gallants!" the cry came, then died, and Caroline saw the ship, full sheets set just as the wind freshened and sent the *Marigold* steady on her tack.

"Three weeks, not more, and we will land at Newport News," said Joshua. "And I will be glad to see the end of sailing. My God, this has been a desperate journey!"

"Yes," Caroline murmured with an aching heart, "desperate, indeed."

They were met at the Ormontons' with glad cries of relief. Caroline thought she would faint in earnest if she were once more to repeat the lie, which had not grown easier to tell—especially with Redleigh's sardonic face always before her.

When she was finally helped to her chamber, she saw that her pallet had been removed and the room was freshly adorned with flowers. Joshua's articles were upon the highboy and his small portmanteau was opened on a bench.

This mute evidence of connubiality added to her despair.

Joshua was a long time in coming to bed himself, and he came, as usual, with the full odor of drink on him. Caroline, still awake although she pretended to sleep, half-hoped that he would be too drunk to think of her. But in this she was disappointed.

He came to her without any clothing and soon had her in his arms. "Sleeping, Poppet," he murmured, "but soon awake." He was covering her face with kisses, which she could not bring herself to return with any spirit.

"A month with your abductor and still unsullied," he said. "No kisses such as these." He pulled her gown roughly from her. "No desire to see such beauties?" he went on. "Never touching you like this?" And he squeezed her breasts until she protested.

"No . . . no," she repeated.

"I cannot believe it." He pried her thighs apart and stroked her. "Then if he has not touched you, nor any other man, how ready you must be for me."

Caught, she tried to pretend what she did not feel. Her disgust and revulsion made her tremble, and he mistook it, as he always had, for passion. If only he would be done with it, she thought. But tonight he seemed to want to prolong the caressing. Her own lack of feeling made his touch painful and she winced. He drew away, half-snarling. "So, so happy to see me you wept? No man for a month, and yet you cannot bear my touch?"

Fear seized her and her stomach contracted. "My . . . my injury," she whispered. "You forget."

"I forget nothing," he said. "Don't lie to me. Was there a man? Hardin, for example, who saved you and died so gallantly?" he sneered. "Was it Hardin? Was he quartered with you in the noble pirate's cabin?"

"No, no! In God's name, Joshua, why do you torment me?"

"Damn me, then, if I thought you were that rogue's woman, I would leave you along the way to Virginia."

Along the way? In the sea? Murder her?

"I swear to you, the pirates never touched me aboard the *Mouette*, and as for Hardin, I never saw him while I was aboard."

The truth of that at least crept into her voice.

"Then why do you pull away from me?"

"I told you—you forgot my injury." She gathered courage from deep within her and said, "Oh, Joshua, I am not a woman of the streets to be taken any way you wish."

With a curse, he flung himself away from her.

"Rest, then," he said thickly. She did not answer, and presently, as she heard him snoring, she thought that, after all, he had been too drunk to sustain his interest in her, anyway.

But as she stared into the darkness, she knew that the scene would be repeated unless she could find some way to allay his suspicions. She thought of the child she carried for nearly a month now. Soon it would be evident, and when it was . . . She shivered. Above all else, Joshua must think it his. Whatever it meant, whatever she had to endure, Joshua must not suspect the truth.

She slept with that knowledge, and when he awakened her in the morning, himself again and eager to consummate the act abandoned the night before, she was able to pretend sufficiently to satisfy him.

After he had dressed, he came back to stand over her.

"Will you stay in bed for a while, or shall I send for someone to help you?"

"I am much better this morning." Her tone matched his in amiability. "I believe even my ankle does not pain me so greatly."

"A husband's attentions, my dear," he returned with lugubrious gallantry. It brought a smile to her face, which he misinterpreted.

That evening, as the Welles party made its way into the captain's launch to board the *Charlotte,* Domino left the shore tavern. He was newly garbed in the costume of a British sailor, having signed on as Andrew Hall of Bristol aboard the frigate *Maid of Coventry,* bound in two days' time for Barbados.

With him was one of the crew from the *Coventry,* an old seaman named Waggers. Stooped, graying, an empty eye socket beneath his patch, he hobbled along beside Domino with a nimbleness that belied his age.

"Uncommon's what I says and says again," Waggers chortled. "Damsel in distress. Ho-ho. Be like her was far more distressed when her husband come fer her. Pirates and storms and mutinies, eh? And her up like a bird and skimmin' off to the *Marigold* to stow away innocent-like with the husband sailin' in. Be the mate's man told me, he did. Cap'n said, 'No need to sail with us and yer own husband comin' behind.' And she says, 'Thankee, Cap'n,' an' when he be in the sheds she skips off to the boat and hides an' . . . "

"Yes, I heard," Domino interrupted him. "Hurry, Waggers. The boat's leaving, and we have the captain to worry us."

"Aye, an' that we do. Hi, hi!" he exclaimed. "Yonder, see? Them's the Welleses. See her wi' the golden hair?" He tugged at Domino's arm with one hand, pointing excitedly with the other.

Domino followed his gaze, his impassive face tight despite the leap of his heart and the blood that rushed up under his bronzed skin.

She was there. Caroline. And not Caroline. The Caroline of his memory was tangle-haired and garbed in remnants, when garbed at all. Now for the first time since he had left her, the physical memory of her body, warm and soft and yielding in his arms, came back to haunt him.

They were close enough so that if she had turned then, she would have seen him. He moved over into the shadow of a building and Waggers, still holding his arm, sidled after him.

Domino's eyes went over her. She wore a gray gown with white around the bodice and neck, like the Puritan ladies of the North. Across her shoulders lay a fleecy shawl, and even as he watched, she drew it up and over her head, hiding the fair curls, leaving her profile turned, pure and pale.

The man with her, her husband, looked familiar, and he saw that it was the one who had led her below when they took the *Charlotte*.

Welles was almost his own height. He wore a white peruke and was richly garbed for such a journey. He bent solicitously to Caroline, touching her with possessive familiarity. The sight of it stabbed at Domino. In that moment, he could have stepped forward, thrown Welles off, and abducted her.

The blinding jealousy shocked him, and as the moment passed he found himself trembling. Her words came back to haunt him: "And will you like thinking of me with another man?"

How cool he had been then. How controlled. How sure. Now he was sure of nothing. Only some logic deep within kept him rooted, and presently he was able to think of the *Mouette,* of his own larger purpose, and of the man beside him, who, sensing something was amiss, had let go his grasp on Domino's arm and was peering around and up into his face.

"Say, matey, what's atrouble to yer? Ye look sick."

"Too much ale, I fancy," Domino answered, his eyes still on the launch. Caroline was seated now, with Joshua beside her as the launch pulled away. When it reached the end of the pier, she turned and looked back. It seemed to him that she looked to the very spot where he stood, but he knew that was only a trick of the eye.

"A pretty wench," Waggers cackled. "Be a strong man —pirate or no—who could keep his hands quiet if 'twere such like in his cabin."

The launch drew out of sight, the stern disappearing into the darkness beyond the pier. "Aye," Domino said absently, "aye."

He began to move forward stiffly, as if his feet were reluctant to obey his commands. He was tired deep in his bones. The long search ahead, once so important, loomed as a futile and ponderous task.

A few steps on, the barmaid of the tavern they had just left appeared in front of him.

"Well, sailor," she said in her hearty voice, "be you blind?"

"Good evening to you, Abby," he answered, stopping. "An' you're bound for bed?"

"Aye."

"Alone, sailor?"

He looked at her, plump and pretty, her manner rough, but her rougish face gentle. Hardly knowing what he said, he replied, "If you refuse me."

She giggled and looked at Waggers.

" 'Tisn't me you'd beg, eh, Abby?" Waggers leered.

"Go along, Waggers," Domino ordered.

"But you, what about the cap'n and you not bein' there?"

"I will be there. Tell him I missed the boat back. Tell him I am swimming. Tell him whatever you please." He took Abby by the arm and said in a low voice, "We will go to your room now."

"Here," she answered, "I haven't asked yer."

"I'm asking you," he replied evenly, moving her along.

Her room was dark and small and the bed was barely enough for two. He undressed her with silent expertise and as silently removed his own clothes. She came to him willingly, impatient at delay. and was soon ready, receiving him with a sharp cry, but otherwise silent.

Above her, he felt a cold detachment. He saw himself as if from a distance, as if his mind were above the bed looking down on her soft, fleshy body, her face slack, eyes half-closed, lips wet and parted as she twisted beneath his even thrusts. He himself was moving like a machine, hands upon her breasts, to a silent military cadence: "One and two and three . . . " The door opened and he felt her start beneath him, but he went on.

"Andy," Waggers called softly into the gloom, "I got ter boat to wait fer yer."

"Uh . . . thank you, Waggers. Uh . . . close the door."

A moment or two later it was over. She was the kind who wept at her climax, and he heard the whimpering as if from a great distance. He waited with her until it stopped and then he left her, rising almost at once and dressing.

"You be comin' back, I hope, sailor," she said with a soft laugh.

"Someday," he answered briefly. Then, after tossing a coin upon the counterpane, he left the room.

Waggers waited outside, and at the sight of Domino he began a little limping jig. "Ho!" he cried. Ben't ye the rogue an' rascal. A woman afore sailin' an' 'twill keep? Nay. Afore Barbados, fever'll be on yer agin."

Domino grunted a reply. His body felt lighter, his thoughts were clearer, and his purpose was once again in the forefront. It was only later, lying in his hammock aboard the *Coventry* on the edge of sleep, that Caroline stood vividly in his mind, but he was asleep before the image caused him any pain.

Part

Four

Chapter Thirteen

Wildwood was set in the middle of grassy lawns. It faced the James River, but its back was toward the rolling, fertile acres that stretched up to the pine forest. It was far grander in appearance than Caroline had expected.

The sloping banks that led to the dock were still studded with late wildflowers, although the December chill had already touched the land.

It was strange to sail to the very foot of one's own home. As the *Charlotte* anchored to unload her cargo for Welles' plantation and pick up the casks of tobacco, an excited cheering and babbling of voices greeted her from the throats of both the blacks and whites who lined the shore.

Above Wildwood, the river narrowed, making passage of a sizable ship impossible, and those small planters who did not own their own docks were forced to roll their five-hundred-pound casks and hogsheads across the fields or down the river roundroad to Joshua's landing.

Sedan chairs awaited their arrival, and as Caroline was borne up the embankment and along the road to the house she felt as if she might almost be on her way to some country home in Kent.

The house itself, tall, columned, and sparkling white in the sun, was composed of a main section and two large wings which, she was to discover, had once been three separate buildings connected by walkways now enclosed.

The main wing contained the reception rooms below and bedchambers above. The left wing housed the kitchen and pantries; the right contained Joshua's offices.

Behind the kitchen was a large vegetable garden enclosed by white fencing. Opposite were the house slaves' white-washed cabins, few in number compared with the long rows near the fields.

"Take care," Joshua said as they alighted. "See over there? We must cross the ha-ha fence."

She followed his gesture and saw that they were crossing a ditch into which had been built a wall.

"How curious!" she exclaimed. " 'Tis like a castle moat without water. Is it to keep out the Indians and brigands?"

"Sheep," said Joshua.

"Sheep?"

"They feed from the lawns and keep them cropped. But 'twould not do to have sheep odors clinging to the house."

"Does everyone have them—those fences, I mean?"

"Yes, I would think so, at least all the planters do. There is too much lawn to keep wasting the slaves' time with scything. Sheep are better and keep the lawns smoother."

"Then I suppose all visitors must be warned," Caroline commented.

"Strangers are sometimes caught unaware," Joshua agreed.

"Is that the reason for the name?" she asked.

"What do you mean?"

"Ha-ha," she said with a straight face, and he laughed, amused.

"You are very witty this morning," he said.

"It is good to be through with voyaging," she remarked. Then she said, "The house is so much larger than I imagined it."

"My uncle had planned to found a dynasty here. Unfortunately, his wife was unable to accommodate him. I hope I shall have better fortune."

"I, too," she said, thinking of the baby within her and wondering at what point she must tell him. Soon. She flinched at the idea. He had not been very demanding aboard the *Charlotte*, for if the southerly routes had caused him to suffer *mal de mer*, the rougher seas of the North and the fierce coastal swells as they neared Hampton Roads had rendered him totally feeble.

As they climbed the wide steps to the roofed colonnade,

Caroline saw a tall, quite lovely girl coming up the side of the lawns between two slaves bearing trunks.

Her complexion was a creamy tan, her nose straight and slightly tilted at the tip, and the hair that peeped beneath her white turban was silky black.

"Who is that?" she asked Joshua.

He said carelessly, "A new slave I bought in Barbados. My headwoman here died before I set sail for England. I needed a replacement."

"Slave!" Caroline exclaimed. "Why, she looks . . . well . . . as if she might be Spanish or . . . or French."

"She might be, for all I know," Joshua replied. "Her mother was a half-caste. She may be, too."

"Oh, I see," said Caroline, not seeing at all. "But if her own father was white, as well as her grandfather, why would she still be a slave?"

Joshua shrugged. "There are many such. One does not generally marry slaves, my dear, nor yet acknowledge their offspring as one's own. Her name is Serena. She will maid you, I think, unless you prefer one of the other women. There is quite a good girl named Charity, the daughter of my carpenter, Andrew. She would suit you. But I believe Serena knows about maiding a lady. It was the reason I bought her."

"Not knowing if I was alive or dead?" Caroline asked.

"I hoped alive," Joshua said. "Buying Serena seemed proof during those dark days."

She looked at him curiously, feeling somehow that despite the lover-like sentiments, he was jesting, but he was regarding her with an amiable expression.

"Shall we go in?" he asked, then beckoned her inside the big door above whose lintel was a carved pineapple painted in the earthy colors of that fruit.

In the weeks that followed, Caroline, who had spent much of her previous time remembering or longing for Domino, found herself too busy to mope very much.

The tobacco plantation, she was soon to discover, was not as seasonal as other plantations or farms. The tobacco not only needed to be grown and harvested, but it required aging and curing. The crop harvested this past year was now drying, and that of the year before was aging. All of it needed constant attention. The plantation was busy from dawn until sunset.

At the Ormontons' she had seen the slaves from a distance, save for those who waited upon her at the house. Here, they were ever present.

Among the house servants there was Abraham, who acted as Joshua's valet and as butler. He was a small, thin, and very quiet man, whose sole preoccupation seemed to be to please Joshua and somehow avoid his quick-tempered rebukes and readiness with his riding crop.

There were four or five maids, one looking much like the other. Caroline soon discovered that they were inclined to laugh and talk among themselves whenever Joshua was out of the house, but they, like Abraham, became silent and self-effacing as soon as his footsteps sounded.

In the kitchen a large, plump woman, who was called only Cookie, presided over what she constantly referred to as "wuthless, lazy" helpers. Of all of them, she appeared the least sullen.

Serena, now housekeeper according to Joshua, moved among the rest, seemingly aware that her elevated station and light skin was despised by one and all. With Caroline she behaved with a deference so precise and aloof as to border on arrogance.

Caroline found her unnerving. In the end, she chose the girl Charity to maid her. Charity was the only one of the household who could be called cheerful, and at that it was an understatement. She was irrepressible. Not more than fourteen, she had an elfin face above a slim, budding figure and impishly merry black eyes that twinkled even when she wore her most subdued expression.

She was delighted to be moved up to such a prominent position and was soon filled with a youthful self-importance that was both touching and amusing. She prattled endlessly whenever she was with Caroline, and the latter began to look forward to seeing her. Charity was a bright presence in a household that for the most part was somber.

Beyond the kitchen, in one of the white-washed cabins, Charity's father, Andrew, not only took care of all the carpentry needs on the plantation, but he was able, as well, to turn his hand to wheel-making, to coopering, or, for that matter, to shoeing a horse. Tall, strongly built, and with an air of quiet dignity about himself, he was the most respected of the plantation's men. Charity's mother was head of the sewing and weaving and spinning women, who worked in a long, low shack not far from the nearby quarters. The older of Charity's two sisters worked with her, as had Charity before Caroline came.

"But ah nevah was no good," she confided to Caroline, "no good atall. Mend a tear be 'bout all ah can do, Mistiss."

"Then you will have to give my sewing to the others." Caroline laughed. "I will keep you, anyway."

"Thank-ee, Mistiss. That Serena, she good. Do mos' anything. Ack lak a lady, so she do. Us be thinkin' her be riz up by some wite lady foh maidin'. Mebbe do bad things an' got dole away fum dat place Massa fine huh."

"She is not very happy," Caroline observed.

"No, Mistiss, she be angry evah day. Don' shout. Don' scol'. Jus' look lak she mout.'

It was true enough. Serena's voice was never raised—not in anger, not in laughter, not in reproach, nor in compliment. Her manners were perfect. Her voice was toneless, her eyes veiled, and her face still. She kept herself apart from everyone, walking a lonely path between the whites and the blacks.

The field hands were kept to their own quarters and the immediate area around them. Each morning the foreman lined them up to await Gideon Taylor, Joshua's overseer. It was Taylor who checked the number of slaves, and often, finding one missing due to illness, decided the man was well enough to work.

Taylor, his face brown and lined from years in the sun, lived in the overseer's cottage near the slope to the river with his malarial-looking wife and an abundance of children. They, too, kept to themselves, as befitted those who were neither master nor slave but only hired help.

Caroline observed that Taylor was both deferential to Joshua and easy enough with the field hands. The whip he carried as he rode the acres in search of laggards was rarely raised, and, as far as she knew, never used. The field hands, out of Joshua's way, were a considerably happier lot than those who came in daily contact with him. Taylor was not cruel; he was firm. And from what Charity said, he was a far better overseer than some.

He might be all that, Caroline thought, and yet she did not like him. He had a way of looking at her out of his small, washed-out blue eyes that made her uncomfortable.

It was as if he knew something she did not and held her not in respect, as his manner suggested, but in mild contempt.

The two she found least pleasant to be around—Serena and Taylor—were the very ones Joshua thought the most of. Taylor, he claimed, was indispensable and so capable of running the plantation as to make Joshua's trips abroad feasible and his long stays in Williamsburg possible each winter.

Serena, he told Caroline, was good enough to ease much of her own work and could be trusted to take over Caroline's duties whenever she, too, journeyed away from Wildwood.

Joshua rose early each morning and Caroline found she, too, was required to rise and dress and begin her duties. In the dark of early morning a tankard of ale began the day, after which Joshua rode the acres or consulted with Taylor or attended to some business in his offices.

The sun was well up before they breakfasted. Accustomed to more delicate fare in England, Caroline found that here in Virginia breakfast was as hearty as supper. There was roasted meat or a baked fowl and cold smoked bacon, a mealy cake called cornbread, as well as fluffy biscuits and gravy and a pie as often as not. At first her stomach revolted at such largesse, but as the days wore on she became accustomed to it and was soon eating with relish.

She discovered that the plantation was practically self-sufficient. The yarn and cloth for the slaves' clothing was spun and woven in the outbuilding and was made into dresses and jackets and breeches for the slaves, and the skilled workers, like Andrew, kept tools, furnishings, wagons, and animals in good repair.

Joshua took care of business and fields and crops, but Caroline was expected to oversee the management of food and all other things pertaining to the household and to the domestic portion of the slaves' lives.

The storehouses, too, were her duty. There, she measured the food for the daily needs. In the smokehouse, with its huge hams and beef preserved against spoiling, she measured the amount of meat necessary to feed so many. At first she was at a loss and multiplied rations until Joshua stopped her.

"We *feed* the hands, we don't stuff them like turkeys. We will be ruined at this rate. Meal and side meat and flour are enough. They have their own vegetable gardens and they keep some chickens. At slaughtering time they receive chitterlings and tripe and other parts not fit for consumption at our table."

She thought of their own dinners at which so much was wasted. What became of that food? She asked him and he said, "It is the duty of a good wife to see that not too much is wasted. What goes back to the kitchen feeds the house slaves. God knows there are enough of them to feed without pampering field hands."

After that, she watched more carefully at her own table. Still, there were always several meats and fishes and vegetables and all manner of hot breads and sweets and savories gracing it in overabundance.

Each day found the small dairy busy churning butter and turning out cheeses, some to eat quickly, others to ripen and age to deep yellow.

Were it not for Caroline's active days, her consumption of food would have rendered her fat. As it was, the growing child within had begun to make her waist thicken so that she was forever in need of letting out seams.

Serena took the garments from Caroline for alteration with the same air of proud acquiescence with which she greeted all other requests.

Always immaculate, however ragged her clothing, Serena learned as quickly as Caroline herself, and despite some grumbling from the other servants at Serena's being shunted into the headwoman's place. Serena soon became indispensable to the household. With Charity, Caroline could banter as one bantered with a child. With the other maids she managed to achieve a pleasant rapport. But with Serena there remained an immeasurable gulf.

When she was not working at her chores or being required to listen to Joshua's harangues on politics, complaints about business, or long stories of the past in which she had little interest, Caroline would read. She had discovered that Joshua, surprisingly. had a fine library filled with books, some of them just purchased on his last trip to England. Almost all of them looked untouched by human hands. She thought this odd. for she had not yet learned that in Virginia aristocracy the fine library was a caste mark, much as were the fine gowns for the ladies and lace on a gentleman's cuffs. Not all members necessarily felt obliged to read the heavy volumes of Plutarch and Sidney and Locke, although perhaps there were far more of the aristocrats here who took pleasure in learning than there were in England, where there were many more amusements to distract one.

Joshua regarded her passion for reading with some disdain, calling it part of her strange, unfeminine side. Nevertheless, many evenings, when Joshua was content to sit staring at the fire with brandy at his elbow, she would perch the petticoat lamp on one knob of the ladderback chair in the library and while away the hour after supper until Joshua roused himself and they went to bed.

His attentions, like the rest of her life, were something she had learned to accept. One day soon, she would confess her pregnancy and perhaps then have the advantage of being able to plead weariness or headaches more often than she dared do now.

She had looked forward to the telling with mixed feelings and was therefore surprised when shortly after Christmas she told him and received only the most cursory questioning.

"I am sure," she said, "nearly three months, I would think—at least two. I was so confused after my capture that I could not remember the last time I had my flow."

"Well, then, summer will see a child in the house."

"July, by my reckoning," she answered, knowing very well it would be June. It would not be too awkward if the child were thought early by a month. But two months! She devoutly hoped it would wait its term and certainly not put in any sudden appearance. Sometimes children were born later than expected. She had been, so her mother said.

The night she told him and on the succeeding nights Joshua remained downstairs after she had gone to bed. By the end of the week, when he moved to a separate room, Caroline realized that he meant to refrain from the marital act until the baby arrived. Freed of this burden, Caroline found her days more agreeable and slept well.

She had loathed submitting to him, yet now that he no longer approached her, her body began to long for a physical touch. Domino swam back into her mind often as she drifted off to sleep and again as she awakened. Her dreams, when she remembered them, were almost exclusively about him. At first she was obsessed with the thought of him, but then, as time went on, the reality of their relationship faded and became as fanciful as the dreams themselves.

Once, lying in bed, his face only vague in her mind, she experienced an overwhelming sense of loss, and with it the full truth of her position, which had been so long suppressed, rose to challenge her.

She was married to a man whose touch was distasteful. She was in love with a man—not her husband—and she was carrying his child. Ahead loomed the actual birth and with it certain proof that Joshua could not have fathered the child. A chilling thought crowded in: Joshua viewing the child, too early born, and finding no likeness to himself. Sweet heaven, if it were like Domino, dark-haired and black-eyed . . . !

She sat up abruptly, shaking. What had she been thinking of? With sudden clarity, she saw Domino's face now —twisted, as it had been that night he left her at the Ormontons'. She had built all her dreams and hopes on nothing more substantial than that. Fool! Had he cared at all, he could never have left her without a word or a promise to return.

What was her life to become? Even if all went well and the birth aroused none of Joshua's old suspicions, she was still tied to this marriage—and to Joshua. She looked down the vista of years to come and could find no joy and no promise. All at once, the child she had carried with such secret pleasure became one more link in the chains that bound her.

If she were not with child, how much easier it would be to plan, how much easier it would be to seek and execute the path of freedom. She would not care how she had to live or what she might become. Any life at all would be better than this one. With a swiftness born of youth, she relegated to unimportance the relative comfort and ease of her life and embraced the notion that rags and poverty were preferable if by that means she would be rid of Joshua.

And then she came back to the fact that wishing was a long way from having. Thwarted, she flung herself down upon the bed and began to weep. Joshua, coming in a few minutes later, found her sobbing. Alarmed that something was amiss with the baby, he tried to calm her.

But the more he sought to comfort her, the stormier her weeping grew, until at last he said, "Fanciful notions—women are given to fancies, especially at such a time. You are too long without society. I think we will venture to spend the rest of the winter in Williamsburg."

Hearing this, her sobs abated somewhat and she made an effort to control herself. Williamsburg. Oh, at least it was a complete town and near the sea. There, a way to end her present misery might be found.

"Spend the winter?"

"Yes. 'Tis near mid-January. Usually I am at the town house before Christmas. There is nothing here that Taylor can't see to, nor anything at the house that Serena is not capable of handling. We will come back in May."

"Five months," she said. This turn of events erased the last trace of her woe.

"I might need to make a trip back, but you needn't," he said. "I shall order the barge made ready for our trip. It's not too long a journey. Several hours will see us there. Tomorrow you must pack whatever items you will need. There are many kinds of entertainment in Williamsburg, theaters and musicales and balls—quite as many, I fancy, as London. Actually, I like the season in Williamsburg even better than I do in London."

"But I shall not be able to socialize too long," Caroline demurred. "Soon, it will not be seemly to appear in public."

"Nonsense. You are not in London now, and a little more latitude is allowed here. Besides, my dear, you are slender enough—so slender I would say you miscalculated and the child will not arrive until August."

"Perhaps you are right," she answered with a flutter of fear.

"Then you will get ready tomorrow?"

"Yes, Joshua, and thank you," she answered and smiled at him.

"I say, you look very fetching, my dear," he said, his eyes on the low neckline of her nightdress. " 'Tis a pity I must play the gentleman."

"Oh, Joshua," she said with downcast eyes as she feigned embarrassment.

"All this talk has quite awakened me," he said, standing up. "I shall have a glass or two of brandy. Go to sleep, Caroline."

"Yes, Joshua," she replied meekly, then settled herself back upon the pillows.

Williamsburg. Town life. Something different. Heartened by the prospect, she told herself that, after all, their stay in Williamsburg might bring good fortune to her.

Three days later, in the early evening, they reached Williamsburg. The river trip had taken somewhat longer than Joshua had anticipated, owing to the fact that two of the eight slaves rowing had proved to be weakened by illness and were unable to continue. Caroline and Joshua, as well as six house servants, occupied the stern section, and with the chests containing clothing and books and supplies from the plantation also aboard, the barge rode low in the water.

Charity, on the first trip outside the plantation in all of her fourteen years, was beside herself with excitement and had been spoken to several times about her sudden movements until Cookie, exasperated, reached out and gave her a pinch hard enough to elicit a yelp. Thereafter, she remained motionless and silent, but her eyes still sparkled impishly, much to Cookie's open annoyance and Caroline's private amusement.

They were met at the landing by a phaeton driven by Joshua's black caretaker, Ethan, an old slave slowed down by his years, whose hair was grizzled. With him were two drays driven by his sons, who looked not much younger than Ethan himself. The phaeton was for their private use, the drays for the slaves and chattel goods.

"How many slaves are kept in Williamsburg?" Caroline asked.

"Six," Joshua replied. "Ethan's family, all of them. There is as much to be done in town as there is at Wildwood. I have an agent who sees to them, but in truth Ethan is more capable than anyone. He was my uncle's valet and majordomo. He's not as active as he once was, and I needed him here at the town house. My uncle did not keep a town house. I built mine shortly after I arrived, and I needed trustworthy caretakers. You will soon see how well the town house is cared for."

As they entered the town the drays separated from them and Caroline asked why.

"I want you to tour the town now while it is still light. 'Twill be your home for all the winter seasons. You may as well become familiar with it. We are coming along Duke of Gloucester Street. Ahead is the capitol."

Hardly London, Caroline thought, but teeming with life after the plantation. She rejoiced in the sight of so many shops and taverns and ordinaries. Duke of Gloucester Street was very wide and tree-lined. To her left, as they neared the center, she saw a long green expanse and beyond its gates an imposing brick residence, looking as if Christopher Wren himself had designed it. "The governor's palace," Joshua said in anticipation of her question. "Fauquier's now. There he entertains those whose views are similar to his own. I vow, were it not for men like Peyton Randolph and some of the others, I would say treason runs rampant in Williamsburg."

"Why treason?"

"All this talk of freeing slaves and taxing the imports from England, and of abolishing rule from London."

"And do all Virginians save Mr. Randolph agree?"

Joshua snorted. "There are many who do not agree, but enough who do. Why, one skipjack has had the audacity to suggest taxation is unfair."

"And what upstart spoke such treason?" Caroline asked, privately delighted but assuming a shocked air.

"Henry, Patrick Henry—a failure at everything he's attempted . . . storekeeper, farmer. He decided to take up law. He has a habit of arguing against the Crown when it comes to the matter of taxes. He fancies himself an orator. I will say for him that he is succeeding at that. Talk was all he was ever suited for. Pish!"

"I see," said Caroline.

"At that," Joshua went on morosely, "he is not as bad as some of the turncoats."

"Turncoats?"

"Traitors to their own families, their own class. Why, one of the august Lees themselves actually proposed not only freeing the slaves but placing a tax on imports to pay them. If that isn't treason, I don't know what is."

"Yes, indeed," she said soothingly. "Oh, I would hope there are less rebellious people in Williamsburg."

"There won't be for long. People like Fauquier and Richard Lee are stirring people up." He cleared his throat. "Yonder is the capitol. The Burgesses sit there. We will turn down Waller Street and you will see the theater. Young Lewis Hallam's company is performing a revival of *The Beggar's Opera* this week, so I'm told. Have you ever seen it?"

"No. It has not been presented in London for years now. Once in a while there is talk of doing so, but it is considered a bit coarse."

"For London tastes? How could anything be too coarse for London's tastes? Between Fielding and Hogarth, one would find all the coarseness possible."

"I thought you liked London," Caroline said.

"Well enough. And it did provide me with a wife . . . and a son."

"Perhaps a daughter," said Caroline, unhappy at the turn the conversation had taken.

"If it is a girl, I shall drown her, as the Chinese peasants do."

"Joshua!" she exlaimed.

"I jest, my dear," he said equably. "Sons will come in due course. There, now, you have had your glimpse of our capitol. We shall soon be at the house." Leaning forward, he tapped Ethan and ordered the phaeton turned around.

"Where is the house?" Caroline asked.

"Just on Nicholson Street, not far from the Blairs."

The town house was set rather close to the road, but behind it stretched the garden and outbuildings, so the effect was that of a plantation in miniature.

Built two rooms deep with a main hall separating them, it was constructed half of brick, half of white timbers. The staircase circled gracefully to the upper story, which boasted four bedchambers.

If the plantation had been allowed to grow somewhat shabby, the town house had not. The furnishings were of well-polished mahogany. The floors were covered with gros-point rugs and the walls with the finest paper, some of it quite elegantly executed.

The first outbuilding was off the dining room and contained the kitchen, over which Cookie was already presiding. There were servants' quarters at the very end of the property, and two ornamental outhouses were set in the garden for the convenience of the males.

There was, in addition to a stable and carriage house, a small barn housing two cows, off which were a microscopic dairy and spring house.

Ethan was all Joshua claimed and evidently responsible for the fine condition of the house and outbuildings. Caroline thought he had done a better job of work than the twenty house servants employed at the larger residence.

"I love it here," she said extravagantly.

"More than Wildwood?"

" 'Tis different," she said evasively. Then, summoning Charity, she went upstairs to change and rest after the journey.

If Williamsburg was hardly London in appearance, it more than made up for it in the variety and lavishness of its entertainment.

Caroline reveled in the theater and the concerts, in the sight of richly dressed ladies and gentlemen strolling about the town, in the balls given in the ballroom of the Raleigh Tavern, on Gloucester Street, and in the private parties. Most of all, she delighted in the frequent visitors to the house and in giving dinners and entertainments of her own.

The Williamsburg residents had no real liking for the English or what they termed the real English, few of whom they had seen before the Indian war commenced. Joshua told her that when he had first arrived to assume his uncle's property, he had been treated with so marked a disfavor that he had nearly given up the inheritance and gone back to England. "It took me the better part of fifteen years," he said, "and then it was largely because I was taken up by the old governor, Dinwiddie."

"And now?"

Joshua shrugged. "I have known Fauquier for some time. I am not an intimate, the way the honorable George Wythe is." There was an unmistakable sneer in his voice. "Leader of the Virginia bar . . . by what vote I can't say. Why, the very land and house where he dwells belong to his father-in-law. In truth, old Talliaferro built it, presumably so Elizabeth would have a decent dwelling place.

"Oh, Joshua, I found Mr. Wythe most charming and intelligent and . . ."

"Charming? Yes, I suppose one could say that is how he has managed to make his mark. But, as I recall, you find many men charming—young Lyons, for one, and Mr.

Hardin, who I understand used to take you for evening strolls during my illness aboard the *Charlotte*."

"Joshua!"

"Do you deny it?"

"Of course not," she said, her temper flaring. "It was well known that one of the gentlemen aboard would escort me as a matter of protection."

"My understanding is that Mr. Hardin was generally preferred."

"Ordered by the captain," she retorted, "hardly preferred."

"But welcome enough aboard the pirate ship?"

"I told you, I hadn't seen Mr. Hardin on board the *Mouette*."

"Yes, I know what you told me." He turned away. "And you had better begin raising your hoops. It seems the child is, after all, as you reckoned." He flung himself from the room and Caroline's wrath gave way before renewed apprehension.

The next morning he announced that he would return to the plantation for two days. She greeted this news coolly, having decided that to act anything but the injured part would surely make her appear guilty.

"You will be safe enough for those two days," he said. "I have asked Mrs. Page's widowed sister to keep you company."

"I need no company," Caroline said.

"It will be best," he answered. "I shall return on Saturday, in time for the governor's ball. Pease remain at the house until Mrs. Goodwin arrives. I would not want her to suffer discourtesy."

"I do not need you to tell me my manners," Caroline said haughtily. "I am not some back-of-the-woods Colonial. . . ." She stopped, appalled.

"So that is how we strike you?" he said angriy. Take care, Caroline. You would soon be without any social intercourse should you make your true feelings public. I fancy Mr. Wythe, whom you found so charming . . . "

"And Mistress Wythe," she interrupted. "Had you not started a quarrel with me, you would have heard so before."

"If Mr. Wythe should know it, I fancy even he would turn cold." Joshua finished as if she had not spoken. He left the house without speaking to her again.

There was a dual purpose in his going to Wildwood just now. They had been two months in the town, and two months was too long without a woman. He dared not approach Caroline. Nothing must occur to bring about a sooner birth. July. The month was burned into his mind. July and the babe was his for sure; any sooner, and it was not. He knew well infants sometimes arrived sooner than expected. In this case, he hoped it was not true. There had been times when he had had difficulty restraining himself these past weeks, but, determined not to give any excuse for a premature birth, he had managed.

It was nearing April, and he noted that Caroline looked not likely to deliver before summer. Still . . . it wouldn't matter. He would be glad when the issue was settled, one way or another.

The longer he lived with her story, the longer his doubts remained. Had she confessed to rape, he could have believed her, at least in part; but to insist on the story that the captain had protected her. . . . A rogue! A brigand! And yet he was more of a saint than other men of nobler breeding.

He would never believe that. Still, if the child proved his, he would let it rest. If not . . . if not, the child would not live to bear his name and thus make him a pointing stick.

That brought him to his other important business at the plantation. He began to think about it, and long before he reached Wildwood he was eager with anticipation.

Serena saw the barge come into the landing and immediately went to make herself presentable. They were back, she thought, but not due for months yet. She had enjoyed being here alone, ordering what meals she pleased and taking her leisure when she felt like it. These days, with her body swelling, she tired more easily. He knew, yet he had behaved as if it had not occurred.

She had been caught unaware and had let it go too long to rid herself of it. The violent purgative had made her wretchedly ill, yet the child remained inside her.

It woud not happen again. She would see to it, by taking the herbs regularly and at the first sign so they could work to purge herself. Meanwhile . . . she must make the best of it.

She had gone up to Caroline Welles' room not only

to check her appearance, but to make certain no trace of her presence lingered there. She had spent many a long hour trying on various garments and reclining on the French sofa or on the bed itself.

From the window she saw the sedan chair borne across the ha-ha fence and to the front of the house. Only Joshua Welles alighted. So his wife had not come. Serena smiled. All the better. She gave a last look around the room and then left it. She was descending the stairs when Welles appeared in the hall.

"I saw you come," she said, "and I have prepared Madame's room."

"Madame is not with me," he answered shortly. "Take my case up," he ordered, and she took the portmanteau with a faint smile. Bringing it to the room, she opened it and removed the articles, putting them away neatly.

He came in a few minutes later and closed the door.

"We will lie here this evening," he said, beginning to remove his clothing.

"Not in Madame's bed!" she exclaimed.

"Why, you impudent black bitch! Do as I say!" he spluttered.

Silently, she began to remove her own clothing, taking off the turban last and letting her thick black hair fall over her engorged breasts and protruding belly.

She advanced toward him as he stood there, her eyes narrowed. He seized her almost at once, bending his head to suck noisily at her straining nipples. She rubbed against him, and then as he raised his head, she pulled away. He liked variety and he liked to fight, she knew that, and today she would give him both and as much pleasure as possible. She wanted something. He could give it to her.

He had seized her again and this time threw her harshly on the bed. She waited until he was nearly atop her and then rolled away, laughing.

"Damn you!" he said, trying to grasp her, but she slithered down so that he reached only air. This time he made no effort to take her. Instead, he raised his hand and brought it down hard on her bare buttocks. She screamed to please him and he struck her again. Again she screamed. She could hear him breathing hoarsely. As he moved to strike her yet again, her mouth came down on him and his hand fell weakly upon the bed. She tried to prolong it, but in a few minutes it was over and he was gasping.

She stayed at the foot of the bed, sitting cross-legged, her hair a curtain over her body.

She watched him through half-closed eyes as he lay there. Not yet, she told herself, not yet—later, when he is ready for me again.

But after a moment he opened his eyes and said, "I want to talk to you, Serena."

"Yes, master," she said meekly.

"I will not have the brat you are carrying in the house. You understand?"

"Yes, master," she answered evenly.

"It will have to be given to one of the slaves to raise, not tagging around your skirts."

"No, master, not tagging around my skirts . . . not here at all. I want to send it away."

"Away?"

"Yes. My brother lives free in New Orleans. I want to send it to him."

"Send it? Sell it, you mean! And not to your brother!"

She shook her head. "Send it," she repeated.

"Go to hell," he said calmly. "And take the brat with you."

She said nothing but got off the bed and began to dress.

"Here, what the devil do you think you are doing?"

"I am going away."

"And be killed for your pains."

She gave a slight movement to her shoulders. "Kill me now if you like." She walked to the side of the bed and looked down at him. "This child will be no slave. It is yours."

"I don't give a damn whose it is. I own no black bastard."

"Black or white, he is your son," she said calmly.

"My son . . . is . . . " He stopped. Damn this woman. He had nearly forgotten what he wanted from her.

He sat up and swung his feet to the floor. "All right." He capitulated so suddenly that she was stunned.

"If it is a boy, you can send it to your brother; a girl, and it stays here. You understand?"

"I understand," she said. If it were a girl . . . but she would take care of that when the time came.

"But I have a condition."

"Yes?"

"We return in May. I want you to take special care of Mistress Welles. See that she suffers no illness, accident, or sudden frights. You understand?"

She nodded, curious.

"I do not want the baby born before July. If it is . . . " He stopped. "If it is," he continued after a moment, "if it is born before July and she has not had any illness or accident, you are to take it and drown it. Do you understand?"

"Yes, master," she replied in the same calm voice.

"Good. See that you obey."

"And my son goes to my brother?"

"He goes to your brother. But not a girl—a girl stays here."

"Why?" she asked.

"A pretty sight she will be," he said. Then, seizing her again, he added, "Like you—a good woman for a man's appetites. Savage—I like that. Oh," he said as her nails raked his shoulders, "you little hellcat. I'll teach you." Grabbing her leg, he bit her sharply on the soft inner portion of her thigh. In retaliation, she sunk her teeth into his shoulder and in a moment they were rolling and snarling like animals until, at a fever pitch, he took her brutally.

Afterward, she thought with a certain dullness of mind that it was a strong child to have remained with her after that. It would have to be strong. And a boy, not a girl. She knew now why he would keep a girl. But she would not let him keep hers. And she knew what the bargain was. All she had to do was drown the child of his wife. In June it would not be his. In July. But by then her own son would be on his way to New Orleans. A few weeks only and that would be over.

In the months since Joshua had bought Serena, she had learned certain things about him. He would do as he promised. He would not be swayed from carrying out anything once he had given voice to it. It was not honor. She knew that. He had no honor. He had pride and stubbornness. And here, where he held sway over life and death, he had ruthless arrogance.

Chapter Fourteen

The palace was alight with hundreds of spermacetti candles flaring from wall sconces and gracing tables in their pewter or silver holders and making each prism of the crystal chandeliers sparkle.

Caroline, sitting sedately with Mrs. Wythe and some of the older ladies, watched the dancers with a certain amount of envy. Her hoops had been raised as far as it was possible to raise them, but dancing was not only impossible, it was socially indecorous. In another week or two, attending such a gathering would be out of the question.

Joshua had long since retired to another part of the palace with several of his friends to engage in a card game. Fauquier, an inveterate gambler himself, always thoughtfully provided such entertainment for those gentlemen who wearied of the ball or the concert or who could not resist a stop at the gaming tables.

Gaming in London was a sport to many, but in Virginia's capital it was virtually the addiction of almost every man. There were cards and races and beyond that a wager on almost anything from when the next ship from England would arrive to how soon the last of the French Indies would fall to the current naval hero, Rodney.

As the cotillion ended, George Wythe left a group of gentlemen to fetch his wife and lead her out for the gavotte that followed. With him was a very tall, strongly built boy who carried his slender length awkwardly and, in fact, gave every appearance of being an oafish bumpkin, save for his face, which was handsomely boned and of a high color.

"Mistress Welles," George Wythe said, "may I present young Thomas Jefferson, one of our students at William and Mary and soon to study law with me." The youth bowed gravely and murmured a greeting over Caroline's extended hand.

"Please don't let his youth mislead you, ma'am," Wythe added. "He speaks with the tongue of the old and learned." Jefferson's color increased and an embarrassed smile lit his sober face.

"I shall look forward with peasure to being instructed," Caroline bantered.

"We leave you then in good company." Mrs. Wythe smiled. "Now, don't tire Mistress Welles with mathematical formulas, Thomas. Amuse her with recitations in French," she admonished as she went off on her husband's arm.

"Will you sit down, Mr. Jefferson?" Caroline asked demurely.

"If it pleases you, ma'am, with pleasure," he returned.

"And shall you amuse me with recitations?" she asked in French.

"You speak well, ma'am," he replied with dawning interest.

"You, also, sir," she answered with a smile.

"Have you visited France?"

"Alas, no. The war prevents it."

"I shall go there one day," he said. "I shall see the France of Rousseau, of Montesquieu and Voltaire and of Racine and Molière.

"I have some knowledge of the playwrights," Caroline said, "but of the rest I confess ignorance, except Rousseau, who is very difficult to read in English, and I have not attempted him in his native tongue."

"Your pardon, ma'am," he exclaimed excitedly, "but you are unusual for a woman. Reading Rousseau and having a knowledge of Molière and Racine, even confessing to finding Rousseau difficult! He is difficult, ma'am, but I am surprised that so charming a lady would have so firm an opinion of him."

"Then you agree with Racine: 'She is all wavering and hesitation: in short, she is a woman.' "

"Not al all," he protested. "I shall do penance for my

unintentional offense by saying, 'Man, I can assure you, is a nasty creature.' "

"Not Racine." Caroline hazarded. "Molière?"

"Yes! *Tartuffe*."

"Is that your favorite play?"

"No. My favorite is *Le Bourgeois Gentilhomme*."

"And mine is *Hamlet*."

"You are loyal to your own countryman." He smiled.

"Your countryman, too," Caroline replied.

His face sobered. "No, ma'am, not truly mine. Mine are gathered in this ballroom."

"All of them?" Caroline jested.

"Or dwelling on farms up in the back country and keeping shops in the towns," he said, still serious.

"Oh, Mr. Jefferson, I was making a joke." She laughed and he smiled uncertainly.

"Forgive me, ma'am," he said, "I am somewhat lacking in humor."

"Indeed, not," she soothed, "for if Molière pleases you, surely your wit must be extremely well developed."

"It is Molière who is witty and I who enjoy and envy his wit," Jefferson said.

"Oh!" she exclaimed, lapsing into English once more. "I must need the wit of a Molière to make you smile." This time he laughed outright.

"Tell me," he asked, "how came you by so much knowledge?"

"I grew bored with sewing and needlepoint and looked for other means to amuse myself."

"And found them in books?"

"And found them in books," she agreed.

"And languages?"

"Oh, they came easily to my tongue: French, of course; Latin and Greek, because my brother's tutors insisted on teaching them, and since I haunted the lesson, perforce they taught me. I should like to learn Spanish, and my German is very meager."

"I mean to have them," he said, "and others. I am preparing now to study Gaelic."

"Gaelic? But, why?"

"For the purpose of reading the *Ossian*. I have read McPherson's translation, but I wish to do one of my own. I have only just sent to him for a copy of the original. It is beautiful poetry, ma'am. Ossian was a great hero of

Ireland in the third century: daring, bold, a splendid warrior and lover."

"I have found you out at last, Mr. Jefferson." Caroline laughed. "You are a romantic!"

"I, ma'am? Fah! I am a practical man, not much given to romance, but to pursuits of the mind. Ah, here comes my good friend, John Page. He is with me at the college. You must ask him my true character." He rose to make the introduction and Caroline rose, too.

"Definitely a practical man," John Page answered her question gaily. "In any case, we Whigs must band together."

"Rebels, then," Caroline said.

"Virginians, ma'am," Page corrected her. "And here is yet another rallying to our support against the lovely English lady," he added.

Joshua, arriving back at the ball just before the end, found Caroline surrounded by six or seven gentlemen, all of them laughing at an apparent sally. Neither Mrs. Wythe nor any of the other ladies were near her. Mrs. Wythe was instead engaged in a hornpipe with her husband. Those of the other ladies who were not dancing clustered together some distance apart.

Caroline, flushed with the pleasure of the witty conversation and the attention, had forgotten everything in the joy of the moment. It was as if she were still a maiden and at the center of a group of gallants, for as soon as each gentleman finished whatever dance he was promised, he returned to the gay and laughing gathering around her.

She did not see Joshua approach but sensed that he was there by the sudden cessation of laughter. A moment later his hand touched her elbow.

"My apologies for my long absence, my dear," he said. "But I see you have not languished for want of company."

"Indeed, not," Caroline agreed. "The gentlemen have been most kind in entertaining me."

"Egad!" Jefferson exclaimed beside her. "It's the last reel, and I am Miss Ludwell's partner. Please excuse me." He bowed and hurried off. With murmured apologies of their own, the rest soon dispersed.

"A lovely ball," Caroline said, sighing. "I do wish I could dance." She turned her attention to the floor. The first strains of "Sir Roger de Coverly" filled the hall as the lines formed.

Jefferson, she saw, was leading off with Miss Ludwell, and she watched him with interest as the reel progressed. It was like and yet unlike the de Coverly at home. These Virginians had taken it and made it their own. The vigor and enthusiasm were more marked, the gaiety more abandoned. And none were so gay or abandoned as young Mr. Jefferson, who cut a remarkable figure.

"Astonishing," Caroline said to Joshua. "He walks and stands like an awkward bear, yet he dances with the grace of a young deer."

"And who is that, pray tell?" Joshua asked sourly.

"Young Mr. Jefferson," she said, then thought: But why do I say young, for he is surely my own age or a bit more?

"Another of Fauquier's pets," Joshua remarked. "In fact, he and Dr. Small from the college, together with Wythe, form a *partie carré* at Fauquier's table. What they discuss I cannot imagine . . . possibly new ways to rob us of the slaves."

"I don't think so," Caroline answered. "They talk of philosophy and literature and poetry and music."

"How do you surmise that?" Joshua asked.

"Mr. Jefferson told me so," she replied. "He's very keen on philosophy, especially the writings of the French philosophers. And literature. And languages. Quite odd for someone so young."

"You, my dear, fancy yourself his superior," Joshua sneered.

"No, of course not. Please, Joshua, don't spoil my pleasure in one of the last parties I will be able to attend."

"My apologies, Caroline," he replied coldly. "Still, it is annoying to find you choosing your companions from the Whig elements. Why, next you will be asking me to bring Richard Lee home for a discourse on the rights of slaves —as if slaves had rights."

"They are human," Caroline said quietly.

"That, my dear wife, is a matter of opinion, and I see, as in so many other things, mine differs from yours."

"Not in many things, Joshua." She turned aside the beginning of a quarrel. "Not in choices of ballad-operas and plays, for example. I quite fancied *The Beggar's Opera* and agree heartily with you about it, and I was fascinated by some of the new plays that Mr. Hallam performs. They should be our export to London."

"Very pretty," he said, not at all mollified. "The reel has ended. We will go in to supper." He offered his arm and led her off even as the Wythes started back to them.

The exhilaration of the ball lingered with Caroline for days afterward. With it firmly in mind, she asked Joshua's permission to give a small supper party for the Wythes and some others. He temporized at first, but when she mentioned the governor as a guest, he flew into a paroxysm of rage.

"And Jefferson, as well, I take it," he roared. "Perhaps every good-looking dandy from William and Mary."

"You are foolish, Joshua. There is no reason for you to refuse entertainment to the governor. After all, he has entertained us at both concerts and balls."

"Officially," Joshua said. "He has not invited us to dine intimately."

"It would be to your advantage," Caroline pressed. "I am sure my father would not let politics stand in the way of advantage. I know that he still maintains a cordial appearance with Mr. Pitt, for if Bute should lose the king's favor, Mr. Pitt may very well recover it."

She saw that the remark had reached beyond his intolerance and was gratified to win the approval of her plan.

She prepared for her party with great anticipation, and, indeed, it went well enough, she supposed. But the confines of the smaller rooms and the intimacy of the gathering prevented the spontaneity she had enjoyed at the ball. Jefferson performed for them on his violin, giving quite creditable renditions of both a Handel sonata and a Bach fugue. Mrs. Wythe played several charming folk ballads on the harpsichord and the governor displayed a fine baritone when the guests joined in singing.

The supper went very well, for Caroline had prepared it lavishly, keeping a firm watch over Cookie when it came to the more intricate dishes and making the sauces herself.

By any standard it was a success, but when it was over and the last guest had taken his departure, Caroline was disappointed.

"You may have been right, Caroline," Joshua said with

a joviality he had not exhibited in some time. "Not a word of politics. Fauquier has actually asked me to join him for a game tomorrow evening—and he hinted at wanting to have my thinking on a number of matters."

"I am pleased for you, Joshua," Caroline said.

"Yes, indeed, it went very well. Jefferson is not the oaf I imagined him to be. Not much humor in the lad, but he is pleasant enough. He needs a bit more spark if he is to make a success of himself. Even Wythe . . . "

Caroline smiled dutifully, no longer hearing him. Joshua had taken the compliments as his own and was even now imagining that he had not strenuously objected to her wishes at first. Yes, it had been successful from Joshua's point of view, but not her own. She had hoped to continue the conversation begun with Thomas Jefferson at the ball and saw now that it was a foolish idea.

Oh, if only she were not married. Then, she knew that Jefferson would be calling and that she would soon be able to discover how much of the romantic was hidden beneath that scholarly mien.

As she looked about the drawing room, she thought that life here would be pleasant if only she were not Mistress Welles, if only there did not lurk in the back of her mind the thought of how life would be with a man like Domino.

April broke over Virginia with soft rains, and by May everything was in new leaf. May, however, was exceptionally warm, and before the first week was over they returned to Wildwood.

The warm weather and the return of many planters to their country estates brought more society so that hardly a day went by that barges did not call at the Wildwood landing dock bearing neighbors paying a call or slaves bringing invitations.

Joshua entertained the visitors willingly, but he politely refused all invitations, so that for Caroline spring was only a little less lonely than the fall and early winter had been.

She had written a lenghty letter to her family before she left the *Charlotte,* entrusting it to Captain Ramsey for delivery. In it, she made no mention of her pregnancy, but she told as many facts of her capture by pirates and return to Joshua as she could. She had also said that

Joshua had turned cruel since her return and seemed to blame her for the misfortune that had befallen her. Of this, she begged them to say nothing, but she asked instead how soon she might come home to visit.

Although she knew that the *Charlotte* was not due again for at least a month, she began haunting the banks daily, hoping to intercept a message from home before Joshua should see it and learn that she was longing to leave Wildwood.

Serena, she had found upon her return, was not only pregnant but very near her time. "One of the bucks," Joshua said indifferently. "I fancy she was with child when I purchased her. A good price, two for one, and possibly more. They have sex among themselves like any other animals and seldom bother about such niceties as marriage."

"But Charity's parents are married," Caroline said.

"Oh, some. The more intelligent ones have picked up our ways."

"I would have said that Serena was far more intelligent than any."

"Possibly, but apparently in her case intelligence did not win the day." And there the matter rested.

At the end of the month Serena delivered her child and a few days later she was back at work, surprisingly strong and slender for one so recently in confinement.

Caroline, asking the sex of the child, was surprised to see Serena's face tighten with what seemed to be distaste as she said, "A girl."

"And have you named her?"

"Yes. Her name is Nicole."

"What a pretty name."

"Yes," she said sullenly.

"If she is like you, she must be very beautiful," said Caroline in a burst of friendliness. "May I see her?"

"If you wish, Madame," Serena replied. But upon seeing the cool reluctance in Serena's withdrawn face, Caroline did not pursue the matter.

"But where does she keep the child?" Caroline asked Joshua later. "Who cares for it?"

"It is kept in the slave quarters. And of what importance is it who cares for it? Serena has her work here. She is still giving satisfaction, I trust."

"Of course," Caroline answered, repelled both by his

callous indifference and by Serena's evident dislike of the daughter she had produced.

It had confounded her that Serena responded not at all to kindliness and, in fact, gave every indication of hostility to Caroline herself. Yet, since her return, Serena, save for the few days of her confinement, seemed always to be at her elbow. Of late, she had taken to cautioning Caroline against long walks, urging her to confine herself to the immediate gardens, and not to risk a fall by going down the lawns to the embankment.

As the weeks went by, dogwood and apple blossoms were wreathed in fleecy blossoms, the wax myrtle, wisteria, and trumpet came into flower, and the June roses climbed over fences and railings. May had been too warm, but June was perfect, the air soft and delicately warm, the skies cloudless and of a particularly clear and gentle blue.

The green tobacco seedlings stretched row upon row as far as the eye could s·e, almost to the forest fence, where their color was swallowed up in the somber green of the pines.

Now, in the softness of twilight and on dark evenings, the slaves' songs took on a less mournful tone. They sang as they came in from the fields and they sang in their quarters. Frequently Caroline would hear a fiddle being played by one or another of the blacks and clapping and deep-throated laughter.

Standing at her chamber window on one such night, listening to the music and laughter, a wave of nostalgia washed over her and her eyes filled with tears.

"How can they be happy, knowing they are slaves?" she said aloud. And then she remarked, "I suppose it's because they have each other, while I have no one."

A movement behind her made her turn quickly, fearful that Joshua had overheard her. But it was only Serena, coming into the room, fresh linens over her arm.

She met Caroline's eyes, and for once her own were not expressionless. Instead, they expressed a curiosity and something more . . . sadness, perhaps. Odd.

"I . . . you startled me," Caroline said, wondering if Serena had heard her.

"Pardon, Madame," Serena answered. "I thought you called for something."

Caroline shook her head. "I spoke aloud. I daydream these days," she said.

"Yes, Madame." The old familiar indifference mantled Serena's face.

"Serena, I would like to ask you a question."

"Yes, Madame?"

"Is it . . . that is . . . having a baby—will it be difficult?"

"It was not too difficult for me," Serena said.

"And did you have someone to help?"

"Old Betsy, a midwife from the quarters. But surely the master will bring a surgeon to you."

"I have not asked," Caroline confessed. "My time is not yet near."

Serena, eyeing Caroline's great belly, thought that the time was very near. So Welles had been right. The child might not be his. She took a grim pleasure in that notion. His own child lay in the slave quarters, nearly as fair of skin as the woman before her, but with bright red curls and eyes already flecked with hazel. Yet slavery was all that fate or her natural father offered her.

And for the child of this woman and an unknown man, there awaited death by drowning—like the kittens that had been put into a sack and flung into the James only the week before.

She felt a rush of pity for Caroline Welles, an emotion she had not allowed herself since her father's death and the horrors that followed. Sternly, she pushed it back. Pity for a white woman, pampered and rich, and one who had made a cuckold of her husband! And even with the punishment of losing the child, she would never know the truth.

"You are staring, Serena," Caroline's voice broke in on her reflections. "Is something amiss?"

"No, Madame. Madame, when the time comes, you must send for me and I will do all else."

"Thank you, Serena," she sighed. "I do wish the child would take a notion to arrive sooner."

"Yes, Madame," Serena said.

"Serena, how is it that you are . . . what I mean is that you are not like the others."

"No, Madame."

"Then what caused you to be . . . " She floundered, not wanting to say the word.

"Sold as a slave?"

"Yes."

For a moment Serena was silent. She did not want this intimacy, yet the question had brought it all back, and the words of hate and sorrow, or half-madness and fury, trembled on her tongue.

"Please tell me," Caroline begged, "please. I want to know."

Serena turned away toward the door, as if she had not heard, but as her hand touched the knob, she spun around, a strange light in her eyes.

"My grandmother was captured in her village's war and taken by the Sudanese," she began in a rush. "They sold her to a French slaver captain and she was brought on his slave ship to Guadeloupe. My grandfather saw her and bought her. She was very beautiful, so says my mother. My mother, too, was beautiful, darker than I. 'The Mulatto,' everyone called her.

"My grandfather sold her when she had but fifteen summers. He sold her to my father. My father loved her and he did not keep her for a slave. She was mistress of his house and he had no other wife. I had three brothers. I am the youngest and only girl. My oldest brother was first sent to France to school, and then my father gave him money and he went to New Orleans. Another brother ran away to sea. The third died defending my mother during an uprising. My mother . . . " Here she stopped what had amounted to a toneless litany, and Caroline saw her throat convulse.

After a moment, Serena resumed in a somewhat shaky and low voice. "My mother died then, too. They hated her—the slaves—because she was of them, but not of them. The whites hated her, too, because she was beautiful and because she was the mistress of a rich man. Then I was twelve. When I was eighteen my father began to think of my protection. He wanted to send me to my brother, who had married a French lady and who was prospering in New Orleans. There, they did not know of his color. My father thought I, too, could pass for French.

"But he died of a sudden fever even as we waited for my brother's reply. My father's family—his cousins— came to the house. They took everything. And me, me they threw into the slave quarters and finally sold me to a slaver calling at Guadeloupe. The ship brought me to

Barbados, and there . . . there Master Welles bought me."

She stopped her recitation, her body trembling. Her mouth tightened to keep back the words that trembled there. *And he, a pig of a man, raped me and told me that my duties were for his pleasure, the care of his house, and maid to his wife, if she were found. And it is his child you wish to know about, not that of some unknown slave, as you think.*

"Serena," Caroline gasped, horrified. "You . . . why, you cannot stay here. There must be some way to go to your brother. I . . . does Joshua know?"

"He knows," the girl said dully. "Even with only some black blood, you are a slave. And your children are slaves, too, as I found out. It was no matter that I was of my father's white blood."

"But you must do something," Caroline urged, her own predicament, even her own helplessness, forgotten.

"I will do something," Serena said, "one day. But I cannot run away. They would set the dogs after me and men with muskets, and I would die, if I were lucky."

Caroline shivered. Rosa had been lucky; she had died before they caught her.

There was no appeal to Joshua. She knew better than to suggest it. What would become of Serena and the baby "fairer than I am"? What, for that matter, would become of her and her own child?

"I am as helpless as you," she said aloud.

"Yes, Madame."

"I am so sorry, Serena."

"Yes, Madame. May I go now?" *I must go,* Serena thought, *before I break down before this woman and tell her everything.*

"I am sorry," Caroline said again, inadequately. "Yes, go, of course. But I will be your friend, Serena."

Friend! Serena had a vision of such friendship and Welles seeing it and then herself and Nicole. . . . With monumental effort she drew herself up. Looking Caroline full in the face, she said arrogantly, "I want no whites as friends. They have done enough to me."

The insolence of it made Caroline recoil. "Go, then," she said coldly. "See if you fare better among the blacks."

Serena turned and left the room hurriedly. Her breasts

were heaving with a mixture of emotions, and she wanted to scream her torment to the heavens.

She went to her own quarters and the old midwife, Betsy, rose from her place near the crude cradle. "She ben sleepin'," she said.

Serena nodded, unable to speak. The door had hardly closed when her passions broke loose and she flung herself upon her cot, weeping and writhing until the noise awakened the baby, who added her lusty infant wails to Serena's own.

Still sobbing, she went to the child and, picking it up, carried it back to her own cot. Seeing the pink mouth opened, the eyes screwed shut, and the pale cheeks flushed with weeping, the child was suddenly an alien in her arms, and no longer hers any more than any infant animal. She thought of the kittens again and of Joshua's commands for Caroline's baby, and a madness seized her. Why not? Why not drown this strange creature that had been forced upon her? She could see the river in her mind and the infant floating in it, quiet at last. "Food for the fishes," she whispered. Hearing her voice, Nicole's sobs lessened and she gulped in an infinitely sad breath. Nicole! Serena shook her head as if awakening from a nightmare.

What had she been thinking? She pressed the child to her frantically. It uttered one sharp cry, then renewed its wailing.

"Hush, hush," Serena soothed, fumbling at her buttons and finally nudging her nipple into the open mouth.

Nicole dug her tiny fists into her mother's breast, making greedy sucking noises of contentment. Serena stared down at her, watching her own tears falling gently on the baby's downy head.

She had soothed the child to sleep again and had begun to undress herself when Charity brought word that Caroline Welles's own time had come.

And June was less than half over, she thought as she left her quarters and hurried after Charity to the plantation house. Coming to Caroline's room, she found Joshua just leaving it, his face a thundercloud.

"You go to Betsy and tell her she is needed," Serena instructed Charity.

"No!" Joshua's voice was like a whiplash. "One is sufficient. Leave her, Charity." The girl scurried away.

"I cannot," Serena said in a low voice. "I know nothing of birthing, save my own. The child will die."

"The child will die in any case," he reminded her.

"But Mistress Welles, she will die, too, perhaps."

"I care not," he answered. "Do as I order." He seized her arm and thrust her inside the chamber, slamming the door behind him.

A dim taper cast feeble light upon the bed, where Caroline moaned with each contraction.

At her approach, Caroline roused herself to whisper, "Serena?"

"Yes, Madame."

"Oh. It will be difficult for me," she said.

"How long are you like this?"

"Right after you left the chamber. I . . . I was too angry to call. . . ." She broke off, gripping the counterpane and pressing her lips to still her cries.

"Only two hours," Serena said.

"How long?" Caroline whispered.

"Soon, now," Serena lied. How long? She had no idea. Hours, perhaps, and already Caroline was sick and weary. She would never last for hours. If only Serena knew what to do. Betsy would know.

She leaned over Caroline. "I will be right back," she said softly. "Try not to be frightened. It makes it worse." Betsy's advice; that, at least, she remembered.

She managed to slip out of the house without encountering anyone, and when she returned some minutes later, armed with scissors and twine and what sketchy information she could absorb from Betsy, she went into the kitchen and asked for warm water to be sent up.

Coming along the upper corridor, she found Joshua once again at Caroline's door.

"Where were you?" he demanded.

"I must have twine and scissors," she said as placidly as she could. "Cookie will send water. I told her to leave it outside the door."

"Good. See that no one enters. When her time is near, call me. I wish to have the first look at the little bastard."

"Yes, master," she answered quietly, then slipped past him into the room.

Serena's hands and voice were gentle, and her face

remained tranquil whenever she leaned over to speak
to Caroline or direct her. But something in Serena's manner beneath the surface calm communicated itself to
Caroline, and between one long and agonizing contraction and the next, she whispered, "Something is wrong,
isn't it?"

"Nothing," Serena answered.

"Please," Caroline begged, "tell me the truth."

"The baby is taking a long time," Serena said reluctantly. "I have heard of such matters when the feet are
born before the head."

"And what does that mean?" Caroline asked.

"Just that it will take longer." Serena's voice was low,
and before Caroline could ask the next question, the pain
seized her again. She could feel a wild convolution of her
belly, a sharper pain, and then it receded, leaving her
spent.

The windows were closed against the evil effects of night
air and the room was stifling. Caroline stirred herself as
Serena wiped her face with a damp cloth and whispered,
"Please, open the window."

"It is bad . . ." Serena began.

"Please, please. 'Tis no matter . . . 'tis bad as it is."
And she began to moan again.

This time, lying in the brief trough between the waves
of agony, she felt the cooling balm of soft night winds and
breathed deeply several times. It eased her discomfort, and
when the next contraction came, as she drew in a breath of
sweet air it somehow seemed less painful. The pains began
to come faster now with less respite in between, so that
for a long time the world became nothing more than a gray
void in which she labored and wept and cried out. Once,
as she tried to breathe, she caught the scent of a night-
blooming flower and was for an instant transported to that
island in the Bahamas. It seemed to her that she could
hear the water cascading down the rocky ledges to splash
into the lagoon and could almost see that paradisical haven
and Domino coming toward her. She whispered his name
and Serena bent over her.

"What is it?" she asked. "Who do you call?"

And Caroline came back to the misery of the present.
"No one," she said faintly. "No . . . oh!" She broke off.
Her body was turning itself inside out as it sought to expel
its burden. Dimly, she realized that the worst of the pain

had diminished. Instead, she could feel within herself a slippery squirming and knew it was her child wiggling free.

Yet the convolutions persisted, stronger and stronger so that she felt as if her entire abdomen had drawn back from her bones like the casing of a sausage.

"It is nearly over," she heard Serena say. "Push hard, Madame. Yes, yes, like that."

Caroline strained and strained. There was a piercing, sharp pain and she screamed against it. It was over—over, and still the small body in her body wriggled and slithered and slipped.

"Head—the head has come first, after all," Serena said, and there was awe in her voice. "Bear down now, please, Madame." Again the effort and again the pain, only each was infinitely less now.

"*Et voilà. Elle est arrivée,*" Serena said, lapsing unconsciously into her mother tongue.

A girl, then, Caroline thought, but the thought drifted away from her. I must see her, she said to herself, but her body would not respond. Her eyes closed and her head dropped to one side. All pain was gone. Peace. She sank into it, scarcely conscious of her surroundings.

Serena, her own body damp, sank for a moment upon the end of the bed and felt the weariness in her muscles. She looked down at the infant in her lap and again experienced the wondering surprise of actual birth. There was more to do. What had Betsy said? Oh, wrap up the child and lay it aside and tend to the mother.

She rose hurriedly to comply. Caroline lay unresisting under these final ministrations. She is unconscious, Serena thought. So much the better for what must follow. She wrapped up the stained bedclothes and deposited them on the floor, laying fresh linen upon Caroline and drawing the coverlets over her. Caroline stirred and murmured unintelligibly but did not awaken.

Taking the baby up, Serena went to summon Joshua and found him just outside the door. He viewed the infant girl, held in Serena's two hands. He did not need to see the child to know; Serena's low murmur told him. And staring at the child who had yet to utter its first cry, any doubts he might have entertained vanished forever. Black curly hair of a thickness uncommon to infants covered its head and long black lashes swept down to meet olive cheeks. This was no child of his, and it did not even have a mark of the Rowland family. He knew now without a doubt that this was, after all, the pirate's bastard. His mouth tightened in fury and he had to force himself not to seize the baby then and there and dash its brains out upon the floor.

"Drown it," he hissed between clenched teeth.

"Yes, master," Serena answered stoically.

"A pity," he said, raising his voice, "that the child is dead . . . born too soon."

The words reached Caroline and she stirred. "Dead!" she echoed. "My baby! Give me my baby!"

At a gesture from Welles, Serena hurried from the room, carrying the naked infant. Halfway down the stairs it uttered its first cry, a cry muffled against Serena's bosom. As she crossed the garden, she heard Caroline's scream, high pitched and desperate, and then came a wild and stormy sobbing that echoed and reechoed as she made the infant ready.

Chapter Fifteen

For two weeks following the birth, Caroline lay weak and apathetic upon her bed, seeing no one save Serena and Charity. The latter regularly brought concoctions made by her mother to help Caroline recover.

She knew that her sickness was less of the body then of the mind, but she could summon no will to fight. Joshua, pleading business in Williamsburg, had absented himself within a few days of her confinement.

At last, under the patient persistence of Charity and Serena, Caroline finally roused herself to dress and go downstairs each morning. She spent most days sitting staring into space, a book, unread, lying on her lap.

On her first venture onto the grounds, she came upon the grave of her child, a tiny mound over which a small stone read: CAROLINE ELLEN JUNE 12, 1762.

The single date, plus the horrified realization that the child had been given her name, broke through her apathetic state. Falling to the ground, she wept uncontrollably, her face pressed into the earth, her arms forming a semicircle above her head, as if she would gather the remains of her child to her.

Time stood still as she lay there, and when at last her sobs eased and she struggled erect, a sense of purpose had begun to form.

She had, she realized, wavered between leaving Joshua and resigning herself to her fate and had taken no opportunity to effect escape. Her wishes and daydreams were only that. If she could hope to flee, she would need a plan and money. She had neither. Always any plan had melted before the fact of her penniless state and the knowledge that there was no place she could run to once she had decided that her dream of finding Domino was merely a dream on which she had built her slender hopes.

At the graveside, she saw that the time for resolution had come: accept her lot and forget her dreams, or put action to her desire and form to her dream.

Leaving, she faced a future she could not see; staying, she faced Joshua and a return to his presence in her bed and yet another confinement. Of the two, she would prefer the blind future.

Accepting that, she rose to her feet, her eyes clearer and her head held high once more.

I have my jewelry, she thought rapidly as she went back to the house. With it, I can book passage on the first ship I can find. South. New Orleans. She remembered that Serena had told her of a brother living there. Or she could go to Martinique, now in English hands, where she might learn something of Domino, or back to England, there, to throw herself on her family's mercy, if necessary. This last course seemed the least likely, for what complaint could she bring of Joshua beyond the fact that he disgusted her by his touch, and bored her by his conversation and his posturing? No, England, which had seemed a haven in Nassau, now loomed as yet another prison.

Having decided on some course, at least, she began to feel more like herself, and her natural strength and vigor came flooding back.

Once, just before Joshua's return, she thought of confiding in Serena and offering to take her and the baby along. But she rejected the idea now, remembering Serena's cold withdrawal from her earlier offer of help and friendship.

She took inventory of her jewelry, selecting only that which had come to her as part of her wedding gifts or which she had been given before her marriage.

Everything lay in her timing; she knew that. Joshua had said he would return on the sixteenth or seventeenth of July. If she left too soon, she risked meeting him at one of the seaports. No, she must leave by barge just a day or two before he would return. In that way she would be reaching Newport News after he left Williamsburg.

With all her plans laid and with the meager, necessary

preparations made, she began to mark the passage of days with expectancy. As the fifteenth approached, her anticipation made her exceedingly tense. No lady, she knew, should travel alone without so much as a house servant. Yet, who could she take? Charity was far too young, and Serena was already discarded as a possibility. The others she would not trust. No, she would have to make the voyage to Newport News alone. There, perhaps, she could hire a white servant or buy an indentured one before proceeding south.

On the morning of the fourteenth, she was ready and sent word that she would have the barge brought to her, as she meant to go visiting.

"Just after lunch," she said. That would give her five hours to sunset. The barge would be well downriver by then and close to Newport News, if not actually there.

She spent the rest of the day in ordinary pursuits and managed to eat a fairly hearty meal. She went to her room immediately afterward and changed into clothing suitable for the voyage. She longed to pack a small portmanteau, but, fearful of giving away her secret, she dared not risk it.

As she stuffed the kerchief containing her jewels down the front of her bodice between her breasts, there was a tap on the door.

"Enter," she called. "I am ready."

"Are you, my dear?" Joshua said. "Ready for what, may I ask?"

At the sound of his voice, her knees turned to water. Too late! Too late! her brain chanted.

"You haven't answered me," he said, advancing into the room and catching her arm in a vise-like grip.

"I . . . I was going visiting upriver to . . . to see the Burrs," she improvised.

"To see the Burrs? And when did you make their acquaintance, pray, tell? As I recall, you were indisposed when they called on us last month, and they have not been back since. I feel certain, since I saw Burr himself in Williamsburg only this morning."

"I . . . I was bored," she continued to stammer.

"Then why not visit the Blairs, who are so close that a sedan chair would take you, rather than a barge? And you have met the Blairs. Remember, they are of the same family you knew in Williamsburg."

"Please, Joshua," she said, "what is wrong with you? You are hurting my arm."

"I will hurt more than that," he rasped. "You are well enough, I see, Mistress Welles, well enough. You have recovered from your ordeal and from the death of the pirate's bastard. Oh, yes," he said as she started, "I know. I saw it. You know, there is an old superstition that whoever a child grows to resemble, the mark of his father is on him in the few moments after birth. I saw that mark, my dear—a fully formed babe, and plump . . . no premature child, and no child of mine." He spat out these last words and flung her brutally across the room. The force of the fall stunned her, and before she could rise he was over her, pulling her to her feet and raining blows across her face and shoulders.

"Whore!" he cried. "Slut! Damn you to hell!"

She could not defend herself against the sudden attack. She cowered, covering her face as best she could behind her crossed arms. Her head was ringing and her heart was galloping through her chest like a mad thing.

"Well, you shall learn what whores are worth. By God, I would strangle you now, would have smothered you as you lay screaming for your brat, were it not for my business with your father. A live daughter has more family ties than a dead one without issue. But you will suffer every day of your life for this."

He was panting heavily from exertion and he ceased the beating, pushing her over on the bed while he stood, holding one of its posts, drawing ragged breaths, his eyes insane with unsatiated rage, his skin patched with red.

She dared not move, fearful of bringing about a fresh onslaught. After a time his breathing returned to normal and he said, "Get up." She obeyed mechanically, coming face to face with him.

He ripped the cap from her head and slashed the front of her gown with one movement. The stomacher fell away and the kerchief containing the jewels was revealed.

"What is this?" he ejaculated. Seizing the kerchief, he unrolled it. The jewels lay twinkling up at him, and he uttered a sharp, cruel laugh.

"Visiting, eh? Where were you going with these?"

She did not answer, and when he repeated the question again and still drew no response, he slammed his fist against her cheek, staggering her with the blow.

"I don't know," she managed to say. "I wanted to go away."

"Go away? Where? To find your pirate? To play woman of the streets?"

She shook her head. "England," she lied. "I wanted to go home."

"You will never see home again," he said with finality, "nor leave this plantation again. Here you are, and here you stay." He advanced on her once more, his eyes deadly. Her bodice was ripped from her and her gown and underskirts, too, each item torn as if he took pleasure in the sound of the ripping cloth. And when she was naked at last, he threw her upon the bed. She lay there unresisting, knowing resistance to be futile. He was at once atop her, fully clothed, save for his breeches. She closed her eyes, thinking somehow she must bear this. Seconds later, he had turned her on her face and mounted her. Her breasts, still engorged no matter how often she expelled the milk, throbbed against this pressure. Her face was pressed into the bedclothes so that she could scarcely breathe. She felt her thighs pried apart. Then a horrible, agonizing pain tore through her body as he thrust himself through the narrow opening between her buttocks.

Her screams were muffled into the bedclothes. Between the lack of air and the unbearable pain, she thought surely she would die.

When it was over, he left her without a word and went to his own room. Shakily, she stood up and realized that she was torn and bleeding. She went to the commode to cleanse herself and suddenly a deep revulsion overcame her and she vomited wretchedly into the water.

If she had strained at the bonds of her life prior to that evening, she was hopelessly imprisoned now. As the days passed, Joshua took an insane pleasure in debasing her. Sometimes it would be only an insult in front of Serena; sometimes it was physical cruelty, such as pinching her throat or breast until she cried out; once, coming to her as she lay sleeping, he tore off the covers and thrust his member into her mouth, himself burrowing between her thighs while she fought the nausea that this act inflicted, and then, at the moment of his climax, he bit her so cruelly she fainted.

She grew thin and sickly under this and would think

with longing of reaching the embankment and hurling herself into the flowing river.

He began to bring guests to the house, at which time he would play the worried and benevolent husband until she thought she must scream out the truth. The Blairs eyed her with gravity, as if she were on the verge of death. The Burrs were similarly pitying, and Mrs. Burr, a quiet, slender lady, was bold enough to say that "a voyage, perhaps, my dear, after your sorrow, would do wonders for you."

"She is too weak yet to travel," Joshua answered for her, "or else we should have visited you before this."

And then, just as she feared her mind would snap and she would begin to scream and scream and never stop, deliverance appeared at her table one night.

Almost every duty at the plantation had been taken out of her hands. Serena reigned over the household while she, Caroline, was its mistress in name only. Joshua ordered their lives otherwise and frequently would not advise her of guests who might be coming to luncheon or supper until an hour before the guests made their appearance. Then, as she tried to prepare to greet them, he would hamper her by sending Charity out while he recited the names and backgrounds of the people she was expected to greet with a smile and entertain as well as her "health" would permit. Failure on her part resulted in one of his nightly visits.

It seemed to Caroline that he was a very different man on those occasions and that he took a voluptuous delight in the pain he inflicted, talking to her in a low, drawling voice, as if he himself had been only lately awakened before he came to tear her rudely from her uneasy slumber.

However, one sultry, sullen evening at the end of July, he came to her room and, settling himself with every appearance of affability, told her that she was to expect seven supper guests the following evening and one house guest who would spend several days with them.

"The Burrs, the Chiswells—the Marshes whom you met in Williamsburg are staying with them—and Byrd Travers. We shall be nine at the table. Travers is a bachelor. You are to be particularly agreeable to him, as I have business with him that I wish to conclude on this visit."

"Yes," she answered tonelessly.

"Travers himself is shrewd but somewhat lacking in

the manners you are accustomed to . . . or perhaps I misjudge you. Tell me, did your pirate have good manners?"

She did not answer and he repeated the question as an order.

"He seemed mannerly enough," she replied.

"Oh, he seemed mannerly enough," he mimicked. " 'If it would please you, ma'am, come to my bed,' and you replied, 'Oh, sir, I shall be honored.' And I reckon you performed a stately minuet before you retired gracefully to his cot?"

"No," she answered almost inaudibly.

He was about to pursue it and then suddenly veered on his course. "We will let that rest for the moment. Please see that you are particularly well gowned for this dinner. I want no suggestion that you are overly melancholy. Travers is important to me."

"If he is such a friend of yours, why have we not seen him before?" she asked.

"Friends? Travers is hardly that. He is a planter of sorts, entirely owing to his mother. Old Travers was a backwoods farmer, some say a former bondsman, who caught the fancy of one of a planter's daughters. I cannot remember her first name. It hardly matters. She eloped with Travers to his shack and was not seen again in society. But on her death her son inherited land left to her by her father. It is beautiful, rich land. Some of it adjoins my own estate, and it is that land that I want. Travers has agreed to negotiate."

"I fail to see how I can be of any assistance," she said.

"You can entrance him. You know so well how to entrance men. And he will be softened by the thoughts of becoming friends and visiting us again. Ergo, I will consummate the contract more to my advantage than otherwise."

"And when I have entranced him, sir, will you come to my chamber and beat me for being a whore?" she said, with a brief return of her old spirit.

"Take care," he answered silkily, "or I will beat you for being a whore today so that your bruises will not be evident tomorrow."

She flinched and he smiled and stood up. "Your best toilet, ma'am."

On the following day, Caroline called Charity to her

early and spent twice the amount of time she had spent of late in dressing.

She bathed as she used to bathe, then washed her hair and had Charity brush it dry in the hot sunlight pouring through her open window.

Charity had yet to grow expert at the powdering, and today, as Caroline sat huddled, her face well into the paper cone, Charity dusted so liberally that a thick film settled on the dressing table and carpet, as well as on Caroline's negligee and Charity's clothes. She choked and sputtered as the starch filled her nostrils but went on without pause until Caroline signaled her to stop.

She herself coughed as she came away from the cone and into the clouds of powder drifting over them. Seeing Charity behind her in the mirror, literally covered from head to foot and looking much like a small and cheerful ghost, she laughed out loud for the first time since her confinement.

"Ah lak yo' laughin', mistiss," Charity said, delighted. "Yo' han't laugh in a long time."

"No," Caroline answered, her face sobering. "No, I haven't, have I?"

"Laugh some moah," Charity begged, and the request was so comical that Caroline laughed again in spite of herself.

"Come," she said, "brush away the powder and help me dress, or else I shall be late."

"Somebody comin' now," Charity answered.

"Where?"

"Up de road fum de rivah."

"You can hear them?"

"Yes, mistiss. Ear lak de fox, mah mammy say; eye lak de hawk." She giggled. "And mouf lak de layin' hen, my pappy say."

Caroline laughed again. "Fetch the pink-and-silver gown," she said. It was the one that she had worn the evening Joshua Welles had proposed to her. Why, it was over a year since then. How gay she had been then, how carefree, how sure of herself and of being able to bend fate to her will. Instead, it was she who had bended, she who was breaking. Pain clogged her throat and her eyes clouded.

"Oh, mistiss," Charity said, tying the hoops, "yo' too

small in de waist an' too big in de bosom. Dis gown don'
nevah fit now."

"Tie the ribbons tighter, Charity. Serena has altered
the gown," Caroline answered, wincing as her breasts
strained against the cloth.

Finished at last, she surveyed herself in the mirror. Her
skin was very white, with none of the color it used to
have. Against it, her dark brows and lashes looked black
. . . and her eyes! Wonderingly, she peered in the mirror.
The eyes reflected there were those of a stranger, the
blue color grayed, as if reflecting the shadows beneath.

The pink embroidery on the gown was the only color
noticeable. Silver and white. All of her. Like a gray lady.
"Goodness," she sighed, "I am much changed."

"Yo' be change, mistiss, when yo' don' smile lak ah
tole yo'. Yo' laugh and then yo' be all pink again. Laugh,"
she coaxed, stretching her lips into a comical grin.

Caroline gave her a shaky smile. "I vow, Charity, you
would make even the hangman smile at you."

"Yo' be a slave, my pappy say, yo' mout will smile
'cause nobody care fo' yo' trouble. Smile an' then yo'
mout feel bettah."

"Very good advice," Caroline said, patting Charity's
plump arm. "I shall try to follow it."

"Entrance him," Joshua had said. Summoning strength
from somewhere inside herself, Caroline went down to
greet Joshua's guests.

It was a merry party that gathered around the lavish
table. Serena, Caroline had to admit, was as well able as
she, if not more so, to oversee a splendid menu.

Terrapin soup was followed by bass smothered in a
delicate sauce, the likes of which Caroline had never
tasted, and it was accompanied by a local vegetable known
as wild rice, which grew plentifully in the marshy sections
of the land. There followed fresh veal from a recently
slaughtered calf, boned and wrapped around a lightly seasoned stuffing, and the smoked ham, so dear to Virginia
hearts, pink and moist and tender and very different in
both texture and flavor from the ones normally served at
supper. Then came snap beans, crunchy with nutmeats,
tiny carrots swimming in butter sauce, and browned
Charleston rice touched with spicy herbs. And among the

rich variety of desserts was a thick, custardy cream, rum-flavored and cold.

"The meal reminds me of my stay in Paris," said Mr. Chiswell at the end of this Lucullan banquet. "Strike me blue, if it doesn't. My compliments, ma'am," he said to Caroline, on whose left he had been seated.

She murmured a reply to his courteous remark and looked at Byrd Travers, who sat on her right.

He had not been easy to entrance. Indeed, he showed no promise of ever succumbing to what charms she might still possess. A heavy-set man of medium height, with dark, thick brown hair he wore unpowdered and shorter than the current fashion, he had confined himself mainly to listening to her forced chatter, making a brief response when, indeed, he spoke at all. He regarded her out of light, clear brown eyes that seemed to see beneath her artificial gaiety.

In a moment she would rise, then the ladies, and they would withdraw, leaving the gentlemen to their brandy and snuff. Luke, one of the footmen in attendance, had just placed Joshua's music box containing the snuff at his elbow, definitely her signal to depart.

Delaying another moment, she said, "Mr. Travers, I have scarcely heard you speak this evening."

"I was enchanted by your witty conversation, ma'am," he answered with heavy gallantry in his first effort at a compliment.

"You are too kind, sir," she answered lightly. "We anticipate your stay with us and hope to hear something of Richmond."

"Ah," said Mr. Chiswell, overhearing this last, "you must take care, ma'am. Mr. Travers will enlist your aid in his campaign to transfer the capital of Virginia to Richmond."

"Not at all," Travers demurred. "I only say it is more naturally suited than Williamsburg. Roads leading to it are better, and it is at the head of navigation on the James, so that approach by land or by sea is simpler."

"I cannot venture an opinion," Caroline said. "I do not know Richmond, and I found Williamsburg most stimulating, if difficult to reach."

"Spoken with the tongue of a true diplomat, ma'am," Chiswell applauded.

"Spoken truly," Travers added, and this time he smiled at her, a spark in his eyes.

At last, she thought, and a moment later she summoned the other ladies with her eyebrows and led them from the room.

She did not have another opportunity to speak to Travers. It was a long day and evening, with a musical entertainment offered between lunch and supper by a harpsichordist and violinist whom Joshua had sent for from Williamsburg. It was too muggy to stroll overlong in the gardens, and even the setting sun did not bring much relief.

By the time supper had ended and the guests had taken their departure up the river on their barges, now lighted by torches held steadily by slaves, Caroline was glad to excuse herself and leave Joshua and Travers alone.

She could not tell how Joshua considered the evening to have gone, but waking up in the morning after a night of uninterrupted sleep, she presumed he had been well enough satisfied.

Between lunch and supper the following day, Caroline found she was too restless to take her customary nap. The heavy weather had not lifted, but the sun had disappeared behind thick, ominous clouds, and from the distance a low growl of thunder heralded the approaching storm long before the rains came.

She prowled through the house like a caged lion, finding each room empty and silent. Finally, she settled in the library, wishing that there were some light fare with which she might divert herself. If Joshua were a reader, there would be such, she thought. Instead, the library had little in the way of amusing novels, and those she had read and reread until their charm was gone. Nevertheless, she selected one and leafed through to find favored passages.

She was thus absorbed when Byrd Travers, in search of diversion himself, entered.

"I beg your pardon, ma'am," he said on finding her there, and made as if to withdraw.

"No, please stay, Mr. Travers. It is very dull today, is it not?"

"No longer," he answered. "You have a magnificent library, ma'am."

"My husband's collection," she replied.

"Do you spend much time here?"

"Yes, more lately, since . . ." She stopped and changed the subject. "Tell me about your life in Richmond," she said.

"Oh, it is not very different from life elsewhere in the Colony. It is a small town, although set, like Rome, on seven hills. It is very beautiful. My plantation lies to the northwest of it."

"But I thought your lands were near our own."

"And that we were neighbors? Alas, no! I have a small parcel that ends at the line of your land. It is a parcel I kept for sentiment, as my mother was born on it, but that was many years ago, and the original house has long since been leveled by fire, and never rebuilt."

"Then you are not truly attached to it?"

He shook his head. "I am more attached to my father's land near the Blue Ridge Mountains. I love the mountains. Perhaps that is why I prefer the rolling hills of Richmond to this flatland."

"Why, Mr. Travers, you are most eloquent once you begin to speak."

" 'Tis the company, ma'am," he returned.

"Oh, Mr. Travers, you are most agreeable," Caroline answered. She was more at ease now that she was on the familiar ground of gallant paying compliments. Consequently, she responded with the coquetry natural to her, smiling, flashing quick looks of admiration, and fluttering her lids. Artfully, she drew him out until she felt that she knew all of Richmond and of his life there and in the woods that he could possibly remember himself.

Backwoodsman his father might have been, but he had been well tutored there and had actually been sent to school in England for a short period. It accounted for the odd mixture of the ordinary and aristocratic that she had noted on first meeting him. He was far from fine-featured. His hands were the hands of a workman, and his body bore the heavy muscularity of generations of yeomen; yet, he was well spoken and, if not brilliant, certainly intelligent. He was correct in his manners, if clumsy in their execution. Altogether he was interesting in his very contrasts.

"I should like to see Richmond one day," she said at last, rising from her chair.

"I should be honored," he answered, coming swiftly to

his feet so that he faced her, his eyes only slightly above hers. She tilted her head and met his glance. She saw the flicker of awakened interest in his face before he lowered his eyes. A tiny spark of awareness shimmered between them and Caroline stood there a moment longer before stepping back.

As she did, she saw his eyes go rapidly over her body and come to rest at her bosom, saw the slight rise of his chest. Then, laying a light hand on his arm, she said softly, "You have been kind to while my lonely hour away with me."

"Lonely, ma'am?" He looked at her searchingly.

"Lonely," she answered softly. "But I have kept you overlong. Please excuse me."

"Hardly overlong," he said. Looking at the hand on his arm, he pressed his own hand over it a moment, then released it, saying, "I trust we shall have further opportunity to speak before I take my departure."

"Oh, yes," she said carelessly, "here or in the gardens. I am generally to be found in either on most days. And then, surely, you will visit us again."

"I hope so, ma'am."

With a last flutter of her lashes, she left the room.

Two days after her meeting with Travers in the library, Caroline awoke to find Joshua standing by her bed, shaking her.

"The *Charlotte* has arrived," he said tersely. As she started to get up in delight, he pushed her back. "You are to remain in your room," he said. "I shall lock you in. I know you are able to secrete yourself in holds, Caroline. I will not have Ramsey at the house. If there be any messages, I shall bring them to you . . . after I have seen that they are messages I wish you to receive."

It was useless to argue; she knew that, just as she knew he would offer some palatable lie to Ramsey about her illness being a reason to keep the house quiet and free of visitors. As for messages, she doubted there would be any he would let her have.

By the following morning the *Charlotte* had sailed again, and Joshua, coming to release her from her day's imprisonment, brought a letter from her mother. It was a silly, inconsequential letter, describing Jane's wedding and Anne's forthcoming festivities and saying the wedding of

King George and Princess Charlotte had taken place amidst much splendor. There was no mention of her own letter. It was signed, "Your affectionate mother."

" 'Tis not a letter that demands a reply," she said to Joshua. "Still, she will think it strange if I do not answer."

"I answered for you, my dear wife," he said with a sneer. "And now, please be up and about your duties. Our guest missed you last evening. Oh, by the way," he added carelessly, "it seems your father has been named earl of Stour at last. Your brother is now Viscount Ashford, and I believe this all gives you and your sisters the right to be called Lady—Lady Caroline . . . hardly a fitting title for a strumpet. You will not use it."

"I care not," she answered indifferently. "May I have Charity, please? 'Twould not do to have Mr. Travers see me in so poor a state."

Charity came to her with an air of such repressed excitement that she seemed ready to burst.

"What is it?" Caroline asked.

For answer, Charity withdrew a letter from beneath her apron, saying in a loud whisper, "Yo' mout say naught, mistiss. Dey cap'n give it to me. Say yo' pappy done say give um on'y to yo'. Cap'n give me a penny." She held up a copper penny, beaming. "On'y whut ah mout buy wid it ah don' know."

"Save it," Caroline advised. "I shall give you another to match it. Now, do be quiet, Charity, while I read."

Her father's letter, while couched in affectionate terms and with many paternal misgivings about her present situation, dashed any faint hopes she might have entertained about succor from that source.

Her complaints had alarmed him and he feared that she would attempt some rash action. It was for this reason that he had sent his letter under the rose with instructions to Ramsey to see that it came to no eyes but her own.

He reminded her that her husband was not a man to be trifled with and that she must on no account antagonize him. "A woman belongs to her husband," the letter ran in part, "and not even the fondest father might legally interfere with that husbandly right."

Were she to attempt to return to London, no justice in the land would uphold her right to leave her husband's bed and board. Divorce was unthinkable, save, of course,

for a husband's right to dissolve the bonds in the case of
adultery on his wife's part. In this last instance, he begged
her to be grateful for her husband's protection. There had
been other cases of abduction by pirates and the like in
which the husband had been unwlling to reclaim "damaged
goods."

In short, she was to count her blessings, obey her husband, and all would be well. He signed the letter affectionately. He confessed to missing her "saucy ways," but
he made it clear that Joshua's wishes were of paramount
importance.

When she had finished reading it, she tore it into small
pieces and threw it into the chamber pot. England and
home were forever behind her. While she had expected
little more, the reality of her position struck her with great
force. She was alone. And if she hoped again to find any
happiness at all, it must be by her own wits.

Byrd Travers was due to leave Wildwood by the end
of the week. Joshua, who had yet to conclude his business,
grew nervous and short-tempered as the week drew to a
close.

Caroline, harried and abjured by him to spend more
time with Travers, found this was not easy to accomplish.
Although he had spent some part of each day engaging
her in conversation, it was always of short duration, and
not again had there been the opportunity that had presented itself in the library.

He was always circumspect and always noncommittal
about returning to visit. She sensed that he found her attractive, but, save for a deepening expression or an extravagant compliment, he gave no indication of more than
a passing and casual interest in this visit.

"I have done my best," she said to Joshua. "He enjoys
our company and would accept other invitations. I can do
no more. The wonder to me is why he came at all, had
he not intended to sell the land to you."

"He will sell it—but at a price I do not wish to pay."

"I cannot see how my efforts will make him lower his
price," she said.

"No, of course not. Even Travers is too much the gentleman for your tastes. Something rough and coarse to
match your own nature, and you would long since have
captured him."

"Is it your intention that I bed with him?" she asked contemptuously and he pressed her wrists together with a harsh twist.

Wincing, she said, "Let me go, Joshua, for if you hurt me now, I will scream, and then Mr. Travers can learn, as well as the rest of Virginia, how you abuse me."

He flung her away from him and said, "You will pay dearly enough when he has left the house, and the more dearly, because I must hold my temper now."

"I have two days yet of freedom," she said, a hot glow in her eyes. "And then shall you kill me, Joshua? For I would rather be dead than remain with you. Indeed, I have often thought of killing myself in these past weeks. It would precipitate a scandal, Joshua, back in England and would perch on my father's shoulder."

"If that is your threat and I am to take it seriously, I shall chain you to your bed until the time when I no longer have any need for you," he grated out and strode from the room.

She paced her chamber after he had left, half-terrified at the thought of what her intemperate words would bring in retribution, half-elated because she had dared at last, if only for a moment, to confront him.

In this mood she joined the supper table with a certain nervous excitement that infected her humor and made her more brilliantly gay than she had been heretofore.

She saw that her mood annoyed Joshua, although he made a great effort to conceal it. Her carefree mood had stimulated Travers. Caught up in her own recklessness, she drank far more claret than she had intended to, and in this heightened mood she found that she was making many a foolish jest.

"My God," drawled Joshua at one point near the end of the meal, "this reminds me of the last evening aboard the *Charlotte* just before she was boarded."

"Indeed," Caroline rejoined gaily, "we were very merry that evening, without a thought of what would follow. And no one was merrier than you, my dear Joshua."

"Ah, that tale has reached even Richmond." Travers laughed. "Pardon me, but it was an adventurous tale."

"With a happy ending," Joshua said, smiling brittlely, "for I recovered my bride without having to pay ransom."

"A most happy ending," Travers agreed, his voice still merry but his face sobering.

"I will leave you now." Caroline rose unsteadily. "Please excuse me."

"We will join you in the drawing room very soon, my dear," Joshua said, knowing she meant to go to her own chamber.

The effects of the claret stayed with her. Left alone in the drawing room, the silence hummed noisily against her ears and she felt light-headed, as if she stood outside her own body, or as if she might at any moment leave it for a more familiar dwelling.

In this state, memories she had steeled herself against, lest they drive her mad, came rushing back to engulf her: the abduction itself and the smothering confines of the sea chest; El Loco falling atop her with his reeking body pressed close to her own; Domino . . . Oh! Domino and those days and nights beckoned her once more. Her heart beat wildly and her body ached with the effort to repress that scream. Were she to scream, she would never stop and would soon be taken for a madwoman.

"That's it," she half-whispered. "He must mean to drive me mad or to do some desperate act. He can't kill me himself, but . . ."

Never. Never. As much as life had lost its glow, never would she give Joshua this last triumph over her. Leave him, yes; let him face scandal and ridicule, yes, and die in that attempt—but not before she had revenged herself.

She was standing in the middle of the room, shaking, whispering to herself like someone demented. Caught in her own maelstrom of panic and rage and fear, she did not hear Travers enter, and his voice, breaking through her utter absorption, made her jump wildly.

"Ma'am what is it?" he asked, alarmed.

She looked at him, scarcely seeing him.

"N-nothing . . . n-nothing," she stammered, trying to recover her senses. "I have drunk too much wine, I fear. I am quite giddy."

"But also quite charming," he said in a low voice.

She looked at him, the haze beginning to clear, and she saw his face sharpen with desire.

"Where is Joshua?" she asked tremulously.

"Called away by some difficulty at the drying barns. He sent me to amuse you, as he may be somewhat delayed."

"Oh," she replied, thinking, so Mr. Travers is not immune to my charms at all; he wants me. Does he want me enough to take me away from this place? She swayed toward him, murmuring, "How fortunate, for I am not quite able to amuse myself any longer." She was very close to him, so close she could see the hairs that his razor had not taken away cleanly and smell the strong odors of brandy and leather and male sweat.

She raised her head, leaning back slightly, met his eyes, and let her own grow soft with invitation. With a muffled curse, he pulled her into his arms and pressed hungry lips upon her own. She had meant only to accommodate him in the hopes of winning him to her cause, but at the touch of his mouth a familiar excitement was reawakened and she pressed ardently against him, returning his kisses with a fervor equal to his own.

"Not here," he muttered at last, wrenching himself away. "Come to my room."

Swaying in the sudden release, she focused on him with difficulty and managed to say, "Sir, you forget yourself."

"Ma'am," he returned with mockery, "no more than you yourself."

"Joshua . . ." she began.

"Your husband, ma'am, is on his nightly absence. I swear, never have I known so many difficulties to crop up in one week on one plantation. No, ma'am, your husband will not return for some time. He makes his usual visit to one of the slave women. Which, I cannot say, nor yet how many. But I know that he has not made nightly visits to your chamber, ma'am."

"You . . . you cannot say such things," she spluttered. "Joshua detests the blacks. With them he is cruel and heartless and . . ."

"Cruel and heartless and he despises them, ma'am, but not the women. Come." He seized hold of her. "Do you imagine I did not see you are the much-neglected wife? Do you think a moment ago you did not reveal yourself?"

"I . . . I cannot," she said.

For answer, he took her once more in his arms, confidently expectant, and he was not disappointed, for she received his caresses as ardently as before. Only this time, she thought coolly, I will bargain with him. And he will take me away.

His mouth moved from hers and he began to kiss her throat and breasts with increasing impatience.

With an effort, she disengaged herself. "I will come to you," she said.

She went swiftly to her own chamber and left him to retire at a more leisurely pace. When she had finished her evening ablutions and sent Charity away, she crept down the hall to the guest room and stepped in.

Her hair, brushed free of powder, fell in ringlets over the silken robe and she advanced toward him smoothly.

"Beautiful," he murmured. " 'Tis a pity the robe must go." He undressed her slowly, stopping to caress her, to run his hands over her whole body, to press her against him. Long before he bedded her, she was alive with passion, so much so that she was scarcely aware of his entry until the wild surging of her body overcame her. "Hush," he whispered at her first cry, and taking the edge of the coverlet, he put it between her teeth so that her cries were muffled in her throat.

I liked it, she thought afterward in some amazement, and yet I have no particular affection for this man, save that he will deliver me from Joshua.

She roused herself on one elbow and looked down at him.

"Your husband wastes himself on others," he remarked, "and leaves you to pine." He stroked her breasts, laughing softly. "A double pleasure," he said.

"A double pleasure?"

"Bedding a woman such as yourself and cuckolding Welles at the same time."

"It pleases you to cuckold my husband?"

"Not as much as it pleasures me to have your body, but well enough." He pulled her down to kiss her breast and she drew back.

"I must go soon," she said.

"Not yet."

"Yes. It is one thing to make a fool of Joshua, but quite another to be killed for your pains."

"Tomorrow," he said.

"Yes, tomorrow, if you will promise me something."

"Anything."

"You sail for England this week?"

"Yes."

"Take me with you."

"Take you . . . but surely you do not imagine such news as that would not reach Welles at once. To be killed for my pains, indeed, that is not the worst. To be shot in a duel is one thing, but to be hanged from the gibbet in Williamsburg at the next public time . . . Why, a man stealing bread would be hanged. A man stealing a wife . . . ha! I might well be castrated first."

"Joshua will not know. I shall leave my clothes beside the riverbank and dress as a common bondswoman and you will take me as your servant."

"Impossible!" he exclaimed.

"You must," she begged. "You don't know what my life is like here. I will be dead within weeks if I remain here." Trembling, she poured out her story, or as much as she dared. "If I can reach London, I can find sanctuary with my father," she said.

"Even a father cannot keep a wife from her husband," he said.

"My father can," she said bitterly. "My father can do just about anything he chooses. Joshua would not dare go against him for that, as well as for other reasons. . . ."

"And how, pray, will I spirit you from Wildwood in bright sunlight aboard my barge?"

"I do not know," she admitted, "but there must be some way. I could wait farther along the embankment. Surely, you who know this river and countryside so well can advise me."

He looked at her curiously. "I think you have come to my bed only to achieve your escape from an onerous marriage."

"No more than you brought me here only for the sake of cuckolding Joshua," she answered, smiling at him.

He laughed. "A very imp of a woman," he said, reaching for her, but she eluded him and sprang from the bed, hastily donning her nightrobe.

"Tomorrow," she promised, "and, after that, many tomorrows."

She spent the next morning making a crude costume from a linen morning frock that had seen much wear and that she had been ready to give to Charity. Patiently, she tore holes and mended them, once or twice patching with bits snipped from a petticoat. She scraped at her shoes with her scissors until the red heels were well marked and torn and the shoes themselves split at the instep. These items she hid carefully at the back of her wardrobe, together with her jewelry. With a mob cap covering her hair, these things, and a dark shawl, she could well pass for a goody.

At lunch, she encountered Travers for the first time since the evening before and was grateful that Joshua was late in arriving, for the sight of Travers brought the color to her face, and the look in his eye was hard to mistake.

She ate silently, speaking only when she was spoken to and causing Joshua to remark that her merriment of the previous evening had left her dull on the morrow.

"Let us pray that your spirits are sufficiently recovered by evening," he said, "for it is Mr. Travers' last night. Will you join me, Travers?" he asked politely as he prepared to ride out to the fields.

"Later, if I may," Travers said smoothly. "I wish to go over those figures once more before we sign."

"As you please," Joshua said. "I did want another word on the matter."

Caroline excused herself and went to the library, leaving them to their talk.

Travers found her sometime later and literally seized her on entering, covering her face with kisses.

"I thought of you all night and morning," he said. "You left too soon last night."

"Just in time," she said, twisting away, "for I heard Joshua come in not long after."

"Come with me now," he said, seizing her once more.

"Have you lost your senses?" she exclaimed. "The sun is still bright and anyone might see us."

"Here, then," he said thickly.

"You have lost your senses," she said. Then pushing away from him, she walked to the door. He came after her, and as she reached the door, he grasped her, spinning her around and pinning her against the wall.

"Stop!" she commanded, but he paid no more attention to her than if she had been a passing breeze. Instead, he pulled her skirts up and her knickers down. Then, pushing her more firmly against the wall, he took her in short, quick thrusts before she realized what he was doing. The suddenness of it, the hard thrust, far from disgusting her, engendered a quick, primitive excitement, and spasms shook her long before he was done.

Having had his way, he reassembbled her clothing with as much gentleness as if he had been a shy and reticent lover.

"You are quick to show passion, Caroline," he said, using her name for the first time. "It would be a good journey to London."

"Would be? Will be," she said positively.

"I was mad last night," he told her. "But my sanity is restored now. I will carry messages to your father for you, but I cannot see any way to bring you with me."

"You promised," she accused.

"Be reasonable," he answered.

"You will take me on the morrow," she said with an icy calm she was far from feeling. "Or as soon as you leave the dock without me, I shall tell Joshua you raped me."

He stared at her. "I shall deny it. He will never believe you."

"Oh, I think he will," she said coldly, "for he has been longing for such a confession from me for months. He has other reasons to believe me. He knows I would not lie for the sake of being beaten yet again. Think about the matter and let me know your decision."

She left him in the library and went up to her chamber. At supper she sent word that she was too ill to join them. She expected that Joshua would arrive and compel her to go down, but he did not. When he came to her chamber after supper, he was glittering with self-satisfaction.

"It appears, my dear, you may be useful to me, after all," he said. "I mind me of Fauquier and only tonight Travers has cut his price. 'For friendship's sake,' said he, but I know well that it is the charm of my wife, for I think him to be smitten. We must keep him a friend. There are other dealings to be thought of. Yes, you may still be of use, after all. I know that courtesans serve kings well. Why not a whore as a planter? I may have misjudged the situation."

When he had left, Caroline lay smiling in the dark. Travers, she knew very well, had cut the price to mollify Joshua and lead him to feel friendly. That was very unwise, for now, should he leave her behind and should she carry out her threat, Joshua would believe that his gesture was made out of Travers' fear of discovery. She got up and crept to the door. Joshua was in the lower hall, preparing to leave the house, and after a time she heard Travers come up the stairs. He paused outside her door and then went on to his own chamber. She waited until his door was closed and then slipped out to follow him. Her entrance brought a swift protest from Travers.

"He will be back soon," Travers said in alarm. "He asked me to wait downstairs. I have only come up to fetch my snuffbox. His is quite empty."

"I did not come to you for pleasure," Caroline said quietly, "but to tell you that by lowering the price, you have given Joshua one more reason to believe me. Now, will you take me"—here she began to pull at her gown—"or shall I rip my clothes and begin screaming?"

"God forbid," he said, "don't do that."

"Answer me," she commanded.

"Answer you!" he growled. "What answer can I give?"

"You used me for your pleasure," she said. "Now you must pay for it."

"I will take you with me," he agreed sullenly.

"How?"

"The least dangerous plan I could think of was that you would manage to take a horse to the end of your land along the rolling road. I will wait for you in the barge until the lunch hour tomorrow."

"No," she said. "I cannot get a horse. I am not allowed one, as Joshua fears I will leave him. Take the barge up-river and send it back so it waits for me above the dock until eleven at night. I have some time to myself after supper and I can slip away then."

"Very well."

"But do not come back yourself, for if I fail and Joshua finds you aboard it, waiting, he will know you aided me. Send it back with as few oarsmen as possible—as if you were sending a message downstream. Instruct your lead man to take my orders, for if Joshua catches me I will lure him away. I must go now. I shall be ill-disposed on the morrow and unable to see you go away in the morning. Do not fail me, Travers, I will do as I say if the barge does not await me."

She left him speechless and returned to her own chamber. Done, she thought in cool triumph. Her earlier excitement had vanished. Now that the die was cast, a calmness descended upon her, and with it came an enormous sense of fatigue. She slept as she had not slept in many months and awoke well past the normal hour of rising.

Joshua, expansive now that he had gained his own ends, was nearly cordial. He came to her room after lunch to inquire about her health.

"I am better," she said. "I shall join you for supper."

"Very well." He looked at her with dawning speculation. "It seems you are more tractable of late," he said. "Perhaps punishment has made you see the light."

"Unjust punishment," she said.

He frowned. "That is what caused your ill use to begin with, Caroline—lies." He held up a hand to forestall her speaking. "I will hear no more of them. It is over. If you continue to behave, we may once again enjoy a reasonably tranquil life. After all, I still need heirs. And there are other advantages to you, as I now see so clearly from Travers' capitulation. Tell me, Caroline, did he make advances?"

"Travers!" she exclaimed, laughing. "Oh, Joshua, it was nearly the end of his visit before he would make any discourse of length with me. And then it was of the dullest sort. He is a ninnyhammer, at best. One can easily believe his father was a rough backwoodsman."

He smiled, pleased with the answer. "I shall see you at supper," he said. "We can talk further then."

The evening meal passed rather pleasantly, and Joshua seemed less inclined to leave the house when it was over. As in the old days, he retired to the drawing room, there to sit with his bottle of brandy, making light chatter with her and finally saying, "I think we will retire early, my dear."

Her heart sank. She had pleased him too much in her anxiety to calm his suspicions. It was nearly half ten. The barge would wait no longer than an hour, and it was a little more than a mile to the trysting place.

Stilling her panic, she said meekly, "I shall go now, then, and ready myself for bed."

"Leave your candle burning," he said idly. "I will follow you shortly." He was pouring out another brandy as she left.

She went swiftly up the stairs and into her room, where she snatched her bundle and hurried out again, going in stocking feet along the hall to the back stairs. She stole down them without a sound and a moment later was in the passageway leading into the kitchen. There she listened for several minutes, but there was no noise. She pushed open the door and found the room deserted. The smell of recent cooking and of washing up still hung in the air. In the vast hearth the fire hissed gently under its blanket of damp wood, its embers glowing faintly beneath.

Caroline crossed the kitchen and stepped out into the vegetable garden. Hugging the fence, she went swiftly down and through the gate leading to the house-slave quarters. She heard the cry of an infant and a crooning voice as she hurried past them. Well behind the quarters, she turned right so that her path brought her out to the line of trees surrounding the front lawn.

How long had she been gone? She could not judge. Clear of the ha-ha fence, she hurried down the dark lawn. Presently, the ground began to slant and she moved more slowly down the embankment until she reached the rolling road at the shore.

A large stand of trees jutted out at a point just below the dock and she slipped into them, twisting and turning in her huge skirts until she was in a small clearing. There, she stopped and with shaking hands removed all but her bodice and knickers and donned the clothes she had prepared. She gathered the removed clothing and threw it into the river, taking care to leave a scrap torn from her skirt upon a bush near the edge. She held the shoes in her hand and, taking a deep breath, then bent her head and scurried along the road toward that point beyond the dock where the barge waited.

On her left, the lawns of the plantation had disappeared and the ragged outcropping of scrub oak and alder hung over the embankment. She straightened up, sure now of her safety, for there had been no outcry behind her. Even if Joshua had discovered her gone, he would not yet have time to summon a search party.

Seconds later, a rustling in the brush above the embankment made her duck instinctively out of sight beneath the overhanging branches. Someone was coming, coming from the trees above her. Yet it was a curious sound, soft and slithering. An animal?

Almost as she thought it, a figure scrambled to the ground in front of her, and before she could move or call out, Serena was at her side, saying, "Hush. Make no sound."

"Serena, what are you doing here? How . . ."

"I have no time," Serena was whispering. "He will soon miss you. I knew what you planned. Never mind how I learned it. I have something. . . ." She stopped. "Your baby," she said abruptly, "it did not die. Do you hear me?"

"Did not?" Caroline said, dumbfounded.

"No. It lies above under the trees, and I must bring it to you. He ordered me to drown it." Caroline made a moan and Serena shook her. "Be clever, Madame. This is no time for foolishness. The baby is alive. I kept her in the slave quarters. I nursed her. I have much milk, enough for two. But he will kill me if he learns of this. So take it and go quickly. I will try to mislead the search as long as I can. Wait here." She was up the embankment in a flash of long legs and down again, bearing a bundle that she placed in Caroline's unresisting arms.

"See? Take her. Is your milk dried?"

"Not yet," Caroline said.

"Good. Feed her and it will come full. That is what Betsy tells me. Go. and . . . for my sake, I hope you are well away before Master Welles finds you gone."

Only half-aware of the fact that the soft, warm bundle against her was actually her own child, Caroline said, "But the grave . . ."

"A dead cat, wrapped in sheeting. Only the slaves know."

"But they . . ."

"They have no love for Joshua Welles," Serena said grimly, "no more than I do."

"Come with me," Caroline urged. "Bring your baby and come with me."

"No. I cannot. You may be looked for, but they will not bring you back in irons or flog you to death or shoot you on sight. Please." she begged as the baby began to whimper in its sleep, "hurry." She was back up the embankment before Caroline could speak again.

Dazed, she stumbled forward until she reached the barge. Four slaves sat at the oars. Upon seeing them, Caroline thought, they will take me to Travers, but Travers will not bring me to London with this child.

She climbed aboard the barge and said, "Take me down to Newport News."

"But, mistiss, Master Travers say yo' come back to Richmon'," objected the head man.

"Master Travers told you I would give the orders, did he not?"

"Yas, mistiss."

"Then row for Newport News," she said. Then, sinking down onto the awninged seat, she drew in a long, sobbing breath.

As they went past the dock, all was quiet. Caroline, looking up at it, thought, whatever befalls me now, I am finished with Joshua Welles forever. And I have my baby. Her baby! The full force of the revelation struck her at last, and she looked down at the sleeping child.

"Mine," she said in wonderment, "and with hair as black as Domino's."

Chapter Sixteen

The journey down the James was endless. The slaves, in the absence of a man to enforce swifter rowing, were light upon the oars. It seemed to Caroline that the lazy gliding through the rushing downstream waters would go on forever.

The baby, finding itself with a new source of food, had cried lustily at the unfamiliar breast and its scant supply. The nursing itself was agony, and only at the very end of each feeding did the milk flow freely and the pain lessen. By that time, the child was as exhausted as she was.

Huddled under the awninged seat in the stern, with her shawl draped carefully around the baby as it suckled, Caroline could only think that it was all some strange dream, hideous in all its implications, save for the child, who, in itself, was part of this alien world of dreams.

For the first half of the voyage Caroline was tense with worry, straining to listen for any sound that would bespeak a following craft.

Toward dawn, the slaves drew into the bank under the shade of slender trees. In spite of her protests, they insisted they must stop.

"We hungry, mistiss," the head man said. "We cain't row less'n we eat. Ain' nothin' but watah and bread, nohow. An' we tired, mistiss. Jonah, here, he almos' asleep."

She could do nothing but acquiesce. The head man leaped ashore and tied the barge's lines to the two sturdiest trees nearest them. The rest clambered out and sat themselves down on the bank, chewing noisily at the bread and gulping the water.

"Yo' needs some, too, mistiss," the head man said before joining the others. And when she shook her head, he urged her, saying tactfully, "Yo' chile need food, mistiss."

She took the proffered bread and water, murmuring a "thank you." She drank the water thirstily and accepted more before she could bring herself to eat the damp bread.

While the slaves stretched out to rest, she sat watching the dawn come up before her. There was no other craft on the water, and save for the water lapping at the barge and the birds' morning songs, the world was still.

It was a sullen dawn, promising a hot and humid day. In the East, the first rim of sun showed deep red and cast an orange-yellow glow upon the water. Scarcely any wind ruffled the leaves and grasses where the dew rose— a steamy vapor that blurred the deep green of the foliage.

The child stirred and fretted and Caroline unbuttoned her bodice to feed it once more. This time the child seemed more content and soon after was asleep again.

Caroline felt stiff and sore and her eyes burned dryly. And yet, with every nerve and muscle alert, she could not doze. She looked enviously at the blacks, sleeping like children who have had a hard day's play, their bodies curved into the earth, as if they lay on feather beds.

She shifted her position and, laying the baby on the seat, painfully pulled herself erect. She would walk a little way and find a tree under which she might lie. She picked up the baby, soothing its sleepy protest, and stepped ashore unsteadily.

Only a few more miles to Newport News, the head man had said. She clambered up the embankment. Reaching the top, she looked back at the river. Across it and a little farther on were ships—one of which would carry her away from this coast, somewhere to the South where she and the baby would be safely out of Joshua's reach.

It was cooler up in the grove of trees at the top. She laid the baby under one of them and settled herself beside it. Leaning back, she closed her eyes and felt some of the tension along her shoulders and back ease.

The sequence of events prior to her escape was too much for her exhausted brain to be able to contemplate now just what she would do on reaching Newport News. Flight by herself alone was easy, but with the baby . . . the baby. "I must name her," she said aloud, and a few minutes later she was asleep.

She awoke to find the sun directly overhead and burning down through the trees. The baby was crying and she herself was parched with thirst.

They had all been sleeping for hours. Oh, surely by now Joshua would have left Wildwood, if only to satisfy himself that she had, indeed, drowned. She could imagine him coursing down the river, his eyes intent on glimpsing some sign of her. She scrambled hastily to her feet and, taking up the baby, went back to the shore.

But as she stepped out to the top of the bank, she saw with a wrench of horror that the slaves no longer slept on the bank and that the barge was gone.

Gone! They had awakened while she slept and left her there. How long had they been gone? She hurried down the slope, nearly catapulting herself and the child into the water. But there was no sign of any barge.

The baby was wailing in earnest now, but Caroline, crushed by this turn of events, hardly heard her. She would have to find a dwelling place and someone from whom to beg help and food and water. She could only hope that whoever it was would not recognize her and send word to Joshua.

Turning downriver, she started to trudge along the narrow path. As she walked, she planned her story: she was a nursemaid and was to bring the baby to Newport News to its parents, but the slaves had left her and run away. No, she didn't know their names . . . oh, Amos was one and Josiah was another and . . . but that was all. In her mind she envisaged the scene. Name—she would have to give a name. Dobbs. She was Mary Dobbs and the baby was . . . was . . . who? Who were these parents and why was she bringing the baby to Newport News and where had she come from?

The baby's cries had reached a frantic pitch and at last broke through her preoccupation. She would have to stop and nurse it. She selected a spot under some overhanging branches and sat down.

As the baby nursed, she realized that it was soaking wet beneath its shawls. She began to peel back the layers, and when the child was finished she laid it down and took off her own petticoat. She tore at it with her teeth until she had enough cloth to fashion a diaper. This she put on the baby, drawing it tightly into a triangle around the tiny hips. The baby came out of its temporary, well-fed calmness to protest vocally at this treatment.

Sometime later the baby was newly robed in crude garments made of the petticoat. Caroline had fashioned her shawl into a sling, passing it over her right shoulder and around her neck. Into this she placed the now-sleeping child and once more set off down the embankment.

She had been confident that in following the river she would soon reach the shore opposite Newport News, from whence she felt sure she could find someone to row her across to it.

However, as the afternoon wore on, she came to a point in the river road where a steep cliff jutted out over the water and she was forced to retrace her steps and climb up the slope and into the trees that lined the edge. If only she could see a house from this point, she would go toward it, but she feared that if she moved too far from the sight of the river, she would be hopelessly lost.

She struggled on, careful to keep the river in sight. Then, just as she saw the first sign of a sail, she was stopped by a forest of alder and oak and beech through which wound a narrow footpath. To her right and past the trees surely there was some house.

She stood irresolute for several minutes, considering which was the best of two poor choices, and she finally decided to go forward. If she kept well to her left, she would surely come through this forest and be once more in sight of the river.

It was the best decision as far as it went, but she had been walking perhaps another fifteen minutes when she realized that the path kept veering to her right. In another fifteen minutes as she continued to follow it, she no longer knew how far inland she had come.

She went deeper and deeper into the woods and farther and farther from shore, and yet she could not turn and retrace her steps. What lay behind was as unknown as that which lay before her.

Around her she could hear the rustle of small animals scurrying at her approach, and from time to time birds swooped before her. It reminded her of the first days on the island, of how fearful she had been to venture from the cave into the brush. At the end of that jungle path, there had been the lovely tranquil lagoon. It shimmered in her mind like a haven of peace and security: the cool waters, the warm sun, the soft breezes. Domino had found her there . . . that first time. Remembering, her body ached and a wild upsurge of longing coursed through her.

She bit her lip until the pain drove all other pain away. Those days, she knew, would never come again, not even if she succeeded in finding Domino. He could be anywhere in the world; he could have died long ago. She trembled at the thought and looked down at the baby, lulled by the gentle swaying of its improvised cradle. Domino was gone, and she was in flight from Joshua, and bumping gently against her was the fruit of her love. Suddenly she stopped on the path, suffused with tenderness for the child, and she hugged it to her. I have this, she thought—at least I have this.

It steadied her, and with renewed courage she went on.

When at last the path ended, she found herself coming out of the trees and onto a sandy marshland. Ahead, well in the distance, was a rim of blue, as if an ocean met the sky. Between that and the forest behind her lay what seemed to be a limitless stretch of beach.

The sand burned against her bare feet, yet when she thrust her feet into the shoes, the heels wobbled and sank into the clinging, wet underbed below the hot, dry grains.

Gritting her teeth, she went on. The sun lay at her back, burning fiercely into her left shoulder. The winds were light, and when a sudden gust blew, it carried a fine dust of sand with it, stinging her eyes and face.

Coming to a fingered inlet of water, she tried to cross it but found it too deep and turned away to the point where it narrowed out.

She lost track of time. There was nothing except the hot sands tormenting her blistered feet, the sun laying burning fingers on her raw back, and the endless, endless walking across flat beach, the struggle over the dunes, and the scratchiness of the scrubby sea grass in the patches here and there.

Once, the sleeping baby, bumping gently against her in the shawl, stirred and awakened, crying. Without pausing, she drew it up to her breast and let it suckle.

After a long time the sun was gone, the sky darkened, and a breeze sprang up, cooling her and drying the perspiration from her body and making her shiver.

She was completely lost now. Beneath her feet the sand and scrub brush had given way to softer grasses. To her right a river ran gurgling back the way she had come. Presently, she came to a grove of trees through which a path wound off to her left, and when she reached the end she knew she was once again near some dwelling. The air was thick with the scent of honeysuckle, and at the stream another path stretched up from its banks.

Peering ahead, she saw a fence surrounding wide, grassy lawns and a garden, and in the middle distance, nestled into the trees, were the lights of a house. Sanctuary at last.

Half-sobbing, she started to run forward, but her legs were wobbly, weary from miles of walking, and she was forced to slow down. The baby had been quiet a long time —too quiet. She stopped and peered down at it in sudden anxiety. It looked so peaceful, lying so still. She bent her head, pressing her ear down toward the child, and upon hearing its light breathing, she relaxed.

This would not do. She had come miles without letting fear take hold of her. Now, in sight of deliverance, was no time to be afraid or to slow her pace.

Yet, however much she argued with herself, her feet moved forward slowly and woodenly. The pangs of hunger that she had suppressed, the faintness from both that hunger and exhaustion, and the thirst that had grown almost from the moment she had left that little stream some hours before—all clamored for her attention.

As if alerted by this, the child roused itself to whimper. It was a feeble cry, as if it had exhausted all of its own strength.

She moved forward in a trance. The river narrowed at one point. Hardly pausing to think of what she was doing, Caroline leaped upon the jutting rocks around which the current swirled and raced. She went from one to the other as if she was ever used to fording streams and rivers this way. Afterward, she would remember that and wonder how she had not fallen into the waters to drown in the eddies.

The smoke rising in the distance had seemed close as she stood at the forest entrance; now it seemed to be retreating, as if in a nightmare. And it was a nightmare in which she longed to run and yet could not, longed to reach a haven and yet it was ever before her, beckoning, promising, but just out of reach.

Presently, she came upon a fence. She attempted to climb over it, but it was too high, and she could not gain a foothold with her sore and bleeding feet. Balked at this last moment, she surrendered to her own weariness and slid down to the ground, her back against the palings, with the baby, still whimpering, pressing its tiny body against her.

It was here that Mr. Thoroughgood found her long after the sky had grown dark. Stepping out of his house, he heard the distant, monotonous sound of the child's hopeless and weak cries. Thinking it to be a lamb that had strayed from the fold, he followed the sound to the fence.

His startled exclamation roused Caroline and she called out, "Who is there?" Her voice was verging on a scream.

"My name is Adam Thoroughgood, ma'am," he said, peering at her. "Is that a child with you?"

"Oh," she answered, "please . . . my baby. We have walked so far."

"Here." He reached down and helped her to her feet. "Come along," he urged. "There is a gate near the house. "Where have you come from?" he asked.

"Far away," she answered. "I . . . the blacks rowed off with the barge and left us by the riverbank. I have been walking for hours, and there was the cliff, and then the sand, and the forest, and I lost the river. . . ." She was chattering stupidly, her words stumbling over each other.

"You are safe now, ma'am," he said. "Yonder is the house, and my wife will make you comfortable."

Caroline looked up, following his pointing finger, and she saw a small stone house, its door hospitably open and its lamplight gleaming upon the lawn.

"Oh," she sighed. With safety suddenly before her, she fell forward. She heard Thoroughgood's startled exclamation and felt him reaching for her, and then she was sinking down, down into darkness, blissful, soothing, and all-encompassing.

She awoke in a narrow bed with the morning sun warm on her face. She twisted away from it and heard the baby's soft cooing sounds near her. Rising on one elbow, she saw a dark polished cradle at the side of her bed and in it was the child, just awakening, waving tiny fists before its face.

Vaguely, she recalled being carried into the house and laid down, of having water brought to her lips and later a strong brew which tasted noxious, but which she had, under gentle prodding, swallowed. Someone had taken her torn and soiled clothes from her. She was clad in a clean cotton gown. Her feet had been bathed and the pain of the cuts and bruises was eased beneath a salve.

The baby, too, had been cleaned and changed. She sat up and swung her feet over the side of the bed, but at the first touch of the floor beneath them she winced in pain.

The baby started to cry and Caroline leaned down and gathered her up, propping herself against the wall above her bed. The baby was soon nursing contentedly, and Caroline, looking at downy black hair that curled gently just at the tip of one small pink ear, smiled.

A strange feeling overcame her, and at first she could not fathom its meaning. It was several minutes before she recognized it as the stirring of a dim happiness.

She had succeeded so far and would succeed yet again now that she had found respite. And there was the baby, still unnamed. She frowned, concentrating, then laughed aloud. "I shall call you Felicity, for what else is my only happiness but you?" she said softly to the baby.

The miracle of Felicity's survival struck her anew. Serena had risked her own life by keeping Felicity alive. How could she ever repay Serena? She would never see her again. Serena was cool, withdrawn, aloof, even insolent, yet it was Serena who had saved Felicity at her own peril and at the peril of her own child. To disobey Joshua was tantamount to signing her death warrant if he should ever find out. Well, he would not find out; that much she must do—for Serena's sake, as well as her own and Felicity's. Four lives in Joshua's hands. She shuddered.

No one must know the baby lived. She gave a little start. The man and his wife . . . What was their last name . . . Thoroughgood? What had she said to them last night in those few moments of awareness? Oh, she must be on her way—and soon. She laid the contented child back in its cradle and, still wincing with pain, walked on tender feet to the door.

The room downstairs was empty, but she saw her clothes folded neatly before the hearth. She slipped down and across the room to snatch them up and hurry back to the bedchamber. As she placed the clothes upon the bed, something dropped from them with a thud—her kerchief, still wrapped around the jewelry! Of course, they had found the jewels. She could not tell them then that she was a nursemaid, for, even if they believed that, they would think her a jewel thief, as well.

She dressed hastily, her stomach rumbling with hunger. She longed to eat, but there was no time for that. She had just placed the clean cap upon her tangled locks when someone tapped on the door. It opened before she could answer.

A tall, cheerful woman of middle years advanced, smiling into the room.

"Well and welladay!" she said cheerfully. "Restored, I see, and none the worse for your adventure."

"Yes, I thank you . . . Mrs. Thoroughgood, is it?"

"Aye, and it has been these past twenty-five years." Mrs. Thoroughgood laughed. "And you?"

"I . . . I am Mary Dobbs." Caroline managed to lie with only slight hesitation.

"And the babe?"

"Felicity," Caroline answered, relieved to be telling the truth. It struck her that if she held as close as possible to the truth, she would do better.

"And where were you bound when the slaves deserted you?"

"To Newport News, to join my husband," Caroline said.

"Newport News, is it? Welladay, Mistress Dobbs, you are on the wrong side of the James for that. You are outside of Norfolk. From how far upriver did you come?"

"I . . . I was visiting a relative at Williamsburg," Caroline improvised, "a Mr. Smith. My . . . my husband had business in . . . er . . . Newport News. We . . . we were going to Charleston. He was to come back for us, but, instead, he sent word that we were to join him."

"And the slaves ran away?"

"I think they mistook my orders," Caroline said, foundering as she was forced to lie. "I stopped some distance up the river and went up near the trees to feed Felicity. I must have dozed off, for when I awoke, it was several hours later and the slaves and barge were gone."

"And when was this?"

Would the woman never cease questioning! Caroline thought. "At noon, and I walked, and then . . . well, Mr. Thoroughgood found me."

"Walked, and in bare feet, and all that way!" Mrs. Thoroughgood marveled. "Oh, but hear me clatter on like a busybody. You must be famished. Come to the kitchen,

While you eat I'll find Mr. Thoroughgood and see if he can take you to your husband."

No food had ever tasted so good to Caroline. She wolfed down smoked ham and biscuits and yams drenched in butter and ate several corn pones, on which she lavished fresh honey.

The black woman who served her stood by to bring her new portions and pour steaming fragrant coffee as soon as the first cup was emptied.

She was on the last sip of coffee when Mrs. Thoroughgood returned to the kitchen with the news that Mr. Thoroughgood would bring her into the town in the carriage.

"How can I ever repay you?" Caroline said gratefully.

"Pshaw!" Mrs. Thoroughgood waved a good-natured hand. "No payment between neighbors in distress. Still, I'd like to ask a favor," she said.

"Yes, anything," Caroline said gratefully.

"You'll think me rude," the woman warned.

"Let me judge," Caroline said, smiling to conceal a sudden anxiety.

"Just tell me how you came to be dressed in those garments and yet possessed of so many jewels. I couldn't help but see them last evening when I washed your garments and dried them at the hearth. And I shall perish of curiosity all winter if you do not relieve my mind."

As the woman spoke, Caroline went rapidly over possible explanations. Seizing the first likely one, she said, "When I first came upriver on one of those barges, I was fairly ruined by the water. So this time I took my oldest dress and shoes and patched them as well as I could, thinking to spare myself another ruined gown."

Mrs. Thoroughgood's face cleared, but it fell into lines of disappointment immediately afterward. "You may laugh," she said, laughing herself a bit ruefully, "but I thought it would be a romantic tale."

"I wish," said Caroline with fervent truthfulness, "that I could tell you one to show my gratitude."

"Pshaw!" said Mrs. Thoroughgood. " 'Tis romantic enough to find a young lady on my doorstep with a hungry, crying baby in her arms. And it is great luck that Letty has a new babe and could give milk to yours."

Felicity, Caroline thought with a rising desire to giggle,

Felicity, you have been nursed by more substitutes than a eweless lamb.

"Who is Letty?" she asked aloud.

"Why, 'tis my woman who gave you breakfast," Mrs. Thoroughgood said. "She's wife to Mr. Thoroughgood's best man, John William."

"I am forever in your debt, all of your debt," Caroline began, but once again her thanks were waved aside.

"Come," said her amiable hostess, "we must ready the babe, for Mr. Thoroughgood will be here at any moment."

The drive into town was not of long duration. Mr. Thoroughgood was as cheerful as his wife, nearly as curious, but not as loquacious. His questions were brief and he seemed satisfied with her answers. He drew up near the waterfront, the busiest section of the town. Looking across the broad expanse of the mouth of the James and eastward, where the deep channel led out to the ocean, Caroline saw any number of ships, ships of all sizes and descriptions: barges, launches, punts, small coastal vessels, large seagoing ships, although none was as large as the *Charlotte* or even a lesser example, like the *Marigold*.

It was a panorama of vessels, with the small ones tied up to the landing docks and the larger ones anchored offshore and the tallest masts rising some distance beyond.

"So many boats," she said, encouraged by the sight.

"Aye, and one is sure to take you across the river." Mr. Thoroughgood smiled. He handed her the reins. "You had best wait here," he said. "The waterfront is filthy and filled with crack-ropes. I will find a good man to take you across."

She watched him stride off and looked around her. They were on a side road with small dwellings. They were modest, with neat gardens, at the top of the street but crowding together with bare gardens where the street neared the docks.

Just in front of Mr. Thoroughgood's carriage was a large bay horse tethered in front of one of the crudest cottages. It was a handsome horse with a saddle of well-burnished leather. It was a gentleman's horse, she knew, and she looked around, wondering why it would be standing in front of so humble a dwelling.

Presently, the door of the house opened and a tall man hurried out. There was something familiar about him, and instinctively Caroline shrank back, clutching Felicity to her.

The man was headed straight toward the bay. Then all at once, as he reached the horse, she knew who it was—Jefferson, young Thomas Jefferson. What on earth was he doing here? She began to pray that he would take no notice of her and bent her head over Felicity as he mounted his horse. She heard him give a command to the horse, looked up, and found that he had turned around, heading back away from the waterfront and thus facing her directly.

He met her gaze full-on, a frown of puzzlement on his face. She quickly looked away, but it was too late. He had drawn up beside her, reining in his mount and saying, "Why, Mistress Welles, what brings you here?"

"Mr. Jefferson," she temporized, "I am as surprised to see you. What brought you to Norfolk?"

"An old matter," he said, "a former bondsman who befriended me once and has come upon hard times himself."

He was still looking at her with that questioning expression in his eyes. She must tell him something, but what could she tell him? He knew who she was and where she came from and was scarcely likely to accept some foolish story.

She raised a pleading face to him and said, "Oh, Mr. Jefferson, I must ask for your silence, for I have had a grievous experience."

She saw him glance at the sleeping baby. Were he to say in Williamsburg that he had seen her with a baby, the news would surely reach Joshua, and then . . . Serena! Hastily, she sought for something that would divert him, but he spoke first, saying, "Your child, Mistress Welles? We had heard falsely that it died."

"Yes . . . no . . ." she stammered, flustered. Looking at him again, she thought, I have no choice but to confide in him and trust his honor not to reveal the truth.

She drew a deep breath and began to speak in a low and rapid voice. "I beg your silence on your honor, Mr. Jefferson, for more than one life is in your hands," she began, and she saw him stiffen at once, his young face tight with astonishment. "You see me like this"—she made a gesture toward her shabby clothing—"and with a child . . . my child . . . we . . . we are running away. My . . . my husband tried to kill the child, but a slave woman saved her and nursed her with her own child, and I . . . I did not know. When I found out, I made plans to take her away. I must find a ship going south. I have friends in Nassau," she said, stumbling over the lie, "and they will help me."

Dear heaven, she thought, what will I say if he questions me too closely? He will want to know why Joshua ordered the baby killed, and she could almost see that ascetic face shuddering with distaste if she were to admit that the father of the child was the French pirate who had abducted her.

"Mistress Welles," he was saying, "what you tell me is of a foul crime averted. Surely such a man deserves punishment. Would you not seek the protection of the governor? I know that . . . "

"No, no!" she cried. "You don't know Joshua! He is a devil! Before you could seize him, the slave would be dead. And seizing him . . . 'tis only my word against his . . . mine and a slave woman's. And he has the Blairs and Chiswells and many other well-respected people to say that he has treated me with tenderness and concern," she finished, half-crying.

Her tears unsettled Jefferson, who said hastily, "There, ma'am, I meant only to help you."

"Oh, if you mean only to help me, Mr. Jefferson, then aid me in my search for a ship to carry me away and say nothing to anyone. Do you think my word would stand against that of Mr. Chiswell, who in all innocence would be forced to admit he saw a happy home?"

"But the child," Jefferson protested. "Surely, when you show the child. . . . Did not your husband say himself the child had died?"

"Yes. And perhaps I would be believed. But Serena would die and her own baby along with her. I could not bring so much as the fear of such a punishment near her. Think, Mr. Jefferson, how noble she was to defy her master's law for the law of God and human kindness. Yet, you know well that Joshua can have her slain and be none the worse off."

This last argument hit its mark.

"We will talk more of this presently," Jefferson said. "But I will aid you in every way I can. And do not fear, ma'am, on my honor, no word of your secret shall pass my lips as long as I am entrusted by you."

At this, her tears began to flow in earnest, and he, alarmed at the abandonment with which she wept and at the wails of the awakened infant, hurriedly dismounted and tethered his horse. He was at her side quickly, urging her to compose herself. Mr. Thoroughgood, coming back to tell her he had not yet secured passage to Newport News, found her being comforted by a strange young gentleman whom he took to be her husband.

"He is a friend of my husband's," Caroline said before Jefferson could answer, "and he will take me to him."

Mr. Thoroughgood was relieved, but at the same time he was not altogether pleased. Too much about this young woman struck him as strange. When he had drawn the carriage up before the house near St. John's Church, where Jefferson had promised she would find shelter for herself and the child, Mr. Thoroughgood said quietly,

"I recognize you as a lady by your manner and voice, ma'am. I am confused by such patched and worn garments, and the cap and shoes are more suited to a goody than to a lady. And I don't understand why your relative had so little regard for your safety as to put you aboard a barge manned by slaves, and with nary a protector to travel with you. Especially am I confused because you bear jewels of the nature my wife and I saw. This young gentleman, a friend of your husband's, you say? Well, ma'am, for your sake, I trust this is true."

Caroline realized that he had not believed her story and knew how much less he would believe the truth. She had fallen low in his regard and it embarrassed her, yet there was nothing she could say, except, "Sir, I trust you will accept my story, for it is true enough. I must go and bring my child to the protection of her father, and I vow on her head that that is the truest statement I have ever uttered." Relieved, she saw that he cast a more favorable look on her.

"I believe that, ma'am," he said, "for I see how you love the child, and I don't think you'd dare risk God's wrath by swearing on her. Yet, all is not as you've told us. Well, anyway, take care." He helped her from the carriage and then laid the baby in her arms. "God be with you," he said.

It was two days before Jefferson reported that he had

been able to sell her jewels and pay for passage aboard a ship going as far south as Savannah.

During those two days, Caroline had been forced to reveal more than she would have liked to, although she feared his disgust at hearing the unwholesome tale of a man convinced the child his wife bore was not his and ordering it slain. She loathed lying to Jefferson, yet, not for anything would she have told him about Domino or the island or anything else that would give credence to Joshua's claim.

If this blackened and damned Joshua forever in Jefferson's mind, she cared not. Joshua could be hanged from the scaffold at the jail and she would be glad. The strain of telling part truth and part lie and trying to remember which was which made her tense.

The rooms Jefferson had secured from a woman named Mrs. Bonnyfeather were small and confining, yet she couldn't risk going abroad. There was too much danger of someone from Williamsburg—or, in fact, any of their friends—appearing in Norfolk, just as Jefferson had.

Therefore, her joy at the news that he had found passage was unbounded. She could gladly have kissed him. He had been chivalrous beyond any claim of friendship, a champion of her distress, and a sympathetic, if reluctant, confidant. She sensed that such cruelty and unpleasantness between people was as foreign to him as the tongue of the Saracens—more so, she thought affectionately, for if he had so known, that tongue would become his own, where cruelty would never be part of his nature.

He was the only man she had ever met aside from Domino who was possessed of such complexities of nature, and, like Domino, there was a side to him that always remained aloof, not out of snobbery or arrogance, for he suffered neither defect, but out of an inner privacy of thought.

"I have proved something," she said to him when he told her of the ship while they sat in Mrs. Bonnyfather's little parlor.

"And what is that?" he asked, smiling and in good spirits now that his search had proved successful.

"That beneath your practicality you are truly romantic. Do you remember that I charged you with that on our first meeting?"

"I remember, and I also remember telling you I am far from romantic."

"Only a romantic man could have come to my aid so gallantly and with such sensitivity to my feelings," she assured him somberly. He met her eyes, his own went suddenly shy and tender, and he said in a strange voice, "You are a beautiful woman, Caroline Welles. A man would need to be carved from stone to fail you in any request."

Touched, she could make no answer. Staring at him, she saw his eyes grow warmer and looked away, thinking: No, I must not allow any further intimacy, for this is a man I would be content with, and that can never be.

As if he knew what she was thinking and the thoughts were his own, he spoke up briskly: "Now to the practical matters, ma'am."

The mood passed and she listened without further fluttering to the story he had prepared for her.

She was, he said, his cousin, and with this in mind he had procured for her suitable clothing. Her husband awaited her in Nassau. She was in the care of the captain himself, who was charged in the name of the governor to see her safely there.

"I will explain as much as I dare to Fauquier if you give me leave to use my discretion," he said. "That way I may procure a letter from him asking all concerned to protect you."

"Yes, yes," she answered. "But request his silence."

"Have no fear. Fauquier is no companion to Mr. Welles. And Fauquier knows too well his abuse of slaves . . . as, indeed, do we all."

Three days later, garbed in a simple but well-made outfit, Caroline stepped aboard the launch that would carry her to the *Nancy O.* When she was seated, Jefferson handed down Felicity, properly dressed for the first time in her short weeks of life.

"Safe voyage," he said. "Should you not find friends waiting in Nassau, seek out my cousin, Mrs. Leigh, and for my sake, she and her husband will aid you."

"I will." She smiled at him tremulously, wishing with all her heart that she were not leaving her one protector behind her.

The launch cast off and in a few moments they were

skimming across the water, buoyed by so stiff a breeze that the oars rested nearly useless beneath a bellying jib-sail. Caroline looked back at the shore, waving to Jefferson until the launch veered and tacked on the course that would bring her and Felicity to the *Nancy O,* a snub-nosed little vessel of sturdy build. At the first sight of the boat, Caroline forgot any pang of parting.

In a short time she would be in Savannah. There, where no one knew her, no longer in fear of Joshua finding her, she would wait until she found a ship bound for Martinique.

She looked up at the clear sky, felt the refreshing wind, and began to think that all misery lay behind her and only better times lay ahead.

Part
Five

Chapter Seventeen

A fine warm rain fell steadily over the sea island south of Savannah. Beneath the brooding cypresses and the moss-hung live oaks, vaporous mists steamed upward to melt into its gray curtain.

Offshore, the bare masts of the *Mouette* appeared and disappeared as she rose and fell with the incoming tide: a ghost ship, riding a ghostly sea.

Tracking westward through the semitropical foliage, Domino's step was light upon the soaked grasses. He was naked from the waist up and his breeches were torn and bloodied above his bare legs and feet. His hair hung thick and black to his shoulders and his skin was bronzed. In his right hand he held a dagger.

On his left cheek there was a long thin cut, still oozing blood where the knife had dug most deeply, although most of the blood had dried. His face was set, his eyes as dark and brooding as the cypresses under which he passed. As he slipped through the trees, he looked more like a lone Indian stalking his prey than a ship's captain.

Behind him, the decks of the *Mouette* were red with the blood of those who had fallen in the fierce fight to regain her. All but two of the willing mutineers lay dead. Half of those who had gladly fought with him were dead, too. Christos was wounded. Manuel and José had drowned in their effort to escape. And somewhere ahead, fleeing like a large gray rat, was Loco. He was unarmed; there was that, at least.

Domino had not thought beyond catching those three who had escaped. He had flung himself into the sea after them, with only his dagger. Manuel had sunk almost at once, and José, struggling against the undertow, had screamed for help until the sea filled his mouth for the last time.

Domino, intent on finding Loco, had seen him stagger from the waves and onto the beach moments before he himself reached the shallow water.

Loco had disappeared almost at once into the trees. He could have gone in almost any direction. Still, Domino stalked him, his eyes sweeping the ground ahead for signs of Loco's passage.

Half a mile farther on, Domino stepped onto the lee-ward sands. Looking down the length and breadth of the beach and water, he finally spied Loco, swimming strongly toward the Georgia mainland.

He hesitated. It was a long swim to the shore. The chances were against Loco reaching it, particularly after the fighting, the swim from the ship, and the headlong flight across the island. Domino was exhausted. Loco must be equally so.

If Loco made it at all, there was still the swamp and forest between him and any town. He would surely head toward Savannah. He had no food and no weapon. And although Domino had heard the Yammacraws were a friendly tribe, he did not think Loco knew that.

The signs were all in favor of his returning to the ship and leaving Loco to another fate. Reluctantly, he slipped his dagger into the waistband of his breeches and turned back the way he had come.

In his singlemindedness the long trek after Loco had seemed to pass swiftly. Going back, robbed of his vengeance, the paths were endless.

Now that his only aim was to rejoin the *Mouette*, the weary fatigue of battle and pursuit crept over him. The thought of the swim that lay ahead once he finally reached the windward side increased his tiredness.

His muscles ached in protest, yet he went stoically on, drawing upon unrealized strength. It was only when he had finally gained the shore and saw the launch rowing steadily toward him that he gave way and sank upon the ground.

It was three days before all evidence of the battle had been cleared from the ship. The two mutineers still alive were in chains and would remain there until such time as they could be put ashore.

"You should have them hanged," Christos urged Domino as he limped along beside his captain, who was facing the forecastle deck.

"No. There has been enough death. Loco was different. I would sink my dagger into his belly now with joy. The others"—he shrugged—"they are stupid men, little better than animals, and, like animals, they know nothing, save their own needs of the moment."

"Ah. When the battle is over the captain once more becomes the philosopher," Christos remarked amiably.

"I have no stomach for vengeance against oafs," Domino said, "not cold vengeance. I need the heat of battle."

He looked at Christos' bandaged leg and said, "You were fortunate, my friend. Had the cutlass struck deeper, you would have lost that leg to a surgeon's knife."

"I would have turned my dagger to my own heart first," Christos said feelingly.

"And how is the wound?"

"It itches," Christos complained.

Domino nodded. "That is good. You will heal without turning gangrenous."

"Could you not remove the bandage and leaves now?"

Domino shook his head. "The leaves keep away the gangrene."

"A bizarre and strange remedy. I thought you mad when I first saw what you intended doing with those leaves. I still think . . . "

"Believe me, Christos, the remedy works. It saved my own leg years ago when I was a boy. My father had the good sense to take me to the Indian village. The old medicine man there had saved many a leg and arm of those who could put aside their prejudices for the sake of their lives." He grinned suddenly. "Eh, Christos," he said, "we talk of everything, but we have yet to rejoice. The ship is ours again. The worst is over. And soon, my friend, the war will be, too."

"And Liberté. That is what you are thinking of—your island. But what is that island paradise with only those of us who join you and no women among them? If we leave the ship for a landsman's life, we take the wife, no?"

Domino's smile faded. "Yes. That is something to think of, but not now. We are only half-manned, Christos. I think we must go into Savannah and try for more crew."

"Are you mad?" Christos exclaimed. "Walk into the English town and say, 'Pardon, kind sirs, I, a French privateer, wish to rob you of your own crews'?"

"I shall not go as a Frenchman. I will take the crew and the longboat and sail into Savannah harbor as an English merchantman. And I shall take only those who are English themselves."

"Why not sail the *Mouette* up the Savannah River?" Christos asked. "We still have the English flag that Loco ran up whenever we met Englishmen or wished to put into one of their ports."

"That was at sea. Can you see my motley crew walking the streets of Savannah? 'Pirates!' the people would shriek at the sight of them, and we'd all be in irons."

"We need stores, as well," Christos said.

"Make the list for me, then, and muster a crew under Haywood for the longboat. I will sail on the next tide. And you, my friend, will take command in my absence. Go easy on the men, Christos. Give them extra rations of food and rum. I want a willing crew for my next run."

"And where is that?"

"Virginia," Domino said.

"Virginia? Into the teeth of the enemy?"

"Into the teeth of the enemy," Domino assured him. "There is something I must do before we sail south again."

Christos looked at him questioningly, but Domino vouchsafed no further explanation, and Christos said, "There is something you must do before you go to Savannah, Captain."

"And what is that?"

"You will not soon be taken for an English captain in those rags. Fortunately, there is the booty from the last encounter with an English vessel—not only the gold, Captain, but chests of everything. Loco left nothing aboard, just as he left no one alive before he scuttled the ship. Six battles, four ours, and every one of those ships lying on the ocean floor with their corpses."

"A dead man's clothes, then," Domino said gruffly.

"And if Loco does find his way to Savannah, another dead man."

"Over a year now," Christos said suddenly, "all because of the Englishwoman. Loco could never have roused the others to mutiny, save on the promise of her as the prize. I wonder if she found her husband . . . if she made her way to Vir—— . . . " He broke off and shot a quick look at Domino. "Virginia," he finished slowly, comprehension dawning on his face.

Meeting his eyes, Domino looked away. "I will go below to make ready," he said, then strode off. Not for anything would he reveal his reasons for daring to voyage into more northerly coastal waters.

He knew that he risked both ship and crew and any hope of realizing Liberté. Worse, he risked death for all of them. Yet, over the year of pursuing the *Mouette* on ship after ship, from Martinique to Barbados, to Hispaniola, through the battles that raged along the Spanish main, the hope would rise before him. As Rodney cut his triumphant swath through French territory, outclassing the small French fleets he encountered, island after island falling to the English when the French ships arrived too late, or, like Admiral Blenac's fleet, were bottled up harmless and helpless, his own unhappiness over what he knew would be the war's inevitable end was pale beside his obsession to see her again.

"Madness," he muttered aloud as he came to his own cabin. His course had been set too long for him to steer a different one now. Yet he knew that he could not rid himself of his fancies until he had found Caroline.

Now he had found the one and was on his way to rid himself of the other . . . and return the gold coins that had gained him his ship.

Then he would be free, and only then . . . a ghost laid to rest, no more to haunt him or to fill even his cabin with her presence and the memories of things past.

He shook himself, as if that gesture would somehow rid him of his musings, and set about preparing for the trip into Savannah harbor.

The inn that stood on the bluff above the Savannah riverfront commanded a wide view of the harbor. It served rum and ale and food to visiting seamen, and here, pirates masquerading as ordinary sailors and officers, mingled in relative safety. Here, too, as in the Tondee Tavern, some streets inland, captains and masters sought to hire crews to replace those men lost at sea or in battle. When hiring failed, an unwary landsman or sailor might wake up from a bout with too much rum and find himself far out at sea.

Seldom were the pirates responsible for this method of manning their ships, since the booty they offered was far more tempting than the low pay, bad food, and cruel and harsh treatment known to prevail aboard an English naval vessel.

For some time the pirates, as well as many merchant seamen, had avoided heavy drinking in shore taverns. The war losses made gang impressment more necessary than ever. These gangs could be seen roaming the taverns and inns frequented by sailors in almost every seaport on the Atlantic.

However, the turn of the tide of war so totally in Britain's favor and the concentration of the naval forces in the Indies had freed the northerly seaports of his particular menace. More merchantmen than ever increased the flow of traffic in the harbor, and if among them were pirates and privateers like Domino and his crew, no one appeared the wiser.

Domino, fitted in the finest of the garments the booty chest yielded, sat at a small table in the public room with Haywood.

"The reports are discouraging," Haywood was saying in a low voice. "We need gunners' mates. Brusac lost all of them during the fight. I have managed only one."

"And the rest?" Domino asked.

"We are ten men short of our needs. In battle we will be dangerously shorthanded."

"One more day," Domino said. "I can spare no more. Try the new crop arriving from the brigantine that anchored yesterday evening. It is a tub of a boat, but it bears the name *Indies Queen*. The captain's name is Sage —a bad captain by all reports. I have heard it said a man can receive two dozen lashes for being late to the watch by as little as two minutes. And no excuse is accepted, nor leniency granted."

Haywood grunted. "I have heard as much myself, Captain, and more. Sage permits little shore liberty. He sends the men in groups of four to six and in company with armed mates of their own mess. They themselves bear neither dagger nor pistol. Nor does anyone dare speak to them while they are ashore."

Domino smiled thinly. "And where is the *Indies Queen* bound?"

"South, Captain, bearing a cargo of goods for the Indies. She is out of Bristol these three months and more."

"And why drop anchor at Savannah?"

"Heavy gales forced her off her course and damaged her masts. She ran for the nearest port. I heard all this at the ship's chandlery only an hour ago."

"When will she be ready to sail?"

"They reckon in a week, Captain."

"Very well. If you cannot man the *Mouette* in port with men from the *Indies Queen,* we will lie in wait for her off the coast and free the seamen ourselves." He laughed. "A sport, Haywood—engaging a merchantman for booty and finding a willing crew."

"In battle . . . " Haywood began.

"Ten men short or not, a first-rater is a match for a brigantine . . . more than a match when it is a brig with a sullen crew."

Haywood stood up. "I will see what I can do at Tondee Tavern. Some of Sage's men might be there."

When he had left, Domino called for another tankard of ale and a plate of food. He was busy eating the meal of cold beef and cheese when the door opened and two men entered. The first was small and fat, with small pig eyes set deep in the fleshy folds of his face. He wore the stained and unpressed garb of a naval captain. The weasel-faced seaman who followed him was dressed in what had once been the white breeches and frock of a naval lieutenant. His blue coat, unlike the captain's, was clean, and Domino had no difficulty in recognizing both as something other than what their uniforms suggested— merchantmen or possibly privateers in English service. He doubted the latter, unless their forays had been singularly unsuccessful. Privateer officers were better dressed. The meanest slop chest aboard the smallest vessel would yield better clothing than that of either of the men. They stood at the counter, a little distance from Domino, and ordered rum.

A moment later, hearing the weasel address the porker

as "Captain Sage," he smiled at his own sagacity. Turning, he took a second look at the man whose crew he meant to have, one way or the other.

Sage, however, took no notice of Domino. He was clearly excited about something and kept rubbing his hands together in unconscious anticipation.

He spoke in a low voice to the weasel, whom he addressed as Mr. Flint, and Domino could catch very little of what they said. He went back to his meal. Finishing it and the ale, he rose and left the tavern in search of Haywood. He was halfway up the road to Tondee's when he realized he had left his tricorne behind, and, swearing impatiently, he hurried back to the inn.

As he passed Sage he heard him say, ". . . a fortune in reward. Her husband has promised two hundred pounds in gold for her safe return."

"I heard of no reward by a Dobbs," Flint said.

"Not Dobbs, you idiot! 'Tis only a name she is using, I'm certain, for she accurately fits the description. There isn't a captain or sailor calling at a Virginia port these past three months who hasn't heard of it. Think of the luck! She has fallen into my hands. With all the ships standing below, she came to me."

"Captain, she says she is Mary Dobbs, and, if in truth she lies about that, still there has been no mention of a babe in Newport News, nor in Norfolk, neither."

"Tush. She is Mistress Welles. Damn my eyes if she ain't."

Caroline! Domino nearly said it aloud. Here in Savannah and with a child? And her husband offering a reward? But, why?

He signaled the innkeeper for a tankard of ale and sat down again, drawing out the list of stores and pretending to study it.

"Tonight," Sage was whispering, "when she comes to meet me here. We dare not wait. She might take it into her head to try a ship going straight to Martinique instead of stopping at Guadeloupe first."

"Aye, Captain," the man replied. "But should the room be filled . . ."

"Not in here, you dolt," Sage growled. "On the road from the church. See to it that she makes no outcry. Seize the infant first. Once you have it, she'll be meek enough."

"Aye, aye, sir," the man replied. "But if 'tis not Welles'

wife, but Dobbs, after all . . . and we sailing back with her . . . "

"She is Mistress Welles, I tell you. As for the child, 'twas born after she left . . . or Welles knew naught and has been roundly rebused by a bedswerver of a wife." He gave a coarse laugh.

Domino's first instinct was to seize Sage and throttle him. With some effort, he forced himself to finish the ale and go out.

Sage and Flint were already speaking of other matters when Domino stood up to leave. As he opened the tavern door, he came face to face with Haywood.

"Good news," the mate said cheerfully. Then, spying Sage and his lieutenant, he said hastily, "The ship is to be ready on the morrow, Captain."

"Good news, indeed," Domino said. "Come, Mr. Haywood, I have some further business with the chandler."

When they were well away from the inn, Haywood, who could scarcely contain himself, said, "I say, Captain, it is a fortune beyond your dreams. Sage is far worse a captain than you'd believe. One of the mates was eager to desert himself, and he has promised to deliver the men we need, and he has asked if you will take twelve instead of ten." At this he slapped his thigh and laughed.

"I'll take the twelve," Domino said quietly. "Listen, Haywood, I have business in town until late. See to the boat's crew and meet me in my room above the inn in the morning. If I have not returned by then, muster the lads and look for me either along the road from the church or . . . "—he paused—" . . . or aboard Sage's brig."

Haywood goggled. "Aboard the brig! But, Captain . . . "

"Don't question my orders, Haywood," Domino answered tightly. "Obey them."

"Aye, aye, sir," Haywood replied. "In the morning, then, Captain."

Domino spent the rest of the afternoon traversing the road between the tavern and the church, noting every house and every possible hiding place. Near the turn to the tavern, he spied a peach orchard and thought it would serve well as a cover. After marking the spot firmly in his mind so that he would easily find it under cover of darkness, he returned to his room above the tavern.

Caroline was somewhere in Savannah, and with her a

child, an infant. So she was not only married to Welles, but mother of a newborn baby, also. Three months missing, and Welles with no knowledge of his own child—a child born somewhere between Virginia and Savannah, or in the town itself.

His mouth twisted. He remembered her saying she hated her husband, and he remembered, too, her passionate nature. Hate him or not, she had borne his child . . . or someone's child, if she hated Welles enough. Either thought bit deeply into him and he grew alarmed at the jealous fury rising inside him.

He paced his room like a caged beast. "Take me to Martinique," she had said, and that was where she now sought passage. To what end? To come to him was the obvious answer, but surely in the eight months since Martinique had fallen, she had heard some mention of it. And, just as surely, she would not expect to find him there, languishing on the shore. Someone else, then.

I am growing womanish, he thought in disgust, and he flung himself from the room to once again walk the streets of the town. "Here . . . she is here. And she could be in any dwelling I pass," he said to himself over and over. If only he knew which one, then tonight's adventure need never occur.

Chapter Eighteen

When she had arrived in Savannah over two months ago, Caroline had little clear idea of what she might expect in the way of accommodations. All down the coast, she had fretted that not only would she and Felicity find themselves without shelter, but that neither would she find a ship to take her to Martinique . . . or, if at all, not for many months.

And in truth, it had taken a long time to find one. Most vessels coming into Savannah were making a last call at the Colonies before returning to England, or else they were coastal vessels like the *Nancy O* and would be sailing back to their home harbors.

Finding Captain Sage had been pure luck. She had almost begun to despair, thinking that after all this she must dare the return to England and from there find passage to Martinique.

As she prepared for the voyage, she was humming lightly. The room in the house that had once been the parsonage of the first rector, John Wesley, was pleasant and cozy in its very smallness.

She had been curious about Wesley, whom she knew to be one of the band of strange Methodists, bent on changing churches and preaching almost as if they were St. Paul himself. She had once gone, as a lark, with Redleigh and Fortescue and a whole band of others to hear him preach in the open air.

The rest had found high amusement in the fervor of Wesley's speech, but she had been caught by it, felt stirred up in a strange way, although she could not tell why, and had been astounded at the response he had received from his more serious listeners, some clearly moved to a fervor equal to his own.

She had not thought of that day again until she had sought aid at the church and the rector's wife had told her the reason why the parsonage contained one more room than the rest of the buildings that were constructed by Oglethorpe's decree during the first two years of Savannah's existence.

"To accommodate visitors," the rector's wife had said. "He was a different sort of man, John Wesley. He could not find a pulpit in the Episcopal Church, of course. A proper radical is Wesley."

Later she found out that Wesley had left Savannah owing to a blighted romance. That such an elderly clergyman as Wesley had ever suffered the pangs of tormented love struck Caroline as highly entertaining.

Each morning she had taken Felicity and walked down to the bluff overlooking the river, searching for a sail. When one came into sight, she would seek out its captain, sometimes with the aid of the rector, to learn what port they would visit next. Each time she had been disappointed—until yesterday evening, when the Reverend Doctor Wright brought Captain Sage to the parsonage.

Sage was an unpleasant little man, she thought herself, and the rector was definitely hesitant about consigning her to his care, saying he would feel better if she traveled with some protection.

But Caroline had no intention of lingering for many more months. The Wrights were pleasant people with a brood of mannerly children, but she had chafed under the stern religiosity of a household in which the busy days left little time for conversation.

She knew she was a source of speculation and curiosity both to the parsonage as well as to the friends and parishioners who called there. Sometimes she had been hard put to remember her story. But the governor's letter and her own mention of the Chiswells, the Lees, and the Randolphs had, she knew, gone far to establish her as a perfectly respectable woman on her way to join her husband in Nassau, and under the protection of no less than the governor of the Virginia Colony. Even Sage would need to respect that.

Dear Thomas Jefferson, she thought affectionately, were it not for his obtaining that letter to the rector from

Fauquier, she scarcely thought she would have found such sanctuary for so long.

Happily occupied with her tasks and still humming snatches of melodies, the hours flew past for the first time since her arrival. Just before dinner Felicity awoke from her nap and lay in her cradle, cooing to herself, waving fists and snatching at the sunbeams dancing in front of her.

"You are growing too big for this tiny cradle," Caroline said to her as she picked her up, "and very fat. Milk no longer satisfies you, does it, my love?"

Felicity smiled and gurgled in response, and Caroline noted for the thousandth time the baby's clear resemblance to Domino. Save for the shape of the mouth and for the deep blue of her eyes, Felicity was so like the man who fathered her that sometimes, looking at her, Caroline's heart would contract in a mixture of love and pain.

"Soon," she whispered as she nursed her daughter, "soon. I have come this far. I am free. I have money and passage. I will find him. I know I will find him."

The long journey, the many islands, the lands beyond them, and the endless seas rose to mock her, but she pushed the images aside. She would find Domino—no matter how many seas and no matter how many lands lay between. Sooner or later, he would go to his island. And she would be close by.

She glanced at the clock on the chest, and noting the hour, she said aloud, "In only seven hours and a bit more, we will be aboard the *Indies Queen*. What do you think of that, Felicity?" But the baby had fallen asleep at her breast, a drop of milk lodged in a crease near her soft pink mouth.

At half past nine that evening, Domino crouched behind the hedges of the peach orchard. His pistols were sheathed in their holders, and his dagger was in his hand. His muscles were tense and ready. There was nothing to do now except wait.

The innkeeper, Mr. Stevenson, was an amiable man and several cuts above the ordinary tavern owner. His speech and manner suggested a man of some breeding and education, and Domino suspected that he had come from a family of means and position that somehow had fallen on hard times. Mr. Stevenson had come to Georgia thirty years before as a lad of sixteen. Orphaned, with his father dying in a debtors' prison, he had been forced to take his place and a "merciful providence," as he himself called it, had sent him to join Oglethorpe instead of languishing in prison. "For life 'twould have been miserable," he said to Domino over a glass of rum that evening. "For none was left of my family to pay my father's debts."

Debtors' prisons, Domino thought. They were a stupid method, even if one overlooked the cruelty of it all. For how could a lad of sixteen hope to work out debts without means to earn a livelihood? He knew the common opinion was that the threat of such was a deterrent to others. In his own view, were that so, debtors' prisons would not exist.

Stevenson had been fortunate. More, he had been strong and clever. He prospered in the Colony, and now he had holdings in land beyond that which surrounded his inn. He had married and reared children, and they, too, prospered.

All of these factors had made possible Stevenson's generous and unquestioning response to Domino's story that his wife and daughter were joining him that evening. He was bringing them in from an outlying plantation where they had been visiting while he made ready to sail. Domino knew that Stevenson did not accept his statement, but he also knew Stevenson would keep his doubts to himself for all time. A gentleman, Stevenson, no matter by what means he came to Georgia.

It remained now to take Flint by surprise and disarm him before he had a chance to make an outcry.

Domino stretched and resumed his crouched position. There was too much he didn't know. Would Flint come alone? Would he pass this way, after all? It was the only logical road leading from Christ Church. Still, he might have reason to approach the road from another street.

Domino drew his watch from his pocket. Holding it at an angle to catch the faint illumination of starlight, he saw it was nearly on the hour. He slipped the watch back in his fob pocket and crept forward, every sense alert.

A few moments later, he heard approaching footsteps and counted at least two men from their sound. He sheathed his dagger and drew his pistols. The men were nearly abreast of the turning, and they came noisily enough. He heard Flint's voice saying, "Mark you, show nothing but courtesy at the parsonage, or else you will alert them."

"Aye, sir," his companion answered. "And be easy when you bind her. Captain Sage don't want an injured woman, nor yet a dead one."

"Aye, sir," the man replied. "But what if she be so . . . " He broke off in surprise, for at that moment Domino sprang from his hiding place, his pistols cocked in either hand.

It had happened so quickly that to the two men from the *Indies Queen,* Domino simply appeared before them like a spirit manifesting itself in an instant.

Before they could react at all, he said in a cold voice that left no room for doubt, "Make one sound or attempt to move and you will die the next instant."

They goggled at him but they obeyed him. "You," he said to the seaman, "bind Flint with this and cover his mouth." Keeping one pistol at the ready, he replaced the other and slipped the coiled rope from his shoulder. This, together with a kerchief, he flung at the man.

"Watch how you move," he cautioned him. "Don't touch the pistol at your side."

The man turned to obey, and as he did, Domino replaced his other pistol and drew his dagger. The sailor started to bend over Flint just as Flint's hand snaked out and closed over his pistol. With a sudden movement, he flung the sailor aside, and at that instant, even as the pistol was raised, Domino's dagger left his hand and sank to the hilt in Flint's throat. A low gurgling, the clattering of the pistol to the cobblestones, and Flint was down. The seaman sprang forward to recover the pistol, but Domino's boot had caught it and kicked it away. At almost the same moment his left hand collared the man, and in his right hand his own pistol gleamed.

"I warned you," he said in an even, low voice. "Now, which shall it be—a ball in your belly, or obedience to my orders?"

"Obedience, sir," the sailor whined.

"Then drag that carcass into the bushes first," Domino ordered. He bent down and retrieved his dagger, stepping back quickly as the pooling blood, finding a new outlet, gave a last forward rush.

The man hurried to obey. When he had finished, Domino said, "Now, you rogue, what is the plan?"

"Mr. Flint, sir," he quaked, nodding toward the bushes, "he be Cap'n Sage's loot'nant. He be on his way to the rector's house to fetch a lady and baby."

"Who you were to seize and bind?" said Domino.

"No, sir, not me. Least 'twas Cap'n's orders, your worship. 'Twas to keep her from knowin' we can't sail yet for a week, and then she be knowin' we was turnin' back to Virginia, mayhap."

"Why?" Domino pursued. "Surely you could have brought her aboard in a week's time, as well, and sailed when you pleased."

"Cap'n Sage be feared another cap'n 'ud spy her and take her hisself."

"I see. And why would that happen?"

"I swear, your honor, I won't know. But I heard Cap'n Sage tell Mr. Flint 'twas prize money on her in Virginia Colony."

"I cannot understand why she must be seized. Why not bring her aboard and seize her then?"

The man shook his head. " 'Twon't be no good. Cap'n Sage was afeared if she warn't the right one, she be able to say he took her up to Virginia so he 'ud have to do away with her. And he didn't want no one in Savannah to know she come aboard—in case there be some big person like that there governor lookin' for her."

"I see," Domino said, not fully understanding, but anxious now to hurry on to the parsonage. If it were not Caroline, he would be able to notify the rector of Sage's attempted abduction. If she were Caroline! His pulse quickened and he ordered the man forward.

"You will say that I am Mr. Flint—unless they have seen him at the parsonage."

"No, sir. 'Twas only the cap'n and meself, sir."

"A stroke of luck," Domino murmured. Then he said, "Mind you, sailor, one false word and all will die."

"Aye, sir," the man said. He trudged forward, leading the way, and a little farther on he spoke: "Beggin' your pardon, your honor, but was you to send me back to the cap'n after this night's work, I be given Moses Law or hanged from the yardarm."

"A fate you well deserve," Domino said.

"No, sir, not me. Was I to do anything but the cap'n's

biddin', 'twould be death long since. Once I seen the cap'n after a man deserted. When they caught him, 'twas more'n Moses Law. 'Twas one hunnerd lashes ordered, with him dead afore sixty, an' the bos'n was still beatin' after that."

"A merchant captain? Sending to find deserters?"

"No, sir, 'twas when Cap'n Sage was a navy cap'n. But even for the navy was he too cruel, and they sent him off. Me, sir, I won't never seen him again, but he got me one night when I was comin' home from the tavern, kinda celebratin' me weddin' an Betsy waitin' and me merry, sir, and singin', and he got me. Next thing I be aboard the *Indies Queen* and not set foot in England since. An' that be near four year ago."

"And would you desert again?"

"Aye, sir, was I certain he won't never find me."

"Then I will take you with me," Domino promised, "but, mark you, only if you do not fail tonight."

"No, sir," the man said fervently.

"What is your name?"

"Carson, sir."

"Well, Carson, look lively, and I will show you a better life than you knew before this night."

"Aye, sir, thank-ee, sir. Be you a ship cap'n, sir?"

"Yes. Here we are," Domino said, and the man turned to look at him, drawing himself up to his full height and seeming less servile.

"You neen't worry, Cap'n. I be a good sailor, and I be better knowin' 'tis no lady I must cosh tonight." A shadow of fear spread over his face. "I neen't cosh her, Cap'n?" And when Domino shook his head, he added, "Nor will ye let Cap'n Sage find me?"

"No. Now, hurry, and, Carson, no matter what happens, remember that I am Mr. Flint. If you hear anyone call me a different name, you must say that I am Mr. Flint."

"Aye, sir," Carson answered.

Dr. Wright opened the door to their knock. His face looked worried beneath his pleasant words of greeting, but as Carson presented "Mr. Flint" and Domino stepped out of the shadows, his expression gave way to relief and a faint puzzlement.

Mr. Flint was a gentleman if Sage was not. It was a curious combination, for it was Flint who looked as if he should be captain and Sage no more than a cutthroat sailor. He coughed mentally in his thoughts at the uncharitable description, then cried heartily, "Come in, sir! Come in! Mistress Dobbs is waiting impatiently."

"Forgive me," Domino said smoothly, "but we are late and the ship is ready to sail. Carson will take the lady's parcels and I shall wait here. Could I impose on your good nature to ask her to hurry?"

"Yes, yes, of course. We will be sorry to lose her. She is a most pleasant young lady. Do you know that she is under the protection of the Virginia governor?"

"Yes, sir," Domino said politely, letting just a hint of impatience into his voice.

"Well, then, Lieutenant, I must not delay you. This way, my good man," he said to Carson, who scurried into the hall after him.

Domino stepped off the doorsill so that his face was well in the shadows. He steeled himself against the possibility that Caroline—if, indeed, it were she—would cry out his name at the very moment she saw him. He could only hope that Carson would remember his orders.

A moment later, Carson reappeared, bearing a small chest and a cradle. "All is well, Cap'n," he whispered as he neared Domino.

The rector was back at the door, this time with the woman on his arm. Domino saw her outlines, saw that she cradled a baby, and then she moved forward so that the light fell on her face. Caroline! His heart jumped in his chest.

"Mr. Flint," the rector called out, peering into the dark garden.

"Now, Carson," Domino whispered, and Carson hurried forward.

"The loot'nant be waitin', ma'am," he said hurriedly.

Caroline moved forward even as Domino bowed low, muttering, "Your servant, ma'am."

"Mr. Flint," she replied on a rising inflection. She hesitated in the doorway. Domino thought, there is no hope for it. I must go forward and offer my arm.

He kept his face to the shadows as long as possible, but when at last he reached her, the light from the open door fell full upon him. He met her eyes evenly and gave a nearly imperceptible shake of his head. Her face went deadly pale and her eyes dilated enormously. She looked ready to faint and he quickly offered his arm, saying anxiously, "I know well the pain of parting, ma'am. Pray, do not concern yourself. You shall reach your destination in full safety, on my honor as a gentleman."

"Welladay, Mistress Dobbs!" Dr. Wright said in a hearty voice. "If you pass this way again, we shall welcome you."

After a moment more for suitable farewells, they were going down the path, Caroline holding firmly on to Domino's arm with one hand and clutching the baby to her with her free arm.

On the dark road, after the door closed behind them, she finally spoke. "Domino . . . where . . . what . . . "

"All in good time, ma'am," he said coolly. "When we are at the inn. You are Mistress Goodfort, my wife."

"Goodfort?"

"Goodfort," he said. "The next few minutes are crucial. Say nothing. Draw your hood well over your curls. Here, I will take the child."

She obeyed him meekly. There were a thousand questions on her lips and her mind was dazed from this blinding change of her fortunes. Domino . . . he was here, dressed like a rich London merchant and acting as Sage's lieutenant. She settled her hood and reached for the baby.

"Congratulations, ma'am," he said, handing it back. "Who does it favor, its father or mother?"

Caroline smiled to herself and said, "She resembles her father."

"Poor infant," Domino said harshly.

"I do not think so," Caroline answered, "for I think her father is quite handsome."

"So handsome that you fled his home?"

"I fled no home of Felicity's father," she replied.

"So it would seem," he answered with a sneer. "Look, here is the inn. Remember, keep your face down and say nothing. Carson?"

"Aye, Cap'n."

"I will get you stay in the barn, for there are no other accommodations—indeed, not so much as an extra room for the lady. See that you keep well out of sight. Tomorrow night we will leave these shores. Until then, stay hidden or Captain Sage will surely catch you."

"Aye, aye, sir," the man answered eagerly. He set down the trunk and cradle at the back door.

Domino tapped and the door opened immediately.

"Well, and you have your good lady with you, Mr. Goodfort," Stevenson said, noting Caroline's half-concealed face with interest.

"Yes. And I would ask a further favor," Domino replied. "My man has no lodgings. He would be grateful for a night in your barn."

"And he is welcome," Stevenson said. "Wait there and I will show you the way, my good man. Come, Mrs. Goodfort. The tavern room is still crowded with all manner of sailors. I will take you up by the back stairs."

Caroline kept her face hidden until the door closed behind the landlord. Then she laid Felicity in her cradle and turned to Domino. "You're here," she said. "I can scarcely believe it." She moved forward, but he stood, watching her, a strange expression on his face. Something was wrong. A thousand times she had envisioned their meeting, and always she had been at once in his embrace.

"What is it?" she asked, bewildered.

"Nothing," he said shortly.

"But . . . aren't you . . . I mean . . . Domino, you came for me, and yet you act as if I were a stranger whom you liked little."

She came close to him, looking up into his face, and said softly, "Oh, darling, how I have longed for this moment."

With a quick movement, he pulled her roughly into his arms and began to kiss her with harsh urgency. She pressed close against him, not caring that his mouth bruised hers, welcoming the pain of it.

Her cloak fell from her shoulders and she uttered a sharp cry as his lips, wandering down her throat, fell upon the soft flesh of her bosom. Behind them, Felicity stirred and whimpered in her sleep.

"I must go to her," Caroline whispered.

But he held her more firmly and she made no effort to disengage herself. The baby made no further outcry.

"Domino," she whispered, "there is so much to tell you, and so much I want to know."

"Hush," he said hoarsely. His hands were busy with her lacings, and as the garments fell from her one by one, passion rose within and thumped along her nerves. Somewhere between the door and the bed, he blew out the candle, and at last he was beside her, as she had dreamed he would be. But it was not the dream; it was the reality. Gone was the tenderness she had recalled with such exquisite agony. He was like a man possessed. His mouth on hers grew harsher and blood spurted from where his teeth nipped her lips.

His hands on her flesh bruised her, and he pulled upon her body as if he would mold and knead it to his own design. When at last he thrust himself between her thighs, it was with a cruelty he had never shown her. Yet she had no will to resist him, and even before the fleeting sense of shock had passed, she felt herself borne along on the high tide of passion, up, up, and up, soaring along the crest until it broke at last on her long-wailing call.

They were both sweating when it was over and she clung to him, trembling in the aftershocks. "I love you," she said at length, and at that he pushed her from him.

"Is that what you say to everyone?" he grated. "Your husband, your baby's father, and God knows who else since then?"

"Domino!" she exclaimed, sitting up and clutching the coverlet around her.

"Domino!" he mimicked. "Not content with a husband alone. Even him you betray with yet another man."

"You were the man I betrayed him with," she said. "Have you forgotten?"

"No." The word was torn from him.

"Then my sin is your own," she said.

"And who, pray tell, is the infant's father?" he said with bitter sarcasm. "Or do you not remember?"

The insult went through her like a bolt of lightning splitting a tree. Her body went rigid with the shock and her breath caught painfully in her throat, so she could not speak.

"I see," he said in the same bitter voice. "You can't remember."

"I can't forget," she answered at last. "No, Felicity is not Joshua's child. She is yours. Do you think that Felicity is but a new infant? She is yours. Yours. Yours. And Joshua tried to kill her. He knew. He knew!" Her breath was choking her, tears ran down her cheeks, and anger, shock, and humiliation struggled within her. "Look at her for yourself." She sprang naked from the bed and, striking a flint, lit the taper again.

"What are you doing?" he said as she went to the cradle.

Holding the taper high above it, she cried, "Look at her, then! Look at her!"

He stood immobile and the tallow wavered in her hand as she trembled.

"She is yours," Caroline repeated, and at this she turned away, letting the arm that held the taper fall. He was across the room in a few strides and wrenched it from her nerveless fingers.

"Are you telling me the truth?" he asked in an incredulous voice.

"Yes," she said lifelessly. Crossing her arms across her bare breasts, she hugged herself to still her quivering body.

She heard him moving toward the cradle, heard him mutter as he bent over it. And then he said, "I would not know who she favors, Caroline, except she has dark hair. A handsome baby." He put the taper down and came back to her.

"Look at me," he said quietly, and she raised her eyes.

"Is Felicity mine?"

"Yes, she is yours."

"Then whoever she favors, I am satisfied." He put an arm around her and said, "Come back to bed. You will die of fever."

She suffered herself to be led back, but when they were once more lying together, she held herself apart from him.

After a moment, he said quietly, "Tell me then what happened and why you ran away."

She began the story slowly, with an absence of feeling, but in the telling her memory flooded back, and long before she was finished the full horror of it—of Joshua's abuse, of thinking the baby dead, of the terrible day she had trod the sand dunes and blundered through the forest —came back to her in a way she had never permitted before.

She was sobbing and shivering at the end of it, held close in Domino's arms, her tears wetting his chest, while he tried to soothe her. He murmured broken words of endearment and comfort until, spent, her tears abated.

"I won't leave you again," he said. "Or if I must, 'twill

be a safe place where I can come for you. Shh!" he added as she started to speak. "You are safe enough now. We will soon be aboard the *Mouette*."

"You have her?" Caroline said, trying to hold back the sleep that was overtaking her.

"I have her, and you . . . and, it seems, a daughter, as well. Christos is there. Haywood is with me. And this time we will try to find a woman to sail with us. I will buy one of Stevenson's blacks or one from among the owners farther down the coast. I can offer a good price in gold. And you shall have someone to help you, and when we reach Liberté, the woman will be freed. I think I might, after all, buy a few slaves before we go to Liberté, and free them. I shall be master of that island and make the laws: no slaves, no debtors. You will like that, Caroline, and so shall . . . " He stopped, hearing her deep, even breathing.

A fine beginning, he thought in rueful amusement. A few hours together and I have talked her to sleep. He drew the covers around her gently and, for a long time before he slept, lay staring into the dark room. Beneath his elation over finding her ran a current of sobriety. It would be many months before they would be able to raise Liberté, and there was much to be done before then. She and the baby could not remain aboard a privateer engaged in battles. He would have to part with her almost as soon as he had found her. But, where? It was a long time before he fell asleep.

In the morning, Savannah was in an uproar. Flint's body had been found, and with that grim discovery Sage let it be known that Mistress Dobbs and her child had never reached his ship; they were missing, along with a scurvy rogue named Carson, who had probably done away with them both.

Caroline stayed in her room above the tavern while Domino went downstairs. His first step was to assure himself that Carson was well hidden in the hayloft of Stevenson's barn, and his next effort was to seek out Stevenson himself.

"Welladay, Mr. Goodfort!" Stevenson greeted him dryly. "It appears that there was yet another lady and her child and yet another low fellow with them who were abducted last night."

"You know well the position, Mr. Stevenson," Domino

said boldly. "And I thank you for keeping silent thus far."

"Tell me your tale, then, Mr. Goodfort. But I warn you, if I do not believe it, I will go to the governor myself."

"I trust you will believe it," Domino said, paling a little. He would not at all relish leaving his dagger in this good man.

As briefly as he could, Domino laid the story before Mr. Stevenson, who listened without comment. When it ended, he said, "An unlikely story, Mr. Goodfort, not one I could readily believe. However, I know that you are a gentleman of some intelligence and imagination, both of which could have given you leave to make a more believable tale than this. I have heard of Sage, as who has not? He has called thrice before at Savannah, and each time his crewmen come ashore with an armed guard. As for the lady, I knew when I saw her last evening, for I have seen her before both at the rectory and coming along the roads with her child. Mistress Dobbs. And I heard Sage talking of a Mistress Welles and prize money. I have heard that before, as well. So, you see, all of it lends credence to this incredible story."

"We must all be thankful for that," Domino said obliquely. "You will honor my request, then?"

"I will honor it and keep Caroline hidden. But I cannot promise there will not be a search instituted. Murder has been committed, whatever the provocation," he added as Domino made as if to speak.

"Should it come to a search," Domino said quietly, "the first men through the door will die by my pistols."

"Of that I have no doubt, Mr. Goodfort—if that is your name, sir."

"As to that, landlord, I will give you my own name before I leave your premises."

Stevenson laughed and held out his hand. "Done, Mr. Goodfort. 'Twill be worth the adventure to learn just who and what you are. I liked you from the first, mind you, or I would not have accommodated you. I will stay with my first opinion until I learn better."

"We'll shake on it. On my honor, I have spoken the truth," Domino said, grasping Stevenson's hand firmly.

"Then I had better take Carson to quarters less likely to be searched than my barn," Stevenson said mildly. "What time do you leave?"

"As soon after dark as possible," Domino told him.

"Hmm. I know the roads will be full of searchers for some time. You, the lady, the baby, and Carson will surely attract immediate attention. You would do well to avoid the riverfront and go by the inland road until you are south of the town. There is a path leading to the river just below the first plantation you come to. Where is your vessel?"

"She lies some five leagues due south of here."

"And your boat?"

"Below in the harbor. I will send word to my master's mate to bring her downstream."

"Well and good. If we do not meet before you leave," Stevenson said, "may fortune smile on you."

"Your servant, sir." Domino bowed.

It was midnight before the party reached the longboat. Carson, who, under orders, had washed himself and grudgingly allowed his hair to be fashioned into a braid, wore breeches and a jerkin supplied him by one of the *Mouette*'s crew who now huddled uncomfortably in Carson's old and filthy garments.

"Take comfort, Fremont," Domino said as they boarded, "you'll get a new outfit from the booty once we are aboard."

"Aye, sir," the man replied, brightening.

Haywood, who had given a long, low, incredulous whistle on spying Caroline, still wore a look of avid curiosity as he held the baby while Domino helped Caroline into the boat.

"Mr. Haywood, sir," Carson called out, "is't a new crew you be holdin' so tender?"

"Belay that!" Haywood cried sharply.

"Aye, aye, sir," Carson replied with a return of his customary meekness. A muffled titter ran through the men.

Domino reached for the child and said mildly, "And now 'tis a new crew member I hold so tenderly. Make ready to cast off, Mr. Haywood."

"Aye, aye, Captain," Haywood said, leaping lightly into the boat.

As they pulled away from the shore, they saw the faint light of torches well to the north but moving closer.

"Not a moment too soon," Domino muttered. "I wonder what Mr. Sage will make of it all."

"Beggin' your pardon, Cap'n," Carson spoke up.

"What is it, Carson?"

"Cap'n Sage, he be thinkin' he sail for Virginia to sell information to . . . "

"Yes," Domino cut him off. "That would be likely. Comfortable, ma'am?" he said to Caroline in a neutral voice.

"Yes, thank you, Captain Domino," she replied tranquilly, and saw his eyes gleam with amusement. How I love him, she thought rapturously and wished that they were at the end of the journey to the *Mouette* instead of the beginning.

They were two weeks at sea, with the *Mouette* nearly in sight of land, before Domino revealed his plans to Caroline.

She had spent those two weeks in a state of happiness so intense that she would awake sometimes to Felicity's cooing morning sound and touch Domino beside her and then think, with a clutch of fear, that such happiness must be paid for with tears.

Where before she had been confined to the cabin in loneliness and fear, she was now free to move from it to the great cabin and out upon the veranda adjoining it. There she spent many a sunny day playing with Felicity or pacing to and fro. She was glad that Domino had been unable to purchase a woman. Her days were filled with duties: feeding Felicity, rocking her to sleep, and washing her little garments. Her nights were filled with Domino, who, as far as all but Caroline knew, bunked in the master's cabin.

All that Domino had withheld during their sojourn on the island he talked of now. And yet, despite his plans for their future, she would sometimes look up and find him regarding her with an almost sad expression.

Once, catching such a look, she said, "It is as if we are married, but we aren't. Does that worry you?"

He shook his head, his face clearing at once and a teasing smile replacing the worried look. "I shall be the head of the island. I shall make Christos the chief justice at once. He will give you a bill of divorcement, and then, of course, he will marry us."

"But it wouldn't be legal," she argued.

"More legal than this," he answered, then put his arms

around her. "This is very illegal," he said against her lips. "Does that mar your pleasure?"

"Nothing can mar my pleasure now," she answered.

At that he drew away. "I have something to tell you," he said.

And the tone of his voice made her say, "No—no, don't tell me anything that will spoil things."

"I must," he said. "I've put it off long enough. "We are in the gulf now that lies between New Orleans and Mexico. In a day or two we will be in New Orleans."

"But I thought . . ."

"I know, I know. But I can't leave you anywhere else. . . ."

"Leave me," she said faintly. "Oh, no, no. You said you'd never leave me again."

"Listen to me," he begged. "I am still under letters of marque. The war is not yet over, although it will soon be. Spain has surrendered. France must follow soon. It is only a delaying action now while they try for better treaty terms. Rodney was too successful," he added bitterly. "The English have made greater demands than before. Otherwise, the war would have ended sooner."

She listened to him, only half-hearing. The war was nearly over and England was the victor, and once she would have been delighted with the news. Now, she cared not at all, save that Domino was going away from her again, and this time . . . She voiced the thought.

He responded by saying, "Nonsense. I am in less danger now than before. I have a better crew. I have a captured English flag under which to run the British blockades. And, most of all, I need not spend half my time wondering if I will find you again. I am taking you to the Gray Sisters in New Orleans."

"Who are the Gray Sisters?"

"Ursuline nuns who were sent out fifty years ago to keep the casquette girls from being molested by women-hungry men until they should be suitably bid for and married."

"And I must stay in a Roman convent?" she cried in dismay. "Why, that is not fit."

He laughed. "Put aside the stories you have heard. This is not medieval Italy, nor France, nor England, for that matter. This is modern times. You will find the Ursulines gentle and pleasant."

"How do you know that? My father says that they—all nuns—are strange women who hate men unless they are priests, and that many of their orphans . . . "

He laughed again. "How ignorant you are about some things, my darling," he said. "Priests do not molest nuns, nor do nuns produce babies with which to people their orphanages."

"How do you know that?" she persisted.

"As to the Ursulines, I have reason to know. Once long ago, when I was much younger, I brought a girl to them for sanctuary."

She looked at him. "A girl you . . . "

"No, not a girl I loved, nor, indeed, bedded. She was a girl I found on the streets of New Orleans. She'd been sent out by her parents to sell herself and bring money home. She was so young and so frightened that she was shaking. Her face bore a bruise that she later told me was given to her by her father for failing on the previous day to do his bidding. She was a virgin, and painfully young—not more than thirteen. I brought her to the Ursulines. They took her in and . . . well . . . eventually she became a nun and went to a convent in France," he finished lamely.

"And is that the fate you intend for me and our daughter?" she asked, unable to refrain from laughing.

"Hardly," he replied, seizing her. "I know you too well for that. In fact," he said, caressing her naked buttocks gently, "I am leaving you in a convent to make certain you are saved for me."

She thought of Byrd Travers, and as quickly put him out of her mind. That secret she would always keep from Domino. He might have another woman, but he would never forgive her having another man, especially not when he learned she had sold herself as surely as that young girl tried to sell herself . . . and had enjoyed it. In that, she was a whore, and she saw it with unflinching clarity. I would do it again, she thought now. If it was the only way to be rid of Joshua and find Domino, she would do it again.

"I don't want another man," she whispered, and between her fear of parting and the thought of all the lonely nights ahead, she pressed herself eagerly upon him, as if in the act of union they would be forever joined. "If we must part," she said, "then stay with me until the time comes—like this, together."

He looked down at her, his eyes unreadable, and for answer he covered her mouth with his own, so that at the climax he seemed to fill every curve and orifice of her body.

Chapter Nineteen

The *Mouette* arrived at her anchorage some miles southeast of the town of New Orleans on an evening that was exceptionally warm for November. The sun was a crescent of blood over the western rim, and the earth was still.

Caroline, standing on the veranda deck and watching the land draw closer, swallowed hard against the sadness that engulfed her. It was over. Soon she would be leaving the ship for the Ursuline convent. Despite Domino's reassurance, she imagined it as a dreary, prison-like place. Even in this steaming, lush land, she could feel that cold.

The water, thick and yellow, was sluggish, driven in spite of itself by the undercurrents that forced it into the deeply blue gulf below.

On the banks, weeping willows and other trees grayed in their shrouds of drooping mosses bent low over the marshy delta earth.

There was a heavy tug as the anchor found its depth. The last of the sail was reefed. The sailors positioned in the mast rigging gave a cheer before scrambling down.

Sighing, Caroline turned back into the great cabin and walked through to her bedplace. Her chest was nearly packed and stood open to receive the last articles in the morning.

Felicity lay sleeping in the hammock Domino had strung for her. Her old cradle was no longer big enough for her. And Felicity was no longer the tiny, helpless infant that Caroline had carried all the miles to Norfolk and cared for in the months in Savannah. Nor was she any longer satisfied to be nursed, and Caroline knew her breasts were drying out. Now that Felicity was able to sit alone, she had begun to snatch at her dish of meal and minced bits of meat, and she struggled to drink from the beakers on the table.

"You can see that a ship is no place for a child," Domino had said on one occasion, witnessing Caroline's efforts to feed Felicity during a brief rough sea, "nor for a woman," he added before Caroline could speak.

"If a woman wore a jerkin and breeches instead of skirts, she'd be every bit as good at sea," Caroline had retorted.

"I can see you in a jerkin and breeches," he had said and laughed. "A bit too full abaft the prow." And he touched her breasts lightly.

She sighed again, and for want of anything better to do she began to rearrange the clothing in the chest.

Her mood persisted and she made no effort to conceal her unhappiness, neither while eating with Domino and Christos nor later, lying in Domino's arms for what she knew would be the last time for a long time. Not even the ardor of his lovemaking dispelled the weighted brooding that hung upon her as heavily as the Spanish moss clung to the oaks on the shore.

In the early morning he roused her gently and made love to her with a quiet tenderness that so underlined her own despair that she wept in the aftermath, her body already feeling the ache of emptiness.

"I will stay with you in New Orleans," he promised in an effort to comfort her, "for another day. Don't cry, Caroline. There, you have awakened Felicity."

He brought the baby to her and watched as she began to nurse.

"She has robbed me of one of my pleasures," he said with a grin.

"Not for much longer," Caroline answered. "My milk no longer satisfies her. Indeed, it seems I have not as much as before."

"Another reason to take her ashore. At the convent, you can give her beakers of cow's milk without fighting a ship's roll."

Caroline did not answer, regarding him out of eyes held wide against the renewal of tears.

He said hastily, "Now, it will be for only a little while. Come, let us be happy today. We've much to do."

"When do we leave the *Mouette?*"

"As soon as we have eaten. We must row inland through one of the bayous and then into the islet, and then we are there. There will be a servant for you and . . . "

"And then the Ursulines," she finished steadily.

"To make arrangemnts. I will take rooms for us at one of the inns, and you shall see how different New Orleans is from the English colonies."

"Better?"

"Much better." He rose and began to dress in the clothes he had worn in Savannah instead of the customary rough breeches and waistcoat he wore aboard.

"And you," he said when he had finished, "you must dress in fashion, too. Don't forget, you are no longer Mistress Dobbs, but Madame de Beaufort. I am known by my own name here."

"And how will you explain leaving your wife and child?" Caroline asked.

"Very simply. I have business for the king, and that is true enough."

"And how came you by an English wife?"

"We met in Guadeloupe, where your father was a representative of the Crown to the neutral government."

"You make up many romances whenever you leave me," she said.

"But this will be the last one. Come, the child is finished. Hurry, now."

New Orleans was very different from the other American colonies. In her interest and excitement, much of Caroline's misery sank into the background.

On Canal Street, Domino hired a horse and carriage and they made their first stop at the open slave market. It was the first time she had seen slaves bought and sold.

While Domino went ahead to the gathering of men at the foot of the block on which the slaves were brought forward, she sat in the carriage and leaned forward to listen to the auction.

The auction had been in progress for sometime, and only half a dozen blacks remained now to be sold. Among them there was only one woman. The men were dressed alike in soiled breechcloths. The woman was clothed in the ordinary garb of slave women, her head wrapped in a worn turban.

As each male was brought forward, the auctioneer

gave his height and weight, as if he were a horse. "Strong, well-muscled, obedient. He caused no difficulty during the voyage. Do I hear ten pounds?"

The bidding went on until the last bid of one hundred pounds was reached. The auctioneer unbound the man's manacles and he was sent down from the block to follow one of his purchaser's other slaves out of the crowd.

Five men remained. The first three sold in varying prices; one, obviously sick and not as tall or strong as the rest, went for ten pounds. He was taken away by a white man with a whip, who, Caroline surmised, was an overseer.

She watched as they pushed through the crowd, and as they reached the open space, the slave stumbled and the overseer's whip flashed out automatically, landing a light but stinging blow across the man's bare back. It was enough to make him fall, and he lay on the ground, retching miserably. Again the whip flashed, this time harder, but although the man cried out, he did not get up. Once more and then again the whip cracked.

The auction proceeded as if there was nothing amiss. Still the man lay there, as if unconscious. The overseer dropped the whip and bent over him to drag him to his feet, but at the first touch he drew back from the slave and said loudly, "Fever! He has the fever!"

The word reached the rest and they drew together so that the overseer, in pushing his way forward to the block, found his passage impeded.

"You have sold me a sick buck!" he cried out. "Mr. LeClerq will be down himself unless you make this good," he threatened.

"Another—take another," the auctioneer said. "Here, a fine buck." He thrust forward the last, a young male who looked half-starved, but who was nevertheless standing tall, his head held proudly, his eyes staring straight ahead above the crowd, his face expressionless.

"Good specimen," the auctioneer wheedled. "Worth every penny of one hundred twenty-five pounds."

"Send him down, then. And he had better not carry fever, as well."

"Your money, sir," the auctioneer said.

"I give you no more," the overseer sneered. "You can take the other slave back."

"Ten pounds is no price for one like this," the auction-eer argued.

"It is all you will get—this one in place of the other, honestly bid and paid for and wrongly sold. Make good, now, or I will report you to Mr. LeClerq."

"Take him," the auctioneer said sullenly, shoving the slave forward.

"Follow me, boy," the overseer commanded, and he set off, the young black at his heels. As he passed the spot where the first slave lay, the overseer kicked him aside. A low, agonized groan broke from the man, and the second black knelt, dropping beside the first with an easy grace. A moment later he rose, with the older man in his arms.

"Here, what the devil do you think you are doing?" the overseer shouted, then brought his whip down with as much force as he could muster, but he was shorter by a head, and without leverage, the blow was weaker than he intended it to be.

The young slave scarcely flinched, but began to move forward toward the overseer.

"Put him down!" he ordered the black. "He has the fever! Keep him away!"

A low, murmuring growl arose from the crowd as they fell back. The young black continued to walk forward with easy strides, his face as impassive as before.

The crowds made way for him, the overseer fell back, and as the young black reached him, the overseer drew his pistol and fired. Once, twice, and still the black went on, and then a third time, and he pitched forward on his face, crushing his burden beneath him.

Almost as soon as the first shot sounded, Domino was back at the carriage, and with the second he sprang to-ward the overseer, trying to reach the hand that aimed the pistol for the third time. He was too late.

Sickened, Caroline turned away, hiding her face against Felicity. She could hear the overseer saying, "Fever! They both must have it! All of them! Who knows?"

There was another low growl from the crowd, and then it began to disperse, leaving the auctioneer and overseer in a heated argument.

Domino came back to the carriage, his face flushed with impotent rage. "It's over," he said to Caroline. "Try not to think of it. It is not a common occurrence, thank God. But there are too many men like that one."

"What will happen to . . . to . . . the blacks?" she questioned.

"They will be carted away. The old one is sick. They . . . never mind. There is nothing to be done. I must see about the woman. I'll only be a moment. Are you all right?"

"Yes," she whispered. "Oh, Domino, my very own father owns slave ships."

"He is not alone," Domino answered and went off.

He was back a few moments later, bringing the woman with him.

"Her name is Jenny," he said. "She was sold south by her master at Charleston for disobedience after her husband died. Her children are still there."

"Oh," Caroline looked at the woman. "I . . . I'm sorry," she said inadequately.

"I have told her that if she stays with you until my return, she is free to go where she likes . . . or to come with us to Liberté. She has agreed."

He turned back to Jenny. "This is my wife, Jenny," he said, "and my daughter."

"Thank-ee, massa," she said.

"Come, into the carriage," he said.

Jenny climbed into the back seat and, reaching forward, said, "mistiss, I take the baby, please."

Caroline placed the sleeping child in her arms and Jenny settled back, holding Felicity with firm competence.

"Cruel," Caroline said in a low voice to Domino.

"Cruel," he agreed. "If I could, I would bring her children to her. She can never go back."

"Disobedience," Caroline said. "What kind of disobedience to merit such cruel punishment?"

He shook his head. "It doesn't matter—something minor. The master needed money or was short on his trading with the slaver. Selling a slave for rank disobedience sounds better. It is more socially acceptable than selling one of a married pair or a mother."

"I . . . I saw slaves mistreated before this," she said.

"So I heard," he remarked. "In Nassau they still speak of you in the slave quarters. You are fortunate you weren't discovered trying to free slaves."

"You . . . you were in Nassau after I left?"

"Yes."

"Then you did come back!"

"Yes," he said.

"Oh, why didn't you tell me that when you left me? If I'd known . . . I . . . "

"I didn't know myself. In any case, it is in the past." He clapped the reins, urging the horse to go faster. "It is the present we must think of now. The convent is just ahead."

Seated in the cool, dim reception room at the Ursulines' convent, Caroline only half-listened as Domino made the final arrangements for their stay with a tall, pleasant-faced nun named Mother Véronique.

The white-washed walls, the lacy iron grilles of the windows, and the dark, polished wood of the furnishings were church-like and somber.

A large, framed oil of Christ dominated the long wall opposite her. Ornamental crucifixes portraying Jesus in his last agony or plain crosses of cypress adorned much of the space on the other walls. A life-like statue of a woman she presumed to be Saint Ursula occupied a pedestal in one corner, and facing it was the Virgin Mary, both carved in marble, with the Virgin wearing a crown studded with jewels.

Through the open door at the end of the room, Caroline could see part of a long refectory table around which were austere, high-backed wooden chairs, all of which bore the same high glossy polish of the reception room furnishings, as if endless hours had been spent rubbing hogsheads of beeswax into them.

She wondered if laughter or song had ever echoed in these hushed chambers. The Ursulines, she knew, taught the daughters of residents and gave succor to the poor and the sick. Idly, she wondered if such as they ever entered the cloister itself.

" . . . it will amuse her, Ma Mère," Domino was saying suavely, "and help pass her time. Madame de Beaufort has received an education unusual in young English women."

Caroline started and turned her glance toward him. "I think you will enjoy aiding in the teaching chores, will you not, my dear?" His eyes signaled that she must assent.

"Teaching? Why, yes. Yes, I enjoy the schoolroom."

"Then it is settled," said the nun, rising. "We shall expect you in the morning, Madame."

Domino, who had risen with the nun, put out his hand to assist Caroline. "The baby," she said.

"Will you not leave her with us?" Mother Véronique asked. "She seems quite content with her nurse."

Caroline hesitated. Felicity, on awakening, had certainly taken an immediate fancy to Jenny and been borne off to the kitchen without a murmur of dissent.

Last day, last day, echoed her brain.

"I . . . if you think so," she appealed to Domino. Meeting his eyes, she was seized with a desire so strong that it caught at her chest, squeezing her heart dry. Blood pounded in her ears and her eyes misted. It was as if she stared down a long and narrow tunnel in which only he was present.

Dimly, she knew she ought to say something more, look away, preserve some semblance of tranquility. She saw his lips move, saw him wrench his own eyes away, and heard him saying, as if from a long distance, "Yes. It is most kind of you, Ma Mère. I shall bring Madame de Beaufort back in the morning."

Morning, she thought, but it is only a little past noon. And there is Felicity to nurse. Still, she could not form the words and permit them to issue from her lips.

Domino placed his hand under her elbow, and again a hot current flowed through her. She never remembered leaving the convent that day, and she had no idea what she said to the nun. They were through the door and down the steps and into the carriage before she spoke at all, and then it was only to say helplessly, "Domino."

"I know," he answered. Looking at him, she saw that this totally unexpected desire had caught him, as well. It is as if we had not been together for years, she thought, dazed, instead of only a few hours.

They said nothing more. They drove through the streets in silence. When they reached the inn, not far from Royal Street, it was all she could do to alight with his assistance.

Waiting while he arranged for their rooms, watching the back of the innkeeper as he led them upstairs to an airy chamber through whose windows she could see the wrought-iron balustrade of the upper gallery, she thought she could not contain herself.

The door had scarcely closed behind the innkeeper when she was in Domino's arms. He covered her face with kisses, and she, half-fainting from emotion, began to pull at his jacket. Somewhere between the door and the bed, their garments were cast off and strewn behind them, and when at last she felt the hot flesh of his body, she cried aloud.

When he sought to caress her, she urged him up on her, opening to him, rising to meet him with a wild abandon, moaning and writhing and calling out, and even, when it was over, trying to hold him to her, far from spent.

"I want more," she muttered.

"I know," he said. "Shh!" And, slipping his hands between her thighs, he touched her delicately and knowingly until another wave of pleasure broke over her, sweet and searing. He stayed as he was, now moving lightly, then, as she began to writhe again beneath his touch, more firmly.

Again and again the passion surged, until at last she was surfeited and murmured feebly, "No more. No more."

She slept after that and awoke to find the late-afternoon sun slanting through the closed jalousies. Domino was already dressed, and as she stirred he looked at her, his face alive, his eyes warm and desirous.

She held out her arms and he laughed. "No," he said. "A wanton. A very wanton. You may live on love, my darling, but I must feed my belly, or it will be poor love you have from me tonight. Come, get up and dress. I am going downstairs to wait. You are too tempting.

She had been languorous in her awakening and in her dressing, yet when she was ready to descend the stairs, she became aware of the fact that she was famished.

The first stroll through New Orleans did little to hold back the hunger pangs, and by the time they reached the French market, with its open stalls displaying every conceivable kind of fish and the steaming kettles spewing forth a variety of delicious odors, she could have consumed anything.

They stood in the street, wolfing down cold bayou crab and warm, freshly boiled shrimp seasoned with spices.

As her hunger abated, Caroline looked around at the street, crowded with all kinds of people: elegantly gowned ladies who painted their faces and wore dark patches of varying designs, now at the side of the lips, now beneath an eye or high upon an elegant cheekbone; gallants escorting them, cuffs thick with lace, stockings snowy white over white breeches; Spanish ladies with hair swept high by combs and with skirts spreading beneath the delicate folds of waist-length mantillas; black servants chattering together in a curious patois in which Caroline discerned French-sounding words, as well as Spanish and alien words.

Walking back through the town, she found the buildings as varied as the New Orleaners themselves: old houses of split cypress wood, roofed in rough cypress bark; brick-and-board houses, almost always with wrought-iron galleries on which people sat, calling to each other across the intervening space, fanning themselves as the late sun burned in the still air. Here and there were houses of a different nature, all stucco, tinted yellow or pink or green with tiled roofs that opened in the very center to look down on courtyards where cool fountains splashed and voices were raised in tinkling laughter.

As the sun set and twilight deepened, the cooling breezes circled in from the surrounding waters and Domino guided her to a public eating place where, to her surprise, she managed to consume an enormous meal of oysters and pheasant and strange roast meat that Domino told her was buffalo. There was with the meal almost every kind of vegetable, some very much like those she had eaten in Nassau. There was also a dish, a mixture of hominy and fish and meat, highly seasoned, that she enjoyed so much that she regretted her excesses with the oysters and pheasant.

Sipping a thick coffee well laced with hot milk at the end of the feast, she said, "I am a glutton today."

"In every way," he agreed. He seemed to be taking a particular pleasure in her enjoyment of the food. He said as they left the restaurant, "It is a wonder to me that with that appetite you remain so slender."

They walked slowly now, turning down by the canal and then away again to seek their lodgings. He slipped his arm around her and she rested against him.

"I love the night," she murmured. "It gives one privacy."

"And today we have need of privacy," he said. "Tonight we will have it." He tightened his grasp and she pressed her head against his arm.

"I wish that tonight would last forever," she said.

"You would soon grow weary," he answered.

Later, resting in his arms, she said, "You will come back for me, Domino?"

"I will come back for you," he answered. "I came back this time not knowing where you were. Now I know where you are and that you are waiting for me."

She was silent, not wanting to give tongue to the doubts that still remained below the surface of her temporary contentment.

For a long time after he slept, she remained awake, in spite of the physical weariness of her body. Her breasts were swollen with the last of her milk, and the pain reminded her of Felicity and the long time that she had been without her customary nursings.

Felicity, who had been her sole preoccupation in the months before Domino found her, had receded along with the rest of the world during this last day; and even now she shimmered in the distance, more phantom than real. All the reality lay beside her. Turning, she buried her face in Domino's strong back, her arms encircling his waist, and fell asleep at last.

Chapter Twenty

Spain had surrendered in August of 1762, and France, holding back her own inevitable capitulation in the new hope of getting a better settlement, finally followed suit.

The news did not reach the Colonies for some months afterward, and when New Orleans residents were finally apprised of it, they shrugged it off. The war had not touched New Orleans during the seven years it raged through the other Colonies and the peace, by whatever terms, could not, therefore, affect the city.

Louis, in a secret treaty the year before, had ceded New Orleans to Spain. Now, under the force of compensating Spain for the loss of Florida to England, he had agreed to give the rest of Louisiana to her ally.

Rumors had cropped up from time to time that such was the case, but no one in New Orleans gave them much credence. New Orleans was still French and still headed by its Creole society. Their rude awakening would arrive with d'Ulloa some two years hence. But in March of 1763, the town was still prospering and was still a law unto itself under the benign rule of the French governor.

Caroline, learning that the war had ended, began at once to anticipate Domino's quick return. Still, March was almost over and she had yet to receive word of him. Only blind faith—baseless, romantic, and hopelessly unrealistic—kept at bay her fear that he had been slain in battle.

Since Christmas, she had hugged to herself the secret knowledge that she was again with child. That and the daily miracle of Felicity growing plump and spoiled and beautiful under the ministrations of Jenny and the nuns' thwarted maternalism were her talismans against a cruel fate. This she clung to during the long and lonely nights.

However, her days were busy enough. She spent the mornings tutoring English to the French-speaking Creole children whom the Ursulines schooled, and in the afternoons she helped Sister Bernadette with her endless gardening.

She particularly like the latter chore; it was one she had assumed for herself. Sister Bernadette was different from the other nuns. They were soft-spoken and gentle and seemed as self-effacing as the gray uniforms that had inspired their nickname. But Sister Bernadette was strong and hearty and her ruddy complexion glowed above her somber habit.

She gave the appearance of a clear-eyed, healthy peasant. She was forthright of speech, to the common despair of the other nuns, and she exuded an aura of earthy courage.

She could skim lightly up a ladder to prune the peach and apple trees or to gather figs, and she could shake a pecan tree free of enough nuts to bake pies for the entire household.

Yet, beneath all that, she had a gentle and aesthetic appreciation for the flowers she cared for as assiduously as she did the vegetable garden. Her roses and the trumpet flowers and hibiscus bloomed riotously, and the two magnolia trees that graced the front lawn were always laden with deep-scented, creamy white blossoms.

"Had I been a man, I would have been a botanist," she once said to Caroline. "As it is, I tend gardens and read all about them."

She had a prodigious knowledge of plants and their relations to each other, and she delighted in instructing. As they worked, she would talk amiably, pointing out different facts about each plant. Caroline learned, among other things, that the hibiscus plants, with their elegant scarlet or pink or white flowers, were cousins of the gumbo, whose fruit produced the okra so widely used in their cooking, or that the lily was a branch of the onion family. She could not imagine when such information could be put to use, but Sister Bernadette took such pleasure from these pleasant instructions that Caroline encouraged her by asking questions.

She had never met a woman quite like Sister Bernadette. She was so little like one imagined a nun to be. Once Caroline ventured to ask her why she had chosen the cloistered life.

"I should tell you that I had a calling," Sister Bernadette replied, laughing. "But in truth, I decided early in life that I would not marry. My family was not desperately poor, but it was not that comfortable. My mother produced thirteen children and then died delivering the fourteenth. My sisters all married, some into worse circumstances. From the time I could hold a needle or turn the churning paddle, I was tied to the hearth. I was the youngest girl. My brothers could think of what they wanted to do. They could ride and shoot and learn. They could choose a wife or not at their pleasure.

"At fourteen, I went into the convent as a postulant. That was thirty years ago. Ah," she had paused reflectively, "perhaps, after all, it was a calling. I could never have lived as my mother did, with no time to myself and no opportunity to learn."

"But did you never want children or . . . or . . ."

"A man to love me?" Sister Bernadette finished. "It is not that I didn't want them, but that I wanted other things more. A woman's lot, at best, is difficult. Even the kindest husband expects much. So I chose God. Some say He is more exacting, but at least He is not nagging me about the housework." Here she had burst into a merry laugh and said, "In mercy's name, say nothing of this. Mother Véronique thinks me impious enough."

Bernadette was like her, and yet unlike her, Caroline thought. I'd love to have a man's freedom, she said to herself. But I always wanted to have a man of my own. If there were no Domino, there would have to be someone else, whereas Sister Bernadette is willing to sacrifice one for the other.

On a pleasant April day six weeks before Felicity's first birthday, Caroline stood in front of the small mirror in her little chamber arranging her cap to conceal most of her curls in preparation for the weekly marketing with Jenny.

This weekly trip outside the convent was the one event she looked forward to eagerly. She never tired of going through the market stalls to select those things that were not available from the convent gardens, dairy, or smoke-house.

Sometimes, as she strolled near the waterfront, she imagined Domino would suddenly appear, and the idea, since it was not totally in the realm of fantasy, delighted her. In her mind's eye she could see the *Mouette* anchored, see the longboat lowered, see Domino stepping into it, and at last tying up at the very dock where the shrimp boats landed.

She smiled at her reflection in the mirror.

Through the open casement she could hear the smaller children, under Mother Véronique's tutelage, singing the "Shepherd's Song."

She followed along with them:

> *Il était un bégerge*
> *Qui ron, ron, ron . . .*

It was a charming little song, and the children's voices made a piercingly sweet sound on the soft air:

> *Qui gardez des moutons, ton . . . ton . . .*

Caroline sang the ending aloud as she left the room. After a short interval, the piping of "Au Clair de la Lune" began.

Crossing the grassy lawn to the schoolhouse to receive final instructions from Mother Véronique, she met Jenny, wearing the freshly starched dress and turban that one of the nuns had made for her to wear on her ventures outside the convent walls.

"Where is Felicity?" Caroline asked her.

"Sistah tek um to dey schoolhouse."

"Sister Elizabeth?"

"Yes, shum tek um."

"The nuns are good to Felicity," Caroline said.

"Yea, dey beem," Jenny agreed.

They stood together peering in the window at the children, who had begun yet another song, a counting rhyme to which they clapped their hands in time.

Mother Véronique stood before them, beating out the rhythm, and held high in Sister Elizabeth's arms was Felicity, clapping her own small, chubby hands and laughing.

"Wait here," Caroline said. "I'll only be a minute. Is there anything needed in the kitchen that I must tell Mother Véronique about?

"No, mistiss, ef um beem, um don shay uh," said Jenny, unconsciously lapsing into the stronger Gullah speech that had eased somewhat during her stay at the convent.

"No, if there is, no one told me," Caroline translated to herself. Jenny's Gullah was beginning to make sense to her.

I am learning another language, she thought, amused, for Gullah was definitely a language of its own. A mixture of native African surrounded by peasant English learned from the white servants, it was nearly incomprehensible to the novice.

She went along to the classroom and met Mother Véronique on her way out.

"You are ready," Mother said, smiling. You look very fresh this morning. I fancy you are plumper than you were when you arrived. You must guard your appetite. Too much food is bad for the digestion."

"Yes, Mother," Caroline said, thinking soon she would have to tell the news, unless Domino returned first. Oh, to have him here and know that there would be no more separations!

She accepted the list, and when she started into the classroom Mother Véronique cautioned, "It is better that you do not say good-bye to Felicity. It will only make her cry."

"Yes, that's true," Caroline agreed reluctantly. "She is happy with the others, isn't she?"

"The adored one cannot be unhappy," Mother answered with a lift of her brow. "We are all spoiling her. We must begin to think of her discipline."

Caroline murmured an agreement that she did not mean. "We must begin to think," she had said, not, "you must begin to think." Too many cooks spoiled the broth, and too many mothers were ruining Felicity. For the thousandth time she cast a wordless prayer to the deity. Soon, soon, Domino must return soon. Her own litany, it was endlessly repetitious and lacking in the fine phrasing of that which the nuns intoned nightly in their chapel, but it was dear to her heart.

Jenny's basket was nearly full, and Caroline was in the process of selecting some bonbons as her own weekly gift to the community when the sun disappeared behind low, dark clouds.

As they passed once more into the street, rain sheeted down and they hurriedly sought shelter in the doorway of an old house.

In front of them people scurried past, seeking shelter of their own, some running toward their nearby homes before they and their purchases were soaked through.

"A sudden storm," she said to Jenny. " 'Twill soon pass."

"Yea, mistiss," Jenny replied. "Um shum wust."

"There was no cinnamon today," Caroline remarked idly. "Sister Bernadette will be disappointed, for she had gathered the first sweet potatoes for pie tonight."

She looked up from the baskets she had been examining to check the items against her list and saw that Jenny was staring straight ahead, a strange expression of fear and disgust on her face.

"What is it?" Caroline asked, following Jenny's gaze.

"Um beem lak dey debbil." She gave a shudder.

"Who?" Caroline scanned the street before her, but she saw nothing but two women hurrying on past them.

"Um. Dey mon dey." Jenny broke into rapid speech and Caroline couldn't follow her.

"I can't understand, " she said.

"Dey mon. Um look at um . . . me an' . . . an' . . . you," she blurted out.

"A bad man?"

"Yea, uh tink. Eye ob dey debbil."

"Where is he?"

"Um gone."

Caroline leaned out from the doorway and scanned the street, but there was no man in sight, and she said in a practical way, "Well, whoever he was, he means us no harm, or he wouldn't have disappeared. Come, Jenny, the rain is very light now. We'll go back."

By the time they neared the convent, the sun had reappeared. The leaves and grass, freshly washed, sparkled in the light, and among the trees jays shrilled the news, drowning out an oriole's music.

The empty streets filled up once more and it seemed to Caroline that the people, like the birds, had been refreshed and invigorated by the brief storm and were hastening to new pleasures.

But I, she thought to herself, am hastening back to the convent. From a pink house up ahead, a lady, dressed in the height of fashion, emerged and glided down the steps to a waiting phaeton. She was laughing, calling back over her shoulder to the gentleman who followed her.

Caroline experienced a stab of jealousy and longing. New Orleans was a wonderful city. The people enjoyed a variety of amusements and an endless array of parties. Sometimes, lying wakeful in her bed at the convent, Caroline had heard the sound of music and the hum of happy voices issuing from nearby homes. At such times she would sigh and turn on her pillow, longing for such entertainment herself.

Now, seeing the woman and man borne off for a happy evening of pleasure, she was painfully conscious of her own plain gown and of the dullness of the evening before her.

"I wish we were away from here," she said aloud to Jenny. "I wish D—— ... my husband would return."

"Yea, mistiss," Jenny said in a low voice, and Caroline was stricken with remorse. At least she had Felicity and this new child, and Domino was somewhere on the sea coming back to her, while Jenny ... Jenny had lost forever what she loved.

"I am foolish," she said lightly. "There are worse things than being bottled up in a Roman convent."

"Yea, um beem," Jenny answered. "Dey de patteroolers an' dey whup an' dey hongry an' cole. Um wust."

"Soon, Jenny, you will be free."

"No, mistiss. Ef uh beem free, uh beem by who chullen."

"There must be some way . . ." Caroline began.

But Jenny said, "No, dey don' beem. Dey massa beem kill um ef um run."

"You don't know Cap—— . . . er, Monsieur de Beaufort," Caroline said firmly, determined to offer hope even if none existed.

"Yea, uh do. Um bes mon."

"Then someday he'll find a way to bring them to you," Caroline said.

Jenny's plight wiped out her own growing discontent for the moment, but that night her mind turned back to dreams of better days, and no matter how she tried to tell herself that such longings for foolish fancies and pleasures were flying in the face of fate, they remained to haunt anew her days and nights.

The brief storm of market day heralded a week's return to heavy rains. North of the forests that edged the city, Lake Pontchartrain swelled with the rainfall, and the Mississippi rose threateningly. Bayou St. John flooded, sending the Cajun families fleeing to higher ground.

The Mississippi, turbulent and angry, beat against the high levee banks and below the town it broke through to rampage across the poorer settlements, sweeping away houses, livestock, and people. Survivors sought sanctuary in the city, and the convent was pressed into full service.

The schoolhouse was closed. All available space was given over to the housing of these families. Caroline, assisting with the endless cooking necessary to feed so many, began to feel the weight of her pregnancy, and one evening, lifting a heavy caldron of water to the hearth, she fainted.

Sister Bernadette carried her to her room and, with Jenny's assistance, managed to undress her. There was no way to keep the secret of the coming baby after that.

The nuns were as excited as if each one bore personal responsibility for the care and feeding of this new arrival and for Caroline herself.

Although she recovered almost as quickly as she had weakened, she was no longer allowed to do any heavy chores and was unable to go to market once the rains ceased.

"It is not seemly," Mother Véronique frowned, and that was that. That pleasant duty fell to Sister Elizabeth, and each time Caroline saw Jenny leaving to accompany the nun, she chafed anew over her confinement.

"I might as well be an invalid," Caroline grumbled to Sister Bernadette at the end of her first week of enforced idleness. "I am not even allowed to weed the garden."

"This tree is badly damaged," Sister Bernadette mourned from her perch on a ladder that was braced against an apple tree. "Of course you mustn't weed. We can't have Monsieur de Beaufort arriving to find you ill."

"But I would not sicken from exercise," Caroline argued. "Please, Sister, speak to Mother Véronique. I know she means well, but it is tiresome to sit all day or, at best, stroll slowly in the garden. It makes me fretful and fanciful. I never ceased doing chores while I carried Felicity."

And if, she said silently, you knew what I endured during that time, dear Sister, you would fall from that perch in horror.

"I'll do what I can," Sister Bernadette promised. "Hand me that saw, Madame de Beaufort, if you will be so kind."

Caroline lifted the saw and handed it up. She stood slightly back from the tree, her back against the bushes that lined the convent wall.

Sister Bernadette, bracing herself in the crotch of the tree, began to saw at a low branch that had split during the storm.

"The wreckage of the garden is unbelievable," she muttered, her face growing redder than ever with her exertion. Caroline looked around. The newly white dogwood and the pink apple blossoms had been stripped from the trees and covered the ground, their pristine beauty soiled by the muddy earth.

"You will have it right again," Caroline said consolingly, "and all the more quickly if I were to help," she added.

"There!" Sister Bernadette uttered a cry of triumph as the broken limb fell to the ground. She skimmed down the ladder after it and bent down to pick it up, saying, "Green wood is not good for fire, but we will let it dry and . . . " She broke off, staring toward Caroline.

"Leave this place!" she shouted.

Caroline jumped in fright and backed away, thinking Bernadette had taken leave of her senses.

"No!" Sister Bernadette shouted. "Run, Madame, run!"

Caroline, shocked by the outburst, needed no urging. She darted forward even as Sister Bernadette charged, the tree limb in her hand.

A moment later Caroline felt herself seized from behind and held, with one arm across her throat, cutting off her breath. Twisting and turning, she saw Sister Bernadette raise the tree limb and bring it down with a whack. The arm holding her fell away. Reeling and coughing, Caroline reached out a hand to the panting nun to steady herself.

"Villain!" Sister Bernadette cried. "Villain!"

Again the tree limb went up, but even as it began its descent something silver flashed in the sun, and before Caroline could move or speak, she saw a dagger arc through the air and embed itself high in the nun's chest.

Whirling about, she saw a second man coming toward her, and in the split second between the scream that rushed up to her throat and its muffled suppression, she had been seized once more.

"My prize!" Loco said, grinning evilly into her face. "I have recaptured my prize!"

This can't be happening, she thought frantically. I must be dreaming. It's a nightmare, a nightmare!

Sister Bernadette lay where she had fallen, blood oozing around the knife blade. Whether she was dead or alive, Caroline could not tell. The man she had struck first was staggering groggily to his feet. Loco spoke rapidly to him in Spanish, and then the man bent and pulled the dagger free. Blood streamed forth, turning the muddy grass into a repellent purple-brown.

He wiped the knife on his breeches and Loco spoke again. Caroline, coming out of her frozen terror, began to struggle, but the hand across her mouth was harsh, and as she fought Loco pinched her nostrils together.

"Quiet!" he hissed. "Or I will squeeze the breath away. *Comprendo?*"

She ceased her struggle, and with that he motioned the other man forward. She felt her legs being lifted, and they carried her between them like slaughtered game until they reached the wall.

There they set her down. While the first man held her, Loco clambered to the top. He turned, barked an order, and the second man lifted her upward toward Loco.

It was her last chance. She knew that. Loco was above, both hands held out to grasp her. Below, the man had been forced to leave her mouth free as he held her by the waist with both his hands to thrust her upward.

Taking a deep breath, she screamed and screamed again even as Loco swung her to the top and dropped her with a sudden jerk to the soft grass outside the walls.

The fall took her breath away and dimly she realized

that her ankle had twisted under her. She tried to move it, to scramble erect and run, but Loco was beside her in the next instant, hauling her to her feet.

The pain of the ankle beneath her made her cry out and he snarled. She saw his fist upraised, saw it coming toward her, tried to duck out of the way, and then a white light exploded behind her eyes and blackness descended.

Somewhere someone was singing. The children. They were singing a song. And Felicity was clapping her hands and the noise made Caroline's head ache. She groaned and tried to look around, but she could not open her eyes. Her lids were heavy, so heavy, and she felt ill. That was it—she was ill and the children were singing. But, no, they had stopped.

With a great effort, she opened her eyes. Sun poured into the place and made her eyes hurt. She blinked them, wincing as fresh pain stabbed her temples.

Where am I? she thought, bewildered, and looked about. A cabin. She was aboard a ship. "Dear God," she sobbed aloud as her memory rushed back.

Loco. He had taken her and killed Sister Bernadette when she had tried to stop him. She attempted to sit up and found she was tied. Thick ropes bound her arms across her breasts and were secured to the sides of the bed; her feet were also tied together, and the rope wound around a nail in the wall.

The full horror of her position engulfed her and she opened her mouth to scream before some instinct, deep within her, made her clamp her lips together so that the bottled-up scream dug at her throat with suffocating fingers.

Random thoughts clawed at her brain. Her head pounded with pain and a feeling of nausea rose over her so overwhelmingly that she twisted her head to the side of the bed and vomited miserably upon the cabin deck.

At this, the pain intensified to such a pitch that she fell back exhausted and slipped into a merciful semiconsciousness.

When she again regained her senses, the cabin was dark, save for a dimly lit lantern that hung above her. Opening her eyes, she heard Loco say, "So, you're awake. That is good."

She peered around the room and spied him coming forward, a knife in his hand. The sight should have roused fresh terror in her, yet she felt nothing. The pain had gone from her head, and with its disappearance her ankle throbbed dully.

I am going to die, she thought with a curious calm. He will kill me. She looked at the knife dispassionately, saying nothing as he bent over her, meeting his gloating eyes unflinchingly.

"A good prize," he said softly, "one that will give me much pleasure and much money in ransom."

He slipped the knife between her arms and slit the ropes. Her arms were free. Still she stayed as she was, leaving them crossed over her breasts. He laid the knife aside and, taking both her wrists, pressed her arms back. Still she lay unmoving and unresisting.

"Soon you will be begging for mercy," he promised, then ripped her bodice in two. His hands fumbled between her breasts until he had cupped each. He squeezed on them until the pain brought tears to her eyes, yet she made no outcry.

That is what he wants, she thought: he wants me terrified and crying and pleading for mercy. She would deny him that much satisfaction. She closed her eyes, the better to concentrate on disciplining her body.

"Look at me," he snarled. When she did not obey, he removed one hand and slapped her across the face forcefully. Her head jerked and the throbbing began again behind her eyes.

"Look at me," he ordered again, and she obeyed, summoning as much courage as she could to meet his hot gaze.

He was snaking his hand downward, ripping at the strings of her corps and then at her skirts. The more she lay unresisting, the more he raged and struck, hitting her indiscriminately wherever he found exposed flesh, until at last she lay naked and bruised before him.

With a curse, he grabbed the knife again and sliced through the ropes that bound her legs together. Opening his breeches hastily, he flung himself upon her as he had once before . . . only this time there was no rescue. She turned her head to one side as his foul breath struck her nostrils and willed herself to acquiescence so that when he tore through in a frenzy of lust and rage, she seemed to exist somewhere above it, as if it were not she bearing the burden of this animal, but a body unrelated to her.

It was over, and with a howl of fury he jumped from her. Seizing the knife, he brandished it.

"Look at me, whore!" he screamed, and she faced him, knowing at last what she must do to save herself.

"If you harm me," she said, marveling at the coolness in her voice, "you will enjoy no ransom. Domino will pay nothing for a dead or scarred woman. And if I tell him you raped me, as I will, you will not live long enough to enjoy the ransom."

He drew back, but an ugly smile broke over his face. He sheathed the dagger and buttoned his breeches.

"I want the gold," he said smoothly. "I will live to enjoy it. It does not matter if you say I rape or not." He uttered a coarse laugh and added, "I take you when I want. But maybe I don't want so much no more. You are fat, a lump of suet. There is better for sale in Basin Street. Even your Domino says that."

He made no effort to tie her up again. He left the cabin and locked the door behind him.

Now that it was over, a trembling took hold of her and for several minutes she shook uncontrollably, her teeth chattering, every part of her body aching unbearably.

The baby in her belly was a hard knot that pushed up against her ribs.

"Dead," she thought with a pulsation of fear and hugged her belly as if she would cradle the infant itself. At last there was a mighty jerk as the child moved in her womb, giving the first evidence of life.

At this, everything melted inside her. Huddling beneath the soiled coverlet, she hugged herself and wept in long, drawn sobs until she could weep no more.

For a long time she lay, staring ahead into the semi-gloom. She tried to concentrate on the fact that Loco meant to ransom her, and that must mean he knew where Domino was. There was that. Whatever she had to endure, she would endure. She dared not think of Felicity, telling herself that at least Felicity was safe.

Presently she heard the sounds of a ship making ready to weigh anchor. They were on their way, then. She pulled herself up and went to the commode. The jug contained very little water. With it, she cleaned herself as well as she could, rejoicing in the sting of the salt, as if its very abrasiveness were purifying.

When she had finished, she put her torn clothing on, and after straightening out the bed, she lay down upon it again.

Above her came the loud cry that meant the ship had cleared her mooring. They were under way. "Whatever happens, I will soon be safe," she whispered aloud. The lamp burned low and then sputtered out, leaving the cabin to the moonlight.

Sometime later she heard a key in the lock and quickly closed her eyes, feigning sleep. Loco's voice spoke loudly to someone else, and a man answered as loudly. After a time, they went away, locking the door again.

She drew a long, ragged breath and then another. There was tomorrow and heaven knew how many more tomorrows before they were once again on land. But she would not think of that now. She would go mad if she thought of that now. Only think of the end, she told herself. Only the end holds any promise. She saw it as a large open space, well lighted at the end of a long dark tunnel, and after a time she was in the dark tunnel struggling to reach the light.

Chapter Twenty-One

Confined to the cabin, with nothing to do, Caroline grew thin and pale on the journey. Three times a day the man who had first seized her, and who, she learned, was named Pablo, entered her cabin and served her meals consisting mainly of ale, cheese, salted meat, and hard biscuits.

He spoke little English, although he appeared to understand most of what she said to him. Twice a day he filled a small tankard with drinking water, and from time to time she was able to persuade him to give her sea water for washing.

Loco had not come near her since the first night, but his presence aboard remained a constant threat. Once when Pablo had been induced to take away the amenity bucket and replace it with a clean one, she said to him, "Is it Captain Loco's orders that I live in filth and stench?"

The remark seemed to amuse him mightily, and he laughed, saying, "Ah, Capitán El Loco. El Conquistador! El Capitán El Loco—*muy importante, muy valiente.*" He went away shaking his head, still laughing to himself and murmuring, "El Capitán El Loco, *ay chihuahua.*"

Of this she understood only the words "important" and "brave." El Loco brave? Brave with a knife, with the abduction of women and the killing of them. She thought of Sister Bernadette, lying on the muddy grass, life flowing from her in an ever-widening pool of blood. Once, the memory would have made her weep, but of late she had withdrawn into herself, hiding behind a barrier that left no room for pity or sorrow. These emotions were luxuries that she could not afford to allow herself and still remain sane.

It was difficult enough to bend her effort and will to occupying her mind with long recitations of passages she had once committed to memory and wrestling with those lines that eluded her.

She slept long hours. It was always a fretful and uneasy sleep. Her brain was grainy from her self-imposed mental exercises, and her body was tense from lack of physical exercise.

Day after day, the sea rolled before her, and she, who had once loved the sight of white-frothed waves and limitless sky, grew weary of it and longed for the sight of land.

Sometimes she thought that if only her cabin were on the port side of the ship instead of starboard, she would see land, for during the entire voyage gulls sported and played, soaring high, wheeling against the sky, only to dive straight down and perch for an instant on the top of the waves before zooming up again.

At night she would repeat her small catechism of hope over and over until she finally slept. Domino waited at the end of the voyage. Felicity waited in the safe haven of the convent. And the child within was alive and healthy.

On those days when she hugged her arms across her belly or sat with hands clasped upon it, the baby would stir and move and kick. At such times, she would talk to it as if it could hear her until the sound of her own voice, echoing in the deep solitude of her empty room, sounded alien and strange and sent flurries of panic along her nerves.

She had steeled herself for a journey of two months. She had marked off the days by scratching notches on the wall beside her bed, using the eating knife as her implement. One day was gone, then one week, then ten days, then two weeks. She longed feverishly for the first month to end, straining toward it in her mind, as if by will alone all of those days would be crossed out all at once.

On the seventeenth day of her capture, Pablo brought her fresh water without being asked and took away the chamber pot, as well. When he returned with a clean bucket, he carried clothing over his arm.

"El Capitán, he say, *por favor, lávese, vístase.*" He pointed to the jug and the clothing, and she understood him to mean that she must wash and change her clothing.

"Captain Domino . . . " she began eagerly.

Pablo quickly nodded his head. "*Sí, sí! Pronto! Pronto!*" He pointed to the porthole and said, "*Tierra, tierra.*" At her uncomprehending look, he pointed to the water and said, "*No agua—tierra.*" Then he raised his arm to the opposite side.

They were near land, she guessed. A land called Pronto? She shook her head. "*Pronto?*" she asked.

"*Sí,*" he agreed, "*pronto.*"

And almost as soon as he had spoken, she heard the high, singing call of a sailor: "Land, ho!" English, unmistakably English.

She said it aloud and Pablo smiled. "*Sí, Inglés,*" he said. "*Por favor lávese, vístase.*" He indicated the jug and clothing once more and left.

Caroline hurried to do his bidding, her hands shaking in her excitement. At last, and far sooner than expected. When she had dressed in the plain linen garments of a serving maid, she stuffed her untidy hair beneath the cap and stood, expectantly, waiting for the door to open, waiting to be taken from the ship.

Several minutes passed before she realized that probably hours must pass before the ship fetched her mooring. And then there would be the time it took for Domino to pay a ransom.

She sank to the bed, pressing her hands together and folding them between tightly clasped knees. What if the ransom was too high? What if Domino was not, after all, at this port? A dozen deterrents to her immediate release scurried through her mind. Don't think about it, she ordered herself, then settled down to wait.

The first feverish minutes limped into hours. Pablo reappeared once, bearing her second meal of the day, but to all questions he only repeated, "*Sí, pronto, tierra.*"

The day dwindled into evening and edged into twilight before the ship jerked and tugged, announcing that they had anchored at last. An hour later, Pablo appeared again, this time smiling broadly and saying, "*Ándele,* Señora. El Capitán say *ándele.*"

She rose on unsteady legs and followed him from the cabin. There was no one in the passageways or near the ladders they ascended.

Going along one passageway, she had a quick glimpse of the harbor and stopped to look shoreward through the open hatch."

"Why," she said, "it's Savannah! Domino is in Savannah again!"

"Savannah, *sí*," Pablo agreed, then motioned her forward to the main cabin. There, he opened the door and stepped aside, saying, *"Señora, por favor, entre usted."*

Three men stood at the opposite end of the cabin. Caroline had a fleeting glimpse of a small, fat man in a captain's uniform, of El Loco, his mouth split in a wolfish grin, and even as she looked toward the third man, tall and broad, he was advancing toward her, his lips stretched into a false smile.

"My dear, dear wife, I had thought you were dead," Joshua said.

The shock of his appearance when she had imagined that Domino was waiting for her was so great that the room began to tilt crazily, and she reached out a hand to support herself. Joshua grasped it.

"It is too much for her," he said. "Please, Captain Sage, a bit of brandy." And to Caroline, he said, "Hold fast to me, my darling. Your travail is at its end."

She suffered him to put a supporting arm around her and to lead her to a chair into which she sank gratefully. The mist before her eyes cleared and the room once more assumed its normal appearance. She sipped gratefully on the proffered brandy, holding the beaker tightly with both hands.

The captain was Sage—Sage, from whom Domino had rescued her. El Loco, apparently, was a sailor under his command. And here was Joshua. She was trapped, trapped more surely and securely than she had ever been. It had all been for nothing: the flight from Wildwood, the endless waiting in Savannah, the lonely months in the convent . . . all for nothing.

She drained the glass, taking comfort from the burning liquor that seared her tongue and throat and spread its fire through her belly.

Somehow, she must not give way under this crushing blow. Somehow she must manage to remain calm and use her wits. After a moment, she handed the empty beaker to Joshua, saying, "How did you know where to find me? And why send so low a cur to fetch me—one who abused me before I had been his captive even an hour?"

"Abuse you, dear Madame?" Captain Sage purred smoothly. "But, I assure you, you must have dreamed it, for you fainted as we took you aboard, and I myself attended you."

"You lie, Captain," Caroline said. "It was Loco who seized me in the convent garden, Loco who beat me and raped me." She shuddered.

Captain Sage said, "I assure you, Mr. Welles, 'tis but fancy. Mistress Welles has not been herself. Indeed, as I have told you, when we found her she seemed to have lost her memory and was wandering near the French market. Indeed, 'twas Mr. Flores who saw her."

"I lost no memory," Caroline broke in. "I remember Loco very well—the crazy one, and well named. He was aboard the pirate ship. Indeed, it was he who captured me first from the *Charlotte,* he who led the mutiny aboard the *Mouette.*"

"Please, ma'am," Sage begged, "do not excite yourself. There may indeed have been such a one as you speak of, but I assure you that Mr. Flores, my lieutenant, comes to me from a Spanish merchantman that sank during the late war."

Caroline stared at him, and meeting his bland smile, she knew that any further protestations were useless.

"You must not excite yourself, my dear," Joshua was saying. He picked up her hand and patted it. "Soon we will have you ashore, and in a little while you will come to your senses. Captain, if the boat is ready, I think we must depart. You can see for yourself that my wife is undone by her illness and by the shock of finding herself safe at last."

He placed his arm under Caroline's elbow and drew her to her feet. "This way, my dear," he purred, and with wooden, jerky steps, she followed him out to the launch.

They landed, but not in Savannah itself, as she had imagined they would. Some distance down the coast from the town they came ashore to a small cottage set in a grove of oaks.

Joshua had spoken no word to her on the trip to the

land, and she, for her part, refrained from repeating her story until they were alone.

The sight of the cottage, dark and isolated, filled her with foreboding. "This is hardly the dwelling you are accustomed to," she said as he pushed open the door.

"But better than you deserve," he answered. Then, grasping her arm, he flung her headlong into the house.

She fell heavily upon the bare, cold floor and lay there, gasping for breath as he blundered about, finally lighting tapers.

In their light, she saw that the cottage was crudely furnished. A wooden bed with straw ticking lay against one wall. A clumsy table and chairs of rough wood were in the center. To her left a cold hearth of rough stone contained a blackened kettle above burned-out kindling.

"Get up," Joshua ordered.

"No," Caroline said. "Why should I rise only to be knocked down again? Beat me if you must; kill me if you will. I care not."

"Killing you would be a pleasure, but not nearly so great as what I have in mind for you. You strumpet, get up."

She lay there, silently staring up at him. A murderous hatred began to form somewhere deep inside her and grew until it filled her being, blinding her to all thoughts of danger.

She saw him raise his booted foot, aiming it at her side, and she rolled as it shot forward. Seizing it with both hands, she pulled so that he was thrown off balance and fell heavily to the floor. Still clinging to him, she raised herself and bent over the upper portion of his leg. It bulged in the tight breeches, and with a low, animal cry, she sank her teeth into it.

He thrashed out, kicking her with the other foot, his hands beating her about the head and shoulders, but still she clung until at last he managed to hit her along the jaw and break her hold.

Reeling from the blow, she struggled to her feet, and as he got up she raked his face with her nails. His howl shattered the silence of their panting struggle and she ran toward the door, wrenching it open and hurling herself headlong down the path toward the shore.

She heard him pounding along behind her and ran faster, but in another moment he had reached her, grasping her with both hands and holding her against him as he went back to the cottage. She squirmed and kicked, but there was no force to her dangling limbs.

Once inside, he threw her to the floor again and stood over her, his eyes blazing with cruelty and his face puce-colored with rage.

"I'll teach you," he said, panting, and this time he kicked her so hard in the side that she fainted. She awoke to find herself in an aching mist. With each breath a stabbing pain shot through her ribs. Joshua was at the hearth, leaning against the mantel, drawing ragged breaths.

"Kill me and be through with it!" she cried out. "I would welcome death if 'twould save me from your foul touch. At least I will die having known the embrace of a real man. Yes, the child was his, and proudly I carried it. Yes, I have been with him, and I would do so again."

As she spewed out the words, she was dragging herself to her feet, sobbing, panting, wincing at the pain, but maddened beyond any rational idea of her real peril.

If she could kill him, she would, and gladly. The mere thought of standing triumphant over his bleeding corpse filled her with such an unholy joy that even the prospect of her own imminent death paled in significance.

"I have endured too much at your hands," she said. "All the evil that has befallen me is evil wrought by you. You're a devil, a vicious, low brute, worse than Redleigh. It is you I would gladly see with your throat slit. You aren't a man. I know what a man is now. Yes, I know."

She finished, standing and facing him, her face hot with the passion of her words.

"Come on, then," she taunted. "Such a man as you pretend to be is surely brave enough to beat a woman. How brave will you be when Domino finds you? Coward, low, scurrilous coward." She spat upon the floor.

He had stood still during her tirade, as if none of her fired-up emotions found similar response in him. He had paled steadily as she flung her insults, and his body was as rigid as granite.

When at length he spoke, his voice was cold. "Kill you?" he said. "I think not. Let me tell you what you can expect. I am selling you, just as I would sell any slave on my plantation. There is a market for white slaves. Did you know that? The Saracens, for example,

prefer white slaves, especially women slaves. And there
are planters in the Indies who buy them. Women—bond-
servants, they call them, only they pay a very high
price for them. They are never free. They keep them for
sport. And there are whorehouses in cities where women
like you can also earn their keep. These are places from
which you will never escape. As for Domino"—he
laughed—"he will never dream of looking for you
where I am sending you."

"He will find me wherever I am," she said steadily.

Joshua laughed again. "He will not search. I will
spread the news that you died, that in a fit of despondency you cast yourself into the sea. I have slaves with
me who will swear that they saw you do it—Serena, for
one. She is here in Savannah. She waits in the house that
I purchased for the sole purpose of waiting for my darling wife to be returned to me. It was Serena who
drowned the pirate's bastard. Did you know that? By my
orders, of course . . . but, then, Serena obeys."

Hot words rushed to Caroline's lips, but she bit them
back. How good it would be to throw the fact of Felicity's survival in his face. But even in her present state of
excitement, she had enough sense left to realize that she
would be signing Serena's death warrant.

"Serena has no choice," Caroline said. "I know how
slaves are treated and what they can expect."

"Then you can see your future," he sneered.

"Whatever it is," she answered, "the lowest cur, the
cruelest Saracen, or the dirtiest sailor would be a joy
compared with your fat, ugly body. If you knew how I
suffered in your loathsome embrace, how little you
pleased me, you would know that at least I will have a
few moments of pleasure, slave or not. Why, you . . .
you could not even father a child."

His face flamed at this last remark and he lunged forward. She dodged, but he caught her by the front of her
dress. The fabric ripped. As if further enraged by the
sound, he clawed at the rest of her garments until she
was standing with her flesh exposed between the tatters.

His eyes went over her body, and as they fell upon
her swollen belly a hoarse cry of frustration burst from
him. As he came at her, both fists upraised, she tried to
defend herself, kicking, clawing, driving her elbow into
his soft belly, but he finally managed to wrestle her to

the floor. There he pinioned her with one hand and struck her over and over in the side and belly until she lay inert under his fists.

With that, he rose and, aiming his foot, delivered a last mighty blow that caught her between the thighs and sent the pain shooting like an arrow straight up through her body to explode in her skull.

When he had regained his breath, he went out to the well and drew up a bucket of water with which he doused himself and from which he drank. Then he filled it again and went back into the cottage to pour it over the senseless Caroline and bring her back to consciousness.

She lay moaning with the terrible pain, still not fully awake despite the splashes of water that soaked her whenever she let herself drift away from the cruel present.

I am dying, she thought, dying, and so is the baby within me. And yet the words held no meaning. She licked at the water around her lips with a swollen tongue. Time stood still. A gray cobweb encircled her, and beyond it there were muffled sounds: doors opening; feet tramping; herself being lifted and carried; Joshua's voice saying, "I have not touched the face. She is marketable."

Voices answering, questions, words such as death and sea and payment, and then Joshua shouting above them, "I care not whether she is ever seen again! I want no payment! I will pay you! Sell her or bury her! Here!"

A clinking sound followed, then a woman's voice, saying, "Thank-ee, sir. 'Twill pay for the trouble."

Caroline moved her lips, trying to speak, and at last she whispered, "Water . . . water."

" 'Twill soon be all the water you'll need in this life," a man answered with a cackle of laughter.

Then a woman said, "Shut up, will ye, Edward? And hurry. 'Tis no good will come of this night's work, damn me eyes if 'twill."

A woman, Caroline thought: What is a woman doing among such as these? It was her last coherent thought. Shortly afterward, she felt herself laid down none too gently, and soon after that the peacefulness of onrushing unconsciousness enveloped her in its embrace.

Part

Six

Chapter Twenty-Two

The August sun beat mercilessly down on New Orleans, sucking moisture from every plant and flower, turning even the canal into thick, molten gold.

The streets were all but deserted. From Chartres to Rampart Streets, along the waterfront and on the German coast, the inhabitants of the town were hidden behind the louvered shutters of their rooms slanted against the sun, while sleeping the heavy, torporous slumber that followed their midday meal.

Domino, walking up from the canal along Bourbon Street, sweated beneath his shirt and jacket. Ahead, a weary dray horse pulled an empty cart, the driver nodding over the reins.

At the corner of St. Ann Street, Domino paused, removed his light jacket, and opened the scarf on his silk shirt. In the absence of wind, the humidity was intensified and the sweat laid a thick, unevaporated film over his skin.

He was nearly there. Another street or two would have him at the convent gates. Now that he was at the end of his journey, a strange foreboding intruded on his otherwise happy mood. It was nonsense, of course. Even if Caroline had not received the letter he had sent her before sailing for France in January, she would surely be waiting, knowing that the war was over.

Aboard the *Mouette*, safe in his strongbox, lay the proclamation and deed ceding Liberté to him. The ship was filled with cargo: cloth and goods of all descriptions; pegs, tools, and nails; seeds; books; parchment. The forecastle deck was crowded with plants, and pigs, cows, and chickens grunted and squawked in their pens amidships.

Sacks of meal and flour and casks of wine were crowded in with the ropes and canvas among the guns, which had been idle these many months, their muzzles staring harmlessly out through the portholes.

He had everything he needed, including the crew that would stay with him on Liberté, and the women, some half a dozen of them, soon to be chosen as wives by the crew. They crowded the available space so that hammocks were slung everywhere there was an inch of room.

The *Mouette* rode low in the water under the combined weight of goods, animals, and humans. They had nearly sunk twice on the crossing during sudden gales. Fortunately, the weather had been fair for the most part. As it was, they had been over three months on the journey.

There had been a singular lack of trouble among the crew over the women. An air of adventure and of anticipation had prevailed, all of it resulting in an unusual bonhomie.

Now all the unmarried men had been sent ashore. The ones with wives remained on duty. "It is the penalty for the pleasures you enjoyed during the voyage," Domino had said and had been greeted by an uproar of laughter. There had been little pleasure available in such cramped quarters.

For himself, Domino acknowledged that it had not been easy to have the women aboard. They were a constant reminder of his own celibate state and thus a constant temptation.

The longer they were at sea, the more his desire for Caroline arose, so that even now it seemed that there was an eternity until he should have her again.

At the convent gates he tied his scarf and put his jacket back on. The doors opened to his knock, and the nun who answered it gave a faint sound of dismay when she saw Domino standing there.

"Monsieur de Beaufort!" she blurted out. "We did not expect you."

"Nevertheless, I am here," he replied. "I have come for my wife. Will you tell the good Mother that I would be most happy if she will see me?"

"Yes, Monsieur," the nun said. "Please come in." She held the door wide open and he entered into the blessed relief of the dim, invitingly cool reception hall.

Nodding nervously at him, the nun hurried away. After

what seemed an interminable amount of time, a door at
the far end of the hall opened and Mother Véronique entered, followed by a tall, robust nun whom she introduced
as Sister Bernadette.

The foreboding that had slithered beneath the edge of
his mind rose to the surface. "Is something wrong?" he
asked at once. "Where is Madame de Beaufort? My
daughter?"

"Felicity is in the kitchen with Jenny. She is splendid.
Indeed, she is a charming and very sweet child. She's a joy
to the convent. We all . . . "

"My wife?" Domino cut through the chattering voice.
"Where is my wife?"

"Oh, Monsieur de Beaufort . . . she is gone. Please,
Monsieur, it is Sister Bernadette who can explain. Poor
Sister Bernadette nearly lost her own life trying to defend
Madame."

"Lost her own life? My wife—she . . . "

"Dead or alive, Monsieur, we cannot say—perhaps better dead, if what Sister Bernadette heard is true. Tell him."
she appealed to the nun.

"Monsieur," Sister Bernadette began, "it was an attack
. . . by surprise. . . . We were in the garden . . . and
Madame was . . . "

As he listened to the nun's story, Domino's face alternately whitened and then blazed. Caroline, pregnant, abducted by Loco, for ransom. Ransom from whom?

He asked the question through tight lips.

"You, Monsieur, I thought. Is it not?"

"Yes," Domino answered mechanically, but he had
other thoughts. It had to be Welles. Somehow, Loco had
learned about Welles' offer of a ransom and found out
where Caroline was. But, how? Chance. Surely it must
have been chance. Even to Stevenson, back in Savannah,
he had not revealed his true destination: Martinique, he
had said.

Suddenly, he had a clear picture of Caroline as he had
first seen her in the hold of the *Mouette:* naked, spread-
eagled, and Loco astride her. The pictures burned his
mind. He could feel his blood pounding in his temples until a red mist obscured the room. He heard a sharp exclamation from Sister Bernadette, then an anxious inquiry
from Mother Véronique, and with a tremendous effort
he brought himself under control.

"I am all right," he said tensely. "I will see my daughter now. I must ask a further favor, Ma Mère. I will go in search of my wife. I will leave my child and her nurse here until my return."

He saw at once the request was happily received, and he surmised that they were delighted to keep the child among them. They went away with pleased smiles, casting happy little sidelong glances at each other.

Domino sat down heavily upon a narrow chair and it creaked under his weight. "Caroline," he murmured, and his chest hurt with the effort to control his emotions. It was four months and more since she had been taken. In April he had been at Versailles, still awaiting Louis' pleasure.

He should have come for her before he sailed for France in January. He had been tempted to, but knowing that the terms of surrender would soon be signed, he had been afraid that whatever extra land Louis managed to salvage out of the New World would soon be spoken for by others at court who were seeking repayment of favors or favors for other political reasons.

The same ship that carried the news of surrender had brought the information that the duchess of Pompadour had not been well of late. A few more months, he had reasoned, and he would go to Caroline with the land secured.

"And months more," he spoke aloud as the door opened again and Jenny came in with Felicity.

"Um dey Papa," Jenny said, coaxing Felicity toward Domino.

But the child clung to her nurse, saying doubtfully, "Papa?"

"Papa," Jenny repeated. "Um Papa. Dey Shum."

"No." Felicity shook her black curls firmly and buried her head in Jenny's shoulder.

"Um skeer dey," she said apologizing to Domino. "Um say 'Mama, Mama.' "

At this, Felicity lifted her head and said hopefully, "Mama?" She stared at Domino with eyes so like Caroline's that his heart twisted.

He put out a gentle hand and touched her small cheek with one finger. "Soon," he promised steadily, "I will bring Mama to you." He met Jenny's eyes, and in them he saw a sorrowful doubt. "I will," he repeated. "Stay with her, Jenny, until I return."

"Yea, massa, uh do."

"Not massa," he corrected, "Captain."

"Yea, Caypun," Jenny replied, but the look of doubt did not lessen, and it haunted him long after he had left the convent to go in search of Christos.

At nine o'clock that evening, Domino sat in a tavern on Basin Street, drinking rum and idly watching two mulatto men dance to the frenzied rhythm of guitar and skinhead drum.

It was the sixth tavern he had been in since Christos brought him the news that Loco had been seen in New Orleans as recently as two days ago. They had separated, Christos to search in one part of town, while Domino combed the other.

"Eh, Domino, it is you. But, *alors,* I think it cannot be." The voice that spoke beside him was soft and throaty and he smiled as he turned. "Solange," he said, greeting the woman, "it has been a long time."

"Yes," she answered. "I heard you were in New Orleans many months ago, but you did not come near Solange."

"That was months ago," he said. She had not changed much, he thought. The delicately olive skin of the octoroon was as clear and unlined as it had been when he met her some seven years before. She must be thirty now, yet she showed no sign of aging. The heavy black hair had not a strand of gray, and the almond-shaped eyes of a liquid brown were as untroubled as if she spent her days in idleness instead of running the most expensive whorehouse in New Orleans. And her body was as reed-slim, as high and full-bosomed as it had been as a girl.

"You are still the pirate king?" she questioned, her red lips parting in a teasing smile.

"No more pirates," he answered. "The war is over."

"*Zut!*" she exclaimed. "Wars are over, but pirates are still at war. Barataria Bayou has three ships now. And out on the water, more come. The war has chased them to us."

He looked at her speculatively. "Have you seen a pirate yourself of late?"

"Many—French and English and Spanish and . . . "

"Any real Spanish pirates—I mean, one who looks like

a ferret?" He added a rapid description of Loco and her eyes widened.

"You are of the witches!" she exclaimed. "He is at my house now, tonight—he and three of his men. They pay in gold for the best girls, but not for me," she said and laughed. She reached out to run a finger lightly along his collar. "Solange hears Domino is in town, and *voilà!* She comes to look for him."

Domino rose and threw down some coins upon the table. "And you have found me. Come, we will go to the house."

Some minutes later, rounding the corner of Basin Street, Domino ran full tilt into Christos.

"Domino, I was looking for you. Loco, he's . . . "

"At Solange's," Domino finished. "I know."

"Solange," Christos said when he saw her, "you had better stay here."

"No. She comes with us. I want to find the room he is in without opening the door of every one."

Solange pulled away a little. "It is not me you come to the house for, no. It is a filthy beast of a sailor."

Domino's lips drew back in an exultant grin. "Both," he said. Then, taking her firmly by the elbow, he steered her ahead of him. "Quietly, now," he cautioned. "I want the bastard taken by surprise."

The house was dark as they entered. In the room at the right two candles burned palely, casting thin fingers of light through the gloom. From above sounded the squeals and moans and guttural cries of the inhabitants.

Motioning Christos to follow him, Domino crept softly up the stairs. It was the third door on the left, Solange had instructed. The other sailors were across the hall and on either side.

Leaving Christos on guard, with both pistols drawn, Domino turned the handle of a door behind which he could hear Loco muttering a string of obscenities to the woman he had mounted, half-cursing her, half-instructing her.

The door swung back silently. On the bed, Domino saw a woman, her fair hair spread out behind her, with Loco astride, still muttering. The woman turned as the door opened, saw Domino and the dagger in his hand, and uttered a scream. Loco laughed low, misinterpreting the reason behind the cry. Before the woman could cry out again, Domino crossed the room and collared Loco, dragging him free of the woman with brutal abruptness and throwing him to the floor, where Loco lay half-dazed, half-maddened by the shock of the interruption.

The woman, screaming out again, fled the room. On all sides there were startled shouts and then doors were flung open. Above it all, Christos' voice rang out, a cold menace in his orders to stand as they were or be shot.

Domino knelt quickly at Loco's naked side, pinning the man down with one arm and pressing the dagger against the scrawny neck with his free hand.

"What did you do with her?"

"Her?"

The dagger pressed until the skin broke.

"I know nothing," Loco gasped, and the dagger pressed again. "If I tell you, you will not kill me?" Loco asked.

Domino did not answer, and Loco, a craftiness replacing his fear, said, "If you are to kill me, anyway, then why should I tell you anything? Let me up. Let me dress. Then I will tell you."

For a long moment Domino did not answer. The hand that held the dagger was tense, the arm above it like steel —steel against which a force seemed to push, as if it would drive the dagger home before Loco could speak again.

All at once, Domino stood up. "All right," he said. "Get up. Put your breeches on. That will do. And tell me. Don't forget, Loco, I am better with the blade than you."

He watched, eyes narrowed, as Loco hurriedly drew on his breeches, buttoning them with hands that trembled.

"Get away from the bed!" Domino ordered when Loco reached back.

"Sí, Capitán," Loco answered, but as he stepped away his right arm came up and his own dagger gleamed in his hand. He threatened to move forward, but Domino did not move. A split second later Loco came at him in earnest, and Domino, standing four-square, waited until Loco's dagger had nearly touched his chest before his own shot out and opened the side of the man's arm. Loco's dagger wavered, nearly dropped, and then with a howl, Loco stabbed again, this time slicing Domino's jacket down the front, piercing the shirt and grazing the skin beneath.

Domino felt the hot gush of blood along the thin wound, and even as Loco's knife flashed once more, he drove his own dagger into Loco's belly. Still Loco came at him, again the dagger flashed, and this time Domino, stepping to the side, watched Loco fall forward from his own impetus.

Then Loco was up again, blood pouring from his arm, spilling from his belly, his mouth thick with foam. Curses poured from his lips. "Never!" he was saying. "Never find her! I took her! Like a lump of suet! Ugly! Her belly swollen! Never moved! Whore! Used to it! Nothing! Never again! I lay with her! I took her! How you like that, Capitán? I, Loco . . . I told you . . . we are even . . . even . . . ev——. . . " His voice gurgled off as Domino's dagger found his throat, stilling the mad flow of words, stilling the life within forever.

He stared at the body, scarcely realizing that he had killed Loco without learning anything of Caroline's whereabouts. When the knowledge of his own stupidity came to him, he uttered a cry of fury and charged from the room.

In the hall he found the three sailors, all in various stages of undress, their hands raised before Christos' aimed pistols. The women had retreated and were cowering at the end of the hall.

"You," he addressed the nearest man, "what's your name?"

"Pablo . . . Pablo . . . no speak . . ." the man said.

"He don't speak," one of the others said, " 'cept Spanish. You kill the captain?" he asked.

"I killed him. I want to know what happened to . . . to the woman he took hostage."

"English woman?"

"Yes."

"He give 'er back to 'er husband. Leastwise, Captain Sage done it."

"Where is Sage?"

"Dead. Mr. Flores says he fell overboard. But we know Flores pushed 'im." He broke off and looked at Pablo. "*Sí?*" he said, and he made the motion of pushing someone. "Capitán," he added.

"*Sí, sí.* El Loco, El Capitán." Pablo made a slashing motion. "El Capitán." He mimed a fall.

"Is this the man who helped Loco?" Domino pointed to Pablo, who seemed to understand and backed off in fear, uttering jerky sentences in incomprehensible Spanish.

"Ain't 'is fault," the third sailor spoke up. "Cap'n's orders. Sage brung Welles to Savannah to wait, an' then 'e run into Orleans. Figgered yer won't go to Martinique. Figgered it 'ud be danger fer yer. Knowed ya was Cap'n Domino. Seen yer in the tavern. Says 'e, 'Domino 'ull head fer Orleans.' That's what Loco said, too. Loco come into Savannah lookin' for a berth. Cap'n found out 'e knowed ya and the lady and took 'im on seein' Flint be dead. An' that's the facts, Cap'n Domino. Pablo, 'ere, 'e was nice to the lady—brung 'er food. Cap'n said jes bread an' water an' mebbe cheese. Pablo, 'e give 'er 'is own ale, an' meat sometimes. An' sometimes 'e talked me into givin' some o' mine."

"Talked to you? You speak Spanish?"

"A word or two is all. But me an' Pablo, we been kind o' friends, ya might say. Eh, Pablo?" he called out. And as Pablo looked at him, he made some rapid hand signs at the sight of which Pablo nodded, looking less fearful.

"*Sí*," he said, nodding vigorously. "Señora Welles, *muy dolorosa*." At this last remark he indicated his eyes, as if weeping.

Domino said gruffly, "All right." He made a signal to Pablo to show him he was safe.

The man said, *"Gracias.* Capitán, *gracias."*

"She is back in Virginia," Domino said to Christos. "We will go there for her."

"And what about these rogues?" Christos asked.

"Let them go back to their women once they have buried that," Domino answered, nodding his head at the room where Loco lay. "I will see you aboard in the morning." He turned and went down the stairs to find Solange still waiting.

"You are covered with blood!" she exclaimed at the sight of him. "Your hands, face . . . " He looked down and saw that Loco's blood covered him and mingled with the oozing fluid from the shallow wound in his own chest.

"Come. Wash." Solange said, then led him to the back-yard. There she splashed a bucket of water over him, then ordered him to remove his clothes while she went to get a fresh bucket of water.

The cool water against his flesh flushed away the last traces of blood, as well as the stench of sweat and battle. Solange took his soiled clothes away, leaving him to find his way into her room, where he sank upon the bed, his muscles aching, his mind still seething.

He could still hear Loco's taunting voice: "I took her! I lay with her! Like a lump of suet! Whore! Used to it!" And he could still feel the blind, unreasoning fury those words had wrought in him.

Angrily, he pulled himself up, punching the fist of one hand into the heel of the other, as if into the dead body of Loco, his thirst for vengeance still unslaked.

Solange found him thus sometime later. "You must stop," she said wisely. "You will drive yourself mad if you don't. Here, come to Solange." She smiled at him, beginning to remove her clothes. Then, going on in a soft, soothing, almost singsong voice, she said, "Here, Solange comes to find you, and you are like a madman. You are satisfied with the killing, but not me—Solange is not satisfied at all." As the last of her garments rustled away, she pressed her body against him, wound her arms around his stiff and unyielding neck, and murmured softly into his ear, "I think of you many times, Domino. It is so good with you."

She was moving in a rotating motion against him, and slowly the tension of his neck and shoulders left him. A hot glow spread upward from his loins and he nearly crushed her waist between his two hands. Still, when she pressed her lips upon his, his own were cold. "What is it?" she asked, but instead of answering, he pushed her back down on the bed and flung himself upon her.

"Too fast," she murmured in a half-reproach that ended in a cry as he thrust himself into her with long, hard, cruel strokes. The initial shock had made her gasp, but almost as soon a certain excitement seized her. The very cruelty of his force aroused her and she began to writhe and twist, pulling well away from him and rushing eagerly back again until it was over in one mighty, final throb of mutual pleasure.

He rolled away almost at once, and she drew in a deep, satisfied breath. There were so many men who had lain with her, but so few who had brought her to the peak of ecstasy.

She was sixteen when the first man in her life had taken her. She could still remember that singular thrill even in the long years after he left her to other men . . .

years in which she used men as they used her and reaped the profits.

Domino had been the first to give her more than money, and there had been perhaps two or three since. They were rare enough.

In between there were the married men whose wives turned their backs too often; married men who could never be satisfied with one woman; young boys, timid and quick, like rabbits, anxious to reach the end and scurry away; and ineffectual men who needed every artifice to achieve union.

Ah, the Dominos were rare. And they never stayed, which was just as well, she thought cynically, or she would long since have found herself scrubbing shirts in some hovel—old and dowdy and poor.

She stretched like a sinuous cat and silently drew one of Domino's hands up between her breasts, where he permitted it to lie quietly. "I said it was always good with you," she murmured sleepily. "Again in a little while, eh, my friend? You won't go away?"

"No," he lied. She was soon asleep, and when, an hour later, he removed his hand and rose from the bed, she did not awaken.

As the sun set the following evening, Domino sat in the main cabin of the *Mouette,* an untouched glass of wine before him, going through the sheaf of documents pertaining to the *Mouette*'s cargo. Christos sat beside him, his swarthy face solemn.

"You have arranged that each of the married men will see me?" Domino questioned.

"Yes. Haywood has gone to fetch them. They know something is afoot and they are anxious—all of them. For those without women, of course, it should be no problem."

Domino slapped the flat of his hand over the manifests. "Whoever says nay, pay off and let him get off the ship here," he said grimly.

"Not many, I think," Christos replied. "Let us hope. It is a long journey to Virginia."

"I reckon a month, at most," Domino said.

"If the weather holds."

"We sail—good weather or not . . . full crew or not." He scowled as someone tapped on the door.

"Enter," he called brusquely, and Carson came into the room.

"Your pardon, Cap'n," he said. "Mr. Christos said you beem wantin' to see me."

Domino leaned back in his chair and eyed the man. This was not the Carson he had taken from Sage's command. That Carson had been a craven serf, pathetically grateful for a decent word, shaking in his tattered and soiled garments. The man before him wore reasonably clean and whole garments. He stood erect, and if from time to time his eyes flinched, they were no longer the eyes of a cur that expects and receives a kick. Carson's hair was neatly pulled back into a pigtail, and a clean kerchief held unruly locks away from his brow. His well-shaved face had filled out and on it there was a look that approached well-being.

"We are not sailing for Liberté yet," Domino began without preamble, intending his words to shock, the better to gauge true reaction. "I am putting ashore all livestock for safekeeping, as well as some of the rest of the cargo, keeping only what is needed for food or for ballast. I am also"—here he paused deliberately before resuming—"I am also putting all the women ashore in safe quarters. You men will sail with me to Virginia."

"Aye, Captain," Carson returned.

"Aye, Captain?" Domino repeated on a rising note. "How say you, Carson? Does this please you?"

"No Cap'n, please me it well don't. An' 'twon't please Sally, neither. But orders is orders, like I tell 'er. Cap'n's got a reason, I says. But 'er beem a land gel too long. Never thinkin' to see me agin an' hatin' the sea that took me away. But, Cap'n, been't ya kind, I'd like as still be wi' Cap'n Sage nor never goin' crossed channel to home. An' been't yer kind, I won't be here, but in Hampshire, wi' nary a livin' to be got, 'cept fishin', an' it ain't good."

"I see. You repay me?"

"No, Cap'n. I ain't never able fer that. But if yer say we sail, I say aye an' be done wi' it. An' I tell Sally orders is orders."

"Well said, Carson." Domino permitted a fleeting smile to cross his face. "You may as well tell Sally it will be a long voyage—two months or three before we return to New Orleans."

"Aye, Cap'n. Cap'n?"

"Yes, Carson?"

"Sally be a mother soon. So she be skeered, it bein' the first time an' her not so young. The women—'ull they be together?"

"Yes. I have rented a house near the church. They'll be safe enough."

"Aye, Cap'n. Thank-ee, Cap'n."

"That's all, then, Carson. The other men—are they waiting?"

"Aye, Cap'n. They be standin' on deck to take turns. We done it by letters. Mr. Haywood said C first, an' that's me. And Couvre be next, an' then Deberdt be third, an' La——..."

"Yes, yes, Carson, I understand," Domino interposed. "Say nothing of this. I wish each man to hear it from me first."

"Aye, aye, sir."

When he had left, Christos said with a lightening of mood, "If they are all like that, Domino, we need have no fear."

"So if I have half the present crew, I will be satisfied," Domino said as the door opened and the next man entered.

Shortly before the bosun's mate piped the eight-o'clock watch, the last of the ship's crew had been informed of the change and, except one married couple and three of the bachelors, there had been no dissent.

The next morning, as the first load of cargo was carried up from the hold to the waiting boats, the five dissenters departed.

"I am not sorry to see them go," Christos observed. "That woman had no love for work, and I think Liberté would have been too much for her. As for the rest," he said, shrugging, "they were not the best of the men. We have kept the best, Domino."

"We need the best," Domino answered. "It will not be easy to rescue Caroline from Welles. We cannot sail the *Mouette* up to his front door without someone noticing." He gave a dry, unamused laugh. "See that Haywood hurries them," he added, nodding to the seamen coming up onto the deck under heavy loads.

The unloading took all of one day and half of the next, and for the following three days the *Mouette*, riding higher now that so much of the cargo was gone, lay in the windless shelter at the mouth of the Mississippi Sound while all aboard prayed for a breeze to send them out upon the blue gulf waters.

When at last the wind sprang up, driving in hard from the northwest, the cheering of the crew could be heard all along the crowded waterfront.

The long wait and enforced idleness had left the sailors primed, and they scampered into the rigging like new midshipmen who had spent their boyhoods dreaming of such a moment.

With all sails set, the *Mouette* raced down the sound and into the gulf in a good imitation of the sea gull for which she was named.

"Ah, she flies like the bird!" Christos shouted as a fine spume from the gulf sprayed over them and the *Mouette* heeled and righted on her course.

"She is a bird!" Domino shouted back. "But let us hope it will be southerly winds we meet around the Keys, or we will be blown to Bermuda before we know it."

His heart lifted now that they were on their way. He looked up at the sheets, as full as a woman's skirts before the wind.

"Sail, ho!" cried the crow's-nest watch. "Englishman!"

"Hoist the Union!" Domino answered. "If she's a privateer, I don't want to give her the excuse that she did not know the war had ended."

"Hoist the Union!" Christos sang out, grinning. "Hoist the Union!"

Haywood picked it up and the boatswain caroled the last call. Above the masts, the English flag rippled out on the wind and was lowered and raised in an answering salute to the other ship.

"Sink me, sir!" said Haywood, hurrying up. "She's the *Lady Dare*. English flag or not, Blanche Chester will open fire."

"Let her fire and be damned." Domino laughed. "We'll outrun her. What's her bearing, Mr. Christos?"

"South and west of us by fifteen knots I reckon, Captain. She's tacking a course for the Indies, I'll bet."

"And we for Virginia," Domino said. "Let us wish her ill fortune and bear well to the northeast."

"Aye, aye, Captain."

"She might be tacking wide around the Keys and coming after us," Haywood suggested.

"Then she will be surprised," Domino promised. "Ready the guns, Mr. Haywood. They may yet see duty once more."

Domino was filled with an exultation, born of the wind and the sea and the fact that he was on his way, win or lose, to claim his last prize.

Chapter Twenty-Three

Serena moved quietly through the rooms at Wildwood, inspecting the finished work of the house slaves, automatically adjusting a bed cover into place or straightening an ornament. Her gestures were mechanical, her eyes those of a sleepwalker. From time to time she stopped, her head cocked, and then moved on.

It would never end, she thought with a darting pain that pierced her apathy. She looked down the long vista of the years and saw herself moving endlessly through the rooms and corridors of Wildwood and always hearing the last faint cry of her child as it died in her arms. Always the vision of Nicole's small face, empurpled with the choking disease that had claimed her, would rise with unexpected clarity to tear at the bands around her heart.

She could hardly remember how long it had been. The days slipped into weeks, the weeks into months, and the seasons had changed. But she had not changed. The web that enclosed her from the night Nicole died had thickened with the passage of time, and she was imprisoned within it so that she saw and heard all, as if it existed in another world.

Welles still came to her, but she had given up the fight. Nothing brought a response, not even the whip that he used to rouse her. Once, lying upon his bed as he beat her, she had prayed that it would be a true beating this time, that her flesh would be stripped, her bones bared, and that her blood, running free, would take her spirit with it, leaving an empty carcass, unknowing and useless to all but the worms.

Sometimes, on awakening, she would for a moment

think herself to be back in her father's house with the soft Caribbean wind sighing through the windows and the easy roll of the surf caressing the beaches beyond them.

Soon, her mother could come to awaken her with a gentle voice and tender hands, and she would rise and dress and go to the table. She would pause at her father's chair and plant a kiss upon the top of his head and he would reach out and pat her in laughing good humor.

And then she would remember that it was all gone. Her mother lay dead and her father, too, and her brothers were scattered and she was the debased prey of the violent man who had bought her. And Nicole was dead. And then the gray cocoon would envelop her, deadening the pain buried within her heart.

As she passed into the master chamber, she found Joshua in the act of buttoning his breeches. He did not look up when she entered, saying over his shoulder, "Is that you, Serena?" And at her murmured assent, he added, "The sewing women grow slovenly. These breeches are not properly mended. See to it. If it happens again, the woman responsible is to be whipped."

"Yes, master." she said tonelessly.

"As for you"—he had turned now and was regarding her through narrowed eyes—"you have grown lax. Perhaps it is you who needs the beating."

"Yes, master," she replied in the same voice as before. His threats had no power over her anymore. He knew that and knew that she was indifferent to pain or love or even hate and that she would welcome death by any means.

A sense of irony stirred. She was safe if only because he would always withhold that which she most longed for.

"You bore me," he said now. "I know I must replace you soon."

"Yes, master."

"I realize it is time to sell you south."

"Yes, master."

"Damn your eyes, you black bitch! Say something besides 'Yes, master.' "

She said nothing, meeting his eyes without any expression in her own. She thought dispassionately that he was the most loathesome creature she had ever seen. He had grown fat during the past year. seldom venturing into Williamsburg. Few were the neighbors who called, and as time went by he made fewer and fewer trips from the plantation.

Serena could have told him that despite his claims that he had been too late to reach Caroline and that she had killed herself in a fit of despondency over the child she had lost, rumors persisted that he himself had done away with her or by some cruelty forced her to flee.

Joshua himself sensed something of this, but he could not fathom how such rumors had arisen. He had been too careful. Serena had not left the plantation. And in any case, she had done as he ordered. But then the brat had been alive, and it was she who had been pliable to his orders and willing in bed.

He missed the excitement of those encounters, the intense pleasure he had derived from her resistance, her fighting, even the clawing and biting, and, most of all, the hard, ringing pain of his hand slapping her bare flesh. Now he could beat her, but her very apathy spoiled his pleasure and left him impotent both in his fury and in the physical sense.

Once, frightened that it meant the end of his manhood, he had taken one of the young girls from the slave quarters to reassure himself. But after the first few encounters she had been too pliant and ceased to interest him.

He fumed within over the way his life had turned. Rowland had taken the news of his daughter's death with shocked anger. In his letter answering the news, Rowland had left no doubt that he held Welles responsible in some way and had made veiled threats to end the very satisfactory and profitable trade.

Joshua had thus been forced to reply with equally subtle threats to expose all if Rowland were to be so rash as to drop him. Since then, there had been only one communication as to business. On the next shipment, Joshua had found a subtle decrease in the amount of goods and a definite drop in actual gold. And Ramsey, damn him, was discreetly pleased at Joshua's protest over so much scrip and so little goods.

There was no way he could retaliate. Rowland controlled the gold. And were he himself to lighten the tobacco casks and so keep Rowland from making a profit without tax, there would go more gold.

"Damn him!" he exclaimed aloud. Then, realizing

Serena still stood there, her blank eyes staring at him, he shouted, "Get out, you pig!"

Without a sound, she turned around and left the room. Rowland at odds and Serena no better than the walking dead, and society's face all but turned against him. The governor had been barely civil on their last meeting, and even his closest neighbors, the Blairs, no longer called. He had, in fact, on his last visit to them been received with punctilious courtesy, but with a marked lack of enthusiasm he could not miss.

It was like that everywhere, and it was like boxing an eiderdown quilt. For all the years he had been in Virginia, he had never been able to penetrate its society in the fully accepted sense he had longed for. And he had never fully understood the people. He had come close to both during that winter Caroline had spent with him in Williamsburg. Caroline.

That, at least, was one satisfaction: dead now at worst, but at best a slave to some man or men. He liked to think of her used nightly in a whorehouse, liked to think of her helpless, degraded, and looking older than her years.

It was a dream that grew especially during the times when he took the opium and could drift off to dreams in a world where he was king, on a day he would have sufficient supply not to ration those dreams . . . nightly if he liked. Wine and spirits were not adequate substitutes. Bascomb had not brought enough opium the last time, and Welles had threatened the doctor again, forcing him to add some of his own supply.

Next year, he would buy directly in London from one of the incoming Orient traders, as Bascomb did. And next year he would have it out with Rowland. Or, better yet, he would start new business elsewhere. Let Rowland pay for his earldom then if he could. And next year he would find himself another wife—a good-looking, submissive young girl who would bear children and be satisfied with her lot. And the tide would turn again in his favor.

He finished dressing and left the house to ride over his acres and take satisfaction—what satisfaction he could— from the long rows of tobacco, the big drying kilns, and the endless bounty that was his.

Serena watched him ride away and a strange feeling of having been deprived of something swept over her. Beneath the layers of indifference a long-forgotten emotion stirred so briefly that it was gone before she could name it. Yet it was something she wanted, something she must have. She tried to think of what it could be, but it eluded her.

Going into the kitchen sometime later, she found Charity standing at the table peeling vegetables for dinner. Cookie dozed fitfully in her chair by the hearth, over which a young suckling pig turned slowly on the spit. The mouth-watering aroma of the cooked flesh filled the room.

Charity looked up with a start as Serena entered. She wore a long, shapeless dress far too big for her thin body and a calico rag was tied around her hair. The garment had been her mother's, and while it had been taken up in the hem it was otherwise left so that no outlines of her young body showed, with the bodice blousing out over breasts that Serena knew had been bound to conceal their true shape. Since the last young girl Welles had taken, many of the others with the help of their mothers had resorted to such subterfuge. And they had stilled their laughter and song when Joshua was anywhere near them.

Charity was half-orphaned now. The fever that had taken Nicole had also claimed the lives of a dozen slaves, Charity's mother among them, as well as her older sister. Her present outfit she owed to her father's fear for her.

"He's left," Serena said shortly.

Charity answered, "But he come back lak always. Big fat massa." She dropped the knife and drew herself up in mocking imitation of Welles. "I be massa head! Yo' boy, yo' wan' a taste o' mah whup? Wait a minnit, I go get me someun as 'ull lif' it foh me 'cause I too fat!" She giggled and Cookie stirred and awoke.

"Mind dem onions, Charity. Ah sweah, I neber seen a chile lak yo'. Giddy. Jus' giddy and das de truf."

"Ole fat massa, he gone ridin' away." Charity said.

"He fall off dat hoss one day and brek his neck an' dere'll be cheerin' in de fields," Cookie prophesied darkly.

"Why?" Serena asked dully. "When a new master will come on the next boat upriver?"

"Cain be wus," Cookie said. "Be bettah. Mistiss Chiswell, de cook, she tell me dey ain' no such as Massa

Welles in dey house. Say huh ole massa don' bodder de girls an' he don' whup no one nohow. Say he be good, an' de mistiss, she be tekkin' keer foh dem when dey sick."

"And slices meat for them from her own roast pork instead of scraps and chitterlings, I suppose?"

"Plenty o' meat," Cookie said resentfully.

"Plenty of what they don't want themselves," Serena answered. "And they are still slaves."

"Yo' talk lak dat, high and mighty, an' yo' gonna git killed same's yo' mammy," Cookie growled.

"Serena don' mean no harm," Charity protested. "An' she wa'n't always no slave, needah."

"No more 'un mah mammy wuz," Cookie said. "But soon's dey tek her, she be slave, an' me, too, an' mine. Das de way 'twuz when yo' lose de war in huh land."

"How is your little sister?" Serena asked Charity.

"Faith? She fine now. Oney mah pappy"—her face fell—"mah pappy, he don' evah be de same agin. Mighty sad at ouah place, Serena."

"Mighty sad all over this place," Serena answered. "Death," she added in a dreamy voice, "that's the smell of Wildwood. It hangs over the house and it clings to the grass. Death."

"Hush yo' mouf," Cookie said. "Yo' be skeerin' dat chile an' yo' be gettin' yo' own self sold jus' as sho' as can be. Death. Death come all de time to evahbody. Ain't no use to talk 'bout it, 'ceptin' it be someun yo' glad to see dead—like ole massa. An' lak I say, den dey be no weepin' but cheerin' in de fields."

"And Taylor's whip across the back of everyone cheering," Serena said. "You think Welles is bad. Taylor'll be as bad once he has all the say."

"Ain't gonna leave no such plantation to Taylor," Cookie snorted. "Be one o' dem fancy people fum acrost de sea."

"It won't matter. Nothing does matter. Charity, fix me a cup of coffee, please, and bring it to the parlor."

"Yo' ain't gonna set in de parlor an' drink coffee!" Charity exclaimed incredulously. "Ole massa come back an' see yo' an he whup yo' to death yo'self."

"No," Serena said. "No. He has no mercy. Bring the coffee."

"Now what she mean by dat?" Charity asked when Serena had gone.

"Don' mean nothin'. Crazy. Been crazy since dat baby die in de spring, weepin' ovah ole massa's chile, dat's what she do. Huh, ah gits me one o' ole massa's children, ah kill it mahself."

"No yo' won'. Serena say once yo' got yo' baby don' much mattah who de paw is. Poah Mistiss Cah-line . . . she dun loss a baby, too, an' she dun kill huhself."

"No, she don' do dat an' she don' lose no chile, needah. Dat ole massa, he think he know, but he ain't know nothin'. Stop gawpin', chile, an fetch Serena dat coffee."

"Ah'd lak a baby o' mah own," Charity said dreamily.

"Yo' bettah not let yo' paw heah yo' talk lak dat. He be weahin' out a whup on yo' hide. Now, hush up an' hurry up." Cookie settled herself back in her chair. "Death," she muttered. "Always talkin' death. One day it come fo' huh, an' das fo' sho' . . . an' come fo' ole massa, too, ah reckon."

The long twilights of summer had come to an end, and once the sun dipped over the western rim of the Blue Ridge Mountains, night fell swiftly.

Stretching back from Wildwood, the pine forests and foothills were blacker than the night itself, and on this night, in the absence of moonlight, the house loomed like a ghostly mansion in the velvet darkness.

A silence lay over the land, hushing the sound of the swift-flowing river and muffling the oars of the longboat that drew in to the Wildwood dock.

As the crew crept up the embankment and filed along the shadowed drive, Domino, in the lead, was struck by the feeling, as if of an invisible barrier encircled the house itself. It was almost palpable, so much so that he paused in his tracks and waited, straining his ear to pick up some sign of life.

"What is it?" Christos whispered from behind him.

"I don't know—a strangeness, as of something amiss, or missing."

"It is fancy," Christos said. "I felt it, too. But it is fancy."

"Forward, then," Domino said after a moment and went on.

It had been no easy task to learn the exact whereabouts of Wildwood. Coming as far upriver as Williamsburg, he had found its inhabitants reluctant to give directions, almost as if he had asked the way to Hell.

He had gathered from bits of conversation that Wildwood and its owner were not favorites in the town. Of Caroline he had heard nothing, as if she no longer existed. The idea chilled him and increased his dogged persistence.

Remembering Caroline's descriptions, he led the men carefully over the ha-ha fence and spread them out in front of the house while he went up the steps alone.

They stood now at the ready: Christos, Haywood, Carson, and the carpenter's mate, Couvre. All were men he could trust beyond question. "Do not enter no matter what you hear until I call you," he had said, and he knew he would be obeyed.

In his own view, Welles would not recognize him, certainly not at first. Their view of each other aboard the *Charlotte* had been brief, and he had been wearing ordinary clothes. Garbed as he was now, in the stolen uniform of a British naval captain, he would have the advantage of surprise.

He patted the pistols in their holsters and the dagger beneath his jacket. Straightening up, he knocked upon the door.

There was no immediate answer, and after a time he knocked again, this time more loudly.

The door swung open and from behind it a young black girl peeped out at him, her eyes wide, as if she feared what she might find.

"I am Captain Thompson," he said to the girl, "of His Majesty's ship the *Redoubtable,* and I am here to see Mr. Welles. Is he at home?"

From the depths of the house a voice roared, "Who is it, Charity?"

The girl jumped and held the door open wider.

"Come in, Caypun," she said. "Ah'll fetch de massa."

He stepped inside, closing the door behind him, and followed the girl to a room beyond the staircase and to the left of it.

"He be a caypun, massa," Charity said. "He be fum de king."

Domino was in the room, bowing low and saying,

"Your servant, Mr. Welles. I come with a message from Lord Stour."

"Lord Stour," Joshua said and laughed. "I hear tell he is skipping between Whigs and Tories now that Bute is resigned and no pet of any of them these days."

"Sir," Domino said stiffly, holding his tricorne in the crook of his arm in such a manner as to throw his face into shadow.

"Never mind." Joshua pulled himself to his feet. "Come into the light, sir, so I may see your face."

Domino stepped forward, pretending not to notice the chair that Joshua offered opposite his own. As he turned, he dropped the hand with the tricorne to his waist, feeling the reassurance of his dagger beneath it.

"So you are Captain, eh? Captain who?"

"Thompson, sir."

"Thompson, eh? Damn, your face is familiar. I'm sure we have met before this."

"I think not, sir."

"Eh, well, perhaps not. And what is this message you have come so far to bring?"

"It is a message for your wife, sir."

"Wife . . . wife . . . I . . . " He broke off and stared at Domino. "My wife, is it? Ah, well, then, Captain Thompson, I must fetch her," he said. "Please be seated."

He walked from the room and Domino kept his back to the door until he heard it close.

So far, so good. Caroline, of course, would give it away, but by that time he would be ready. He crossed the room and stood with his ear against the door, listening for the returning footsteps, his hands resting lightly on his pistols. It would be better if Caroline could suppress recognition. In that way he might contrive to get her alone long enough to take her away without rousing the plantation. But he did not have any real hope of that.

Presently, he heard Joshua returning, his footsteps sounding on the bare floorboards of the hall. There was only one set of footsteps. Hurriedly, Domino crossed the room and was standing once more before the hearth.

"My wife is indisposed," Joshua said, coming forward. "Such a pity. She asks me to bring her father's message to her."

As Joshua spoke, he advanced toward Domino, a smile upon his face, strutting a little, his hands behind his back. *Hands behind his back!* The warning flashed too late in Domino's brain. His own pistols were sheathed and he managed only to dodge aside so that the bullet from Welles' pistol hit a figurine on the mantel and shattered it and the gold-framed mirror behind it.

With a cry of inarticulate rage, Joshua swung around, but Domino, coming around the side of the chair, his hand now holding his dagger, was upon him, knocking the pistol from his hand and seizing him around the throat.

"Where is she?" he asked hoarsely.

"Where you will never find her, Captain . . . Captain Domino! Yes! I finally recognized you. You see, there could be no message for my wife from her father, you brigand, he thinking her long dead these many months."

"Where is she?" Domino rasped, his knife pressed against Joshua's throat.

"I don't know," Joshua gasped. "Dead for all anyone knows. She was very ill the last time I saw her."

"Ill with what? Where did you leave her?"

"In Savannah. I sold her. Kill me if you please, but you will not leave the plantation alive. I have already sent the slaves to rouse my overseer and the head man."

"I have many more men than that outside," Domino said.

"Then it will be a bloody battle, but you will not find Caroline even if you do survive it."

Shifting his grasp on Joshua, Domino laid the dagger aside.

"Then, Mr. Welles, it appears I shall have to beat the truth out of you."

As the words left his mouth, he spun Welles around and jabbed him beneath his breastbone. The breath went out of the man's body and he sank, gasping, to the floor.

Domino was upon him in an instant, his knees pressing into Welles' belly, one hand holding his cravat in a tight, squeezing grip, the other systematically slapping Welles' face. And with each blow, he demanded again to know Caroline's whereabouts.

At last, his head pounding from the repeated blows, his throat burning with bile, Joshua managed to blurt out, "She ran away again. I found her clothing by the river. I thought she had . . . "

"You lie!" Domino said savagely, striking him again.

"All right, I lie. She ran away, though. I heard it said she booked passage aboard a ship bound for Barbados, a ship called . . . the . . . *Marigold.*"

Domino got to his feet and hauled Joshua up. "If this is the truth, we will know soon enough. You will come with me, Welles. And I had better find her in Barbados —or at least hear word of her there." He flung the man from him and said, "Go on, move. I will take you as you are."

"You will take me not at all!" cried Joshua, diving for the pistol that lay on the floor some feet from them. He had it in his hand, had the weapon cocked and was on his feet, laughing, gloating, raising the pistol so that it pointed at Domino's face. Domino had no more time to think anything except that he stared at certain death.

The shot reverberated through the room, and then Welles was sagging down, his eyes wide in disbelief, the pistol clattering to the ground.

With an curse, Domino started forward, and a woman said, "Don't touch him."

He looked up and saw a female advancing from the doorway. Behind her, cowering near the doorframe, was Charity.

"He is mine," the woman said, and as she reached Joshua, she primed the pistol again.

"You should have killed me," she said to Joshua. "I would gladly have died."

"Serena! No! No!" Joshua gurgled.

"I waited a long time for this," she answered in a dreaming voice. "I didn't know it. I never understood it. Once I thought I wanted to live. So I didn't know I had to kill you. Death in this house. Death in this house. I didn't kill Caroline's baby. Did you know that, Joshua? The baby lives. Somewhere, that baby lives. But you are going to die."

"No!" he cried even as the pistol went off. She pulled the bolt, aimed, and fired again and again until the gun was empty, and then Domino was beside her, wresting the gun from her hand.

Still she did not move, staring down at the bloody mass

that had once been Joshua Welles' face, her own face still devoid of expression.

Behind them, Charity finally moved, running and screaming. There was a quick pounding of feet coming from the kitchen. Domino thrust Serena behind him and unsheathed his pistols. They fired in rapid succession as Taylor and the head man came in through the door. One, two, and they were down, Taylor with a bullet in his head, the slave clutching his shoulder.

"Pappy!" Charity came running back, and with a long, wailing cry crouched over the slave. "Oh, please!" she said, trying to shield her father as he tried to shove her away. "Please, Caypun, don' kill mah pappy."

Domino drew in a deep breath. "There will be no more killing," he said. "What is your name, man?"

"Andrew, Caypun."

" 'Tis only a flesh wound," Domino said, looking at the shoulder. "I saw too late that you were unarmed."

He lifted Charity to her feet. "Fetch your mother, Charity."

"She dead," Charity said.

"Then bring clean cloth and water to fix this wound. Hurry. Who else is in the house?"

"No one." Serena spoke from behind him. "No one, save Cookie, and by now I am sure she has run away." Her voice had lost its toneless quality. She sounded cool and assured and as if what had transpired was none of her doing.

"Help Andrew," Domino said. "I will open the door for my men."

"When they come, they will blame the slaves," Serena said, indicating the bodies.

"My men?"

"Whoever comes," she replied.

"No, no, they won't," Domino answered. "You are Serena?"

"Yes."

"Caroline told me of you."

"Caroline is on the pirate ship," Serena said, "a pirate ship with women. Welles sold her."

"Sold her?"

"Yes. He told me so. He boasted of how he beat her, but not on the face. She is to be sold to someone. I don't know who . . . a Saracen or a madam of a whorehouse. She would be a slave."

"When?" Domino asked, a gnawing sickness spreading through him.

"Nearly four months ago. It was the end of May when they brought her to him. He paid ransom for her, only to beat her and sell her to Blanche Chester."

"Blanche?" Domino saw the *Lady Dare* as she had sailed after them around the Keys and towards the Indies. They had left her far behind and Christos had reckoned she was on a course to intercept a merchantman, a sea raider still, haunting the waters offshore for fresh booty. And Chester was not only a pirate, but a procuress, taking good-looking women and girls from vessels she captured or from her raids along the shore and selling them to the highest bidder. Caroline, in her hands! And to think he had been so close to her as they passed each other at the beginning of his journey.

"Come," he said, his voice still steady in spite of his churning mind and body. "See to Andrew. You will have to come with us," he added, then went to open the door and called the men in.

The party that had crept so quietly up the path to the house at midnight went without caution back to the dock just before dawn.

Serena, clutching a shawl around her as if to ward off a chill only she could feel, walked beside Christos, her arm stiff beneath his guiding hand. Andrew, supported by Carson, followed Charity, who held her younger sister.

Behind them, pistols in their stiffening hands, lay the bodies of Welles and his overseer. Elsewhere on the plantation the slaves slept on. If the sound of shots had awakened any, they had not appeared at their doors or come out to learn what had happened.

Only Cookie had been awake and in the house when it began, and she had not returned from wherever she had fled to during the shooting.

Andrew had not been eager to leave with them. It had taken the combined persuasion of his daughter, Domino, and even Serena to make him see that were he found wounded, he would be suspected of murdering at least one of the men who died.

"Slaves have been hanged for far less a suspicion,"

Domino advised him, and at last Andrew had gathered some of his belongings and awakened the younger girl.

Serena carried nothing with her. "I will take nothing," she had said to Domino. "I want nothing from this place."

Christos had argued that they should break into the offices and take what gold was there, but Domino vetoed the idea. "If it looks like burglary, then the slaves will be suspected. And if not, the authorities will know someone else was here. They will surely know I was. I do not care to have a price on my head now that I have come at last to the end of buccaneering."

He had been hard put to think of how to advise the authorities of the double murder, and at last he settled on docking in Williamsburg long enough to pay a boy to take a note to the governor.

The note, hastily scribbled at Wildwood, now lay in his breast pocket. It read:

> I must hasten back to my ship. I have lately come from Wildwood, where I found both master and overseer dead from a struggle. They appear to have shot each other in an argument. I know nothing more, for the slaves were in their quarters, save for three I saw running off through the woods.
>
> Captain Thompson

As they boarded the longboat, Charity said, "Pappy, what gonna happen tomorra when Mistuh Taylor, he don' be deah, and de massa, he don' come?"

"Gonna be feastin' an' shoutin' till de white folk come."

"Cookie, she be skeered," Charity went on. "She run soon's de massa send huh fo' Mistuh Taylor. She say death come fo' sho' dis night."

"Hush," said her father.

"She be tellin' white folk how Caypun come an' den de shootin' start."

Domino swore under his breath. He hadn't thought of that or he would have made a search for the woman. Too late now. He gave a signal and the boat pulled away from the dock, the oars splashing gently in the river.

It would be useless to leave the note now. He took it from inside his jacket and shredded it, letting the pieces fall over the side to sink in the water.

"We will go straight to the *Mouette*," he told Christos, "and then I will go into Norfolk."

It would be easier to see the authorities in Norfolk. There was less likelihood of his being detained. He had not questioned the whereabouts of Joshua Welles in Norfolk.

It would be a simple enough matter to say that he had called with a message from Lord Stour about some irregularities in shipment and that when Welles sent for the overseer, a battle had ensued, one he had been powerless to stop. Some of the slaves had run off, but most were unaware of the shooting. Yes, much better. He only hoped that whatever revelry Welles' and Taylor's death inspired, it would not go too hard against the slaves.

"Why not leave the plantation to them?" Serena asked, as if she read his thoughts.

"Because sooner or later, someone would come looking for Welles," he said, "and they would all suffer."

"And does that matter to you?" she asked curiously.

"Yes," he said curtly. "As it should to you, Mademoiselle," he said.

"Once it did," she answered.

"Once it will again," he insisted. "Your days of slavery are over forever. It remains for you to decide how it will go after that."

She did not answer. Looking at her, he saw that she had bowed her head over her clasped hands and he sensed that she was weeping.

"Why do you speak to her that way?" Christos asked, accusation in his voice.

"She weeps not for what I say to her," Domino replied.

Then he said to Serena in a gentler voice, "It is well for you to weep, Mademoiselle. When the heart hurts, it is better cured with tears. Caroline told me of your life before. It can never be that way again, but it will be what you yourself wish now. Come, when you have finished weeping, say to yourself: I go at last to freedom and take courage once more. For you have courage. I owe my life to you now, as well as my daughter's. And . . ." He stopped. He had been about to say that if there were any hope for Caroline, that, too. But the words would not come.

Even if Caroline were alive, what could she be after all that had happened to her? What he had learned since he began his search for her and what he knew from Loco and from Serena was all evil and degradation. She, who could not bear the touch of an oafish husband, was now in the hands of men perhaps worse than Welles had been.

He knew she had spirit and fire and passion. He knew that she was brave and resourceful and intelligent. Yet she had vulnerable emotions and sensitivities. And in spite of everything, she had a need for protection. She had not been reared to expect brutality, and she had known nothing but shelter until the day he had sighted the *Charlotte* two years ago.

With a groan, Domino cursed himself for that day, and as soon thrust the guilt from him. There had always been Welles. Sooner or later, a woman of Caroline's passions would have fallen in the way of Welles' special wrath.

His thoughts were unbearable. He longed for action, any kind of action. He concentrated on the task ahead: the finding of the *Lady Dare* and the boarding, and women would once more be aboard the *Mouette*. Not only would there be women, but a child, as well, and one scarcely more than a child. Yet there was nowhere he could leave them. Their fate was cast with his and had been from the moment his pistols had been fired. To put them ashore would mean death for them more certainly than any fate they might find at sea with him.

The dawn had intensified its light, and ahead of them the sun edged over the horizon.

Tense from his musings, helpless for the moment in the clutch of fate, Domino rose and made his way to Carson.

"I will take your place," he said. "Do you move into mine?"

"Aye, aye, Captain," Carson replied, surrendering his oar.

It was better to use his body, to feel his muscles stretch as he pulled against the surging current.

Charity sat with her sister in her lap, their heads touching as they slept. Serena, too, had ceased her weeping and was leaning against Christos' arm, asleep, as well.

Indeed, all save the rowers rested, and the oarsmen pulled with an automatic motion born of their own fatigue. Only Domino was alert in this silent land-banked stream, and with each pull of his oar he could only think that for all he must yet do, in the end he had lost Caroline forever.

Chapter Twenty-Four

Caroline had been sick for a long time. The screaming nightmare of the miscarriage had blurred in the aftermath of raging infection and fever. For weeks she had hovered between life and death, and when at last she awoke to the strange new world in which she found herself, she was at first dazed and uncomprehending.

In the months of her recuperation, she felt like one recently restored from the dead, and she was resentful over having been snatched from the bliss of oblivion. It occurred to her that in all the rejoicing over Lazarus, there had been no mention of Lazarus being especially delighted.

Whatever the makeup of the crew of the *Lady Dare,* whatever their way of life, they had tended her as carefully as if she were rare and precious cargo.

It was strange to think of Bianche Chester as a captain. In looks she was nothing more than a robust goody, rough of speech and full of bawdy good humor. A woman of perhaps forty, with protuberant brown eyes and bucked teeth, she resembled a rather amiable hare. It was hard to imagine her being bold enough to wage war against armed merchantmen and to board vessels and engage in hand-to-hand combat with a cutlass as a weapon.

In her first few encounters with Caroline, Blanche had been alternately grave, with almost maternal concern, and roughly jesting, as if by the force of her own good health she could transform Caroline from the pale and sickly woman she had become.

Often she would come to sit beside Caroline's bed and talk to her of her own life as a child and of how she became a pirate. Dressed in a shirt and breeches and waistcoat, with her well-shaped calves encased in black hose, she could have passed for a man. It was the hair that gave her away. Thick and chestnut-colored with no visible gray strands, it was her one true mark of beauty, and she wore it pulled back and bound with a black ribbon from whence it hung in heavy rippling waves down her back.

At first, Caroline heard little of what Blanche said. The voice going on and on acted like a sleeping potion and Caroline's eyes would grow heavy and finally close.

As she recovered her strength, however, she began to take an interest in the tales. Blanche spared nothing in the telling, talking as freely and frankly as if what had occurred was mere commonplace fare.

"Bedded me mother, an' her a chambermaid, but fond of her, he was," she would say of her father, "and fair broken-hearted when she died. Had his own wife, he did, but never loved her. Loved me better than he loved his other children. Aristocrat, he was." Here she laughed. "But I took none of that from him. He put me in a school after my mother died, but I soon had enough of it and ran away with the boy who used to bring the milk to the school."

"And didn't your father look for you?"

"Where 'ud he look? Christ, he had enough of a problem to keep me a secret as 'twas."

Blanche's easy profanity came as a shock to Caroline, used as she had been to a society still retiring behind puritanism in speech, even if it did enjoy Restoration morals.

"And was it the milk boy who took you to sea?"

"Hell!" Blanche exclaimed with a roar. "He was only a lad hisself. I soon tired of him, I tell you, and of going hungry amidst plenty. We was begging for scraps at the gate.

"No, this is not for Blanche Chester, said I. And then begging in a tavern down by the river, I met Bill Stone. Tall, he was, and a man, and just home from months at sea. A pirate, then, he was, but I never knew it. Took a fancy to me and I to him. Took me with him that night and bedded me and wedded me and brung me to sea. Learned from Bill, I did. And smarter than him I was. Terrible stubborn man, Bill was. Took chances he could see were too dangerous. And one of 'em got us captured and got him hanged."

"And they let you go?"

"Aye, thanks to Molly Nettlor. Did I tell you she was for all the world like a man?"

"No, you didn't," Caroline answered, vaguely recalling some such tale but unable to think of details.

"Well, Bill's mate, she was; master mate, she was. And I sailed with her near four years before I found her out. Bill knew. He had her, too, you see. One woman 'ud never be enough for Bill. Found him more than once with a shore gel, and him only leaving my own bed not long afore. Well, but be that as it may, Molly—we called her Mark then—was always good to me, and me in my innocence thought 'twas a fancy she'd—or he'd—taken. Fair pleased with myself, I was. A bit of my own back for Bill and his wild ways. Strike me blue! And when I found out she was a woman, I near died."

"How did you find out?"

"Why, 'twas the day Bill thought himself better than a first-rater with thirty guns and runs his little sallie alongside her and tries to board her, and we near got blasted out of the water.

"Molly, she come running to me and tearing off her clothes and putting on a gown and saying, 'We was captured, Blanche, and don't you say nothing different, or our necks'll stretch same's that crackrope of a husband you got. Damn fool!' she says. 'Serve us right,' she says. And I'm standing there open-mouthed to see Mark turned into Molly, breasts and all!" Blanche gave a mighty guffaw at the memory.

"And feeling worse'n a fool, preening myself, 'twas my charms as had caught the eye of a handsome fellow, and all the time 'twas no more than my own husband's whore being friendly like, and bearing no malice, as we shared the same man."

"And you? How did you feel?"

"Me? Damn, it was the best joke. We was good friends after that, Molly and me. Still good friends. Oh, if you had seen us in that court in Nassau and the judge, all solemn, and us crying and saying as how we was kidnapped and abused and forced into carnal acts as near killed us! Ha! And Bill was grinning like a fool to see us make such a jackanapes of the judge. Walked out clean, we did. And all the good ladies of Nassau fixed us up with clothes and a place to stay and gave us money and bought us passage back to England. Sailed away, nice as you please, and when the ship dropped anchor at Barbados we was soon off her and getting ourselves into breeches again and signed on with a pirate ship."

In the telling of her adventures, Blanche was so pleased to find a willing audience that she adopted a friendlier manner toward Caroline, treating her as if she were an old friend instead of her captive.

Then, one day, having finished describing how she and Molly, with the hoard of their share in booty money, finally managed to buy their own ship, she paused and looked ruefully at Caroline.

"Heigh, ho," she said easily. "And me thinking you a friend and knowing I must soon sell you off. You be looking better now, though your hair be fouled and you be as dirty as any pirate I've ever seen. I think we'll put into Barataria and give you a wash and try you on the Orleans market; see if you be ready. If not, well, we'll keep you and try for one of the Indies. Like as not we'll place you well. You be sure of that. 'Twill be better for you than for some others: maybe a planter widowed and not wanting to marry again and not wanting to go to a whorehouse in town, or maybe not having one and not wanting a black woman, as others do with. Treat you good, then, he will—maybe even wed you in the end if you be clever with him."

Caroline had frozen during this speech, and when Blanche rose to leave, Caroline said, "You saved me only to sell me?"

"Aye, you could say so. Business be business, and a corpse brings no money. But even do we not sell you, we'd save you, just the same. We been't cold-hearted."

"But what of the girls you take in raids and the helpless women you abduct from other ships?"

"Aye, and what of them? Think you the girls in the hovels along the shores fare better bedding with the likes of themselves? As for the ladies on the ships . . . well, we hold them for ransom, but 'twould surprise you how many are never ransomed by their husbands or even their fathers. 'Used,' they says as an excuse, 'and no good to us anymore.' 'Tis the same with the husbands and fathers, don't you see? Business be business for them, too, nor would any merchant buy damaged goods back, could he escape it. Rest easy, Caroline. Whatever we find for you, 'twill be better than the husband who paid us to take you away."

"I'd rather be a pirate," Caroline said.

"Aye. 'Tis a good life and full of excitement and money-making for those as has the stomach. Be you sure you could put cutlass to belly if need be? Ah," she added with a laugh at Caroline's scarcely repressed shudder. "See you? Not a pirate, then; a cook for pirates, maybe. And there is those in the crew as would fancy having you theirselves. Do we not find a buyer for you, 'twill be something to think on."

The very nature of this speech—bizarre and improbable —lessened its effect on Caroline. She had heard Blanche talk of her as if she were a mare to be sold for breeding: troublesome in her sickness and unlikely to fetch a high price owing to her current appearance, but not to worry . . . a good grooming and a good master would soon fix her up. Then she would be gamboling in fields of pleasure, and if she achieved the proper balance between friskiness and obedience, she would soon prove too valuable a pet to mistreat.

The ludicrousness of the imagery overcame her and she fell to giggling foolishly until weak tears began to course down her cheeks.

When they had come ashore at Barataria, Caroline, knowing she was so close to Felicity, began to imagine that in the course of their stay she would find an opportunity to escape surveillance and make her way upriver and into New Orleans.

However, she had reckoned without Molly, who might have been kind to a young Blanche Chester, but who had evidently soured in the intervening fifteen years.

Blanche was inclined to believe that Caroline, weakened by her long illness and timid by the facts of birth and breeding, required little supervision. How could she escape the compound of crude huts surrounded by trees and islets in which river snakes abounded and where cotton-mouths and water moccasins could usually be found sunning themselves near the banks?

Molly believed otherwise and set herself to guarding Caroline, for whom she entertained little liking. A tall, broad-shouldered, and deep-chested woman, Molly wore her iron-gray hair cut to the shoulders and swinging free beneath her tricorne. She looked rather like a man in her breeches and jacket, and her low voice added to the over-all effect. Her face was lined from age and weather, and the smudgy, dark moustache common to many women past their middle years increased Molly's masculine appearance.

Although she was senior to Blanche in years and in her navigational knowledge, and taller, stronger, and rougher, Molly could not equal Blanche's hold over the rest of the mixed crew. Of the thirty-odd crew members who sailed the *Lady Dare,* a dozen were women, some squat and ugly, some clearly attractive, and all as hard bitten as their mates. Liaisons between them and the men were common enough, and Blanche once said coarsely that when the sea voyage lasted too long, even the oldest and ugliest among the women could choose her bed partner. "Be their need great, men don't see a woman except below the waist," she had said, and Molly had grunted a crude assent.

The sojourn on Barataria, as a consequence of Molly's ever-watchful eyes, had been as confining as the months aboard the *Lady Dare.*

It required many washings before Caroline's hair shone once more with its original golden luster, but by the end of the first week Blanche pronounced her fit for viewing.

Garbed in pirated finery and surveying herself in a mirror that was also part of the last booty, Caroline hardly recognized herself. She was very thin and her eyes looked larger and brighter, as if fever still lingered there. Her brows were startlingly black on her white face. But a bit of color had begun to creep back along her cheekbones. Her lips had lost their paleness, and if not the deep, rosy color of before, they were nevertheless pink and less drawn.

The gown, a pale-blue brocaded satin, with a stomacher of a deeper shade embroidered in silver leaves, was too hot for the sultriness of the weather. Still, the color was complimentary.

Hoops, she observed, were not as wide as they had been, and the corps was less restricting, being stiffened at wider intervals and bending lightly over her breasts.

She had not been dressed like this for a very long time

—not, in fact, since the night before she ran away from Wildwood. Her shoes, a bit too big, were new, and the red heels showed brightly beneath the cloth-of-gold uppers.

Blanche was delighted with the results of her efforts, and even Molly gave a grudging compliment. "We be selling you soon, I reckon," she said, satisfaction in her voice.

The first of the buyers was an old, balding, fat man whose clothing looked none too clean and whose mouth was set from the spittle that frothed as he spoke.

Caroline, sickened at the sight of him, could only pray he would not meet the asking price. He asked for and received an audience alone with her. "Five minutes," he was told. As her guards left the hut, he advanced smilingly toward Caroline and then grasped her cold hands in his hot, dry palms.

He smelled of stale grease and tobacco and some sweet scent, as if he had doused himself with a mixture of flower waters to conceal the acrid odor of a long-unwashed body.

If he so much as touches me, I will die, she thought, and from somewhere a mad impulse seized her. As he bent toward her, she began to titter like an insane person and said, "Oh, it be I now for you not so I sang. I laugh."

Hearing this, he stepped back and stared at her, whereupon she crossed her eyes and tittered again, mouthing fresh insanities. She saw the alarm and revulsion on his face and repeated her mumbled incoherencies. He backed away, truly frightened.

At that she broke into a peal of laughter and he bolted away. She was still laughing with sheer amusement when Molly hurried back into the hut.

"What have you done?" she cried. "He thinks you be daft. And you look daft! Stop that! Stop that!"

Molly's tricorne slipped in her agitation and landed comically over one eye, giving her the look of an outraged parrot. At this, Caroline laughed harder and only Molly's stinging slap across her cheek stopped the helpless flow of laughter.

"I am sorry," she managed to say. "But he was so . . . so comical that I could not help but laugh. He took me for a madwoman."

"I take you for a clever wench," Molly said. "One trick, but not two, or you be whipped."

"Here, here," Blanche remonstrated, coming into the hut. "We talk no more of the whip. Caroline is right. He took her for daft. He be comical, right enough. No more would he pay a good price. There are others, Molly."

Others, Caroline thought, shuddering. I cannot do this each time, nor will I. The next one I will try to charm, for surely once I am in New Orleans I can make my way to the convent. They will not chain me, and thinking me a bond-servant, they will imagine I dare not run.

But the stay on Barataria ended with none of the would-be buyers willing to meet the price. "Not a virgin," was the general reason given, and nothing Blanche could say about how much better was experience for pleasure altered their views.

In a few days they had left the island and sailed for the Florida coast. There they met with even less success than before, the Spanish finding her too thin, as well.

"We must fatten her up," Blanche said to Molly.

"Aye, and sell her to the best offer. I think you ask too high a price. Is it to keep her aboard?"

"Keep her? God's wounds, think you I be mad? What good is she to us, save for ransom?"

"Then I say we should sell her for the highest bid, no matter if it fall lower than what we ask."

"Very well," Blanche capitulated suddenly. "We fatten her and we sail into the Indies and there we sell her —if not to a planter, then to a whorehouse. Precious little we get from one there, though."

"So we are finished. It don't matter," Molly said, scowling. "Now that she be clean and combed, there be mumbling in the quarters as to who will have her if she not be sold."

"Aye, and I can take care of that," Blanche said.

"Aye, and end up like Anne Bonney. You remember the tales of Anne Bonney? Soft heart, soft head, Blanche. I be telling you that these many years gone."

"So you have," Blanche agreed. "But which of us do be captain? And which of us do find the best prizes, eh, Molly?"

"Aye, and so 'twas with Bonney till she grew soft-hearted. Dead by a rope is Bonney."

" 'Twas a man she fancied done her in," Blanche said.

"Aye, and 'twill be a woman as does you in. She be trouble. Aye, and I know it."

"Enough!" Blanche roared suddenly. "Christ, you be foolish in your years. We sail from Florida tomorrow. Six weeks be long enough, and five ports too many. How say you, Molly," she added in a quieter voice, "a prize on the way, perhaps, and the wench sold in Barbados' open market, if need be?"

"Done." Molly stretched out a grubby hand and they shook on it.

Learning that they were once more setting out to sea and this time for the Indies, Caroline's heart sank. Better to have endured the fat little porker and escaped into the streets of New Orleans than to find herself chained in Barbados or Martinique with nowhere to run.

That night, lying awake in her bed, listening to the waves slapping against the sides of the ship as the tide rushed toward the shore, she thought briefly of slipping over the side and swimming for the land before the ship weighed anchor. From Florida she could find her way back to New Orleans.

But she discarded the notion almost at once. It was too great a distance to risk, and when once she would gladly have exchanged life for death and thus dared all, something new had been born in her.

I have endured much, she was wont to think as each fresh peril rose before her, and I will endure this. Two years ago, she could not have conceived of one-tenth of what had happened to her. Now she saw those two years as periods of bright happiness broken by those of intense misery, of oases of comfort and safety before the next desperate adventure across trackless, unknown deserts.

She had endured having Joshua as a husband and lasted through his brutality; she had survived Loco and his vile intrusion of her. Somehow, during the period she believed Felicity to be dead, she had found the strength to go on. Abduction, rape, storm, gale, desert island, and dank ship's hold—she had come through all. She would come through this. If a way was not clear before her now, it would become so, and when it did she would seize the opportunity and find the courage to use it.

Sold in the market at Barbados? Let them. Her chin lifted and she smiled to herself. I may look timid and weak to Blanche Chester, who understands little save

coarseness and fighting, but I will outwit her and her ilk
yet.

Suddenly, thh room was alive with ghostly images of
her life and of her former self: her father giving way before her, her wishes granted, her persistence winning for
her almost always, save when she allowed herself to believe she had no weapons.

"Why," she said aloud, "I have always been strong. I
only *thought* myself weak and helpless." Her heart
pounded and she almost laughed aloud.

With the surge of self-realization and of courage, her
tensions evaporated and her body relaxed. As she drifted
off to sleep, half-remembered fragments of things she
had read came back to her, all having to do with courage. Free, she thought, I am free in myself. She tried to
think of the significance of that, of the deeper meaning
below the surface of those words, but it eluded her, and
in the morning she could not remember how it went.

Smooth sailing took the *Lady Dare* out beyond the
Bahamas in record time. Seeking prey, she haunted the
offshore islands and then sailed back out along the best-
known shipping routes and returned closer to shore and
out again.

Caroline, wrapped in the warm blanket of her renewed
hope and self-encouragement, even found it possible to
enjoy the cool breezes, warm sun, and even this delay in
reaching land.

Under Blanche's orders, the best of the fare aboard was
fed to her and she ate it gladly, feeling the life sperm
quicken with each hearty meal. She was a goose being
fattened for the Christmas of their prize. Gold. They were
asking gold for her, some fifty pounds of it.

In the light of all that had transpired, and weighing it
against a life much like her sisters, she found the scales
tipped in her favor. At least I am living, she thought,
and I have known as much ecstasy as I have known pain
. . . and I will again.

As the days passed her body filled out, her face
rounded, and her eyes lost their feverish look and sparkled
once more. Now when Blanche would stop to speak to her
as she paced the decks, Caroline went out of her way to
urge the older woman to tell her more stories.

With Molly, her efforts at amiability were still met with

suspicion. In Molly she perceived an intelligence Blanche did not possess, and it was that intelligence coupled with a native shrewdness that kept Molly wary of her.

Molly knew without knowing why that Caroline was far more capable and resourceful than her outward show of wide-eyed helplessness. Blanche, far less analytical, took Caroline's friendly curiosity and seeming acquiescence at face value.

Molly should have been the captain, and save for the abrasiveness of her personality and her open contempt for the men beneath her, she would have been.

At the beginning of their voyages on the then new *Lady Dare,* Molly had automatically assumed command. Her reign was short-lived. A mutiny arose before they had been at sea a month, and save for the fact that Blanche had learned of it and taken steps to secure arms and some crew for defense, the career of the new lady pirates would have ended sooner than the legendary Anne Bonney's.

Quelling the mutiny and executing the leaders had been Blanche's triumph. Where Molly would have hanged every last one, Blanche promised amnesty to the poor rabble who had followed the leaders. She had been elected captain then and had remained so.

Much of Molly's antagonism toward Caroline was also due to Blanche's liking for her. Dethroned as captain, feeling cheated out of position when it had been she who saved Blanche to begin with, she was jealous of any camaraderie of which she was not a part.

"Come to a man, and Molly don't mind. Come to one of the women, and she do," Blanche said to Caroline. "Jealous streak in Molly. Now I be different. Come to one of the women, and I don't care. Come to one of the men —if he be my man—and I be ready to slit her throat."

"Yet you shared a man," Caroline reminded her.

"Aye. But 'twasn't something I knew then. And when I found it out, sweet Jesus, the man been hanged. No cause to be jealous of a cold body—only the warm ones." She slapped Caroline on the shoulder and added, "Somewhere you be finding that for yourself. Somewhere, you be finding a man you won't want to run from, too."

It was on the tip of Caroline's tongue to say, "But I have found that," then spill forth her story. However caution prevailed. She had an idea that were she to

mention Domino and tell of how they met, of how he
rescued her once, and of Felicity, she would somehow
bring not only more danger to herself, but to them, as well.
Why this should be, she didn't know. Still, she trusted her
instincts and kept her own counsel.

"How long before we reach land?" she asked instead.

"I reckon in another week on this career before we
turn landward. The pickings be poorer now. I know not
why. War be over. Reckon we be coming across something
soon. Merchantmen from the Colonies be not so rich in
gold and goods and fine clothing as them that be coming
out from England."

But the week passed without sight of another sail, and
they turned south at last, running between the southerly
Bahamas and bearing a course that led them through the
strait between Hispaniola and Cuba.

Blanche's intention was to run close to shore past the
Leewards and into the Windward Islands of the Lesser
Antilles, coming into Barbados from the West.

The calm weather of the past month had been unsea-
sonable, and as September passed its autumnal equinox, a
shifting of the currents below the clear, smooth surface
of the sea bespoke a storm somewhere to the south.

Now that they were headed into Barbados, taking a
route unlikely to meet a ship that might bring booty of
any size, there was a relaxation of tension among the
crew. By the time the *Lady Dare* was roughly thirty
miles southwest of Dominica, even the dour Molly showed
signs of well-being.

Not searching for ships themselves beyond the customary watch to avoid collision, they were taken totally by
surprise shortly after noon on what should have been the
third day out of Barbados.

The watch had sung the warning, the crew had prepared, but by the time the ship had been identified as
English, it was nearly upon them.

Caroline, who had been walking the afterdeck, could
not see the sail. Hearing the call, she had drawn back
against the bulkhead, fearing that she would be taken at
once to her cabin below.

Sailors rushed past her unheeding as she cowered in
her shelter. All around her rose the hoarse shouts of men
and the shriller cries of the women. Battle cries.

"She's upon us!" someone shouted. Too late, the *Lady Dare*'s guns spoke and the shells fell harmlessly into the ocean on the port side.

There was no answering fire from the other ship, and Caroline, not seeing, imagined that the broadside had crippled her too badly to defend herself.

Again the *Lady Dare*'s cannon roared, and again there was no answering fire. A split second of silence followed the last dying echoes of the guns, and then the shouting began in earnest. There was a bump, as of the ship running aground, and at this, Caroline left her shelter and made her way forward to the prow.

Coming close to it, still behind the midships hatch, she had the eerie feeling that she was reliving the capture of the *Charlotte* by the *Mouette*.

The bowsprit was secured to that of the other ship, and from its bowsprit men leaped to the deck of the *Lady Dare*. Cutlasses flew as the crews of both ships were locked in mortal combat.

Long afterward, Caroline was to marvel that she had not sought safety below decks but had stood, transfixed, as knives sliced through throats and breasts.

She saw Blanche Chester fall, her back a mass of blood, then saw Molly rush to her only to be sliced down.

The shouting, the screams of the dying, and the blood that spurted from slashed throats and flowed from the mouths of men whose hearts were pierced seemed to go on for an eternity, and then at last the shouting died away and the battle was over.

More than a dozen bodies sprawled on a deck covered with blood and gore. At first Caroline could not tell who had won, but then she saw four of the women of the *Lady Dare* backing up against the wall, their arms raised, and she knew that the *Lady Dare* would haunt the Spanish Main no more.

She looked up as a voice boomed out, "Stand easy!" Her heart stopped, jumped, and then began to race crazily in her chest, for there on the bowsprit of the captured *Lady Dare* stood Domino, his legs spread wide, pistols in his hands, just as he had stood upon the *Princess Charlotte*.

Chapter Twenty-Five

For a long moment their eyes locked, and quite unconscious of what she was doing, Caroline took a few running steps forward.

"Another of um!" a voice shouted, and two sailors she recognized as being from the *Mouette* ran toward her, weapons raised.

Caroline stopped, shrinking back, and then Domino called out, *"S'arrêtez-vous! C'est mon prix!"*

The sailors fell back at once and Domino leaped upon the deck and hurried to Caroline.

"You are unharmed, I see," he said in a low voice, his eyes blank.

She nodded without speaking.

"They gave you freedom of the ship?"

Again she nodded.

"You are one of them?"

"No," she said. "I was to be sold in Barbados."

He stared at her, his face still unreadable, and presently he said, "Carson, take this lady aboard the *Mouette* and see her to my cabin."

"Aye, aye." Carson hurried up and stopped short as he saw Caroline.

"Why 'tis you, marm," he said with a pleased smile.

"Belay that," Domino said curtly. "Take her to my cabin."

"Domino, please," Caroline said in a trembling voice.

He did not answer but wheeled away to oversee the search of the prisoners.

As Carson led her past the carnage, she heard a voice murmuring. Looking down, she saw Blanche Chester feebly trying to rise. Oblivious to the rest, Caroline knelt beside her.

"So, 'tis you who is a prize once more," Blanche said. "Molly be right. You was trouble in the end."

"I'm sorry," Caroline said, and she realized she meant it. Right or wrong, Blanche had treated her well. She had seen her to restored health, and whatever Blanche's motive was, Caroline owed her that much gratitude.

"Be you the woman Domino wants?"

Caroline nodded.

"If I be knowing that, I'd as lief have let you die and be buried at sea, so I would."

"I know," Caroline said.

"He never lost a ship of his own, nor a prize ship, save the ship be sunk."

"Don't talk," Caroline begged.

"I am dying," Blanche said. " 'Tis better than death by hanging from the *Mouette*'s yardarm." Blanche gave a low sound halfway between a laugh and a sob. "Be as well dead and all aboard captured and Molly . . . " She made a feeble gesture toward the body lying near her.

"Get up Caroline," Domino said above her. "Carson, you have your orders."

Carson bent and helped Caroline to her feet. Her skirts were streaked with Blanche's blood.

"She is low and wicked," Caroline said to the silent Domino. "But she saved me and she treated me decently when she could have let me die or given me over to the men of her crew." And turning away, she followed Carson up toward the bowsprit.

Alone in the cabin, Caroline paced back and forth nervously until the ship began to move. Some fifteen minutes later there was a mighty explosion and following it a cheer from the crew. Domino had scuttled the *Lady Dare*.

She had a swift vision of men and women drowning and she shuddered. Domino had done what he swore was inhuman. Had he changed that much! Men do change.

Caroline had dreamed of this day, dreamed of finding him, of her joy, of his arms around her. His aloofness had hurt, and her heart was heavy with the pain of it.

It would be good if he had changed. Men did change. She lifted her chin, swallowing back her emotions. She would greet him with dignity, then. If she had lost her love, she would save her pride.

She was standing thus as he entered a moment or two later, but at the sight of him her control broke and she ran forward, words of love rushing to her lips, words that were never spoken as he drew her to him and stilled them forever with kisses.

They stood like this for long moments, locked in an embrace, savoring the sweetness of the reunion, passion still slumbering beneath the joy of tenderness and of the wonder of actually touching each other.

He was holding her gently now, her face pressed into his shoulder, his cheek against her hair. In the distance, she heard another roar from the crew on the deck. Hearing it, she pulled away. Looking up at him, she said, "You scuttled her."

"I did, yes."

"And left them to drown who did not die in battle or the burning of the ship?"

"No. They are in the ship's boats. Only the dead went down with the *Lady Dare*.

"And Blanche?"

"One of the dead. Does that grieve you?"

"No, it does not grieve me. But I am sorry for her."

"Sorry for her?"

"Yes, sorry for her. Does that surprise you? She was a common and cruel woman, and she sold women to be prostitutes, but she knew nothing better. And how much worse is she than the men who own slaves and the countries that grow prosperous on slave trade?"

He smiled faintly. "So, you become a true philosopher now, eh, Caroline? You see good and evil inextricably woven together?"

"I don't understand that well," she answered. "But I see the lowest can be kind and the highest cruel, if that is what you mean."

"Yes, that is what I mean. And Loco, have you an excuse for him, as well?"

"No, never," she said with sudden heat. "He killed Sister Bernadette."

Domino shook his head. "No, she lives. It is she who was able to tell me he had taken you."

"Alive. Then you . . . you saw Felicity." Her voice trembled.

"Yes. The darling of the convent. We shall have to rescue her soon, or else she will become a nun," he said with some amusement.

"Oh," Caroline said on a long breath, feeling ready to weep.

"You must get out of those bloodied rags. I will send someone to help you."

"Domino?"

"Yes?"

"What is it? You are strange with me. I . . . all these months . . . "

"Yes, all these months," he said obliquely.

"How did you find me? Captain Sage ransomed me to Joshua and he . . ."

"I know."

"But how? Loco?"

"Loco is dead. I slit his throat."

"Joshua?"

"Dead. Serena shot him—at Wildwood."

"But . . . how . . . "

"Later," he interrupted her. "We will talk of all this later. You have friends aboard. I will send them to you."

"Friends? Who, then? I have seen Carson and Christos. . . . "

"Other friends . . . from Wildwood—Serena for one, and Charity for another."

She was bewildered, "But, how, why?" she asked.

He gave her a quick hug, saying, "Let them tell you. Charity particularly is perishing to tell you." He laughed and then his face grew sober. "And Serena," he added, "be very gentle with Serena. She has suffered much, and I think 'twill be many months before she is restored."

"Please don't leave me yet," she said suddenly, clutching at him.

"I must. There is too much to see to before we are on the right tack for Liberté."

"Liberté," she repeated. "Then it has really come to pass. We will always be together now."

"Yes," he said brusquely, and his face darkened.

"What is it?" she asked.

"Nothing . . . nothing at all. I will send Charity to you." He left quickly then, as if anxious to forestall further questioning.

Charity had not changed at all. Not even the recent encounter with the *Lady Dare* could halt the bubbling flow of her words or dim her happy nature for long. She was ecstatic over seeing Caroline again and said so. "Yo' sho' be purtier den befo'," she caroled. "Dutty as yo' be."

For her own part, the sight of that sweet, humorous face lifted Caroline away from her own concerns and made her smile.

"I be free now," Charity said. "De caypun, he done free us den an' deah . . . 'cept mah pappy. He don' know what to mek o' dis freedom. Look lak he been so long used to 'Do dis' and 'Do dat' dat he kinda miss it. An' Faith, she jus' cling to Pappy lak dis freedom gonna come git huh in de night."

"But not you, eh, Charity?"

"No, mistiss, not me. Ah lak it. Caypun he come an' say polite-lak, 'Charity, efen it please you, Miss Cah-line need yo' help.' Efen it please me? Sho' do! Be a happy day yo' come home, mistiss. Think yo' be dead fo' sho'."

Home. She looked around the old familiar cabin and thought with surprise: Yes, this is home . . . more home than any I have known.

"I hope," she said when she was dressed in clean clothes, "that I may soon have garments that are my own and not stolen from some poor woman in a raid."

Charity giggled. "Dese heah be stolen fum dat ship Caypun sunk. Yo' oughtta see dat. Lak a bonfiah, it wuz. An' all dem pirates in de boats, dey stop rowin' an' dey look back and we cheer."

"I heard you," Caroline said dryly.

"Be a powuhful man, de caypun. Evuhbody say 'Yessuh' an' 'Nosuh,' an' dey lak 'um. Seem when yo' don' be a slave, seem yo' lak to say 'Yessuh' and 'Nosuh' an' 'Please, suh.' Seem yo' don' mind doin' efen yo' is asked polite-lak. Seem yo' purely enjoy yo'self den."

"It is good for you, Charity," Caroline said. "Freedom was made for the likes of you. And Andrew will learn to like it."

"Hope he do, mistiss. Caypun, he say wait till us gits to ouah new country. Says wait till Pappy be busy mekkin' funnitoor fo' de folk an' have his own place an' don' need to wuk efen he don' feel good. Say he be mekkin' things an' teachin' how to mek things. Say Pappy be a diffrunt puhson once he see how 'po'tant he be."

"Yes," Caroline said slowly. "Yes, we all will be."

Charity went away with the rags bundled under her arm and Serena came in soon afterward. If Charity had not changed, Serena definitely had. The cool aloofness was gone, but she looked out from eyes so filled with pain that Caroline could have wished to have the old Serena back.

"Tell me everything," Caroline begged after they had exchanged greetings. "Domino gave me so little information. And Charity.. . . well, she knows so little of it all. How do you and Charity and the rest come to be aboard? What happened at Wildwood?"

In the telling, Serena lost some of the bleak look. Her words, powerful and awesome, welled up from deep recesses so that by the time she had reached the point where she shot Joshua, she was standing, feet wide apart, braced against the ship's roll, reenacting the deed, shooting again and again into the floor, her face alive with passion.

At the end, she turned to Caroline and said, "I enjoyed it. I would do it again and again if need be. Now you see me for what I am. It was not to save Domino that I shot Joshua. It was something I had meant to do always, something I was afraid to know. I was in the bedchamber when Joshua came in. I saw him take one of his pistols and then I knew. I took the other and followed him. I have no desire for repentance."

Caroline could not speak. Any words seemed foolishly inadequate now.

"And I told him I saved your baby. You call her Felicity, Domino says. A good name."

Still Caroline could think of nothing to say. Whatever she herself had suffered seemed insignificant in comparison to Serena's tragedies.

"You see, you think me as vile as I think myself," Serena said suddenly.

"No." Caroline found her voice at last. "I should have known why Joshua bought you, should have seen you would not be able to live like that. I should have made you come with me that night."

A smile crept over Serena's tormented face—wry and fleeting, but it was a smile.

"It was well you did not," she said with irony. "From what I know of your adventures, I can see I would soon have been dispensed with. When Joshua ransomed me, as indeed he would have, I'd have been cast into the water at once. And my . . . " She stopped.

"Nicole," she went on dully. "You see, he wouldn't let me keep her with me. He . . . when she was ill and I wanted to nurse her, he kept me with him, and when I . . . when finally . . . "

"Don't think of it anymore," Caroline said sternly. "You must not. I know. I lost a child, too, one I never saw. One day it was alive and moving, and the next day it . . . " And she, too, stopped, unable to go on, remembering the fierce beating and the final brutal kick that had killed the child within her.

"Yes," she added with quiet venom, "I can see that you have no need for repentance. Nor would I. Had I the opportunity, I would have killed myself." Her eyes met Serena's, and between them there was welded a bond of friendship that both sensed would never die.

Some of the pain left Serena's face and some of the torment faded.

"It is over," she said very quietly, and Caroline nodded.

After Serena had left, she made her way to the bed, too weary to wait for Domino's return. She lay down and almost at once fell into a deep sleep.

When she awoke, it was night. A lantern swayed above her and in her confusion she thought she was aboard Sage's brigantine and that Loco was coming into the cabin. But the lantern was unlit. Where did the light come from?

With a quick breath she sat up abruptly, but her darting glance showed only Domino, sitting at the table, a taper lighting the papers over which he pored.

"It is you," she said foolishly, and at the sound of her voice he turned.

"Yes. Did you expect someone else?"

"No . . . I . . . oh . . . " She swung her legs over the side of the bed. "It was how I awoke once on the *Indies Queen* —when Captain Sage was taking me back to Savannah."

He laid down his quill and blew out the taper. "You must tell me now," he said, coming to sit beside her, "and I you. There is much to talk of."

"I can't," she answered. "Serena told me all. I know now what happened. I don't want to hear more. It is enough that Joshua can never harm me again. It is enough that I am here with you." And so saying, she turned and reached out her arms.

At that moment she sought only the tenderness so long denied her and lay contentedly in his encircling arms. His lips moved gently over her brow and cheek and she returned the kisses in quick little touches against his neck. But when at last he reached her lips, her own parted eagerly and they sank back against the pillows, pressed greedily together, the old passion renewed and flaming between them.

How good it was to feel him, his warm flesh melting into her own. Briefly, they clung like that, fitting themselves together. Caroline felt the old aching longing well and spread and engulf her so that she was carried out of all thoughts, half-delirious by the time he took her, weak and nerveless when at last they were spent.

She lay in his arms as the bittersweet feeling of the aftermath engulfed her and made her want to weep and laugh together.

Presently he stirred and said in a quiet voice, "Tell me now, Caroline. I will sleep better when it is all finished."

Reluctantly, she complied, skimming over the more horrible aspects, telling him that in truth she could not remember much of the long weeks after the loss of the baby.

When she had finished, he got up. She heard him walking almost aimlessly around and she said, "What is it?" She was raising herself on one elbow to peer through the shadows. She saw him, his body a light blur against the dark.

"Loco," he said tightly. "Loco. You say nothing of him. Yet he boasted of what he did to you even as he lay dying."

The ragged anger and outraged pride were plainer in his voice than any feeling for what indignities she herself had suffered. It made her feel unclean. A clammy feeling of humiliation crept over her and hot words rushed to her lips. What had he expected? That she and she alone could protect herself against such a murdering beast as Loco had been? No matter that she had known later fighting him would have brought help, that Sage would have rescued her merely to ensure his ransom; and in fact he must have dealt hard with Loco when she and Joshua had left the ship. At the time, Loco had had power over her, and all she could do was lie there so still and so unfeeling that she had spoiled what pleasure he had.

But below the humiliation and the need to defend herself, reason and caution stood firmly, stilling the words before she could utter them."

"Then he told you falsely," she lied. "Sage was bent on his ransom—two hundred pounds in gold. Loco was only his man sent to take me aboard. Had I been harmed, Loco would have been whipped as surely as he was once before."

There was some truth in what she said. And after that night Loco had never come near her cabin. Only Pablo, gentle and obedient, had ever entered.

"Sage was waiting at the ship," she went on after a moment. "When I saw him, I knew that Joshua was the one paying ransom and not you, as Loco tried to make me believe."

She lay back, and after a moment he came back to bed, drawing her to him and saying, "I am sorry. I could scarcely live with the thought that Loco . . . " He left the sentence unfinished, pressing her closer to him.

There was a coldness in her that had taken the place of her humiliation "There has been no other," she said. "I told you that Joshua cared only to damage me, and then Blanche Chester protected me if only to get her price."

Can you say the same? she wanted to add, but she knew how futile that would be. In the year since he had left her, she knew there must have been women, if only women he paid.

He can come to me with the perfume of a hundred other women clinging to him, yet be indignant if I admit even to brutal rape. I must bear knowing he had not been celibate, but he cannot bear thinking that with or without my own consent, another man has used me.

"I love you too much," he said in a rough voice, and she dimly perceived that somehow his love was her burden, as well as her joy, that her power to hurt him was, in its way, greater than his to hurt her.

She had seen little evidence of the boy in this man, and upon finding it, her coldness melted and a warm flood of love swept over her.

She would never tell him of Loco because he could not bear it. Had he loved her less, he would not have been withdrawn on finding her again, nor would he ever have touched her without proof that she had not been violated.

No, she must keep Loco a secret, just as she must never tell of Byrd Travers, although the former had been but a disgusting rapist and the latter had been a man who had at least given her physical pleasure.

Every man wants a virgin, she thought. And every woman wants a man who is experienced enough not to deaden her sensibilities with selfish and clumsy advances such as those Joshua had made upon her in the early days.

And therein lay a large part of all the differences between them. Understanding this, a tender superiority was added to her love. He was her protector, but in this one way, at least, she would have to protect him.

Caroline lifted her head and kissed Domino sweetly upon the lips. "And I," she said, "I have never loved another."